TYGERS
OF
WRATH

A NOVEL

Also by Philip Rosenberg

The Seventh Hero: Thomas Carlyle and the Theory of Radical Activism
Contract on Cherry Street

TYGERS OF WRATH

A NOVEL

PHILIP ROSENBERG

ST. MARTIN'S PRESS | NEW YORK

Library of Congress Cataloging-in-Publication Data

Rosenberg, Philip
    Tygers of wrath / Philip Rosenberg.
        p.   cm.
    ISBN 0-312-05528-5
    I. Title.
PS3568.07877T9 1991
813'.54—dc20   90-49213
                                                                          CIP

First Edition February 1991

10 9 8 7 6 5 4 3 2 1

For Matt and Mark and Charlotte
For my mother and father
With love
And gratitude for love.

The tygers of wrath are wiser than the horses of instruction.

WILLIAM BLAKE, *The Marriage of Heaven and Hell*

MONDAY

B OOKS don't keep secrets, that was what he wanted them to understand. Everything that happened happened for a reason and the reason was written on every page.

Not one of them understood it. He would have settled for a solitary pair of eyes looking back at him with comprehension or even interest. But he could tell from their faces that they didn't recognize a single idea, didn't remember a single thing they'd been discussing for a solid week. There was boredom and impatience in some eyes, a wasted, druggy haze in others. A few showed something that might have been mistaken for curiosity but was in fact no more than a thin layer of courtesy over a deep pit of well-intentioned confusion. None, in any case, understood.

Steven took a deep breath to keep his voice under control and turned to the window so he wouldn't start throwing things. *Patiently. Patiently*, he said to himself, reminding himself that he was a teacher.

At the same time he knew it couldn't be true, because you cannot claim to have taught something if no one has learned it. That is axiomatic, true by definition, and you're only lying to yourself if you try to argue with axioms.

What now? he asked the bleak and unforgiving stone landscape below the fourth-floor window. Admit that the last three weeks were a hand job and pass out copies of the *Weekly Reader*? He refused to accept that. Then go back, he told himself, all the way to the beginning if necessary, remind them of the things they knew last week, show them the connections.

Yes, that was it, he told himself. They *had* learned something. It was there in their heads, some of it anyway. They just needed help putting it together.

He whirled at the sound of the door opening, ready to take on all comers. How did they expect you to teach anything in a zoo like this anyway, with the animals coming and going at will, no one exercising control over any of it? They wandered into class half an hour late, wandered out whenever they felt like it. If you called them on it, they had written excuses for everything. Because nobody had the guts to stand up to them.

But Steven's mind was made up. He was going to *take* control. He wasn't going to accept excuses no matter who signed them. That shit might work in other classes, not in this one, baby. You get here when the class starts or you're absent. Period.

Except it wasn't a student at the door, it was Rita Torres. She seemed out of breath. She said, "Steven, quick!" and then she was gone.

Steven raced across the room after her. He could hear the kids moving for the door behind him but he knew that he'd never get out if he took the time to stop them. As long as he beat them to the door and made it out, he figured somebody else could worry about what to do with them after that.

Rita was halfway down the corridor, a couple dozen yards ahead of him, her heels drilling the cement floor as she ran.

Christ, there was no one around. The hall was empty. And the hall was never empty. He raced to catch up.

As he flew past Hal Garson's room, Garson stepped out wearing the bewildered look he put on first thing in the morning and never took off until he left Fiorello La Guardia Junior High behind him for the night. Garson was a small, almost scholarly looking black man with a curious knack for always knowing what had to be done. And then he did it. If he hadn't been a teacher he could have been a cop. He had a certain kind of toughness that had nothing to do with physical strength or even presence, the kind that gave small men the power to make hardened criminals shit in their pants. Steven asked him once how he managed the kids so easily and Garson said it was because they could see in his eyes that he didn't care what happened.

Behind him, Steven could hear Garson barring the way, ordering Steven's class back into their room. Garson would stand in that hallway as long as necessary, looking confused but doing what he had to, keeping at least those two classes, his and Steven's, where they were supposed to be.

Rita was halfway up the stairs when Steven caught up with her. It was remarkable how fast she could move in those heels, he thought. But with legs like hers anything was possible. (*Anything*. The thought flashed in and out of his mind like a reflex.) They reached for the door at the fifth-floor landing together and she let him open it.

"It's Timothy," she said, breathless. A light wash of sweat made her face glow.

The minute Steven opened the door he knew why the hallway on four had been empty. They were all up here on five. The corridor was thronged with kids. (*Thronged*? No one used words like that. It was *mobbed*.) Steven and Rita had to push through them, a soft but solid mass, dense and sticky, resisting but malleable. Rita stayed a step ahead, twisting through the gauntlet as she led the way. A hand grabbed for her breast but she brushed it off as if it were a spiderweb. She had told Steven once that she got groped at least half a dozen times a day. All the female teachers said the same thing, even the shapeless middle-aged ones, but it always happened so fast and surreptitiously that the men almost never saw and harbored a secret suspicion that the women were making it up.

This time there wasn't any doubt. Steven whirled in time to see the smirking gloat on Bedrosian's face. He grabbed the boy by the shirtfront. "Watch your hands, Bedrosian," he snarled.

"Steven!" Rita called sharply from ahead of him, a rebuke for his needless protection. Feeling oddly childish, he flung the boy away to hurry after her. Behind him he could hear a chorus of braying adolescent voices and he would have liked to hit all of them.

The only other things he could make out in the chatter were the names Timothy and Ophelia, but there were too many voices talking at once and he didn't learn anything about what was happening. Timothy was Timothy Warren. Everyone on staff knew he was unstable and needed help, but he never got any. Ophelia James was thirteen years old, a tiny, almost doll-like girl raised in that kind of clenched and unworldly Baptist environment where the daughters are kept under moral lock and key until one day they get mysteriously pregnant.

Rita Torres reached the door to the equipment room at the end of the corridor, where the mob of students was being held back by Charlie Wain, a hulking sixteen-year-old ninth-grader, Rita's pet gorilla. "I didn't let no one in, Miss Torres," he muttered through his teeth, opening the equipment room door for her. She slid through and Steven followed. The door closed behind them.

Rita slumped back against the wall and closed her eyes to catch her breath. Steven, who was breathing hard himself, refrained from questioning her, as much out of vanity as consideration. If he had tried to say anything, he would have sounded like a terminal asthmatic.

All around them, the equipment room was stacked with towels, mats and mountains of unsorted junk that had been there forever. A door on the other side led to the weight room, which was one of the few improvements made at La Guardia Junior High in the last fifty years, the personal gift of Tal Chambers, the only La Guardia alumnus ever to make it to the NBA. In Chambers's day La Guardia had been a senior high.

Rita took a deep breath, spoke in an urgent whisper. "He's in the weight room with Ophelia," she said. "Don't ask me how she got there."

"Or him," Steven said.

In theory, no one was allowed in the weight room without faculty supervision. That had been the rule ever since the weight room was the scene of a gang war in which ten-pound weights were thrown around like discuses and one boy was left paralyzed from the neck down. Obviously this rule counted for about as much as most of the other rules at La Guardia.

"Barry found them in there," Rita went on. "He told them to get out and Timothy told him to leave them alone or he'd hurt her. Barry ran downstairs to call the cops. That's all I know."

Barry was Barry Lucasian, one of the gym teachers.

Steven tried to form a mental picture of the scene so that he could figure out what he was supposed to do. But he had never been inside the weight room and had no image of it in his mind, no sense of where he could expect to find Timothy and the girl once he opened the door. The only thing clear was that he was expected to open the door. Otherwise Rita wouldn't have run downstairs to get him. He was close to Timothy, as close as a teacher could get to a boy like that, closer certainly than anyone else at the school including the other students.

"Has he got a knife or something?" he asked.

"I don't know," she said. "He probably does."

Steven considered and quickly rejected the option of doing nothing, of letting the cops handle things when they got there. It was possible, he realized, that he might have given the idea more serious consideration if Rita hadn't been there, but he didn't think so. It was his school, not the cops'. And Timothy Warren would listen to him. He was reasonably sure of that.

"When the cops get here keep them out," he said. "As long as you can."

He moved to the door to the weight room and tried the knob. It turned with a click he knew could be heard inside so he waited to hear if Timothy would say anything, holding his breath tensely. He could feel Rita Torres holding her breath beside him. When there was no sound from inside he carefully inched the door back.

"Get out!" he heard Timothy call. The boy's voice was shrill, over the edge, that frighteningly familiar tone of ice-cold suspicion that warned Steven how careful he would have to be. Sometimes, when Timothy got like that, it took days of gentle pressure, like luring a frightened animal, just to be able to talk to him. This time Steven didn't have days.

"It's Mr. Hillyer, Timothy. Is Ophelia in there with you?"

"Get out of here, Mr. Hillyer," the boy cried out, somewhere between anger and pleading.

"We have to talk, Timothy. Is Ophelia okay?"

"She's okay."

"Let me hear her say it."

He thought of calling out to her, but that would amount to calling Timothy's bluff. It was the wrong way to start.

"She's not saying nothing. I'm doing the talking."

Then the girl *wasn't* all right. There was a new urgency to getting her out. Steven felt as though a clock in his head had just started to tick.

"Okay, you do the talking, Timothy," he said. "I'm just going to come inside."

He didn't wait for an answer but eased the door back just enough to slide through, then pulled it closed behind him.

He looked around for Timothy but didn't see him. The room was much smaller than he had expected, its walls covered in gleaming white tile. The walls facing him and to his left were studded with weight racks, their thick iron armatures comfortably cradling the heavy bars. There were a few benches, some mats on the floor, and five machines standing side by side, looking somehow both crude and futuristic, with odd, spindly projections thrusting improbably from the jointed frameworks.

It seemed a long time before Steven located Timothy sitting on the floor in the narrow aisle between two of the machines, his back to the wall. Steven couldn't actually see the boy from the doorway, but he could see his shadow on the tile. He couldn't see Ophelia James at all.

"What do you think we ought to talk about, Timothy?" he asked, starting to move forward.

"Stay there," the boy ordered.

"I can't talk to you if I can't see you, Timothy."

"That's your problem."

Steven held his position.

"All right, fine," he said. "What do you want to talk about, Timothy?"

"You're the one that wants to talk."

"Well, something's bothering you. That's why you're in here, isn't it?"

"Never mind why I'm here."

"What about Ophelia? She's here, too, isn't she?"

There was no answer.

"You know, sooner or later you're going to have to come out, Timothy."

"Did you call the cops?"

"I didn't, no."

The evasion made Steven uncomfortable. He would have felt on firmer ground if he knew what Timothy had done with the girl. It also dawned on him that she might not even be there anymore, which would really make them all look like idiots when the cops got there and found an entire junior high school tiptoeing around a skinny teenage headcase sulking in a corner.

"The hell you didn't," Timothy challenged, seeing right through him.

"I didn't call them, but they were called," Steven conceded. "That's why we have to talk now. Before they get here."

He took three quick steps while he was talking so he could see into the space between the machines. He stifled a gasp. The girl *was* there, all four-feet-eleven of her, curled up in Timothy's lap like a child or a cat. She wasn't moving and it occurred to Steven Hillyer that she might be dead.

As soon as he had called the police, Barry Lucasian went outside in his shirtsleeves to wait for them. He expected to hear a siren but instead an unmarked Plymouth pulled up and two men in gray suits got out. It was typical of the Bronx police to send detectives instead of uniforms. The school was full of men in suits and they didn't do a damn bit of good.

"Are you Lucasian?" one of the cops asked. He introduced himself as Detective Donadio and his partner as Detective Franks. Franks was black, but not the kind of black that would do him any good with those kids inside. He had close-cropped hair and a neatly drawn mustache. His suit was depressingly nondescript. For all practical purposes, he might as well have been white. Besides, the Italian cop did all the talking. Donadio had that standard Italian cop look the Police Department seemed to come up with in an endless supply, short and wiry, dark-eyed, dark-skinned, lips in a perpetual sneer.

"What seems to be the trouble?" Donadio asked.

Lucasian wasn't sure whether he was imagining the insolence or it was really there in the detective's flat, nasal voice. He decided to give the man the benefit of the doubt and explained as succinctly as possible that a male student was holding a female student hostage in an upstairs room.

"Black boy?" Donadio asked.

"And girl," Lucasian answered.

Detective Donadio took this in as if it was a story he heard every day of his life and then said, "You're not the principal, are you, Mr. Lucasian?"

"I teach gym. He's got her in the weight room."

That meant less than nothing to Donadio. "I think we ought to talk with the principal," he said.

Help yourself, you supercilious little fuck, Lucasian thought. I'm the one who called you and I'm standing right here. What he said was, "I don't think he's here, officer."

He didn't add that the principal never spent more than six hours a week at the school and hadn't been there since last Tuesday. Or that the assistant principal took her phone off the hook and hid in the washroom near her office whenever there was trouble. Or that the whole so-called administration was about as useful as tits on a bull.

"Awright, let's have a look," Detective Donadio said.

HEROISM wasn't Steven Hillyer's thing. His mouth was dry and his palms were wet. He had trouble thinking of what to say next, so he said the first thing that came to his mind. So did Timothy. Steven suddenly realized that Timothy didn't have any more experience at this sort of thing than he did and that they were both saying what the situation seemed to dictate. Knowing this made Steven more comfortable, and within a few minutes he felt as if he could predict Timothy's responses before the boy made them.

"Why don't we let Ophelia go and then the two of us can talk," Steven suggested.

"What? Me and the cops?"

"No, no. Just you and me. I won't let them in."

"You're gonna keep 'em out?" Timothy jeered.

Steven knew he deserved that. Of course he couldn't keep them out. Teachers were supposed to be authority figures, part of the "System." In reality they weren't, and every kid in the school knew it.

"Maybe I could keep them out for a little while," Steven said. "If you just let Ophelia go."

He took a step closer.

"Hold it right there, leave me alone," Timothy snapped.

He held up a knife, thrusting it in front of him where Steven could see it. A year or so ago Timothy had carried a razor all the time, but eventually he surrendered it to Steven. Now he had a knife. Timothy was in the ninth grade, fifteen years old, but he looked younger, delicate and fine-boned. He had a gentle face. Once he tried to kill himself, and he kept notebooks in which he wrote poems about strangling his mother "like a cat in an alley."

"You hurt her already, didn't you, Timothy?"

"No."

"Why isn't she moving?"

"Passed out or something."

Steven moved a step closer.

"I have to check," he said. "I have to make sure she's all right."

"I didn't cut her, give me some space," the boy screamed in rage, daring him to challenge the claim, the knife point flashing in the harsh fluorescent light.

Steven froze where he stood. Not a figure of speech. He could actually feel his blood stop moving. The paralyzing shock of the moment surprised him. There was a cold and frightened menace in the boy's eyes he had never seen there before and he realized that perhaps he didn't know Timothy at all.

"What is it you want, Timothy?" he managed to say, standing his ground without moving.

"I don't want nothing."

"You want to stay here?"

"Yeah."

"You don't really think we can do that, do you?"

"I'm just telling you what's got to happen, Mr. Hillyer. I don't want to use this thing. I just need a minute to think."

There was something oddly discrepant about being called "mister" by someone who was making threats with a knife. "She's hurt already, Timothy," Steven said.

"Shut up, just shut up!"

"She needs a doctor, Timothy."

"Shut up."

"She needs a doctor."

This time the boy didn't answer, so Steven said, "You'll only make it worse, Timothy."

"How the fuck is that gonna happen?" the boy screamed. "It's worse, man. It's already worse."

Behind him, Steven heard the door to the equipment room open but he didn't think Timothy could have heard it. He focused his attention on staying ready, because if Timothy made the slightest move with the knife he was going to have to jump him and he didn't have the least idea how to do it without getting himself and the girl killed. Then he realized that he'd stopped talking and knew it was a mistake so he said, "Do you come up here a lot, Timothy?"

RITA rushed across the equipment room to intercept the two detectives even before they were through the door. "There's a teacher in there with him. He's talking to him," she said.

"That's fine, we'll take it from here," Donadio told her, trying to sound professional rather than brusque. But the dismissive gesture of his hand came automatically and she tensed, taking immediate offense.

"I think Mr. Hillyer has it under control. They know each other," Rita said. She had dark eyes and long dark hair that seemed to flow like a tide. A woman that looked like that, with a body like that, wouldn't have lasted a minute where Donadio went to school, and that was in a relatively civilized part of Brooklyn. She had to be one tough broad if she could make it here.

"The name's Donadio," he said, managing something that passed for a smile. "And this is Detective Franks. I appreciate what you're trying to do, miss, but we're trained for this kind of thing."

There was a swagger in his voice, but that was all right because he knew he could back it up and knew that she knew it.

"Yes," she said, hesitating slightly, not quite impressed but at least willing to be impressed. She had full lips that pouted slightly as she chose her words. "He trusts Mr. Hillyer," she said. "They've always been close."

Donadio nodded with a look that said he was evaluating this. "I don't believe you told us your name, miss," he said.

"Rita Torres."

"And what's the boy's name, Miss Torres?"

"Timothy Warren."

"Is he armed?"

"I don't know."

She flushed slightly, realizing this was something she should have known.

"Well there's your problem right there," Donadio said. "He could be armed. We don't want anyone getting hurt."

As he stepped to the weight room door, Rita reached out to detain him. But Detective Franks was between them as deftly as if even this move had been part of their training.

"You don't want to get in the way, miss," Franks said, his tone as condescending as if he were talking to a child.

Donadio gave her a wink and slipped open the door to the weight room.

"Get out!" Timothy shouted. A moment earlier he had lowered the knife, holding it loosely by his thigh, but now it flashed up again.

"It's all right, Timothy," Donadio said. "I just want to talk with you."

The boy stared straight at Steven, refusing to deal with a stranger. "Tell him to get out," he said.

"Just wait in the other room," Steven called back over his shoulder. "Timothy and I are working this out."

Steven was hunkered down like a catcher at the end of the aisle between the weight machines. Timothy and the girl were only four or five feet in front of him. Over his shoulder Steven could see two cops just inside the door.

"I can't do that," Donadio said.

"It's gonna be all right, tell him it's gonna be all right," Timothy cried.

Steven hesitated, torn. The boy had been talking to him before they came in. All he needed was a little more time and it could end the way it was supposed to. Timothy would put down the knife and Steven would pick up Ophelia James in his arms and they would walk out together like that, side by side, Steven carrying the girl.

That was what he wanted to happen. But, Christ, even more than that, he wanted to be out of there before he lost control of the situation. *And in short I was afraid*, he thought. Why the hell shouldn't he be afraid?

In spite of this he heard himself saying, "Let me just talk with him. He'll come out in a little while.—Isn't that right, Timothy?"

"You've got a girl in there, don't you, son?" Donadio asked.

Steven looked back over his shoulder again and was surprised to see only one cop. He couldn't imagine what had happened to the black one.

Timothy didn't say anything so Steven answered for him. "He's got the girl with him," he said, his eyes darting around quickly, trying to find the black cop without letting Timothy know he was looking. He thought he saw something move around behind one of the machines but couldn't be sure.

"She's got to come out of there, son. Then we can talk," Donadio said. He had moved around and stepped into the clear space directly behind Steven, confronting Timothy with his presence.

"What the hell!" Donadio gasped. He hadn't expected to see the girl curled up like that on the boy's lap.

"Get out!" Timothy shrieked. "Get out! Get out!"

"That girl's dead, son. I'm taking her out of here," Donadio barked, stepping forward, shoving Steven roughly aside.

As he fell over, Steven caught a glimpse of the black cop up on top of one of the weight machines. There was a gun in his hand but Steven didn't have time to shout anything or do anything.

When Donadio lunged for the boy, a shot like an explosion inside Steven's eardrums drowned out everything else, so loud he could feel the impact of the noise against the inside of his head. The next thing he saw was the black cop dropping down from the machine into the narrow aisle, blocking his view of Timothy. He jabbed the gun into a holster under his arm and leaned back out of the way as Donadio grabbed the girl's ankles and dragged her down the length of Timothy's body until she was flat on the tiled floor.

Steven had to scurry backward like a trapped insect to make room for them, the girl flat on the floor now as Donadio pounded on her chest and then bent his mouth to hers to breathe life into her.

The square white tiles behind Timothy were splashed in bright blood and daubed with pieces of white and pink matter that glistened like bright globs of spittle. There was no sign of Timothy Warren's face.

TUESDAY

THE meter was up to fourteen dollars already and Philip Boorstin only had a twenty in his pocket. It would be embarrassing if he had to borrow money to pay for the cab when he got there.

He looked up the avenue for a bank and saw something up ahead called Lion of Judah Fidelity Trust. Was that a joke? It looked like a bank from a distance, and when he got closer he saw that it was a bank. Who in their right mind would put money in anything called the Lion of Judah Fidelity Trust? *People who don't have money*, he thought wryly, not to be smug but because that actually was a pretty fair summary of the problem in underdeveloped communities like the Bronx.

In any case, the chance that Lion of Judah had automated tellers, or if it did that they would honor any of the cards in Philip Boorstin's wallet, was so slim he didn't even bother asking the cabby to slow down so he could take a look even though the meter was now at sixteen dollars and counting. He leaned forward and spoke through the small vents in the bulletproof partition separating him from the cabby. "How much farther is it?" he asked.

The driver, either because he didn't speak English or didn't care to at the moment, agreed that it was farther. The meter ratcheted past seventeen dollars and kept going.

You could get to the airport for less, Philip thought, beginning to suspect he was being taken on a tour. In a way he found that prospect encouraging because it would solve his cash problem. You don't have to tip a cabdriver who is trying to cheat you.

Then he realized it wouldn't solve anything. He was still going to have to get back to the office after the meeting. The prospect of standing on a street corner in the Bronx, five feet nine and a half inches tall, with his neat, sharp-featured Jewish face and his Italian suit, was enough to take his mind off his problems of the moment. He wasn't a coward but he was realistic enough to know that this was no place for a small and unathletic Jew in expensive clothing.

Where were they? The taxi had turned off the boulevard onto a side street. (For some reason he never understood, they called avenues *boulevards* in the Bronx.) A large building loomed ahead, so formidable that it gave concrete reality to the highly abstract and figurative quality of *looming*. It was a fortress the length and breadth of the entire block, and if it wasn't actually made of granite, then it was some rocklike material with much the same effect. Architecturally it was a monstrosity that made one numb just looking at it, because the sheer weight of it, the *un*sheer, looming, oppressive, weighty weightiness of so much stone seemed capable of suffocating a stranger from two blocks away and there was no telling what it could do to anyone unlucky enough to get sucked inside.

And yet it was a school, or had been a school before it took on its present identity as the home of Community School Board Sixty-one. What kind of people would build schools like that? Philip asked himself. (Philip had attended a private school, bright with windows and promise and learning.) Did they hate children? Were they afraid of their own kids even back then? It seemed so long ago. . . .

"Eighteen ninety," the cabby said, sliding back the partition.

That sounded about right, although Philip would have guessed just after the turn of the century. And to think it stayed in use as an elementary school until the late seventies, almost eighty years of small feet grinding grooves in the marble stairs.

"This is it, isn't it?" the cabby growled.

"Yes, yes, this is it." Suddenly aware that he had been daydreaming, Philip groped into his pocket for the twenty as he craned to read the damage on the meter. Eighteen ninety. (Of course.) He hated the idea of borrowing money from someone at the meeting just because all the drivers on the City Hall staff had been tied up getting the mayor to the airport, but a buck ten for a tip on a nineteen-dollar fare was out of the question.

"Look, I've only got a twenty," he said, handing the bill across. "Let me just run inside. . . ."

The cabby looked at the bill uncomprehendingly. "Eighteen ninety," he said.

"I know. That's what I'm telling you. I'll just run inside. . . ."

The cabby had lapsed back into foreignness. He didn't seem to understand a word. "Get out," he said.

Philip's hand was already on the door handle. He tried to think if there were something he could give the driver to make up the difference and settled instead for taking another crack at explaining, even as his feet reached for the sidewalk.

"I'll get a couple bucks inside, I'll be right out," he said.

The driver stepped on the gas, ripping the door out of Philip's hand. "Fuck you, mister! Fuck you!" he called back as he sped away.

Fuck me? Philip thought. *I'm a goddamn deputy mayor. Do you think I'd be running around without any money in my pockets if there wasn't a damn good reason? Read the papers, for Christ's sake. Don't you know that some trigger-happy Bronx cops blew away a black junior-high-school kid on school property yesterday afternoon? Would it surprise you to learn that the polls rate Mayor Ehrlich's popularity somewhere between gingivitis and cancer? Or that a race riot would just about guarantee someone else would be mayor on New Year's morning? You thought you had problems, how do you like those for problems? Fuck me, mister? Fuck you!*

VICTORIA James was thirty-six years old. She had bones the size of a bird's and was no taller than her daughter had been, a fraction under five feet. She sold tokens in a subway booth for a living and was at work when a policewoman arrived to tell her her daughter was dead. In fact, the policewoman hadn't said that at all. She said she wanted Mrs. James to come with her. Then the male cop with her had to get on his radio to the Transit Authority to have her supervisors send a replacement before Victoria could go with them.

The least they could have done, if they had an ounce of consideration, was bring someone with them so she could leave right away. No one ever thought.

They didn't tell her it was about Ophelia but it had to be about Ophelia because there wasn't anyone else in Victoria James's life. For forty-five minutes her stomach was tied in a knot and she thought they must have arrested Ophelia on some ridiculous charge. Ophelia would never do anything to get arrested, but the Bronx police made mistakes like that all the time. The thought that Ophelia was dead never once crossed her mind.

It wasn't until they pulled up in front of the hospital that Victoria James knew what had happened. She screamed and started to cry. She fainted when an attendant took her to see her daughter's body. Now she was home, heavily sedated, in her doctor's care.

The doctor didn't know what had happened in the weight room and didn't know a thing about Timothy Warren. All he knew was that the police opened fire in a predominantly black junior high school and that a little girl he had treated since infancy was dead. He also knew the way the cops had treated his patient. Dr. Carlisle told the reporters who rang the doorbell all afternoon that Victoria James couldn't talk to anyone and that the people of the Bronx would demand a full investigation. He said this was one more reason why no one in the Bronx trusted the police.

THE Police Department is a bureaucracy first and a law enforcement agency only second. As such, it specializes in all those institutionalized forms of stupidity that help bureaucracies achieve the only two goals they ever have—permanence and stability. A healthy and mature bureaucracy is impervious to outside influences, among which can be included the ostensible purposes of the organization the bureaucracy allegedly serves. A police department, in other words, measures its success and failure in terms of how well it *runs,* which has little or nothing to do with how well it polices anything. And how well it runs, in turn, is measured largely in terms of how well it takes care of the men who run it.

Once in a while, however—once in a long while, and usually by accident—someone will rise to the top because he is actually and demonstrably good at whatever it is he is supposed to be doing. Such was the case with Al Terranova, who got himself appointed Chief of Detectives without ever asking for the job and without owing anyone anything for it. He was fifty-two years old, weighed twice what he had when he first put on a uniform and was through and through what cops called his own man. Al Terranova waddled to his own drummer.

One consequence of his independence was that he never cared whom he kept waiting. He didn't keep track of things like that any more than he kept track of the route his driver took whenever he had to go anywhere. Those were things he took for granted because it was simpler to assume, when the car stopped and the patrolman behind the wheel lunged out to open the door for him, that he was where he was supposed to be at that particular moment. You don't worry about being late for a meeting when you're the Chief because the meeting won't start without you.

Terranova was due in the Bronx to meet with Lieutenant Commander Klemmer and assess the damage. His secretary, who held the rank of lieutenant, had called for the car and sent the Chief downstairs in plenty of time to get him to the Thirty-ninth Precinct on time. He rode down in the elevator with the Chief and just before putting him in the car handed him a thick file folder containing all the reports so far received on the Warren-James homicides. All these steps were necessary because

Terranova's mind, as his critics liked to say, was constituted in such a way that he could find himself with his tool in his hand at a urinal and not remember why he had come there. But give him a case file and twelve minutes to read it in, he could make the facts line up like the Radio City Rockettes and kick their heels in unison. It was said that he had solved cases simply by reading the paperwork of the people who hadn't solved them, and although it wasn't true, the fact remained that it was said.

He was one of those men blessed with the ability to read at phenomenal speeds and had once come across the fact that John Stuart Mill could go through a book literally as fast he could turn the pages. Terranova wasn't in that class, but he wasn't far behind and was as a result remarkably well read for no other reason than the fact that it cost him little trouble. He was able to finish the entire Warren-James file long before his car made it to the Willis Avenue Bridge and so had nothing better to do than pop open the small refrigerator he had installed in the backseat. He took out a milkshake, jabbed in a straw and started to drink.

Two sips later he let the straw slip from his mouth and cocked his head quizzically, going back over something in his mind. "Get me down to the coroner's office, Billy," he said.

"Now, sir?" the driver asked.

"And fast."

Billy had been driving the Chief for almost a year and knew his duties. "Lieutenant said I was supposed to take you up to the Three-nine," he suggested diffidently.

"I'll straighten it out with the lieutenant."

The bright young patrolman shrugged his shoulders and slugged the button that turned on the siren as he executed a sharp U-turn. Terranova leaned back in his seat and rested a hand on the file folder next to him, stifling an impulse to check the medical examiner's report again to see if his hunch was correct. He prided himself on never missing details and resented the soft whisper of self-doubt that urged him to check up on himself as though there were the possibility of a mistake.

"Do you want me to call the Three-nine, sir?" Billy asked after a moment.

"What for?" Terranova asked.

Twenty minutes later his car pulled up in front of the ancient wing of Bellevue Hospital that housed the medical examiner's office. Inside, the area was much like any other hospital except that it had been ruthlessly stripped of all pretense that death was merely one of the possible outcomes of the human condition. Missing were the fetid smells of convalescence, the grim faces and slow, preoccupied movements of friends and family, the mere bystanders of decay, disease and injury. All that was left was the naked fact of mortality.

Terranova marched past the reception area, where he was known and never questioned, through the staff-only door leading into the catacombs of corridors giving access to the offices of the medical examiner's staff. Left, past two doors, right, past three more brought him to the office of Lyle McCulloch. He knocked as he stepped through the door.

McCulloch shared Terranova's interest in milkshakes and intellectual puzzles, so they got on well together. Of the two, McCulloch was far more efficient at metabolizing carbohydrates, which meant he didn't pay for his excesses by carrying them around on his body for everyone to see.

"What's this about?" Terranova demanded in lieu of a greeting. He threw the Warren-James file down on the desk.

McCulloch glanced at it just quickly enough to read the name on the file tab and went back to completing the questionnaire he was working on. "How long have I been at my current residence?" he asked.

Terranova shrugged. "Couple years at least," he said.

"Can I put down 'couple years at least'?"

"Put down four years."

"I haven't been there four years."

"What are you applying for?"

"A loan."

"Put down five."

McCulloch compromised and wrote *4 yrs.* in the little square, then tossed down the pen. He picked up the file folder and held it out for Terranova to take back. "What you see is what you get," he said. "Do you have reason to question it?"

"I have questions."

"Pull up a bench," McCulloch said. "I'll answer them."

He leaned back in his desk chair and put his feet up, leaving the Chief to divest the only other chair in the room of its collection of periodicals and reports before he could sit. Terranova looked at the situation with distaste and elected to stand. He didn't like straightening up other people's messes. "Aren't you assholes required to notify the police of anything unusual in your findings?" he asked.

"It's all in the report."

"Everything you found?"

"Everything."

"What about what you didn't find?"

McCulloch was forced to clear the chair himself, because it made him uncomfortable to be talked down to by someone standing over him. "You mean the undies?" he said, circling around the desk and scooping an armful of literature off the chair. As he looked for somewhere to deposit it, the Chief slipped around behind him and settled into the desk chair.

"That's exactly what I mean," Terranova said. "Has anyone else asked about it?"

McCulloch heard the chair groan as Terranova's bulk tested its capabilities.

"You're the first," he said, jamming handfuls of magazines and papers on top of the books on the bookshelves. "I don't think these so-called detectives of yours do much detecting."

The Chief took the slur on his department in stride, for he often thought the same thing himself. "That's why you're supposed to help them out," he said. "If you would put down in your report that this girl wasn't wearing any underwear, then everybody could be in on the secret."

McCulloch got defensive. "I can't put down everything I *don't* find, you know."

"Underwear? On a fourteen-year-old girl?"

"Thirteen," McCulloch corrected. "And just for the record, she had on an undershirt. No bra because she didn't have tits. It's just the pants that were missing. But your point is well taken. I shall try to be more informative."

Terranova passed over the apology with an almost imperceptible nod. "Any chance you or your people misplaced these underpants?"

"None."

"How about in the wagon? Paramedics or whoever?"

"DOA. They never touched her."

These were the answers Terranova had expected. He thought for a moment. "It's possible she didn't wear underpants," he said at last.

McCulloch shook his head. "She was a thirteen-year-old intact virgin," he said. "Besides, there was a panty line on her thighs."

Then they had to have been taken off somewhere else. But where? And why? And what did it have to do with her death? "Was she tampered with?" Terranova asked.

"I don't think so," McCulloch answered thoughtfully. "There were minimal vaginal secretions but I doubt it means anything. You see that a lot with asphyxiation. Just to be sure I checked out the dead boy, swabbed his genitals, his hands. No traces of sexual contact."

"What about orally?"

"Beats me," McCulloch said. "Your guys didn't leave him a face."

* * *

"THEY'RE expecting you in the conference room," the secretary said the minute Boorstin walked in.

She was the first thing you saw when you stepped through the door, which wasn't an accident because no one hired a girl with tits like hers and then stuck her in a closet. She was a black girl with acres of glowing auburn hair. Her upper eyelids were a shade of sparkling purple and her sweater must have been bought before she started to develop because it looked about to burst. She was, interestingly, the third secretary the Board had hired in the last four months, and if all three of them had been put in a lineup it wouldn't have been possible to pick this one out.

Boorstin asked if there was a phone he could use and she handed him the one on her desk. He would rather have been sent into someone's office but it wasn't worth making a fuss over so he called downtown and asked for a driver to pick him up in an hour and a half. Rachel, his own secretary, who had merely presentable physical endowments, told him there weren't any cars or drivers available but Boorstin knew how to deal with that. If he had learned one thing after three years in city government it was not to argue. You demanded what you wanted and then hung up the phone. This worked especially well when you were out of the office, where no one could get back to you to tell you why you couldn't have it.

"I'm not standing on any damn street corner in the Bronx looking for a cab," he said. "Steal a car if you have to, just get it here."

He slammed down the phone and handed the instrument back to Miss Congeniality, who looked at him as if she were impressed with his forcefulness. It was, he decided, the only expression she had. If he had been less aggressive, she would have been impressed with his gentleness or with his diplomacy or merely with the fact that he was there at all. Still, it was nice to be appreciated. He told her to keep up the good work and hurried for the wide marble staircase leading to the conference room on the second floor.

The room obviously had been someone's office in times gone by, for it was far too gracious to have been a classroom. The original half-paneling was long gone but it was still possible to make out the decorative moldings under the heavy coats of paint ruthlessly applied from baseboards to ceiling. The floor was fine-patterned maple from a day when floors were as neatly laid as a ship's timbers, a mosaic of richly stained, tightly fitted slats designed with decades or even centuries in mind. The windows were high, and one looked about in vain for the burnished oak rod with the heavy iron fishhook at the end for lowering them from the top. The lights were globes like bloated basketballs, dangling from long brass rods set into the ceiling in parallel lines that ran the length of the room.

The center of the room was occupied by a massive table, easily twelve feet long. Four men and three women were seated around it, but the only one who mattered was Artemis Reach. Almost twenty years earlier, when New York City decentralized its school system, removing control of all but the high schools from the monolithic Board of Education and vesting it in scores of virtually autonomous local boards, Community Board Sixty-one inherited one of the most backward collections of schools in the entire system. Located in a desperately poor area, the Board served a population so listless and demoralized that for a dozen years they dutifully returned the same Jewish and Irish principals and superintendents who had been running the schools like outposts in the Indian Territories since time immemorial. But when the tide of radicalism finally and belatedly reached the district in the mid-eighties, it hit hard. Artemis Reach, then a young criminal lawyer who had just narrowly lost a bid for a congressional seat, caught the entrenched educational bureaucracy off guard by announcing his intention to run for the chairmanship of Community Board Sixty-one and launched a magnificently well publicized campaign that made control of the schools a hotter issue than police brutality and budget cuts. Whoever controls the schools controls the future, he declared over and over, pitting his uncompromisingly radical rhetoric against the blander promises of a Jewish junior-high-school principal and a Puerto Rican math teacher.

His first administrative acts on taking office set off all the fireworks his campaign had promised, and even before the fledgling Community Board had found itself office space it was in the middle of a pitched battle with the powerful United Federation of Teachers over the firings and transfers of almost half of Sixty-one's white teachers.

While the rhetoric of radicals and former radicals in every other sector of public life mellowed into nonexistence, in keeping with the changing temper of the times, Reach never let up the pressure. He quickly proved himself a master of the Machiavellian art of ingratiating himself with the people he antagonized the most. Operating out of his command post in an abandoned schoolhouse, he quickly elevated his unsalaried position as Community School Board Chairman into one of the most feared and powerful offices in New York City, where every issue from taxicab licensing to sales tax has racial overtones and no racial policies could be set without first consulting and appeasing Artemis Reach.

A tall man, well over six feet, Reach had smooth chocolate skin and a precisely trimmed black beard that followed the line of his jaw the way a hedge follows the contour of the land. As Deputy Mayor Boorstin entered the room, Reach's double bass voice, capable of rattling windows (and lesser men), rolled across the high-ceilinged space, a physical force that could have propelled Boorstin right out again.

"Boorstin," he boomed. "We were just speculating about whom His Honor would send."

This was followed immediately with a deep-bellied laugh intended to set a tone of friendly and pleasant cooperation, just as the words themselves had been carefully chosen to put Boorstin in his place, to remind him that he was, at least as far as Artemis Reach was concerned, merely an interchangeable cog in a much larger machine. No one in the city politic made better use than Artemis Reach of the fine art of communicating through a sequence of contradictory messages, the truth of his position lying anywhere in the spaces between them, sometimes at the arithmetic mean of the pluses and minuses but just as likely at either extreme. Here was a butterfly who would wind up in no one's collection for the simple reason that he could not be pinned down. Here was a powerful and dangerous butterfly.

"I wouldn't have missed it for the world, Mr. Reach," Boorstin answered, managing to be both arch and glib at the same time.

The meeting opened with introductions. Seated opposite each other, in the positions closest to the chairman, were two women. Betty Gleeson was short and stout, nearing fifty from one direction or the other. In 1960 she had run either the one hundred or the two hundred meters in the Rome Olympics but hadn't won any medals. When she ran for the Board, Wilma Rudolph actually came to the Bronx to put in an appearance on her behalf. Mrs. Gleeson wasn't considered a power on the Board but she never missed a meeting of any sort and was used for public statements whenever the Board wanted to look reassuring and mainstream.

Opposite her, to Reach's right, sat L. D. Woods, born Linda Dawson but always referred to, when it wouldn't get back to her, as Long Dark. She was both of those, tall and slender, with the sultry beauty and cool bearing of a Fulani princess. As administrative assistant to an ineffectual Bronx Jewish congressman named Bert Kellem, she collected on the obligations he never bothered with, the way a dog finds crumbs around the table, and had run for the school board two years ago to give herself an independent platform from which to launch herself when she was ready to run for Kellem's seat. Her ambition was an open secret and *Time* magazine had already listed her as a political comer in an issue on urban politics. This was one of the reasons Artemis Reach kept her as close to his side as he could manage, her looks being the other.

Next to the two women, as neatly as if they were at a Park Avenue dinner with place cards on the table, sat two male members of the Board. Davis Deeks made his money through a string of fast-food restaurants in Harlem and the Bronx. A high-school dropout himself, he made scores of appearances every year urging black children to stay in school, had given more than one fortune to community recreation centers, and brought to the Board a commitment to education utterly unencumbered with ulterior motives. "I'm not a complicated man," he liked to say. "People don't understand that because no one knows what to make of a rich nigger."

As a regional sales manager for IBM, Eufemio Sanchez had wide contacts in the Bronx business community. A Puerto Rican Babbitt, hearty and helpful and friendly, he ingratiated himself to customers and non-customers alike by providing them with the names of other customers or noncustomers who could do their books or their printing, straighten their kids' teeth or supply them with shelving, neon, cutlery or life insurance. He was everyone's free-lance unpaid sales rep, and there was scarcely a small businessman in the Bronx who didn't know him and think he was a terrific guy. He wasn't married and didn't have children, but no one questioned his interest in education or his ability to get them office equipment at a good price.

In the last two slots, closest to the door, sat Lewis Hinden and, opposite him, Florence Hill, who sent three children to the Bronx public schools even though, as a financial officer at CitiBank, she could afford not to. She was the only member of the Board with children in the system.

Lewis Hinden, who actually remained on his feet until Boorstin was seated, wasn't a member of the Board. He was the principal of La Guardia Junior High and as such was more or less the subject of the meeting. Slender and nervous, he brought few discernible qualifications to the job other than a master's degree in education from a southern university few had ever heard of. Obsessively well dressed, with a refinement to his manners and a gentleness to his speech that in another day would have made him "a credit to his race," Hinden knew that Artemis Reach had chosen him for the job because he was above all manageable and at the same time could symbolize to the outside world the enlightened and progressive aspects of community control under Reach's stewardship. The fact that the same qualities that made him seem to be the right person to run a predominantly black urban school utterly disqualified him from actually running it was a drawback that Hinden had solved by having as little as possible to do with the school on a day-to-day basis. He was window dressing and he knew it.

The seating arrangement looked to Boorstin like a Thanksgiving dinner at which half the guests had been detained by a snowstorm. The half of the table toward the door was utterly unoccupied, presenting him with his choice of seats next to either Hinden on one side or Mrs. Hill on the other. He picked neither, dropping into the chair at the foot of the table where he was directly facing Artemis Reach, separated from him by four yards of mahogany. He set his briefcase on the floor and bent down to take out a yellow legal pad, which he slapped onto the table without looking up, acutely mindful of the fact that he was the only white man in the room.

For that matter, the dead girl was black, the dead boy was black, and so was the cop who did the shooting. Indeed, when the first bulletins reached City Hall, the unmistakably ethnic flavor of the incident suggested that the best policy for Mayor Ehrlich and his administration was to stay out of it entirely, to deplore the incident without otherwise commenting and let the chips fall where they might. Without a white man in sight, so the argument ran, even professional demagogues like Artemis Reach would be hard put to make a racial issue out of the killings.

Boorstin had immediately pointed out the danger of letting others decide what the issue was going to be. The situation called for the kind of troubleshooting he had been hired for, the kind of advice he specialized in giving. He was certain Reach would blame the police for their reckless handling of the incident and the Police Commissioner would retaliate with lurid accounts of the chaos in the schools under community-controlled school boards. The minute the Police Department and the Community School Board got into a pissing contest, Boorstin explained to the mayor and the rest of the staff, the only one sure to get wet would be the mayor.

Mayor Junius Ehrlich, who had a plane to catch for a mayors' conference in Phoenix, listened and nodded his head. He liked the fight-back realism of Boorstin's scenario and immediately dispatched his young deputy to the Bronx to handle it. Accordingly, the message Boorstin had come to deliver was that there was no issue here. The police had done everything they could. The officer (who loved black children and in fact had three of his own) fired only when he thought it necessary in order to save the girl's life, even though it was later learned she was already dead. The Board and the school had done everything they could. The dead boy had a B-plus average and the dead girl was a quiet child who had never been in trouble in her life. In fact, it was an English teacher who kept the situation under control until the police arrived. In short, no one was to blame.

That was the party line and Boorstin had come to the Bronx to make sure Reach and Community Board Sixty-one followed it. He had the ammunition in his briefcase to guarantee that it happened. But first he had to listen, if only so that later no one could say he hadn't. He slid a fountain pen from his breast pocket, uncapped it and noted the time, place and participants of the meeting. At the head of the table Reach was leaning back in his chair, hands splayed on his chest, the posture of an older and much heavier man. He waited until the deputy mayor looked up.

Reach's opening speech was predictable, down to the drawling accent he habitually affected when he wanted to appear either injured or aggrieved. The Police Department, he announced, saw itself as little more than an army of occupation in the Bronx. The racism of the organization was a matter of indisputable public record and Reach wasn't about to rehearse it again now. They were all grown-ups in this room and knew the score. Nothing short of the Second Coming could change the big picture (Mrs. Gleeson, who was a God-fearing woman, winced perceptibly) and in any case the big picture wasn't Artemis Reach's concern. (Like dinner wasn't a pig's, Boorstin thought.)

What was of the utmost concern to Reach, the Board and educators throughout the city (was he making this up or had other school boards already been canvassed?) was the shameful relationship between the police forces (he actually used the plural) and the schools.

Reach went on for another minute or two about response times, liaison and unrelated incidents until Boorstin figured he had heard enough. Although listening was mandatory, too much listening conveyed an impression of weakness. "Are you aware of some police wrongdoing in this incident, Mr. Reach?" he asked with almost senatorial courtliness.

Around the table, people looked at each other. In this neck of the woods, police wrongdoing went without saying.

"Two of our children are dead, sir," Reach answered in kind. "In my book that constitutes prima facie evidence of wrongdoing."

Boorstin was ready for him, having already made up his mind to stake out the high ground of provocation rather than lie low in the swamp of conciliation. "Well, let's take a look at it," he said. "We certainly can't blame the police for the girl's death. And the boy seems to have had access to an area that was off limits to unsupervised students. Is it your contention that the police are supposed to do corridor patrol?"

"No, sir, I'm not telling you that," Reach answered, making a mental note to find out who had briefed the deputy mayor. (In fact that piece of information, like almost everything Boorstin knew about the incident, came from Steven Hillyer's statement to the police, which Boorstin had had faxed down to City Hall as soon as it was typed and signed.)

"Okay, then our first question is how that boy came to be in that room without a teacher present," Boorstin continued, pushing his advantage. "Our next question is how he came to be in school. From what I gather, the Warren boy was emotionally disturbed. Deeply disturbed. I believe that was common knowledge."

According to Hillyer's statement, various faculty members had submitted requests for psychiatric evaluations of Timothy Warren, claiming that his continued presence at La Guardia Junior High was disruptive, counterproductive and dangerous both to himself and other students. No action had been taken.

Boorstin leaned back in his chair and let the Board members sound off about the unresponsiveness of city agencies. But he sat up attentively when L. D. Woods started to speak. She was reading from a report she didn't identify, holding the pages before her with her long, slender fingers. She had a deep, husky voice that filled the room like the warm scent of a fire in a fireplace, and above all the kind of smoldering sexuality that made it possible for Boorstin to imagine for a minute that there was no one else in the room. As hard as it was for him to take his eyes off her, he managed to glance over at Artemis Reach and noticed that the Chairman was watching her with a gloating and proprietary smile.

Is that bastard fucking her? Boorstin wondered with a pang of jealousy. Maybe yes and maybe no. It didn't matter either way. What was clear was that if anyone on this Board other than Reach would have to be taken into account, it was going to be L. D. Woods. He let her finish her presentation about the difficulties schools throughout the city had in getting the appropriate agencies to provide treatment for students with diagnosed disorders.

When she finished her attack on social service agencies under the Ehrlich administration, Boorstin asked her what she was citing and she scaled a copy down the table to him with a gesture of magnificent contempt. It was a mimeographed document written under the auspices of the District 61 Parents Action Coalition. Boorstin had never heard of it but he could guess what it was.

"Are you a member of this coalition?" he asked.

The color in her cheeks darkened and she tilted her head slightly backward. "No, sir, I'm not," she said. Her voice almost took Boorstin's breath away.

"Do you mind if I keep this?" he asked.

"By all means. You might learn something."

He dropped the report into his briefcase and when he straightened up again he asked how often and how insistently the administration at La Guardia Junior High had pushed for treatment for the Warren boy.

"That's not the issue here," Lewis Hinden answered quickly. Davis Deeks, the fast-food man, jumped in immediately to declare that the school had enough to do educating the children without chasing after every other city agency to get them to do their jobs. In his mind it was as simple as "knowing who fried the fries and who scraped the grill."

"And whose fault is it if the grill isn't scraped, Mr. Deeks?" Boorstin asked.

At the opposite end of the table Reach stifled an impulse to cut off the discussion right there. He elected to let it go, confident that Deeks could take care of himself.

"The grill man's."

"And if he doesn't do it?"

"He's fired."

"But what if he isn't fired, Mr. Deeks?"

Davis Deeks wasn't about to be bullied. "That's what we have managers for," he shouted back. "The work gets done or they get rid of the people who aren't getting it done."

"Well, that's my point, isn't it, sir?" Boorstin smiled. "If there are no pencils or books, the manager picks up the phone. That's what he's there for—to make sure other people do their jobs."

Deeks leaned back in his chair, nothing further to say.

"Now let me repeat the question," Boorstin said. "The staff of La Guardia wanted Timothy Warren taken off their hands and put in a program where he could receive psychiatric treatment. How often had they requested these services?"

Mrs. Hill said, "The Board has no way of knowing that."

This was the moment Boorstin had so carefully set up, with all their responses falling neatly into place. He turned to Hinden with the self-satisfied feeling of an animal moving in for the kill. "No, the Board doesn't," he said. "But Mr. Hinden does. You're the manager here, Mr. Hinden. How many times?"

Hinden looked down to Reach as though the Chairman could give him the answer, but at the far end of the table Artemis Reach was smoking like a grill that hadn't been scraped.

"I really couldn't say offhand, Mr. Boorstin," Hinden answered softly.

Boorstin ran a quick check of his facial muscles to make sure he wasn't smiling. "In fact, you never requested these services, did you?" he asked.

"I'm sure we must have."

"I think if you'll look into it you'll find that the staff repeatedly made the recommendation, Mr. Hinden, but it never left your office."

There was silence around the table. For all practical purposes the meeting was over. Where was the race issue now? What was left of black outrage at a police killing? The people of the Bronx had no one but themselves to blame. It was their Board that appointed their principal who kept that boy in that school until he snapped. Case closed.

"You have a press conference scheduled for this afternoon, Mr. Reach," Boorstin said.

It wasn't a question and Reach didn't answer it.

"I think a simple statement expressing the Board's condolences might be the most appropriate position for the Board to take," Boorstin said, pushing back from the table.

A Lincoln Town Car with a city driver behind the wheel was waiting downstairs to get Boorstin out of the Bronx.

LIEUTENANT Commander Paul Klemmer didn't look at anyone as he crossed through the squad room on the way to his office. He didn't have to, because he could feel and smell and hear the muffled quiet that sat on the room like fog, the way it always did when something went down the wrong way. The detectives in the room were quiet because they all liked Donadio and Franks and it was hard for them to imagine how either one of them was going to come out of this in one piece.

Franks was at his desk, Donadio at the file cabinet. Both of them followed Klemmer with their eyes as he steered a straight course for his office door. "Just give me a minute," he said, punching through the door and swinging it closed behind him.

Their reports on the incident were right where he had left them, in the middle of his desk, so he took the time to look at them again even though he knew exactly what they said. One page each. There was an art to writing these things and it wasn't an easy art to master. For a novelist the shooting at La Guardia Junior High was easily a chapter, for a sociologist a whole book. In a court of law each of the detectives could count on a full week on the stand. And in this morning's newspapers (except the *Times*, which hadn't made up its mind yet) there was column after column on the story. But a good cop could get every last piece of pertinent information onto one typewritten page, distilling it all down to only the facts that mattered.

Donadio and Franks were both good cops. They paid attention to details, like the way they avoided using the same phrases in their reports. It was a small touch, but it meant no one could say they put their heads together on a story.

A damn good thing, Klemmer reflected with a sigh, that the black one did the shooting. If it had been the other way around, Donadio would be history already. Klemmer didn't like thinking that way but it was realistic and he believed in being realistic the way other people believed in the resurrection of the flesh or that Jesus loved them. In New York City politics took precedence over everything, and there wasn't anything more political than two dead black kids.

What did it come down to? Internal Affairs would probably give them a clean bill of health because the dead boy had a knife. But a grand jury inquiry was mandatory on a fatal shooting and the only thing you could count on with a Bronx County grand jury was the fact that they didn't like cops. A few years ago a patrolman had been indicted for fatally shooting a woman who attacked him with a butcher knife. Only a few months ago a Bronx trial jury acquitted a coked-up killer on all charges stemming from a running gun battle with the police. When he thought about such incidents, it was hard for Klemmer to be optimistic.

He slid the reports into a folder and went to the door to call Franks in, gesturing him toward the aluminum chair with the vinyl cushion that faced his desk.

In no other business, industry or corporation would a forty-two-year-old administrator who had risen to an equivalent rank not have a decent chair in his office to offer anyone who might enter. The chair Franks sat in belonged in a bus station.

Klemmer asked the detective if he wanted coffee and knew the answer before he heard it.

"I don't suppose you got much sleep last night," he said.

"Not much," Franks said flatly, with little appreciation for the fact that the lieutenant commander was trying to break the ice. There had always been something aloof, almost aristocratic, about Franks, which made him a hard man to target for benevolence. He didn't act as if he wanted help and he made it clear from the outset that he wouldn't be grateful when he got it. Life would have been easier, Klemmer thought, if Franks had been one of those dime-a-dozen, fast-talking, high-rolling, down-and-dirty players off the street, as rakish as Harlem, as shabby as BedStuy, the kind of black man people were used to and understood. But Franks wasn't and that was that. You played the hand you were dealt.

Klemmer looked down at the report again, then reclosed the cover and slid it an arm's length to the side, a gesture that said *Let's forget this bullshit and talk.*

"The problem you're going to have," he said out loud, "is that the M.E. says the girl was good and dead when you got there."

Franks didn't answer. He knew that was the problem. He would have to be living down a well not to know it.

"The question everybody's going to ask you is whether you knew she was dead."

Franks still didn't say anything.

"Your partner said she was dead, didn't he?"

"I'm not sure what he said."

"It's in the schoolteacher's statement." Klemmer pulled out a copy of Hillyer's statement.

"You don't have to read it to me," Franks said.

Klemmer read it anyway. " 'That girl's dead, son,' " he quoted. "Isn't that what your partner said?"

"Something like that."

"And then you shot the boy."

"About the same time, yeah."

"Are you telling me he said the girl was dead *after* you fired?" Klemmer challenged, his voice dripping with sarcasm.

"That's not what I'm telling you."

"Well he couldn't have said it *while* you were shooting or the teacher wouldn't have heard him."

"Okay, so what?"

"So what? So he said it *before* you shot!"

"Right," Franks said. "At about the same time."

Klemmer was out of his chair and around the desk so fast that the chair clattered onto its side as he sprang up. It was a calculated move, intended to shock, and it worked to the extent that even an iceman like Jim Franks looked shaken as his commanding officer stood over him, glaring down.

"Listen to me now, Franks, and get this straight before anyone gets here. Not 'about the same time,' not 'after,' not 'while.' *Before.* Detective Donadio said the girl was dead *before* you fired." The lieutenant commander's words were aimed right between Franks's eyes. "That's the teacher's statement and that's what you're damn well going to have to explain. If you duck it, if you tiptoe around it, if you play games or get evasive, they will eat you alive, Detective Franks. Could I make this any clearer?"

A bitter smile spread slowly across the detective's face. It couldn't have been clearer.

AT EIGHT o'clock Klemmer gave up and called the Chief of Detectives' office to find out what had happened to the meeting he had been told would happen that afternoon. The phone call caught Lieutenant Brucks, the Chief's secretary, by surprise. All he knew was that Terranova had set out for the Bronx. He must have been sidetracked. It didn't seem likely he was still on the way.

"If he checks in, tell him I sent Donadio and Franks home," Klemmer grumbled. What he was thinking as he hung up the phone was that two men making approximately thirty-one thousand a year had just wasted an entire tour confined to the office waiting for a meeting that didn't happen. Any kid with a pocket calculator could have figured out how much that was costing the city.

Instead of going home when they were dismissed, Donadio and Franks made their way to a bar a few blocks from the station house. The place offered whiskey, beer and little else for amenities, adding only just enough light to let them see the stains on the tables.

The two detectives ordered drinks from the bar and carried them to a table. The music playing from a radio over the bar was the kind of heartless rock kids listened to, not a song worth remembering. Their distaste for the music made both men feel older than they were. "Who the hell picked that station?" Donadio wondered out loud.

They talked for a while about the Chief of Detectives, starting with his nonappearance for their meeting and going on to swap legends they had heard about him. Neither had ever met him, but there wasn't a detective in the Bureau who didn't know someone who knew him or worked with him and had a Terranova story he swore was true. The one thing they didn't talk about was what happened at La Guardia Junior High. They had compared recollections over coffee immediately after the incident and before they got back to the station house. Neither had mentioned it since.

Franks went back to the bar for another round of drinks. As he sat down and slid one glass of whiskey across to his partner he said, "You know they're going to jack me up on this thing, don't you?"

Donadio hadn't been able to think of anything else for almost thirty-six hours. "It'll work out," he said.

"I iced a kid," Franks answered softly. "How's that going to work out?"

Until that moment it was as though Franks had cancer and it couldn't be talked about despite the fact that it was the only thing possible to think of when you were with him. More. The rule of silence held even though the two of them had been partners for more than a year, even though they had been through everything together. And now Franks came out and said it, *I've got cancer, Vince,* and it was out in the open and they could deal with it.

"He had the knife, he was holding the girl," Donadio said. "If I had the chance to take him out, I would have used it."

"Would you?"

Donadio thought about it a minute without answering. Then he finished his drink. The basis of the bond between partners was that they answered each other honestly. It was why there were always so many silences, so many things that never got spoken of, the sorts of things that most people found it convenient to lie to each other about. It would have been easier to answer his partner's question with a clear affirmative—*Yes, that is what I would have done myself, what any cop would have done, and you did it because the situation didn't give you any choice*—but Donadio didn't in fact know that he would have done it that way, so his only choice was not answering at all.

"Twelve years," Franks said. "Twelve fucking years." That was how long he had been on the job.

"It's not gonna come to that, Jim."

Franks looked back at him from across a wide space littered with pain. "What else can it come to?" he said, his deep voice haunted. "She was dead, she wasn't dead, I knew it, I didn't know it—it doesn't matter. The first thing they're going to ask me is why I fired."

He stopped speaking, leaving his partner poised across the table expecting the rest of the statement, expecting the answer to the one question Donadio had been asking himself but hadn't dared ask Franks since it happened. Why had he fired?

And now in the silence he had the only answer there was, and it was enough to make a grown man cry.

Franks didn't know either. As often as Donadio had been over it in his mind, Franks had been over it a hundred times as often, replaying it so carefully he could see the air move in that tiny room. And no matter how hard he questioned himself, he still didn't know why he fired that gun. He was going to have to live with not knowing.

WEDNESDAY

WHATEVER Steven Hillyer had in mind when he first thought of teaching, it wasn't this. He knew it wasn't going to be Mr. Chips, with decorously shabby tweeds and comfortable pipe smoke, but that was all right because comfortable and decorous weren't important words in his vocabulary. He had been brought up to believe in style because his mother believed in it, but he had long since reconciled himself to the kind of genteel poverty his choice of a calling entailed. It meant something to be a teacher, especially in places where the children had so much to learn.

That, in any case, was what he told himself on his good days. And on his good days it was true. Sometimes a child understood what he was saying, not just about a book but about a world and a mind behind that book. Sometimes, over the course of a year, a child learned to express himself better, to focus and control his thoughts, to put them on paper, or even (more simply but no less thrillingly) to write a grammatical sentence.

But lately it seemed the good days came farther apart as the crushing weight of defeat threatened to bury his small victories like gardens choked under a mountain of volcanic ash. Perhaps it was only the accumulated burden of years of frustration, but it seemed clear to him that every year less and less was getting through. Like farmers taking note of weakened crops from increasingly depleted soil, many of his fellow teachers swore the kids had changed, but Steven didn't believe it for a minute. The problem was in himself, and he was sure that facing this fact, admitting his own failure, would somehow tell him how to fix it. It didn't.

He was only thirty years old and still had the same open, boyish look, the same tousled charm he had brought to La Guardia eight years earlier. But inside, sometimes, he already felt old, the way even a young man can feel when he's met with rejection often enough. Over the past few years he had tried everything he could think of, including lying to himself, to rekindle the energy he felt when he first accepted the assignment to La Guardia Junior High. But sooner or later the doubts always came back, stronger and more insistent than before. He had begun to feel sorry for himself, even though he recognized it was a luxury a man could scarcely afford when he was doing something no one asked him to do, making sacrifices no one asked him to make.

The literature talked about burnout, but the word had an apocalyptic ring, like a jet going down with its engines aflame, that didn't correspond to anything Steven recognized in himself. Instead, he felt only a growing numbness as it became harder and harder to convince himself that the glacial progress of his classes counted for anything in a world that was moving faster than they were, harder and harder to believe that salvaging one or two children could ever balance the dozens upon dozens who fell by the wayside in the process.

In any case, the best of those was dead now, a brilliant and tormented child whose violent end seemed to signal the end of Steven's dreams. Perhaps it was no loss, and he could do without dreams that hadn't turned out to resemble the reality of his eight years at La Guardia. "That is not what I meant at all," he thought. "That is not it, at all."

In point of fact, this was the nub of the problem. Quoting T. S. Eliot was part of what teaching was supposed to be. But try to imagine assigning "Prufrock" at La Guardia. It couldn't be done. It was out of the question. At La Guardia Junior High they scrape brain matter off the walls with paper towels.

The memory of that scene nauseated him and he looked up from the papers he was grading to take in his apartment walls, mercifully bare. He stared straight ahead, trying to fill his mind with the blank whiteness in front of him, swabbing the blood out of his mind with it. For a minute it worked, and he could feel the churning in his gut subside. But only for a minute. Then the cracks in the plaster, a random, wandering web of fine lines like aging skin, started to move and shift, shaping themselves before his eyes into heavier horizontals, then neat, plumbline verticals. Fascinated, even hypnotized, he watched with a kind of numb indiffer-ence, making a game of abetting the process, the way as a child he used to tease a picture out of dappled patterns of sunlight through curtains.

The difference now was that he wasn't doing it so much as it was happening by itself. Even his own complicity was no more under control than his mood, the lines forming themselves against his will into perfect rectangles, the cracked, imperfect wall rapidly becoming a smooth surface of precisely reticulated tiles.

There was blood in the troughs and he looked away, sickened, fighting the force in his brain and eyes and neck that made him look back.

A fountain gushed blood low near the base of the wall—Timothy Warren's throat, gaping like disconnected plumbing.

Steven sucked in his breath and grabbed blindly for the stack of papers on his desk, clutching them as though they were something he had to salvage from the wreckage. He raced from the room into the bathroom, pulling the door sharply closed behind him and leaning against the sink to collect himself. His mouth and throat were dry but his rapid breathing came quickly under control and his mind began to form a plan. First a drink of water. Then he would stay in the bathroom awhile and read a few of the essays. In half an hour he would go back out.

He tossed down the papers and turned on the tap, filling a plastic glass with cloudy water, which he gulped so fast it splashed his face and ran from the corners of his mouth, dribbling onto his shirt and chest. Startled by the tepid wetness, he dropped the glass clattering into the sink and stared down, half in horror, expecting to see the water gushing from his open throat as fast as he was drinking it. He closed his eyes and told himself he was going crazy, but the thought calmed him because he didn't imagine that people who were going crazy could contemplate their own disintegration.

Read the essays, he reminded himself.

He retrieved the glass and set it back in its receptacle, then picked up the stack of papers from the top of the toilet tank, lowered the seat cover and sat down to read. Thank God he had a pen in his shirt pocket. But he didn't have his watch and wouldn't know when half an hour was up.

Forget the half hour, he told himself. A half hour was about five essays. He would read five essays and then go out and get himself something to eat.

As he picked up the first paper, three stapled sheets, and folded back the cover sheet, a slip of paper fell to the floor and he bent over to pick it up.

It was his grand jury subpoena.

THURSDAY

WHEN Steven's father died, his mother put their house on the market, asking over a hundred thousand dollars more than the real estate agent thought she could possibly get. The high price was the only compromise she offered Steven, who was halfway through his junior year of high school and desperately wanted to stay in Litchfield until he graduated. She didn't explain her thinking to Steven, who knew only that the house was for sale and that they would leave Connecticut if a buyer were found.

Looking back now, Steven was able to joke that his senior year in high school had been like living in a museum. They were invaded at all hours by an implacably cheerful tour guide conducting curious strangers through the bedrooms and closets, the kitchen, the laundry, the grounds. While the agent chatted them up relentlessly, the client couples said almost nothing aloud, confining themselves to whispered conferences with each other. Still, Steven, who followed them grimly, skulking a room behind like the house's resident ghost, could read in their meaningful gestures and their pointed questions that he was now no more than an uninvited guest in his own home and that already these strangers were hatching plans for which walls were to come down, where a window was to be let in, how the house could be transformed into something it was never intended to be. If he could have done anything to scare them off, he would have done it, but it didn't prove necessary, for they all came and went and were never heard from again, frightened off by the price, the only thing that frightened such people.

In the end, of course, the house was sold, and sold so suddenly that Steven dressed for his senior prom in a bedroom filled with mover's boxes and posed for his prom picture in his white dinner jacket in a living room from which every stick of furniture had been removed. A few days after the prom Steven and his mother drove to the Cadillac dealer from whom her late husband always bought his monstrous El Dorados and sold the car, the last thing of his father's Steven ever saw. They took a taxi to the train station, and that night they finally slept in the spacious Upper West Side co-op Evelyn Hillyer had bought almost a year before.

That first summer in New York was like a prison term for Steven, who quickly grew to hate the off-white walls of the apartment and the windows that looked out over streets on which nothing ever seemed to happen except an unchanging flow of traffic. And yet he was at such loose ends that it was all he could do to go to the corner market for groceries once in a while or drop off the laundry when his mother asked him to. They spoke Spanish at the market and Chinese at the laundry, deepening his sense of having been uprooted to another country.

Before his father's illness, Steven had planned to go away to college and had applied for early acceptance at Oberlin after visiting the campus with his mother. He liked the old stone buildings and the shaded hills, which seemed to him very much what a college should be. The letter accepting him arrived a few weeks after his father died, and he spent his senior year dreading that his mother would pull up stakes and move while at the same time counting the months until he was free to leave on his own. Once both eventualities had come to pass, with the house in Litch-field sold and college only a summer vacation away, he found that some-how the paradoxical logic of his life seemed to dictate that the less bearable life became at home, the less he was able to contemplate leaving. He wrote to the dean of admissions at Oberlin, announcing that he wouldn't be attending the fall semester, burning that particular bridge to the water-line before he so much as mentioned his decision to his mother. When she learned what he had done, she refused to speak to him for two weeks, during which time he cooked his own meals and did his own laundry in the coin-operated washing machines in the basement, mother and son moving through the spacious apartment like troops behind enemy lines, pausing at doorways to make sure their paths didn't cross.

Curiously, it was an accidental by-product of these two weeks of utter isolation that began to bring Steven out of his shell. He had seen Sonya once or twice in the elevator but they had never talked. She was older than Steven, probably in her twenties, and had long blond hair that she pulled back severely. She wasn't especially pretty, with a narrow face and watery eyes set much too close together, but it wouldn't have mattered if she had been beautiful because Steven at that time had no desire for any of the complications involved in starting a friendship.

Nor did he have any when she came into the laundry room pushing a shopping basket loaded with dirty clothes while he was waiting for the dryer to finish. He looked up from his book and then went back to his reading, offering no more than a terse hello of his own to answer her greeting. His mind, though, wasn't on the book. He found himself wondering if she were looking at him, expecting her at any minute to start the conversation he didn't know how to begin. Of course it didn't happen. He looked up after a while, thinking that perhaps if she looked even the least bit receptive it wouldn't hurt him to go first, but the washing machines she had loaded were churning away and she was nowhere in sight. He hadn't even heard her leave.

A few days later he met her there again. He waited awhile, then lowered his book and looked around thoughtfully, giving her the chance to say something if she chose to.

"What do you read?" she asked.

She spoke with an accent he couldn't place. He assumed it was Scandinavian on account of her blondness.

"Some stories by Fitzgerald," he said, and then explained, "F. Scott Fitzgerald," because of her accent.

Her smile may or may not have been mocking. "I know F. Scott Fitzgerald," she said. "Do you like his stories?"

He had picked the book because it was on the freshman reading list at Oberlin, but so far he couldn't make much of it. He found the writing irritating because at the most crucial points in the stories the characters never seemed to come up with anything more clever to say than what he or any of his friends would have said under the circumstances. He was sure he was missing the point or the stories wouldn't have been taught in college.

"They're okay I guess," he said, flushing with embarrassment at the awful banality of his answer when the words were right at hand for a response that would at least have been provocative. He blamed himself for not having picked a book he could have sounded smarter about.

She asked him if he were a college student and he heard himself say he was planning to go in the fall. They talked through the whole wash cycle and while the dryers ran. They exchanged the titles of the books they loved and denounced the ones that disappointed them as ruthlessly as if the authors had personally let them down. She struck Steven as very wise and very well educated, with clear opinions about everything. Her eyes didn't even seem so close together anymore.

By the next week the basement laundry room had become a full-time literary salon. Steven learned that her name was Sonya and that she was an exchange student from Switzerland working as an au pair for a couple in the building. She was a graduate student at Columbia. Sometimes she was accompanied by the little boy she was caring for, a sullen but undemanding child named Adam who could be set down at the sorting table with a coloring book and left there interminably while Sonya and Steven talked about everything under the sun. If he had been even the slightest bit less self-centered Steven might have felt sorry for the child, whose ferocious absorption in his coloring book seemed almost to border on autism, who never so much as asked either of them to look at the pictures to which he applied himself hour after hour, his tongue poking from the corner of his mouth as he scribbled away.

Through the summer their relationship remained as passionate as it was chaste, with Steven looking in vain for any sign that their afternoon encounters in the laundry room were anywhere near as important to Sonya as they were to him. For a while he tried various stratagems to get to see her outside the laundry room, but he gave up when it became clear to him that she would reject all such offers. Once or twice he ran into her in the elevator, brief, serendipitous encounters that were for him like finding the hidden pockets of sweet brown sugar at the bottom of his oatmeal when he was a little boy. He even ran into her once at the market and struck up a conversation as he fell in step beside her while she did her shopping. But after a few minutes he was thrown into a panic by the sudden fear that he was being a pest. She was a graduate student, after all, and he wasn't really more than a high-school kid. He made a quick excuse and hurried home, promising himself to pass in silence the next time they met so that she wouldn't think he was chasing her.

One afternoon in the middle of August he took the subway to Eighth Street and walked around until he found the NYU campus, where he presented himself to the dean of admissions with his letter of acceptance from Oberlin and a copy of his letter declining to attend. He explained about the death of his father, then lowered his eyes as he fabricated details that made it clear why it wouldn't be a good idea to leave his mother alone at a time like this. His pulse pounded with the exhilaration of his lies, his consciousness divided equally between terror and a sense of command. He had never done anything even remotely like it in his life. In twenty minutes he won the dean's sympathy and admiration and walked out of the office with the understanding that he would be permitted to enroll as a freshman at NYU, pending the receipt of his high-school transcript. He hadn't, thank God, lied about any of his grades.

But if he expected his relationship with Sonya to improve now that he was about to be a college student, he quickly learned otherwise. The first time they met after classes started she put her wash in the machine and left with an excuse about chores and homework. She returned briefly to switch the clothes to a dryer and hurried right off. A few days later it was the same story. He saw her in the elevator but she was with the couple she worked for and barely said more than hello. The next time he saw her she was with friends from school, a girl and a pair of boys who made Steven feel like a child when he compared himself to them in his mind. Almost a week passed before they had another chance to be alone together in the laundry room, and he made a point of asking when they would get a chance to talk about the Hesse novel she had urged him to read.

"I am sure there will be time," she said.

But there wasn't. He saw her less and less as the year went on and she was almost always surrounded with her graduate-student friends. At the end of his freshman year she got another job with a family on the East Side. He called her a couple of times, but he could tell from her distracted tone that she didn't really have any interest in talking to him so he stopped calling. Later he learned she had finished her graduate work and gone home to Switzerland.

THE Bronx County Courthouse dated from about the same period as many of the Bronx schools. As Steven came out of the subway and walked toward it he felt himself on familiar ground, the massive courthouse looming over him no more oppressively than the school he walked into every morning. They had, those early twentieth-century Bronxites, a sense of empire and permanence and dignity raised to a reckless level of intensity, as though they dared both time and history to undo what was here so majestically done in stone. *My name is Bronx, borough of boroughs. Look on my works, ye Mighty, and despair.* Confident and optimistic, unable to imagine the future as anything but a broadening boulevard of progress and prosperity, they hadn't reckoned on population shifts, demographics run amok or obscenely belligerent graffiti scrawled on every flat surface in two languages. They hadn't reckoned on being mocked in their own front yards.

The inside of the courthouse was at least as formidable as the exterior, beginning with the cavernous foyer, its ceiling so high that one lost entirely the sense of being in an enclosed space. At ten minutes to nine in the morning the floor was so thickly crowded with felons, lawyers, witnesses and victims scurrying about with sullen urgency that the floor itself seemed to be alive, like a microscope slide that reveals the unimaginable turbulence hidden within a drop of water or the flow of blood.

Playing the role of a truculent corpuscle, Steven shouldered and jostled his way across the stream to a directory set into the wall in a dull brass frame. Grand jury should have been under *G* but wasn't, and for a moment Steven considered the possibility that he had come to the wrong building. Then he found it, inexplicably hidden under *B* for Bronx County. Had anyone, he wondered, done a study on the number of crimes that annually went unpunished in the Bronx because key witnesses were unable to find the grand jury room?

The ride up to the eighth floor was like a rush-hour trip on the subway, except that on a subway only a small percentage of one's fellow passengers might be criminals while here it was a clear and certain majority. When he got off the elevator he found himself facing a row of windows that extended to the left and right the full length of the building. The corridor circled the floor like a moat, the outer wall a continuous series of windows, the courtrooms and chambers huddled within this protective perimeter so that there couldn't have been a single room in the building with so much as a single window. Was this, Steven wondered, a draconian precaution against the allure of Bronx rooftops, which offered distractions that would otherwise have ground the wheels of justice to a halt? Or had some misguided architect taken too literally the notion that justice is blind and had therefore no more need of windows than a cave salamander has of eyes?

A sign pointed him toward the grand jury room, which, judging from the room number, would be at the far end of the corridor. Ahead of him he saw a cluster of perhaps a dozen people apparently waiting to get in. He checked his watch. It was five minutes to nine.

"Excuse me," he said, addressing anyone in the crowd who would answer. "Is this room eight sixty-two?"

"That's right, grand jury," a man answered. "Are you scheduled to testify?"

"Mm-hmm," Steven muttered, slipping past him. None of the people in the hall seemed interested in going in.

"You wouldn't be Steven Hillyer, would you?" the man asked.

"That's right."

He realized his mistake even before he had a chance to wonder how a stranger knew who he was. As though his name were a cue, the crowd surged toward him, all of them calling questions. Three or four flashbulbs went off and a row of microphones jabbed at his face.

"The Warren kid was your student, wasn't he?"

"Do you think you could have talked him into surrendering?"

"Any idea why he killed the girl, Mr. Hillyer?"

"Wait a minute, hold it, just back off," Steven protested, trying to push through them. "I don't think I'm supposed to be talking about this."

"But he was your student?"

"Yeah, he was my student. Could you just let me through."

He made headway slowly, running up against a buxom and insistent woman who stepped directly into his path.

"Could you have got him to surrender, Mr. Hillyer?" she asked.

"I don't know what I could have done. Excuse me. I'm supposed to be inside."

"Is that why the police shot him?"

"I've got no idea why they shot him. Please get out of my way."

"Mr. Hillyer!" a voice called sharply enough to catch Steven's attention over the tumult. He could see a small but determined man in horn-rimmed glasses shoving his way through the crowd of reporters with rather surprising ferocity. He was at Steven's side in a moment, grabbing his arm with one hand and the doorknob with the other. A second later they were on the other side of the door.

"Do you have any idea what you just said?" the man asked in a tone of inexplicable annoyance.

"I said I didn't know anything."

"You said you didn't know why the officer fired. That's not the same thing."

Steven considered this a moment. "All right, I shouldn't have been talking to them," he conceded, but that was the most he would concede. "That probably means I shouldn't be talking to you either."

He glanced around to see where he was expected to go. They were in an anteroom or reception area of some sort filled with surprisingly modern furniture. A few benchlike couches covered in a gray, nubby fabric, four upholstered chairs in the same fabric and a rack full of magazines were the basic furnishings. A door behind the receptionist's desk led into what he assumed was the grand jury room itself. A coffeepot, steaming exuberantly, nestled on a table among Styrofoam cups. Except for the fact that coffee was on, there was no sign of human presence. It seemed odd there was no one around to tell him what he was expected to do.

Steven started toward the coffeepot but stopped when he heard the little man say, "You've got to talk to me. I'm your lawyer."

Steven looked at him with the incomprehension the statement deserved. He didn't have a lawyer and didn't need one. The man was holding out his hand.

"I'm sorry, I should have introduced myself," he said. "Martin Margolis. I'm with the UFT."

Steven had never had much to do with the United Federation of Teachers. Nominally it was his union and dues were deducted from his paycheck, but he had never trusted the UFT, which always seemed to be less concerned with education than with protecting the jobs of incompetent or indifferent teachers.

"How does that make you my lawyer?" Steven asked.

The little man's eyes seemed to cloud over and he looked awkwardly down at his shoes. "Well, actually," he said, "you're technically not allowed to take an attorney into the grand jury so I guess it doesn't matter."

"What doesn't matter?" Steven asked, genuinely perplexed.

"That I'm not . . . that I don't . . . actually represent you."

Margolis had seemed so forceful in the hall, but it was quickly becoming clear that forcefulness didn't come naturally to him.

"To tell you the truth," he went on, confessing his inadequacies with a sort of hangdog candor, "I really don't know all that much about criminal law. Mostly I do labor things but I guess that's okay."

"Somebody's got to do it," Steven answered, less than kindly.

"I mean about my being here."

The conversation was getting bizarre. "I don't really care why you're here," Steven said. "You're not my lawyer."

"Not per se. I mean in the sense that I *represent* you. But I can *advise* you." And then the little man quickly added, "If you need advice, that is."

There was something elflike about this lawyer, but he was a fuddled elf. "No, I think I can handle it," Steven said.

"No offense, Mr. Hillyer, but you weren't exactly doing terrific in the hall. Anyway, it doesn't cost you a thing. That's what you pay dues for."

The click of a lock interrupted their unpromising discussion and a woman, slender and attractive, entered from an inner chamber and sat behind the receptionist's desk. Curiously, she didn't ask either of them who he was.

Annoyed, Steven sat down on one of the couches while Margolis headed for the coffeepot and came back with two cups of black coffee. "There's milk and sugar if you want," he said, but Steven didn't.

In the next few minutes, without being asked to, Margolis outlined the principles of the grand jury system as though he were teaching a junior-high civics course. He explained that Steven was being called to testify as a witness and that the rules of evidence that applied at trials didn't apply here in the sense that conjecture and hearsay testimony were permitted. Also, the grand jurors were permitted to ask questions. Steven listened without understanding how any of it affected him. In fact, it wasn't even clear how it affected anyone. Timothy Warren killed Ophelia James and Timothy Warren was dead. Who was there to indict?

"I guess they're looking at the cops," Margolis answered.

For some reason this made Steven swallow hard and sent a distinct shiver down his back. As surprised and shocked as he had been by the shooting, he had never questioned it. It was a cold and heartless act, sudden yes, but so clear and overwhelming that it seemed built into everything that led up to it, as inevitable as death in tragedy or wet sidewalks after rain. As often as he had gone over the incident in his mind, from the moment Rita Torres called him out of his class until the blinding, deafening explosion in the narrow alley between the weight machines, he hadn't once been able to picture or even consider the possibility of a different outcome. Yet someone, he realized for the first time, was considering precisely that.

For the next few minutes Steven and the lawyer found themselves locked into a brooding silence. Steven didn't have any questions and Margolis didn't seem to have any advice. The impasse lasted until the sound of voices from the hallway made them turn their heads to the door. A moment later two men stepped in, one black, the other white, pushing through the braying pack of reporters. Steven recognized them at once as the two detectives from the weight room. They seemed smaller than he remembered them, the white cop in fact not much bigger than Steven, who was only a shade over five ten.

They recognized him as well, walking past him without an acknowledgment, their looks severe and unfriendly. It was beginning to dawn on Steven that he was the only living witness to what these two men had done in the weight room. He followed them with his eyes to see if they would look at him, but neither of them did. Still, he couldn't help feeling both conspicuous and uncomfortable. Just to have something to do, he tried to get the conversation with Margolis going again, asking him how long he had been working for the UFT. They quickly discovered that they both had graduated from NYU, but it only took a minute for them to explore all the possible connections and come to the conclusion that they didn't know any of the same people and hadn't taken any of the same classes, leaving them again with nothing to say.

A few minutes later Barry Lucasian pushed his way through the media gauntlet in the corridor and slammed the door heavily behind him. He turned, posing for a moment in the doorway in pressed slacks and a sports jacket over a tight polo shirt obviously selected to display his gym teacher's physique. He glanced at Steven and nodded a greeting, then walked straight to the secretary and introduced himself. She told him to help himself to coffee and have a seat.

The way the man moved had always struck Steven as somewhat hostile and arrogant. He was popular enough with some of the tougher kids in the school but he had a reputation for mindless bullying among all the others who had to take P.E. with him. Over the years Steven had tried to talk to him a few times about problems some of his students were having in gym, but Lucasian was cold and unreceptive with Steven, then quickly let the kids know he didn't appreciate their running to other teachers with complaints. Still, he was from La Guardia, and at this moment in this place it gave him more of a bond with Steven than anyone else in the room. When Lucasian gestured for Steven to join him at the coffee, Steven was glad of the chance to break the tension of waiting.

"What time is your summons for?" Lucasian asked.

Steven said nine.

Lucasian checked his watch. "It's already nine-thirty. I guess I can forget about ten," he said.

"The law's delay," Steven said with a shrug. "We'll probably be here all day."

Lucasian stirred at his coffee. "Listen," he said, lowering his voice to a kind of conspiratorial whisper. "This thing's not supposed to be complicated, is it? What are you going to tell them?"

The question caught Steven off guard. "Just what happened," he said.

"Right."

"Why did you ask that?"

"No reason," Lucasian said. "I just don't think we ought to be going into a lot of shit."

Whatever he was trying to say, Steven didn't understand and he wasn't sure he wanted to. It was beginning to sound like a conversation they shouldn't be having. "I'm just going to answer their questions," he said.

Lucasian looked uncomfortable with that answer. "Hey, if it happened in your room you'd be jumpy, too," he snapped defensively. "There wasn't supposed to be kids in there. I could lose my job."

So that was what he was worried about. Somehow Steven thought he had meant more. "I don't think that's what they're investigating," Steven reassured him.

"Don't kid yourself. They need some fall guy and they're not going to fuck with the cops. They'll make a big deal out of what those kids were doing up there, how they got in. I got three classes at the same time, y'know. I can't be everywhere at once."

"Don't worry about it," Steven said. "They're not going to start asking me how they got in or why they were there. If they do, I don't have any answers."

Lucasian looked down at him from the advantage his six feet plus gave him. "I thought you were talking to Timothy," he said.

From the doorway to the grand jury room, the secretary called, "Mr. Hillyer."

"Look, I've got to go," Steven said. "Don't worry."

He took a deep breath and started for the door, glancing at the lawyer for a little last-minute encouragement, a fighter looking back to his corner at the bell. Margolis smiled wanly.

Beyond Margolis, the eyes of the black detective followed Steven like radar, eyes that gleamed like a cat's in the night, cold and distrusting and ultimately unforgiving.

THE assistant district attorney was younger than Steven, with blotchy skin that looked as if he irritated it every time he shaved. His name was Felder—he didn't say his first name—and he held a pair of glasses in his hand, putting them on whenever he consulted the typed pages he held like a wand, gesticulating with them as though they were a crucial piece of evidence. From the questions Felder concocted out of those pages, Steven was able to figure out that they were a typed copy of the statement he had dictated to the police when he was brought to the station house the afternoon of the killings, but knowing this only made him more acutely aware of the advantage Felder had over him. With every question, Steven's mind split in two, like water flowing around an obstacle, half of it focused back on the etched images in his memory while the other half whirled ahead to reconstruct what he had said in the statement. He thought he was clear on everything and had been clear all along, but the fear of contradicting himself gripped him by the throat and wouldn't let go.

The questioning started badly when Steven inadvertently answered a question in such a way as to suggest that Timothy Warren hadn't been his student. He thought Felder was asking whether Timothy was in his homeroom and his answer came out sounding as if he were trying to minimize his connection with Timothy, who had been in his English class the last two years. "Then he *was* your student," Felder said with a distinct sneer when he finally got it straight. He gave the impression he had just caught Steven in a lie.

From there Felder went on to ask a lot of questions about Timothy and Ophelia James. Was Timothy her boyfriend? Steven didn't know.

Was Timothy in love with her? Steven didn't know that either. What kind of relationship did they have? Steven didn't know that they had a relationship. Each answer sounded like an evasion in his own ears and must have sounded even worse to the grand jurors, who looked at him with steady concentration. They were all seated at small tables arranged like students' desks in a semicircle facing him. They had notepads in front of them and glasses of water, and they didn't take their eyes off Steven even when the prosecutor was talking. He had expected to find himself in the familiar geography of a courtroom, where the judge was the centerpiece and the jury sat to the side. Instead, his chair was virtually in the center of the room, the space behind him empty, unused. The arrangement reminded him of an operating theater, in which case he was the patient on the table.

He tried to remind himself that he wasn't on trial, wasn't accused of anything, but it didn't help. He felt as if he were, and Felder seemed to be doing everything in his power to make him feel that way. "Are you saying Timothy Warren didn't have a relationship with Ophelia James?" the prosecutor asked in a tone that sounded as if he didn't believe Steven's answer even before Steven gave it.

"I'm not saying that," Steven answered. "If there was any relationship or connection or friendship, I simply didn't know about it."

"But you knew Timothy Warren quite well?"

"I was his English teacher."

"You weren't especially close to him?"

"I was very close to him. He was my best student."

"And he was closer to you than to any other teacher, would that be a fair characterization?"

"I suppose so."

Why did he *suppose* so? He knew it. Rita Torres knew it, too, when she came looking for him. The room, the jurors, the way Felder questioned him made his answers come out sounding as if he were trying to hide something even when he knew what he wanted to say. He was sure Felder would spot the evasion, but the prosecutor surprised him by nodding and walking to a desk piled high with papers.

"He kept a notebook, didn't he?" Felder asked.

Had they read Timothy's notebook? Did they have the right to do that? Steven wondered.

"Yes, he did," Steven answered from a distance, his mind already sorting through words and phrases that came unbidden from some of the poems Timothy had asked him to read.

Felder rummaged among the papers briefly and then, with an unnecessarily dramatic flourish, held aloft a spiral-bound notebook with a frayed brown cover that Steven recognized at once.

"And he wrote poems in this notebook, isn't that right?"

Steven nodded without answering. He felt as though he were violating something.

"And from time to time he showed you these poems?"

Steven nodded again. The notebook was open in the man's hand and he was reading, his voice singsong and mocking.

> *Forty ways, Ophelia,*
> *Like streets belonging to a foreign gang,*
> *Hostile streets,*
> *Forty, O,*
> *Down into your Manhattan,*
> *The parts we never see or touch,*
> *Is that the way you want it, O?*

Felder stopped and stared at Steven for what seemed a long time before continuing his questioning. The eyes of the grand jurors were locked on Steven as though the poem were his, as though he was the one with fantasies about touching a thirteen-year-old girl in parts we never see or touch.

"Are you familiar with this poem by Timothy Warren, Mr. Hillyer?"

"No," Steven said numbly.

"You've never seen it before?"

"No. I haven't."

"But it does suggest, doesn't it, a relationship of some sort between Timothy Warren and Ophelia James?"

Steven's head was swimming and he took what felt like a very long time before answering. He knew what the district attorney wanted. He wanted Steven to tell the grand jury that Timothy Warren was depraved and dangerous, because if they could see him that way they would understand the necessity of shooting him. But the poem reminded Steven of too much else, and for a minute he put the scene in the weight room out of his mind and concentrated instead on an image of Timothy in an empty classroom, the boy's head bent over the notebook Felder held in his hands as he mumbled his poetry aloud for Steven's response.

"It might suggest a relationship," Steven said. "That would depend, I think, on when it was written."

"Why would it depend on that?"

"We studied *Hamlet* about two months ago."

Four or five of the grand jurors laughed, abrupt and mocking laughter that startled Steven with its harsh, abashing suddenness. His eyes scanned their faces, trying to pick out the ones who had laughed. A black woman, wide and immobile, her face and posture as stern as a statue, stared back at him defiantly, looking through him as easily as if he were glass. She had laughed, he was sure of it. A slender black man fingered the corner of his mouth insolently, a silent-movie gesture of cynical detachment that declared in pantomime that Steven wasn't fooling anyone. Most of the others hadn't understood at all but Felder was going to make them understand.

"You mean this poem might have been written about the character named Ophelia in Shakespeare's play *Hamlet*?"

"It might have been inspired or suggested by that, yes."

"Did Timothy Warren write a lot of Shakespearean poetry?"

"He wrote about things he read."

"But there's nothing about Manhattan in Shakespeare's *Hamlet*, is there? The character Ophelia didn't live in Manhattan, did she?"

"I think that's a sexual reference, Mr. Felder," Steven said. There was a ripple of embarrassed laughter from the jury.

"I see," Felder answered smugly. "And this sexual reference may have been directed at a fictional character in a play or it may have been directed at an actual girl Timothy Warren knew and had these sexual thoughts about?"

"Yes," Steven said, feeling slightly more assured, ready to meet the challenge, unwilling to give so much as an inch. "That's why I said it depends on when it was written."

Felder hesitated, took stock and then jolted Steven by asking, "Did you consider Timothy Warren dangerous, Mr. Hillyer?"

"Dangerous?"

"In the sense that he presented a threat to the well-being of the school? Its students or teachers?"

"No, I didn't consider him dangerous," Steven said flatly.

Felder seemed shocked, almost angry. The heavy black woman stared at Steven with a look of intense concentration.

"But it's true, is it not, Mr. Hillyer, that you filed a report suggesting that he be given a psychological evaluation?"

"Yes. There were other teachers who submitted that request and I subscribed to it."

"I see. What was done as a result of this request?"

"Nothing, as far as I know."

"And you later filed another report suggesting that Timothy be removed from the school and put under psychiatric care? Is that true?"

"That isn't really the way it was," Steven said.

"You mean you subscribed to what other people were recommending again? You just went along with them, is that what you're saying?"

"That isn't what I'm saying. Timothy needed help and he wasn't getting it. We wanted to get it for him."

Steven wanted to say more but it all seemed to be going in the wrong direction. Against his will, he was painting a picture of Timothy that he didn't recognize, and he was afraid that if he said anything else he would only make it worse.

Again Felder surprised him by dropping that line of questioning and moving in another direction. "Would you say you had a good relationship, student-teacher relationship, with Timothy Warren?" he asked.

If there was a trick to the question, Steven didn't see it. "We had a good relationship," he answered cautiously.

"You communicated easily?"

"Sometimes."

"I mean, you're the one he shared his poetry with. Isn't that correct, Mr. Hillyer?"

"Well, it wasn't that simple," Steven said. "Sometimes he would show me poems and stories he had written, and then he would feel vulnerable because I had seen them and I think he resented me for having seen them. He was basically a very private boy. So there were times when he would accuse me of tricking him and he would get angry."

"Did he make threats when he was angry like this?"

"Sometimes."

"I thought you said you didn't consider him dangerous?"

"I thought he was more dangerous to himself."

"More dangerous to himself?" Felder asked.

"He's dead, isn't he?" Steven said.

The black woman with the statue's face looked at Steven for the first time as though he were someone she knew. Her brown eyes were suddenly warm and moist and compassionate. The man next to her nodded his head.

Felder looked as if he had been hit somewhere and the pain had taken a long time to register. Before he could regroup, the heavy woman in the front row of jurors spoke up. "Did you feel sorry for him?" she asked Steven.

Felder wheeled around to face her as though he wanted to object. The last thing in the world he wanted was the jury feeling sorry for Timothy Warren, because the only way they could express that was by indicting the cops, which would serve no purpose other than multiplying the political damage and saddling the district attorney's office with a prosecution the mayor didn't want, the D.A. didn't want and that couldn't in any case be won. For the moment, though, his hands were tied. He couldn't comment on the woman's question because the only things he could have said would have antagonized the jurors. He had no choice but to let Hillyer answer the question and then be ready for him when he was finished.

"I don't know if I felt sorry for him," Steven said. "I don't think I did. I was worried about him but that's not the same thing. It's hard to explain if you didn't know Timothy. Sometimes he was very friendly. In the sense of being open. He was very bright. And creative. If you're a teacher that's what you look for. At other times he was withdrawn and tense. It seemed very clear that he was in a great deal of torment. He was confused, he seemed to be filled with self-loathing. Is that what you wanted to know?"

"Thank you, yes," she said.

Felder said, "I think we're all rather touched by this picture, Mr. Hillyer. And in a city where the education system comes under so much criticism, it's very reassuring to find such a sensitive and dedicated teacher."

Steven flushed red and mumbled an acknowledgment of the unexpected praise. At the same time, he noticed that Felder still had Timothy's notebook in his hand and was leafing through it as if he were looking for something.

"Timothy Warren showed you a lot of his poetry, didn't he, Mr. Hillyer?"

"I wouldn't say a lot. I think there were a lot of things he never showed me."

"If I read you a passage, do you think you'd be able to tell me whether you had seen it or not?"

Steven knew what was coming.

"If I had read it I'd be able to tell you, yes," he said.

Felder read down the page in his hand before he started to read aloud.

Born of your body, Mother, Cunt.

He lowered the page and addressed the jurors. "I'm sorry," he said. "These are Timothy Warren's words. I think it's important that you hear the language."

The stenotypist's fingers clicked like castanets on her miniature keypad as Felder resumed his reading.

> *Born of your body, Mother, Cunt,*
> *Thinking what? Thinking? No way.*
> *None of that shit.*
> *Thinking nothing,*
> *nothing at all and you know it.*
> *A mindless hump-fuck, no thinking involved,*
> *that gave you me,*
> *Like v.d., clap, the last word in gonorrhea,*
> *The ultimate disease.*
> *What's the cure for life, bitch?*
> *A sharp knife? A little hollow bullet?*
> *An ice pick or an ax?*
> *I think I like an ax.*
> *It fits you better, doesn't it?*
> *Ax not. But I will, mother-bitch,*
> *Trust me for that much.*
> *I will.*

Felder lowered the page and the room seemed darker than it had been, as if a cloud had passed although there were no windows. The air hung in the room, wet and lowering.

"Are you familiar with that poem, Mr. Hillyer?" Felder asked in a hushed voice.

"Timothy showed it to me."

"This wasn't a mother in a play he was talking about, was it? It was his own mother?"

"It wasn't a mother in a play."

"And he threatens to kill his mother in this poem, doesn't he? 'Trust me for that much. I will.' Isn't that right?"

"That was how I understood it. Yes."

"This boy you felt sorry for wanted to kill his mother. At that point didn't it cross your mind that Timothy Warren was dangerous?"

This wasn't right. It wasn't the picture Steven wanted them to have in their minds of Timothy.

"It crossed my mind that Timothy was very angry," he said. "That he was in despair. That he needed help."

"But he had threatened to kill his mother?"

"It's a poem, Mr. Felder."

"You mean you didn't take it seriously?"

"He didn't know where his mother was, Mr. Felder. He couldn't find her. How could he kill her if he couldn't find her?"

W H E N Albert Terranova was growing up at the water's edge on Staten Island, the cops used to come into his father's shop late in the afternoon almost every day. They would move a few crates around and use them as chairs, leaning back against the wall while they drank ice-cold sodas they took from the vending machine, unlocking it with the key his father kept hanging from a string next to the machine. They usually brought sandwiches, which they got on the arm from a shop down the street. For Carmine Terranova it wasn't a bad deal since he got a free lunch for the cost of the sodas they drank in the course of the afternoon.

For an hour and a half, maybe two, they talked and smoked cigarettes, dropping the ashes into an oily coffee can that was kept on the floor between the crates for that purpose. In those days cops didn't carry radios, but since everyone in the village knew where they could be found if they were needed, it didn't really matter. Occasionally it would happen (not often, but often enough for Albert to remember the drama of those moments long after he had contributed his own share of exciting incidents to the history of the New York City Police Department) that someone from the village would rush into his father's bicycle store, panting and dripping sweat, sounding the alarm about a local emergency that required the immediate presence of their authority. The first question the cops always asked was whether or not anyone was hurt, and only when they had the answer did they stub their cigarettes and hurry off.

Usually the emergencies involved no more than a traffic accident at the edge of the village or a brawl in one of the shops. Once Mrs. Pagnelli, fat and well into her sixties, lurched through the door breathless from running all the way down from the houses at the top of the hill. "Come, you come right now," she panted, sobbing even in her breathlessness. "Old man Buffone, he shoots himself and his wife."

They asked her if both of them were dead and she said they were. So they finished their cigarettes because the two old people would still be dead when they got there.

Albert worked in his father's shop from the time he turned twelve until he graduated from high school. More than anything else, it was those long afternoons with not enough work to keep his father busy, let alone the two of them, that convinced him he wanted to be a cop. It wasn't the laconic way of life he saw in those daily police visits that drew him to the job; their freedom to drink sodas with their feet up on crates all afternoon held no appeal for a sturdy, energetic boy aching for something bigger than the enclosed and in-closing life of the island. What drew him instead was what the small number of urgent summonses—barely half a dozen of them in as many years—became in his imagination as they grew and bred and multiplied.

Each time it happened, as though by magic, the cracked sidewalk outside his father's bicycle shop filled instantly with curious customers from the surrounding shops. The neighbors waited for the police to come out and then hurried after them like a volunteer constabulary, racing them on foot to the scene of trouble, once in a while piling into their own cars to follow.

Only Albert, because his father didn't believe there was any valid reason for the boy to leave the shop while it was open for business, remained behind, his only vision of the scene of the crime a picture he had to draw for himself on the basis of what he had gleaned from the police programs he listened to at night on the kitchen radio.

There was magic, too, in the very look of them, with their heavy bellies and their massive arms, bare in their summer blouses, covered with thick black hair like pelts, the majestic weight of the equipment they wore at their belts. Their guns were the least of it, for those three-inch bands of black leather also supported their nightsticks and summons books, their flashlights and extra bullets and memo books. He never forgot the day, although he couldn't have been twelve since he hadn't yet started working in the shop, when one of them unhooked his belt and handed it to him. The weight of it caught him by surprise and his hands dropped to his flanks in failure, the belt banging to the floor. His father joined the cops in mortifying laughter, turning a moment of small cruelty into an aching memory guaranteed to insure that this kid, if he had any balls at all, would one day wear a belt like that.

Still, in the boy's mind the cops in his father's shop were shadows of shadows, ordinary and even boring men who shared only the smallest jot of the power of real police. He knew they were little more than small-town constables despite the fact that they were actually officers of the New York City Police Department, technically liable to find themselves transferred, at the merest whim of a commanding officer, to precincts as far away as the jungles of Harlem, where there were no white men to be seen, or the teeming ghetto of the Lower East Side, where a cop could walk the streets for hours without hearing a single word of English. The truth is it never happened, for Staten Island in those days before the bridge was adamantly its own world, a world that had to be policed by its own people just as its schools had to be taught, its garbage collected and its fires put out by its own teachers, collectors and firemen.

Later, as Albert became part of the force and moved off the island so as not to be sentenced to a perpetuity of patrolling its villages and hamlets, as he worked his way up in the Department through detective and detective sergeant but long before he became Chief, he learned to recognize in those indolent afternoons in his father's bicycle shop, where even the motes in the air moved dreamily, a pattern that was not only endemic to police departments everywhere but was so profoundly built into the system and the psyches of the men that only the most superficial aspects of it could ever be changed. From time to time, the Department hierarchy would crack down on gratuities, favors, leaving the post, cooping. An apple off a stand became a felony; a cop who so much as set foot in a retail establishment was required to have an entry in his memo book detailing the reason.

But nothing changed, not in the slightest. Because the essence of being a cop never changed. Becoming a cop meant becoming the law, embodying in yourself and your uniform, in your blood, in the way your eyes looked at the world and in the words that came out of your lips, the only civic authority most of the people who saw you would ever know. Cops were gods, and gods don't give change.

To be sure, most cops didn't understand this, any more than most civilians. Easily, almost inevitably, they assumed that the respect that sometimes came their way unbidden, sometimes had to be demanded, was their due in some direct or personal sense rather than an offering to forces they merely embodied. From this profound and arrogant misconception, a system of comfortable privileges easily decayed into the rampant, pervasive and virtually universal corruption that came to govern all aspects of police operations, dictating not only what the cops did but what they didn't do, not only when they kept their eyes open but also when they looked the other way. For so many free meals, so many free suits of clothes, whatever it was he was selling, a shopkeeper bought the privilege of closing up for the night and going home comfortable in the assurance his store was being looked after. Conversely, for so many bucks a week, so many blow jobs for the boys in blue, a man was given a license to run numbers, run girls, run drugs without undue worry about either the law or unlicensed competition.

Al Terranova knew as well as the reformers did that this was what it had become, but he also believed in the possibility and even the necessity of what he liked to call the gentle and benign forms of corruption. The apple off the stand, the bowl of free noodles in the Chinese restaurant, the suit of clothes for your kid's confirmation, and even—yes, especially and above all—the hours in the back room of a crusty old guinea's bicycle shop with a can of soda and a cigarette and your feet up on a box. These not only had to exist but should exist because in the best of possible worlds a cop shapes the physical and psychological space of his beat the way wind and gravity shape a planet. It wasn't a question of giving or taking but simply a matter of the way things *flow* in the shaped space of a cop's beat. The moment people forget it—cops and civilians alike—the gratuities become graft, the lost hours derelictions, and the police themselves an occupying army to whom no one in fact owes anything.

The relevance of these reflections wasn't completely clear to Chief Terranova as he stepped off the elevator on the top floor of Headquarters and headed for the Commissioner's office. The connection, if there was one, and he knew his own habits of mind well enough to expect that there always would be, lay in the fact that two good men were being badly fucked. Anything that threw light on why had to be relevant.

It was a long way to come around to the conclusion that what was wrong with the Department, with the city and with every other political subdivision he cared to consider was the fact that cops didn't count anymore. The Commissioner's office had phoned down to warn him that it looked like Franks and Donadio were about to be indicted in the Bronx for their roles in the shooting of Timothy Warren. Not much of a surprise there, despite the assurances he had been given that it wouldn't happen because everyone from the Bronx D.A. to the mayor was looking to get the two dead kids buried as quickly and quietly as possible.

Except for the flags of the United States of America and the City of New York, which dominated the wall behind the immense reception desk, the top-floor foyer at One Police Plaza could have housed the head offices of any modern corporation. The look was clean, modern and antiseptic despite the use of earth colors to blend with the brick architecture of what was still called the new headquarters although it was almost twenty years old. The men moving through the area on their way from one set of offices to another were for the most part in their forties or fifties, but a surprising number of them were in shirtsleeves, giving the impression of youth and vigor, or at least of middle-aged men who appeared youthful and vigorous.

"He's expecting you," the female officer at the reception desk said as Terranova moved toward her. She pressed a button to buzz open the door behind her. On the other side of the door, numerous corridors, many of them short enough to be little more than bays, radiated out in all directions, testifying to the size of the Commissioner's staff. The doors to the individual offices were unnumbered and unmarked, an indication that few people got this far who didn't already know their way around.

The door to the P.C.'s office was at the end of the hall. Terranova knocked once and stepped through it into the presence of the most powerful man in the life of any police officer.

Simon Pound didn't look the part. Small, slender and balding, he moved with almost birdlike timidity, his eyes constantly darting from whoever had his attention at the moment to any other listeners in the area, as though he were endlessly monitoring their reactions. In public he kept his intense nervousness under control with a mask of benign and noncommittal impassivity that, more than anything else, marked him as a man few people liked and even fewer trusted. Born and raised in Tennessee, he had come to New York in his early twenties and still looked as though the city made him uncomfortable.

"Come in, Al," Pound said, accepting Terranova's growl as a greeting.

Behind the Commissioner, a young man with curly hair and dark, Semitic features rose from a chair and moved to join them. The Commissioner introduced him as Philip Boorstin, "from the mayor's office," and then asked Terranova if he wanted anything to drink. He gestured with an almost imperceptible toss of his head when the Chief declined, and a young officer at the side of the room silently and obediently left the bar and disappeared through a doorway.

"It looks like the D.A.'s throwing us a bit of a curve," Boorstin said.

The note of weary insolence in his voice rubbed Terranova the wrong way. "Is that what you call it?" he asked sharply.

"What do you want me to call it?" Boorstin answered, stiffening.

"Are you familiar with the term *cluster fuck*, Mr. Boorstin?"

The Commissioner blanched and cleared his throat. His distaste for strong language was well known and many wondered how he had made it through more than thirty years in the Police Department. "This cuts all of us, Al," he said in mild rebuke.

"Not all in the same place, sir," Terranova shot back.

The Commissioner's eyes narrowed and his lips tightened into a straight hard line. Three years earlier, when Junius Ehrlich appointed him Commissioner, Pound had tried hard to come up with a reason for naming someone other than Al Terranova Chief of Detectives but surrendered in the end to reality. If he didn't pick Terranova, he'd be vulnerable to second-guessing every time anything went wrong. Terranova in that sense was an inevitability, a force of nature, and Simon Pound was a civilized man with little fondness for forces of nature, which in his mind were synonymous with earthquakes, blizzards, thunderstorms and decay. Of all the service chiefs under his command, he had least contact with his Chief of Detectives and was invariably reminded why every time they met.

He turned and walked to the window, leaving Terranova to dump his verbal refuse on the young deputy mayor's front porch. For all practical purposes Pound was signaling as clearly as if he put it in words that the Commissioner's office was washing its hands of the whole affair.

Terranova had no trouble reading the message. The P.C. washed his hands regularly. He had very clean hands. Terranova hadn't expected help from that quarter and wasn't surprised not to be getting it. The man who mattered here was Boorstin, who spoke for the mayor.

"I was told," Terranova said, "that the mayor wanted this taken care of."

"You were told right," Boorstin agreed.

"Then why the hell wasn't it?"

"All due respect, but you're looking at the wrong guy," Boorstin said. "I spent a whole day in the Bronx trying to make that happen."

"And?"

"And nothing. I got Artemis Reach in a hammerlock and made him promise to be a good boy."

"Reach isn't the problem."

"He would have been. If he wanted your detectives' heads on a plate, they would have been on a plate."

"They are on a plate."

Boorstin shook his head. "I don't know what to tell you," he said. "It was supposed to be easy. You go into the grand jury, you show them the knife, you draw them a picture of how this psychotic kid was holding this cute little girl, no bigger than a kitten, and that's the end of it. Righteous shooting."

"And?"

"Some goddamn schoolteacher comes in and tells them the boy with the knife was Keats or Shelley or something like that. His mother abandoned him, et cetera, et cetera. And all of a sudden everyone is melting over this knife-wielding psychotic. All of a sudden it's a big deal that the little girl was dead already. Forget the fact that the only reason she's dead is that Timothy Warren killed her, snapped her neck and let her suffocate to death. Forget the fact that Keats and Shelley didn't break girls' necks. They're crying for this kid. The D.A. trots in two more teachers who were involved in this thing and they tell the jury the kid was trouble. But you can't get the shit back in the goose. All the grand jury wants to know is, if the girl is dead already, then how come the cop has to take Timothy Warren's head off? It's not over till it's over, but the word I get is it looks like they're going to indict."

"Both of them?"

Boorstin shrugged.

"How many shooters do they think there were?"

"Well that's exactly what we're up against. We're talking Bronx here, they don't like cops. Believe me, as soon as the papers pick up on this gentle poet angle there's going to be no end to this thing."

"That's your problem. Mine is what I tell Franks and Donadio."

"I wouldn't tell them anything yet," Boorstin said. "Mayor Ehrlich is still committed to preventing this incident from turning into an issue."

"It's an issue for every cop in the city," Terranova said.

Boorstin smiled. For the most part he found it easier to deal with cops than practically any other brand of city functionary. They were instinctively political, more political even than most of the politicians, because power was their stock in trade. In turn that meant they almost always got the point.

"Does that mean you're going to make it an issue?" Boorstin asked.

"I don't have to. They've got lawyers, they've got a union. If you stick him, doth not a cop scream?"

"Why do I get the feeling that if they did their screaming to the press or started demonstrating, you wouldn't stop them?"

It was Terranova's turn to smile. He didn't have to make threats if Boorstin was going to make them for him. "I couldn't stop them if I wanted to," he said.

At the window, the Commissioner turned. "There will be no police demonstrations," he said crisply, stating what he took to be a fact.

"With all due respect, Commissioner," Boorstin said, "there'll be demonstrations you'll be able to hear all the way up here."

All due respect was the way he told men who outranked him that they didn't know what they were talking about. In Boorstin's mind all crises were simple and called for simple management techniques. When people didn't understand that, things got out of control. In this case it was a matter of keeping Artemis Reach and Community Board Sixty-one quiet, keeping Terranova and the Police Department happy. Once anyone started screaming, the others would get into the act and it would be the nineteen-seventies all over again.

Terranova said, "And I assume you're here to tell me how you can keep that from happening?"

The tone was sarcastic but there was a hint of both realism and respect behind it. Boorstin elected to respond to the realism.

"Oh, I know how to keep it from happening," he said. "All we have to do is keep your detectives out of court."

A RABBI, a priest and a minister go to their first hockey game. A rabbi, a priest and a minister are marooned on a desert island. A rabbi, a priest and a minister are standing in front of a brothel. There are over a hundred thousand rabbi-priest-and-minister jokes and not one of them is funny. The least funny of all was Congressman Bert Kellem, whose entire philosophy of government was based on the principle that elected officials should be photographed as often as possible with the maximum number of rabbis, priests, ministers, and secular representatives of the various racial and ethnic groups in the Bronx. He regularly had his picture taken with Democratic candidates from all over the country who came to the Bronx to be videotaped making vague promises in front of desolate ruins and then went away.

Only a week ago his office was filled with Haitians, Cubans, Puerto Ricans, blacks, Jews and Irishmen gathered together to deplore the desecration of a synagogue in Congressman Kellem's district. They ate lunch, drew up a joint statement, posed for a group picture with the congressman and were on their way to their respective homes when a pack of teenage monsters sprayed swastikas on the gates of a Jewish cemetery and turned over a dozen tombstones.

For years, such irrelevant ad hoc multiethnic alliances had been issuing statements and evaporating without accomplishing anything other than keeping Congressman Kellem's name before his constituency and adding to his reputation as a man committed to the regeneration of the Bronx. Today a new set of community pillars had gathered together to address the problem of equal access to construction contracts in the borough.

L. D. Woods, Kellem's administrative assistant, led them into the conference room to get the meeting started. Kellem himself wouldn't put in an appearance until the statements were all drafted and it was time to take pictures, but no one minded his absence. On the contrary. Sleekly attractive in a blue-black dress that caressed her hips and buttocks like body oil, L. D. Woods was quite capable of making seven old men feel young enough to remember why they wished they were even younger.

"What's a girl like you wasting your time with a goat like Bert Kellem for?" Harry Lipsky teased. Monsignor Fennecy reminded him that he wasn't supposed to say *girl* and Clifford Johnson said, "Woman, right, L.D.?" in a tone that made it sound as if she would be agreeing to go to bed with him if she said yes.

L.D. laughed when she was supposed to laugh, slipping away from their hands with practiced skill, giving them just enough to make them feel good and let them know she was a good sport. She was a woman in her thirties after all, old enough to know the score, old enough to know what she did to men. Being a woman meant being one of the guys, no more schoolgirlish blushes at lascivious remarks, no shrieks of outrage at an uninvited touch or a quick feel.

Those were the rules in this man's world and L. D. Woods played by them and knew them for the bullshit they were. In an out-of-the-way closet of her mind, where the data could be stored for use tomorrow without getting in the way today, she kept track of all the loathsome liberties and indecent touches, tallying them up against the day when she would present the bill. She hated the world of men without hating men, just as she despised the men she worked with without losing her ability to love her lovers.

As she moved about the table distributing copies of Congressman Kellem's memorandum on the current state of construction contracts in the Bronx and listening to the smarmy banter, the door to the conference room opened and Debbie, a mouse-haired nineteen-year-old secretary who was classified as an intern because Kellem paid her less than the minimum wage, leaned in to tell L.D. she had a phone call in her office.

L.D. suggested that the conferees familiarize themselves with the congressman's memorandum while she was gone.

"Hurry back, hon."

"Not gonna be much fun without you, L.D."

"Can't just leave us alone like this. Whatdya say you let Debbie stay? Whatdya say, Debbie?"

As L.D. closed the door behind her and headed for her office, Debbie walked with her. "They're such pigs," the girl said.

"Are they?" L.D. asked, hollow and noncommittal. It was a point of pride with her that no one, not even a girl who could have used the lessons, was allowed so much as a glimpse into her private thoughts.

The call was from Charles Dollenfield, who covered the Bronx political beat for the *Post*. He wrote well enough to get himself space in the paper whenever he needed it if not quite well enough to get himself out of the Bronx. "Quick question. Can we have lunch?" he asked as soon as L.D. got on the line.

"I'd love to, Charlie," she said. "Today's impossible. Is this social or is there something I can help you with?"

"Mainly I just like looking at you," he said. "But I'll settle for a quick word on how come no one's saying anything about the La Guardia school thing."

"Could it be there's nothing to say?"

"Artemis has nothing to say? Since when?"

"Artemis is a smart man, Charlie."

"You mean he's been asked to keep quiet?"

She didn't say anything. Dollenfield took the silence as a confirmation. "By the mayor?"

Again she didn't answer.

"Okay, I've got the picture. What I don't get is why he's going along with it. What have they got on him?"

"I'm on the Board, Charlie. I can't answer a question like that."

At least she was confirming that he was on the right track.

"Why is it," he said, "that nothing gets a reporter interested faster than a story that everyone wants to go away?"

L.D. was just as interested. In the first place because she didn't like the smart-assed deputy mayor who came up to the Bronx to strong-arm Artemis Reach into silence, but it went deeper than that. Congressman Kellem hadn't yet and wouldn't ever say so much as a word to indicate that he knew two children had been killed in his district. The police wanted to get off the hook for killing the boy, Reach and the Board for leaving him in school long enough to kill the girl. And to the mayor's office the whole incident was nothing more than a sticky mess to be contained like an oil spill.

"It's not going away," L.D. told Dollenfield, choosing her words carefully. "Once the indictments come in, I'm sure people will have a lot to say."

This was news. She could almost hear his pulse accelerate over the phone line. He had been told that the Bronx district attorney's office wasn't going for an indictment. L. D. Woods seemed to be saying otherwise.

"Is this something you know?" he asked.

"Charlie, I can't do your job for you," she said.

"Right," he agreed. "You're a wonderful person and I owe you a lunch."

Dollenfield hung up the phone and called Artemis Reach's office. He had it on good authority, he said, that the police officers responsible for Timothy Warren's death were going to be indicted. Reach answered carefully, choosing his words to let uptown readers relish the pleasure he took in seeing the police in trouble without giving downtown readers anything they could put their fingers on as the latest example of his demagoguery. If the reports were true, he said, then he was both shocked and distressed to learn of still more wrongdoing in a police department that seemed to specialize in wrongdoing. What he took away with one hand, he gave back with the other, commending the grand jury for refusing to let the incident be swept under the carpet merely because the victim happened to be an emotionally disturbed young black man.

It was vintage Reach, an inflammatory statement that said nothing. Dollenfield took it down verbatim and hopped a cab to One Police Plaza so that he could read it to Commissioner Pound in person.

The Commissioner gulped audibly but quickly answered that it wouldn't be appropriate for him to comment at this time. This was a judicious response and might have defused the matter for the time being if he had been able to let it go at that. But Simon Pound was an articulate and rational man who couldn't resist the temptation to clarify himself when Dollenfield asked whether or not the Department at this time stood behind Detectives Franks and Donadio.

The first minute and a half of the Commissioner's response was exemplary, citing the concept of due process, the fact that the Police Department's Internal Affairs Division was conducting its own investigation of the matter, and the principle that the Department always stood behind its men unless and until evidence of wrongdoing was properly established. But like most men when they begin to be afraid they have said too much, the Commissioner said more. "The important point to keep in mind," he said, "is that it's a complex situation. We're not talking about some little red schoolhouse. There are students walking around there with knives, they're molesting girls in rooms that are supposed to be locked, it's potentially explosive and an officer responding to a situation like that . . ."

A reporter normally doesn't interrupt a police commissioner but Simon Pound had said the magic word. Dollenfield broke in to ask if Ophelia James had been molested.

Pound realized his mistake at once and quickly backtracked. He remembered reading, in one of the Chief of Detectives' communications, a reference to something about the girl's underwear that was supposed to be checked out. But he wasn't clear on the details and had a vague though nagging suspicion this information wasn't supposed to have been released.

"There are some indications suggesting this possibility," he said but wouldn't comment further except to say the matter was "still under investigation."

Dollenfield, eager to file his story, went away without pushing it further, leaving the Commissioner to congratulate himself, at least until the morning editions came out, on successfully getting the cat back into the bag.

T H E knob felt strange in his hand and the key turned loosely in the lock, as if the works were missing. When he bent down to look, Steven could see deep gouges in the door frame and scratches all around the lock. Apparently someone had gone at it with a pair of pliers. He took a deep breath and tried to think what to do, his stomach in a tight knot as his mind raced with images of what he'd find inside.

Putting his hand on the knob, he pushed at the door. It slid back more than he wanted it to. He stopped moving, every muscle in his body tensed in dread, and then slowly opened the door wide enough to step through. The sight in front of him was enough to make him cry.

His apartment looked like the scene of a terrible accident, the wreckage strewn everywhere as though some powerful force had churned through it with random and reckless violence, shattering and scattering everything it met. He didn't know where to look first.

Books, tumbled off the shelves, lay everywhere, on the floor, on the windowsill, under the tables, spines up, pages splaying out under them like the contents of so many spilled vessels. Handfuls of loose sheets, ripped and twisted from their bindings, lay in scattered clusters. He picked his way across the room, weaving forward as though he were wading through a battlefield strewn with disembodied limbs, here and there the sight of familiar pages sickening him anew.

Ahead of him he saw his Blake, the large folio, its cover bent back and broken. He sucked in a gasp of pain that shuddered all the way down his body, and stooped to pick it up. The pages had been crumpled up and tossed aside, and many were gone entirely. He ran his hand gently along the top sheet, smoothing it with the wet-eyed tenderness of a child fixing the fur of his rain-wet bear. *"The tygers of wrath,"* he read, *"are wiser than the horses of instruction."*

Setting the book carefully on the arm of a chair, he looked around, slowly taking it all in. Everything he owned had been swept up in the vortex, the walls were stained with the contents of the few bottles of wine he owned, the bottles themselves lying smashed and empty on the floor, the furniture slashed and overturned, even the plant on his desk ripped, leaf for leaf, stems and vase strewn on the floor. There were chunks of white stuff spread across the floor like globs of soft dough. He didn't recognize them and moved closer until he could see that they were stuffing from the couch. For some reason, this made him cry out. The wreckage was so complete he wouldn't even have known how to begin putting it back together and hadn't the strength to try.

He didn't dare go into the bedroom or kitchen. Not yet anyway. He knew they would be much the same, and even if they weren't, what did it matter? He wanted to run away but instead he found himself standing by his desk and dialing the police. He reported a burglary without knowing whether anything had been taken, and it hardly seemed to matter. The woman at the other end of the line took his name and address and said that a detective would be there shortly.

He hung up the phone and realized that until the police got there he probably shouldn't touch anything. That was what the police usually said, although the policewoman on the phone hadn't mentioned it.

While he waited Steven began checking to see if anything actually had been stolen. The television was gone. And the tape deck and tuner and amplifier. He hadn't noticed at first because of the wreckage, but he noticed now. It didn't matter. If they hadn't been taken, they would have been destroyed. Then he remembered having read about burglars who trashed rooms and urinated and defecated on the floors. Instantly, his despair gave way to a rage so unlike anything he had ever experienced that it frightened him. He strode quickly across the room and down the short corridor to the kitchen, knowing in his heart that if the men who did this were ever caught, he wouldn't feel satisfied unless they were ground down to the floor like everything before him, their faces buried in their own filth.

He stopped short at the entrance to the tiny kitchen. There were no signs of disorder. Everything was exactly as he left it. They hadn't been there. It hardly seemed possible.

Maybe it was a trick. It had to be a trick. They had left the kitchen alone in order to fool him, so that he would think everything was all right in there. Then in a day or two he would open a drawer or take a pot from the cupboard and find inside a rotten stinking mass of shit.

Impulsively, he began yanking open drawers and cabinets in a frenzy of looking for what he dreaded to find. Five minutes later, short of breath and on the edge of hysteria, he had taken out everything, looked everywhere and found nothing. It wasn't a trick. They hadn't got to the kitchen.

He stood in the center of the room, catching his breath, teetering on the brink of gratitude for being spared this horror. Maybe, please God maybe, they didn't get to the bedroom either.

He didn't hurry now but walked with an almost glacial calm, poised between hope and fear. The bedroom door was closed. Was that good or bad? He didn't know whether to pray or scream or walk away, but before he could make a decision it seemed to be made for him and his hand was on the knob, which turned and swung away from him.

All his senses reeled in a drunken riot at the sight of such blinding disorder it actually looked as if the whole room were in teeming motion. The bitter taste of vomit burned at the back of his mouth. A vile stench rising from somewhere in the room like a toxic steam sickened him and a ringing in his ears sent him staggering back against the door frame.

Through his tightly closed eyes he could still see the broken lamps, the shattered mirror, the slashed mattress, its bowels spilled across the floor like dirty snow. He held his breath but couldn't lessen the fetid stink that filled his nostrils. The ringing noise went on and on. Paralyzed, he was almost glad not to be able to move, not to be able to do anything, not to have to address the question of what there was to be done. When the ringing wouldn't stop, slowly the notion filtered up into his consciousness that it was a real sound, not something in his head. The doorbell, he realized with an effort. The police. Of course. It was the police.

He turned and ran to the front door, which swung slowly open as he neared it. Two figures stood framed in the doorway. A man and a woman. "Steven Hillyer?" the woman said.

Steven agreed.

"You reported a burglary."

It couldn't have been a question. Unless she was blind. He didn't know how to respond.

"I'm Detective West," she said. "This is Detective Mullaney. Do you mind if we look around?"

"Whatever you have to do," Steven said.

They were both young and attractive in a conventional way, her hair in tight curls that settled down over her forehead, his smooth-shaven, square-featured face as bland and open as a picture in a yearbook. They moved into the room and drifted apart, each taking in the damage with the studious detachment of archaeologists. They looked so young and inexperienced, yet acted as though they had seen the destruction of a thousand homes before. It struck Steven suddenly that they must on occasion come upon scenes like this where a dead body or even the bloodied bodies of an entire family were strewn amidst the wreckage and he felt ashamed of the excessiveness of his own feelings.

He watched as Detective West stooped to pick up a book and turned it over in her hand. "Don't you look for fingerprints?" Steven asked.

"In a mess like this?" She looked around the room and glanced to her partner. "Fred?" she asked.

The other detective pursed his lips and shook his head.

"It wouldn't do any good," she said, resuming her search.

He wanted to ask why it wouldn't do any good but didn't get a chance. "You're a schoolteacher, aren't you, Mr. Hillyer?" Detective Mullaney asked from behind him.

The question startled Steven, sending a vague and unclear alarm sounding through his nervous system.

"How did you know that?" he asked.

The detective shrugged. "Thought I recognized the name," he said.

How could he have recognized the name? Steven's name wasn't familiar. He started to say something but Detective West spoke before he did.

"Was the door locked, Mr. Hillyer?" she asked.

As Steven's head turned toward her, she smiled prettily. Was she trying to distract him? Had she jumped in on purpose to keep him from questioning Mullaney?

"Yes, I always lock it when I go out," he mumbled.

"And what time did you discover the break-in?" She had her memo book in her hand and was recording his answers.

"I don't know," he stammered, looking over at Mullaney, who was returning his look. "When I called. I don't know what time it was. I don't even know what time it is now."

She checked her watch. "It's eight o'clock. Your call came in at seven forty-three."

She seemed friendly. She was helpful. Whatever unformed suspicions Steven felt had to be crazy. He told himself they were crazy.

And then Mullaney said, "These things have a way of happening, Mr. Hillyer."

Steven swung around. "What do you mean?" he demanded.

The detective smiled blankly. "Just that they happen," he said.

"Why are you saying that?" His voice sounded shrill even to his own ears.

"Because this is a dangerous city, Mr. Hillyer," the pretty cop with the curls on her forehead said, smiling again. "I guess that's what we need the police for, isn't it?"

"It could even happen again," Mullaney said.

"Is that some kind of threat?" Steven demanded.

"We're police officers, Mr. Hillyer," Mullaney said. "Is there some reason police officers would want to threaten you?"

FRIDAY

T H E trucks arrived a few minutes before seven while the streets were still empty. There were two of them, blue and white vans, and they glided almost soundlessly to a stop in front of La Guardia Junior High School, their engines and lights cutting out at once as though this were a clandestine operation. The sky was light, clear and pale to a bleached and sickly whiteness, and the sun stood only a few degrees above the horizon, glaring down the avenue between grotesquely long shadows.

Two dozen troopers, their visored helmets under their arms, slipped from the trucks silently, nervous young men in their early twenties moving along the early morning avenue as though they had been dropped behind enemy lines. There was little conversation, and the few men who ventured to say anything at all were answered for the most part by dark looks.

A radio car rounded the corner and stopped alongside the first of the vans. Borough Commander Dwayne Norland stepped to the street and scanned the scene, expecting to see before his eyes an embodiment of the deployment scheme he had outlined on his blackboard hours before the sun came up.

His jaw clenched in anger as he saw that the random milling of the men on the sidewalk no more resembled his planned formations than a pig and a chicken look like bacon and eggs. He spotted Lieutenant Eugene Larocca in their midst and began moving in his direction. Before he had taken two steps Larocca hurried toward him on the run. The lieutenant greeted the Borough Commander with the limp salute, barely more than a brush of the cap, employed by police officers in public places.

"The men have been briefed?" Norland asked in a tone of unmistakable displeasure.

"Yes, sir," the lieutenant answered.

Norland checked the scene again, trying to square the chaotic clumps of police officers with the ordered picture in his mind.

"Shall I deploy them now, sir?" Larocca asked.

"Unless there's something you're waiting for, Lieutenant."

Larocca turned and hurried back to the men. A few brief orders were all it took and the little knot of men began to move and shift, passing each other this way and that like a marching band spelling out letters on a football field. As Norland watched from his vantage point in the middle of the street, lines formed, points took on meaning, a pattern crystallized out of the chaos.

Norland himself seemed to change as he watched, his short, square body stretching taller and thinner, his spine striving for and attaining an unnatural rigidity. By the time his troops were fully deployed in front of the school's main entrance, the Borough Commander was virtually a filament. As often as he had done this in the past, he never failed to be awed by the geometrical beauty and irresistible force created by the proper arrangement of properly trained men.

Satisfied at last, he nodded his approval and turned to his car. Across the boulevard, a derelict shambling in the shadows like a werewolf seeking its den before the full light of day stopped long enough to wonder at the maneuvers. For an instant his pale, runny eyes met Norland's across the widest conceivable gulf, each seeming to ask the other what possible use his existence there on that Bronx street might serve. Then the derelict broke the contact, turned and continued on his way, while Borough Commander Norland slipped back into his car and let it take him quickly away.

He had ordered this exercise on no one's authority but his own. As the commanding officer of all uniformed services in the Bronx, there was no one for him to ask, unless one counted the brass downtown. Norland didn't. He took orders from downtown but he never asked for them. The notion that the police interface, as he called it, with the school system might involve diplomatic niceties beyond the ken of a uniformed cop, no matter how high his rank, simply didn't occur to him. More than that, it couldn't even have been explained to him. Commissioner Pound himself had been unambiguous in his account of the lawlessness inside the school. Under such circumstances, the duties of a Borough Commander were obvious.

The walls of La Guardia Junior High were Dwayne Norland's Yalu River, and Dwayne Norland knew what to do when he got there.

* * *

THE powerful sedatives prescribed by Dr. Carlisle did nothing for the pain. All they could do was put her to sleep, but even sleep did no good because there was no way for her to turn off the dreams, no sleep deep enough to drown awareness. Victoria James swallowed the pills and turned off all the lights, then padded softly through rooms lit only by street lamps until the medicine began to take effect. Then it was time to climb into bed and pull the covers up to her chin the way she used to tuck in Ophelia when Ophelia was a little girl.

In the dark, hiding from herself, she fell asleep like falling through space, drifting endlessly backward, out of control. The drugs gave her that much, but no more. They helped her stop thinking about her daughter. But the pain was there, unfocused yet still as real and reckless as before. She felt a tremor in the bed as though it were being shaken by large, gentle hands, and knew that she was sobbing. An awful hollowness spread out from her chest as everything inside her that kept her alive was scooped and scraped out, until even in her drowsiness she knew that something terribly vital had been lost.

This was the worst part, her fears and sorrows turning in her artificial delirium into dreams of rats and worms and unclean animals gnawing at lungs as pink as cotton candy, at twisted viscera that gleamed like strands of wet, raw dough. In her dreams the body lived and moved, squirming like a halved snake until it jerked upright and she thought she heard a scream from its broken throat, only to find that she was sitting up in bed, the echoes of her own scream fading away in the darkness, taking the nightmare with them as her eyes opened on the empty walls.

And so she would think of Ophelia, gentle, sweet Ophelia, who was her heart and her life. The tears that dripped into the clumped bedclothes were Ophelia's tears, the tears that used to spread like ointment from Ophelia's cheeks to her own when she held her little girl.

Her night passed in alternating fits of wretched wakefulness and tortured sleep, until finally the steady droning of the radio drifted into her consciousness, dragging her slowly back to the awful ache of another morning and another day. In the next bedroom Ophelia's alarm would be ringing too.

No it wouldn't.

A woman's husky voice floated through the room, filling it with meaningless news about a mayors' conference in Phoenix and a fistfight among baseball players. In the other bedroom Ophelia would be dressing to the propulsive rhythm of her music.

No she wouldn't.

Victoria James turned on her side to roll away from the nagging voice, fighting to keep her eyes closed just a little longer. It was then that the words stabbed at her, sending a blinding flash of fresh pain straight through her skull. She wrenched around violently, eyes staring, breath coming instantly hard. Her mind was clear, focused like a powerful beam on the radio and the words she had just heard. *The possibility that Ophelia James had been sexually molested before her death Monday in a Bronx junior high school.*

She flew from the bed, her hand jabbing out to stop the hateful voice. In her wildness she sent the radio skittering from the nightstand, plunging toward the floor. A collection of voices chirped inane jingles as the cord caught on the lamp and the radio swung in midair.

Victoria James raced to the kitchen and grabbed the phone, her fingers fumbling as useless as sticks as she tried to dial the number. On the fourth try she made it.

Dr. Carlisle answered the telephone himself.

"It's Victoria James," she said. "Why are they saying my little girl was molested?"

PHILIP Boorstin's day started with the phone ringing while he was in the shower, which had never once meant good news since the day he got the cordless phone for the bathroom. He stepped out from under the water enough to extend the antenna on the damn thing and answer it, but Rachel's voice came through as if she were calling from the bottom of the East River.

Rachel in turn had just got off the phone with a staffer on the City Hall night desk who thought Boorstin should know about the police action at La Guardia Junior High. City Hall etiquette dictated that in the event of any emergency short of nuclear attack, junior staff members reached their superiors through their secretaries, presumably so that those who chose to spend the night where they weren't supposed to didn't have to worry about anyone other than their secretaries knowing.

Philip took the news about the police action without comment other than that he would be right in, set the phone down on the shelf and stepped back under the water, which had maliciously turned cold. Adjusting his shower was the curse of his life, a daily torture that required virtually imperceptible taps in a clockwise or counterclockwise direction. The slightest excess of force changed the water temperature from scaldingly hot to instant hypothermia or vice versa. Two generations of superintendents and an army of professional plumbers—the witty oxymoron of the phrase *professional plumbers* amused him every time he thought about it—had wrestled with the problem and failed to eliminate it, except by periodically curtailing the flow of water for days at a time while they worked on it. Long before this, Philip had resigned himself to spending the worst part of his mornings performing his ritualistic appeasements of the shower gods.

He rewarded himself for success by standing under the running water for as long as possible, with the adjustable shower head turned all the way to "massage" and the water pulsing onto the back of his neck with soothing and insistent steadiness. Hearing that the police had declared war on Community Board Sixty-one entitled him to a moment of relaxation, and he hadn't even finished his first cup of coffee. There were mornings he would have welcomed the chance to stand under the shower all day, and this had the earmarks of being one of them.

Realistically, that wasn't an option. It was a condition of his job in particular and of life in general that the things you can always duck out of are the things you don't mind doing, while the ones you desperately want to escape will follow you anywhere. He used his time under the shower to try to figure out how this morning's catastrophe might have come about. His operating assumption was that Simon Pound was too spineless to have ordered such an inflammatory action but was perhaps just spineless enough to have let himself be talked into it by someone in the Borough Command.

With a sigh of resignation that bordered on self-pity, he stepped out from under the water again and reached for the phone. He dialed Simon Pound's private number, which would automatically reroute the call to wherever he might be. (Unlike deputy mayors, the police had the budgetary wherewithal to keep even their secretaries from knowing where they spent their nights.) After a few clicks and buzzes he had the Commissioner himself on the line.

"Simon, it's Philip Boorstin," he said. "What the hell is going on?"

"Boorstin," the Commissioner repeated as though he were trying to place the name. Then he said, "I don't know. What are you talking about?"

Philip hadn't even considered the possibility that the Commissioner didn't know what his own police force was doing, because in the real world it shouldn't have been a possibility. In a few quick sentences he told Pound the little he knew about the situation and Pound asked, "Where are you calling from?"

"Home," Philip said. "I want to see you in your office as soon as you get in."

"Have you got water running there?"

Stringing together a half-dozen curses in his mind, Philip turned off both taps. "I have to know," he said. "Are you telling me you didn't authorize this?"

"It's the first I've heard of it," Pound answered. "Are you sure your information is correct?"

"Damn sure. I want you to get on the phone right now and call it off, Commissioner. What time are you going to be in your office?"

"I'll be there in a half hour but my morning's pretty well booked."

"Booked!" Philip almost screamed. With the shower off, the air in the bathroom was cold enough to start his teeth chattering. "I'm not talking about an appointment for a goddamn haircut. We've got a crisis here. Someone in your department fucked the duck and I think we'd damn well better get to the bottom of it."

The Commissioner's voice came back even colder than the beads of water on Philip's goosefleshed skin.

"I'm sure there must have been a sound reason for the action, Mr. Boorstin. I'll look into it and get back to you."

The phone went dead, which gave Philip the opportunity to grab a towel and rub himself dry, scraping at his skin with enough energy to generate a little warmth. He called Rachel back and asked her to set up a meeting with Artemis Reach, then got dressed and hurried to the office.

Rachel, who had called him from home, was in the office when he got there. She had already called Community School Board Sixty-one enough times to convince herself that Artemis Reach wasn't taking her calls, so she took the precaution of contacting a few friendly reporters who promised to let her know at once if Reach scheduled a press conference or issued any statements. If she couldn't get in touch with him, she could at least monitor his public moves.

Meanwhile, Philip tried to reestablish communications with the Commissioner with no better luck until shortly after ten o'clock, when Simon Pound called to say that the police action at La Guardia Junior High had been a field decision taken in response to reliable information concerning lawless activities within the school, especially the presence of weapons. (He neglected to mention that the source of the "reliable information" was nothing more than his own petulant comment to the press about conditions at the school.) He considered the action justified since two arrests had been made already on weapons charges. On that basis alone, he flatly refused to call off the guard unless directly ordered to do so by the mayor.

"I want to set up a meeting. You, me and Artemis Reach. How does noon sound?" Boorstin asked, and then corrected himself before giving the Commissioner a chance to respond. "Never mind how it sounds," he said. "Just be there." He named a restaurant near City Hall with a private dining room and hung up the phone with that feeling of satisfaction that can only come from hanging up on someone who has recently hung up on you.

Rachel snatched up the phone and called the restaurant to reserve one of the private rooms for a party of three, on the optimistic assumption that Reach would be available. Less than five minutes later a staff intern rushed in with word that the wire services were carrying a story reporting that the Bronx grand jury had found no grounds for indicting Detectives James Franks and Vincent Donadio.

Philip's eyes felt as if they were rolling loose in his head. Less than twenty-four hours ago the grand jury finding would have been the best possible news. He had gone up to the Bronx and personally spent four and a half hours coaching the young A.D.A. handling the case. The kid's name was Felder and he was convinced he had lost control of the grand jury, which seemed determined to indict. Philip managed to get some backbone into him, even coached him on how to examine the two detectives so they would come out sounding like the Lone Ranger and Tonto. It was a tough job, blowing that kid away, but somebody had to do it. There were a lot of hard questions that could have been asked, questions about the timing of Franks's shot, for instance, but Boorstin showed Felder how to avoid asking them. By the time he was finished with Felder, the young A.D.A. was convinced it wasn't too late to get the grand jury turned around. Apparently it had worked.

If there isn't a saying to the effect that we are more likely to be destroyed by our successes than our failures, there should be. The timing couldn't conceivably have been worse. The front pages of the afternoon papers would have pictures of armed troops massed around one of Artemis Reach's junior high schools as though it were a Latin American polling place, with a leader to an inside page for the story about how the cops who killed one of Artemis Reach's students had beaten an indictment. It was a complete wipeout, the perfect antithesis of the something-for-everyone diplomacy upon which Philip Boorstin's philosophy of government was based. Artemis Reach, he had every reason to assume, would be pissing fire.

It didn't take long to find out. The intercom buzzed and Rachel's voice advised him to pick up his telephone at his own risk.

"Mr. Reach," he said with as much heartiness as he could muster, "I've been trying to get you all morning."

"I think you morons have been getting me pretty good all morning," Reach corrected. "What the fuck do you people think you're doing?"

It wasn't the time to admit that the mayor's office had lost control of its own Police Department. "It's preventive," Philip lied glibly. "No one's set foot inside your school."

He hoped this was true. If it weren't, he was prepared to admit that an overzealous officer had overstepped his authority. But that was all he was prepared to admit.

"That's no answer and you know it. Tell Mayor Ehrlich that if he wants a war, the Bronx is ready for him," Reach snapped back.

"We have to talk about this," Philip countered. "Do you know Abernathy's on Spring Street? I'll bring the Commissioner. Twelve o'clock."

Reach didn't sound happy about it but agreed to attend the meeting.

Shortly before noon Mayor Ehrlich called from Phoenix to ask what the hell was going on. "I leave the city for just three days," he lamented, "three goddamn days, and things go crazy."

The truth of the matter was that if he hadn't been out of town the mayor would have been looking for a way to get out. His passion for survival dictated that the best way to deal with trouble was to hide out until it blew over. Experience had taught him that most forms of trouble did in fact blow over. Of course the wind currents had to be right, but that was why he had a staff of people like Boorstin. It was their job to put the fans in the right places and turn them on at the right times. To be on the safe side, in case anything hit the fan, the mayor made it a practice to be as far as possible from the fallout zone. "The best offense," he was fond of saying, "is a defense"; and "You win elections by not losing them."

"I'm addressing a whole roomful of mayors over lunch," he whined into the phone. "My police are invading my schools. What the fuck am I supposed to tell them?"

"Tell them how important it is to take prompt action," Boorstin suggested, perhaps a touch too flippantly. "Or don't tell them anything. I'm working on it."

At about the same time Boorstin hung up the phone, Artemis Reach finally succeeded in getting through to the principal of La Guardia Junior High. His secretary had been leaving messages for Lewis Hinden all morning and finally reported that she had him on the line.

"Where's he calling from?" Reach asked.

"He didn't say."

It was a safe bet it wasn't the school. "Tell him to get his black ass up to that school where he allegedly works as fast as he can," he said.

The girl had been working for Reach almost two months and still couldn't tell when he was serious. "Do you really want me to say that?" she asked.

"No, sweetie, don't say anything," he said, punching the lighted button on his phone.

Hinden was already talking by the time Reach got the phone to his ear, whining that he had just heard about the situation and was on his way to the school when he got a message that Reach wanted to talk to him.

"Save me the bullshit, Lewis," Reach snapped. "Get yourself out of whoever's bed you're in and get up there."

"There's a logistics problem," Hinden wheedled. "I'm in Manhattan. It could take me an hour, hour and a half to get up there."

It took an hour and a half to get to the Bronx only if you counted showering, shaving and getting dressed. Or if you didn't want to get there.

"And you were wondering if I might smooth things over in the meanwhile?" Reach asked. "Sorry, Lewis, but this is not a morning I choose to get arrested in front of your school."

"I doubt it will come to that, Mr. Reach," Hinden said, missing the point entirely.

"You can bet your black ass it will come to that," Reach said brittlely. "That's exactly what it will come to because you are going to personally see to it that your students can enter and leave the building without interference from the police. Do you understand what I'm telling you, Lewis?"

Hinden thought that he did.

"Good," Reach said. "Call me from jail, Lewis."

EVEN before he came around the corner, Steven sensed that something was wrong. He slowed his pace, conscious only of that vague uneasiness one feels stepping into a familiar room where the furniture has been moved. Something felt out of place but he didn't know what.

He was getting to school a full forty-five minutes later than usual, having taken the wrong train from his mother's apartment, and for a moment he thought that he had simply become disoriented by the unfamiliar look of the street at an unfamiliar hour.

But it couldn't be that. The first period started in ten minutes. Why were there so many students still outside, loitering by the corner?

"Let's go, come on," he said as he approached the students, but they answered only with dismissive gestures. None of them were in his classes. He stepped past them and turned the corner to find at least a quarter of the student body collected on the sidewalk in a sullen, unfriendly mass. There seemed to be police everywhere, some with helmets in place, sticks in use as they herded the students toward the doors, others detaining students already at the door, administering searches with the cold efficiency of an assembly line.

Some of the kids who were shoved toward the doors submitted to the searches with glaring resignation but many tried to bull their way past the cops into the building and were handled roughly in response. At the same time, a number of students still on the sidewalk tried to move away from the school, calling to others to join them. They were quickly rounded up by the police and shoved into the growing logjam at the doors. It was a mess, a chaotic exercise in cross-purposes. The handful of students gathered at the end of the block, away from the action, contented themselves with shouting curses at the cops, who elected to ignore them.

Adding to the confusion, half a dozen remote news crews were clustered together at the curb, shouting out questions aimed at anyone who could stay put long enough to answer them. The police kept them penned within a narrow perimeter, chasing off any students who tried to talk with them as well as the ones who clustered around them antically mugging for the cameras.

Angry and bewildered, Steven plunged into the crowd in an effort to find someone who could tell him what the hell was going on. A few students recognized him and set up a cry that reflected the anarchic pleasure they took in finding a teacher subject to the same shit they were facing. "Good morning, Mr. Hillyer," someone called in a mocking sing-song.

"Tell 'em to get outta here, Mr. Hillyer."

"This sucks, Mr. Hillyer."

"Hey, sign my late slip, Mr. Hillyer."

The press contingent heard his name and picked up the call. "Are you Steven Hillyer? Can we have a comment, Mr. Hillyer?" he heard them shout but kept moving, concentrating hard to blot out the sound of his name, hoping that none of the police heard it.

When he got close enough to the doors he could see that girls as well as boys were being subjected to the searches and that the contents of purses and pockets were being dumped on a pair of tables set up between the doors. Three kids Steven didn't recognize were being shoved straight toward him, against the flow of the crowd, their hands cuffed behind their backs, setting off a chorus of angry shouts.

Steven reached out a hand for one of the cops. "Where are you taking them?" he demanded.

Something hard hit him from behind, knocking him off balance as the police and their prisoners moved beyond his reach. He stumbled but didn't fall, then whirled around to find his own face reflected in a cop's riot visor.

"Just keep moving," the cop said, the voice muffled by the visor, as though there were a machine inside that did the talking.

"Look, I'm a teacher here," Steven said. "Now what's going on?"

The cop's hand took his elbow. "Awright, let's go," he said.

"I'm not going anywhere until you tell me what's going on," Steven shouted back angrily, yanking his arm free.

The kids around him shouted their approval.

"Take it easy, pal. I'm just taking you into the school, that's all."

It would have been pointless to resist. Pointless and impossible. In the wave of passivity that washed over him at that moment, Steven suddenly felt as distant from his own actions of a moment ago as if they were the acts of a stranger. With a sharp twinge of regret he realized that whatever had moved him to charge into the crowd was something far better and more admirable than what was happening to him now as he let himself be led like a small child being taken to school.

"This guy says he's a teacher," the voice behind the visor said.

Steven smiled in spite of himself. *Of course I'm a teacher*, he thought with self-mocking irony. *Why would anyone lie about a thing like that?*

The visored cop at his elbow disappeared back into the crowd, leaving Steven with a tall Hispanic cop standing at parade rest next to one of the tables. "See some I.D.," the cop said in unaccented English.

Steven reached for his wallet.

"Don't show him nothing, Mr. Hillyer," someone shouted from behind him.

Steven asked if his union card would do.

"That'll be fine."

He shuffled through the cards and odd slips of paper in his wallet until he found his UFT membership card. The officer studied it for what seemed a long time considering there was no mystery to it. Steven's name was typed in on a blank line and another line gave an expiration date. There was a signature at the bottom.

"Steven Hillyer?" the cop asked.

Steven tensed for a repetition of the scene with the detectives in his apartment. But what could they do here in public, with so many students around and the press less than thirty feet away?

They could do anything they damn well pleased, he thought. *They were the police.*

"That's right," he said.

The cop handed back the card. The name apparently meant nothing to him. "Awright," he said, gesturing with his thumb. "Get inside."

"What's going on?" Steven asked as he returned his wallet to his hip pocket.

"Step inside, Mr. Hillyer," the cop said flatly, turning to the student behind Steven and ordering him to empty his pockets on the table.

UNLIKE the Police Commissioner or even the smartass deputy mayor who wouldn't in any sensible world have been more than a junior executive taking the subway to the office, Artemis Reach didn't have a driver to take him from one meeting to the next. Hell, the job didn't even provide him with a car, or even for that matter a salary. But you drop your lines where the fish are, he liked to say. He meant that if the best place to be was in an unpaid position on a community school board, so be it. He had been Chairman now for eight years and by his own calculations, which were on the conservative side, he had made himself into one of the half-dozen most powerful men in New York City. So much for the difference between appearance and reality. So much for the fact that the number one deputy to the mayor and the Commissioner of the entire Police Department had drivers taking them to the restaurant and waiting for them while they met and ate, whereas the man every damn politician in the city had to take into account before they could so much as shit, piss or wipe their asses walked across the parking lot behind the restaurant from his own two-year-old Lincoln.

The irony didn't escape him because he was a man finely tuned to apprehending irony. If you're a black man with no more education than what this sty of a city passes out like a farmer flinging slops to the pigs, you had damn well better be able to grab both ends of any ironies that come your way. You had also damn well better be good at making something out of nothing. You learn early to throw your weight around, even when you don't have anything to throw. Guess what? It doesn't matter in the least. People get out of the way just the same. No matter who they are, no matter how much power they like to pretend they have, they duck and cringe and scurry for cover.

Because in New York City everyone is scared. Everyone. The smell of the city is the acrid, noxious smell of diarrheal panic, the sound of the city the squeak of churning bowels. New York runs on fear the way a beetle runs on dung. At the top of the pile sits the mayor, scared of the press, scared of the electorate, scared of the eighty-seven councilmen and councilwomen and commissioners of this and that who are always sharpening their spikes to run against him. Below him sits the Police Commissioner, afraid of the mayor, afraid of the press and above all afraid of his own cops. The biggest city in America is in reality governed by a pack of candy-assed politicians who talk tough and run scared.

But Artemis Reach isn't afraid of anything. Because he is black and because he knows that the biggest, bottomest, onliest fear that keeps all the others in line, the one that gives them their thoughts for the day and their nightmares for the night, is their fear of black people, their fear of Artemis Reach and the three million blacks who read the newspapers every day and watch the news every night to hear what he has to say.

Which was why it was all right that he had to park his own car and walk out of the parking lot right past the two drivers who sat in their cars ready to pop out like Kleenex the moment they spotted the pair of white men whose balls Artemis Reach had in his pocket.

LEWIS Hinden wasted no time doing what was asked of him. As his taxi eased around the corner, he took in the scene from the backseat and ordered the driver to continue down the block until he was past the school. That put the knot of reporters between himself and the entrance and would take him right past them as he approached the police. Although he rarely wore his glasses except for driving, he slipped them on before he got out of the cab.

Impeccable in his three-piece gray suit, he posed for a moment on the sidewalk like a commander on high ground, analyzing the situation through the wire-framed glasses that added the finishing nuance to the image of almost magisterial dignity he conveyed. The three students who had been placed under arrest earlier in the morning were still in handcuffs on the sidewalk in front of the school, awaiting the arrival of a police van to take them to the Thirty-ninth Precinct for processing. Hinden straightened his shoulders and marched toward them with a slow and measured stride.

One or two reporters with experience on the Bronx scene recognized him and called to him for a comment, but he made a point of not looking in their direction, his face a mask of oblivious purpose. A flicker of disappointment crossed his face as he registered the fact that the highest-ranking police officer on the scene appeared to be a lieutenant. He wanted Norland, the Borough Commander, and would have settled for a captain. Still, he knew what he had to do.

"I'm Lewis Hinden, the principal of this junior high school," he said. "Why are these students in custody?"

Behind him, the reporters surged to the edge of the area where they were confined, microphones and cameras pointed at Hinden's back.

It was instantly clear to Lieutenant Larocca, and would have been clear even if the cameras hadn't been running, that Hinden was someone whose question was going to be answered.

"They were found in possession of weapons," Larocca said, as stiffly as if he were reporting to his commanding officer.

"All of them?" Hinden asked.

"No, two of them. This one here is charged with resisting arrest." He indicated the smallest of the three, a boy Hinden didn't recognize.

"On what grounds did you search them, Lieutenant?"

"My orders were to search all incoming students, sir," Larocca said. Under his shirt, large drops of sweat trickled distractingly down his sides, reminding him why it was never a good idea to get drawn into this kind of discussion.

"I'm not interested in your unlawful orders, Lieutenant," Hinden almost purred. "On what *legal* grounds did you search them?"

"My orders were to search all incoming students," Larocca repeated doggedly.

All three of the students were smirking, and for an instant Larocca would have traded his badge and his pension for one minute of privacy to knock those looks off their faces. But Hinden beat him to it.

"Is any of this amusing, Robert?" the principal said sharply, addressing the only boy in the group he knew by name.

The boys exchanged glances and instantly adopted more appropriate expressions.

Satisfied, Hinden turned to the lieutenant. "Unless you can give me some legal reason for detaining them, I will have to demand that you release these boys immediately. They are late for school," he said.

"I'm afraid I can't do that, Mr. Hinden."

Behind his back Hinden sensed the reporters surging forward, dancing past the distracted cops assigned to contain them at the curb. He couldn't see them but he could hear them coming.

"You're late," Hinden said, turning to the boys again. "Get into that school at once."

They looked at him as if he were crazy. Their hands were still cuffed behind their backs.

"You heard me," he snapped. "Now."

The one he called Robert took a tentative step forward and the others followed suit. The two patrolmen, one on either side of the little group of prisoners, glanced to Larocca for orders but none were forthcoming. The boys started to walk.

Larocca threw himself in front of them, spreading his arms. "Hold it right there," he shouted, quickly swinging around to glare at Hinden. "You're outta line, mister!" he barked.

Hinden stepped deftly around him. "Don't be upset," he said to the boys, the way a grade-school teacher might soothe terrorized children. In point of fact, two of the three boys had arrest records that would have made a gangster blush and Hinden knew it. "He has no authority to arrest you," he added. "We'll get those things off you in metal shop."

He took one of the boys by the arm, leading him away. Cameras clicked.

Already Larocca could imagine the pictures in the newspapers. It would look like some kind of goddamn civil rights march and he was going to look like the cracker sheriff throwing himself in their way. The thought infuriated him because he had seen with his own eyes the ten-inch pig-stickers they took off these kids. Go tell that to anyone. Who gave a shit anyway? He had a job to do. He dashed around to put himself once again in their path as a contingent of patrolmen closed ranks, blocking their way.

"Right there, pal!" Larocca shouted.

There were at least three or four microphones between him and the principal. For an instant Larocca felt as if he were going to puke, and the thought that this black bastard with the dainty spectacles had probably planned the whole thing didn't help any.

Hinden stepped deftly to the side to move around Larocca, even though the cops behind the lieutenant left him nowhere to go. He thought of repeating "These children are late for school" but quickly decided that would be overdoing it. The dignity of not answering at all was better than anything he could have said.

He took another step forward and Larocca swallowed so hard his Adam's apple bounced twice before any sound came out. "Mr. Hinden," he said, "I am placing you under arrest for interfering with a police officer in the conduct of his duty."

Hinden offered no resistance and let himself be led to the van, which arrived a moment later.

The principal of La Guardia Junior High rode to the Thirty-ninth Precinct in the back of the van with three La Guardia Junior High students facing weapons charges and a charge of resisting arrest. He didn't say a word to them on the way and they couldn't think of anything to say to him.

T H E school's downstairs lobby looked like a rush-hour train station in the throes of a wildcat walkout, crowded beyond capacity with people going nowhere. The high, excited voices of the students melded together in an indecipherable buzz of anger and bemusement, outrage and mockery. Some of the students, the looser and less bitter of them, contented themselves with making fun of the cops and asking each other if they thought they had managed to get on television. The sullen, the militant and the disaffected gathered in angry knots and shouted their bitterness back and forth.

In the first few seconds after he stepped through the door Steven heard enough to know that a connection was being forged in the students' minds between the garrisoning of La Guardia Junior High and the death of Timothy Warren, who was being transformed in those frantic minutes from a friendless loner into a martyr. Steven picked up words here and there about boycotts and counterattacks, mixed with a smattering of mindlessly brave and violent threats. It wouldn't take much time or much provocation before the simmering rhetoric exploded into a doomed and dangerous assault on the police.

Still, virtually no one was doing anything to stop them. Over the heads of the students, on the far side of the lobby, Steven could see Hal Garson darting among them, grabbing anyone he could grab, spinning them around, barking orders that sent them grumbling toward the staircases. The intensity with which Hal went at it gave him the authority to make it work, but there were no other teachers helping him out. The rest of the teaching staff was apparently holed up in their empty classrooms, laconically noting eighty- and ninety-percent tardiness rates on their attendance sheets.

In the middle of the floor Mrs. Mann, a birdlike middle-aged secretary in the administrative offices, and Joel Goldstone, a first-year teacher's aide, followed Garson's lead, eddying through the area, pleading and cajoling. There was no reason for either of them to be there, Goldstone because he was in over his head with these kids, Mrs. Mann because it wasn't her job. Except by default.

Steven plunged in, grabbing the first student he recognized and ordering him upstairs.

"There ain't nobody up there," the boy protested.

"There will be in a minute," Steven shot back, holding tight to the boy's elbow while he called to others to join them as he pushed and led and bullied the boy toward the stairs on the far side of the milling sea of students.

"Can it, William!" Steven shouted loud enough to be heard ten feet all around, cutting off the boy's protest in mid-sentence. "Don't you know a fucking mess when you see one?"

A ripple of laughter locally defused the tension just enough to get a cluster of students moving with him. "Tell him, Mr. Hillyer! Fucking right!" kids around him called back.

Steven pushed on, making converts with every step, here a trio of popular girls the other girls would follow, here a knot of kids from his own homeroom, the group snowballing almost magically, but without making an appreciable difference in the landscape. He knew he would have to do it again and again, going back for another group as soon as he got this one to the stairs.

He was making progress when he heard a shout behind him. He wheeled around just as a kid named Terry Kravacs shoved Mrs. Mann away from him hard enough to send her staggering backward, tripping and crashing to the floor among a cluster of tangled feet that danced and skipped out of her way, giving her just room enough to fall. The children who stood over her, looking down curiously as if she were a sack suddenly and unexpectedly tossed from an upstairs window, saw her as a piece of the administrative machinery, neither more nor less than the file cabinets and telephones.

"Keep going, it doesn't concern you," Steven barked at the kids with him, darting away from them to get between Kravacs and Mrs. Mann, who picked herself up from the floor and started back toward Kravacs. Beads of sweat stood on her forehead. Kravacs tensed, waiting. He was a white kid with a reputation to protect.

"Get upstairs, Kravacs!" Steven ordered.

"Stay out of this," Mrs. Mann snapped sharply, stepping past him as though he were one of the guilty onlookers. Her eyes were like points of concentrated rage.

"Do you want to push me again?" she demanded, looking straight at Kravacs.

Kravacs hadn't expected her reaction. "You keep your hands off me, you don't get pushed," he sneered, dull and mindlessly insolent.

"You're going upstairs," she answered quickly, "if I have to take you up there myself. I asked you if you were going to shove me again."

Steven held his breath. He wanted to do something but she didn't want his help, and the sufficiency of her anger kept him in his place. Most of the students in the lobby had collected in a circle around them waiting for Kravacs' answer.

Kravacs' eyes darted around, taking the measure of his audience, and in that moment he realized he didn't have an answer. The bitch had foxed him. His face darkened as the truth of this hit home and his jaw worked for a moment without a sound coming out. "I don't want to mess with you, lady," he said at last.

"Then get upstairs," Mrs. Mann said. Her voice was calm and surprisingly soft, as though she had taken the same measure he had of his lack of choices.

Kravacs hesitated a moment, then turned and slouched rapidly toward the stairs as a lobby full of kids erupted in a spontaneous cheer.

Outside on the street the cops heard it and swung open the door enough to look in. They were greeted with a roar of obscenities while a barrage of textbooks and notebooks catapulted toward them from all over the lobby. There was something oddly electric about the moment, not in the action so much as in the suddenness and unity of it.

The door swung closed, the avalanche of books splotting against the cold metal with a soft and sodden sound like rain.

"Listen!" Steven shouted at the top of his voice. "We've got to keep them out there! We can't give them a reason to come in!"

He could hear his name being whispered among students, passed around like a toke in the john, those who knew him telling those who didn't. He knew they were saying that he was the one with Timothy Warren when the cops blew him away. And he wanted them all to know it, because for better or worse, from now on that was above all who Steven Hillyer was.

"They came in the other day," he shouted, silencing the whispers, "and they're looking for a reason to come back. Don't give it to them!"

A girl's voice shouted, "Don't give them anything!" and someone else shouted, "Don't give 'em shit!" The crowd began to part, split up the middle, half heading for the east stairs, half for the west. The noise in the lobby now was a steady drone of indecipherable shouts and mutterings, more like the sound of a machine than human speech. Slowly it faded as the machine that made it rumbled onto the staircases and powered its way up to the classrooms above.

In twenty minutes Steven was alone in the lobby with Hal Garson and Mrs. Mann and Goldstone. They didn't even look at each other until it was all over and the last of the students had disappeared up the stairs. Then Steven started toward the front door and the other three came forward to join him.

Stooping like peasants in a field, they began gathering the harvest of books in their arms.

HANDBALL was Tal Chambers's game these days. Dr. Carlisle hadn't been to the athletic club on Lenox Avenue in Harlem in almost a year, but when Chambers' office said he was playing handball, the doctor knew where to look. He watched in silence a moment until the players finished their point.

Chambers was thirty-four years old, with the body of a man ten years younger. He played with the same ferocious intensity that had made him the Portland Trailblazers' third-round draft choice a dozen years earlier. But now his bare legs were scarred like plowed ground from three knee operations that never succeeded in reassembling the inner workings of his powerful legs.

About a year after the last operation he had flown back to New York without even closing out his Portland apartment. A Los Angeles surgeon had just told him he agreed with the Trailblazers' team doctor that there was no point in further surgery. Tal Chambers hadn't picked up a basketball since. With two years left on his contract, the money kept coming in and he spent the first year of his retirement feeling sorry for himself and ostentatiously doing nothing at all, like a prizefighter between bouts. By the start of the next basketball season, however, he had pulled himself together enough to retrieve his belongings from Portland and open an office in the expensive tower opposite Madison Square Garden. Newspaper accounts of the office opening, which appeared in all the city's sports sections, described him as a "consultant," a euphemism for the fact that a lifetime devoted to throwing a ball through a hoop had left him a lot of friends but few marketable skills.

Tal flipped the ball to his opponent as soon as he saw Dr. Carlisle standing in the doorway and hurried across the floor to pump Carlisle's hand. "You wouldn't be thinking of coming out of retirement now, would you?" Tal asked. "You look like you could still beat me."

Carlisle laughed as he was expected to at the display of the famous Chambers charm. Even as a high-school phenomenon recruited by the country's leading basketball powers, Tal Chambers had always made great copy with his eerily mature gift for saying the right thing, and he had been pegged as the black Bill Bradley long before he played a minute of pro ball.

"Still beat you?" Carlisle said. "When did I ever? I need ten minutes of your time."

"It's yours," Chambers said, mopping his face with a towel. It took him only a few seconds to reschedule his interrupted match and then he led Carlisle toward the locker room. "Are we going to need privacy?" he asked on the way.

"I believe so."

Chambers stopped in the short hallway a few feet from the locker room door. A gesture expressed the fact they would be able to see anyone moving to or from the locker room. "Shoot," he said.

"Those two children who were killed at La Guardia Junior High. I'm sure you've followed the case?"

"I read the papers," Chambers answered evasively, tensing at the mention of the incident. His forehead and cheeks felt hot and he rubbed at them with the towel to conceal the flush of anger. The killings had taken place in the weight room that he had donated to the school. The chancellor, the borough president, a state senator and all the dignitaries from the Board of Education and the Community Board had been present for the dedication ceremonies. Artemis Reach had read a message from the mayor praising the spirit that led an alumnus to make such a contribution to the school that shaped his promising career. It had been one of the proudest moments in Chambers's life.

Now, when people thought of that room they would think of the two kids killed in it. They would think of blood on the tiles. He didn't say any of this to Carlisle but waited to hear what the doctor wanted.

"A news report this morning suggested that the girl may have been molested."

"Is that a problem?" Chambers asked.

"Her mother's my patient, Tal. She's beside herself. I want to know where this is coming from."

Chambers shrugged. "The autopsy," he suggested, sounding tentative only because the answer was so obvious.

Carlisle shook his head. "I read the report," he said. "There's nothing."

"What does the coroner say?"

"He doesn't return my calls."

Chambers took a deep breath to put the picture of his blood-splattered weight room out of his mind. Barry Lucasian, the gym teacher and basketball coach, invited him to La Guardia for a talk and a clinic every year. And his current lady was on Community Board Sixty-one and worked in Congressman Kellem's office. Between his own connections and hers, it shouldn't be hard to answer the doctor's question.

In the back of his mind, at a level he didn't even have to consider, was the possibility that some good could come of it. He didn't know what and didn't ask himself, but he knew there was an art to getting in the middle of these things in the right way. He reminded himself that when people came to him because he had the connections to fix things, it was important to fix them.

"I'll make some calls," he said. "I'll get back to you."

ALBERT Terranova hadn't gone into the field himself to ask questions for years. There were detectives for that. It wasn't a thing chiefs did. But he missed it, and the fact that the radio had been alive all morning with communications to and from the forces camped outside La Guardia Junior High gave him all the excuse he needed. This was something he wanted to see for himself.

As his car glided to a stop, Terranova took in the scene from the backseat. The front of the school looked like the staging area for the St. Patrick's Day parade. Things must have been popping earlier, before the kids were all chased inside. Now a few dozen cops were lounging pointlessly against the street signs and the fenders of their cars, chatting up the remnants of the press corps assigned to cover the story. The cops looked around, indolent and indifferent, but the reporters charged the Chief even before his driver got the rear door open, squawking questions the moment his feet hit the pavement.

He pulled himself out of the car and faced them down, saying nothing until they were quiet. Behind them he could see a uniformed lieutenant making his way toward him.

"One question each," he growled. "Start with you."

He pointed to a small, graying man in a rumpled brown suit. The top reporters had left when things got quiet and probably would be back at the end of the day, looking for incidents when the kids filed out past the cops. The only ones left were the Bronx stringers scavenging for journalistic leavings.

The man licked his lips nervously as he tried to form a decent question. "Yes, sir. What are you . . . I mean, are you conducting the investigation, sir?"

"Just trying to get an education. Next."

"Are you going into the school, Chief?"

"See for yourself. Next."

"Are you going to turn your findings over to the grand jury?"

A good question, since the grand jury had already weighed in with its findings. It was asked by a girl who hardly looked old enough to be out of college and probably wasn't. Very clever. The implication was that either the investigation was too slow or the grand jury too fast.

"I don't have any findings," Terranova said. "I just got here. Next."

The lieutenant Terranova had noticed before stepped around the reporters and saluted sharply. "Sir," Larocca said, in the tone one uses for issuing commands.

Terranova's meaty fingers brushed his brow in response. "I'm sorry, that's all I've got time for," he told the reporters, who took the news with sullen but silent disappointment. The first team wouldn't have let him get away that easily. He stepped past them to confer with the lieutenant, but beckoned to the girl with a quick, small gesture. She hurried up eagerly.

"That was a good question. Don't let people get away without answering," he said and turned away, leaving her to ponder the advice.

"Everything under control, Lieutenant?" he asked, addressing Larocca as he started toward the school doors, where a pair of officers flanked the entrance like statues in a portico. Larocca fell in step beside him.

"Pretty quiet now, sir. You should have seen it about an hour ago," the lieutenant said. "You're going inside, is that right?"

"That's the general idea."

"If you don't mind, sir, I think I'd better send a couple of men with you."

A field officer who let a visiting headquarters type get damaged would have a lot of explaining to do.

"I'll be fine, Lieutenant," Terranova said, deciding he was better off alone than surrounded by uniforms. When he reached the entrance to the school the pair of officers on duty glanced to the lieutenant for approval before opening the door, even though neither one of them would have dared to challenge the Chief of Detectives if the lieutenant's nod hadn't been forthcoming.

Inside, the Chief found the central foyer deserted. The space felt old and hollow but substantial, like the schools he remembered from his own childhood, but he doubted that the resemblance went beyond the architectural. He located the administrative offices, where he was told that the principal was still in jail and where all efforts to find the assistant principal proved unavailing. "Perhaps I could help you?" a stern but attractive black woman from the principal's office asked.

"The gym teacher who was the first one on the scene in the weight room—I think his name is Lucasian—I'd like to talk with him."

"That shouldn't be a problem. I'll send someone for him."

The Chief waved off the offer. "Just tell me where he is. I'll find him myself."

"That would be the gym. I'll send one of the children right up for him."

She seemed not to have heard what he said. "Is there some kind of problem?" he asked.

"It's . . . it's on the fifth floor," she answered with some hesitation, looking down at her feet, not quite sure how to tell the behemoth in front of her that she didn't think he could handle four flights of stairs.

"Trust me, I'm in better shape than I look," he said, showing two rows of small white teeth when he smiled.

She flagged down a small boy hurrying down the corridor with an armload of posters, took the posters from him and told him to show the Chief to the gym.

The boy set a quick pace, which Terranova was able to match for only a few seconds. He paused at the first landing to get his breath. "If you kill me going up these stairs, there's gonna be hell to pay," he said. "What's your name, son?"

"Jamal," the boy said. "Are you the police chief?"

"*A* police chief. The Police Department has lots of chiefs."

The boy looked at him as though he couldn't decide whether he was being kidded or not. It didn't seem reasonable that there could be more than one chief of anything, but Terranova didn't elaborate. Instead, he asked Jamal why he was delivering posters instead of sitting in class.

"I do stuff," the boy offered. "They're always sending me somewhere."

"Don't you have classes?"

"Some."

"I see."

But he didn't. They did things in schools nowadays that made no sense to him. He waited until Jamal started up the stairs again and then said, "You must get around a lot."

"Some, yeah," Jamal said, a guarded tone creeping into his voice.

"So if a person had some questions, you might be the one to ask."

Jamal looked up at him with the same bright smile as before, but the Chief had interrogated enough people over the years to recognize that instant when the ground rules changed. They learned how to talk to cops early in neighborhoods like this. The boy was twelve or thirteen years old at the most, small, with a childish quickness and movements that made him seem even younger.

"I get around," Jamal conceded, "but I don't pay all that much attention."

"Did you know Timothy Warren?"

Jamal quickened his pace, moving a few steps ahead of Terranova. "Everybody knew him," he said. "I didn't know him no more than that."

"I'm not looking to make trouble, Jamal. I'm just trying to find out what happened."

"Some cop blew him away."

"Wait! I'm talking to you."

Jamal stopped half a dozen steps above Terranova and turned to face him with a look of impatient resignation. Terranova knew there was no point in questioning the boy further but he tried anyway.

"Before the cop blew him away," he said. "What was he doing with that girl?"

Jamal shook his head. "I wasn't there."

"But you get around. You hear things."

"Not about that. Look, I got a class next period."

"Was she his girlfriend?"

"If I'm late, I gotta go all the way downstairs and get an excuse."

Terranova said nothing more until they reached the fifth floor. Jamal led him into the gym, where he pointed out Barry Lucasian running a phys ed class through a game that seemed to be some sort of cross between dodge ball and soccer. "That's him," Jamal said, but when the Chief turned to thank him the boy was already on his way out the door.

Terranova had his badge in his hand as he approached Lucasian. The teacher handed over his whistle to one of the taller children and led the Chief to a corner of the gym where they could talk away from the class. He walked with a chest-out swagger that Terranova would have been willing to forgive in a cop but not in a gym teacher.

"Look," Lucasian began, standing so close when he turned to face him that their chests practically bumped. "If this is about what happened Monday, I already talked to the cops."

"Not to this cop."

The gym teacher seemed to back down an inch, or at least to bank his fires. "All right," he said. "But I got a class." He gestured toward them with his thumb.

A gym class wasn't high on Terranova's list of priorities. "They're doing fine. I want you to walk me through it," he said. "Step by step. Where you were, what you saw."

"Like I said, I went into the weight room," Lucasian began.

Terranova cut him off. "Show me," he said.

Lucasian mumbled something and went off to leave instructions with the kid he had put in charge. When he came back he led Terranova out of the gym and down the corridor to the weight room. About a dozen adolescents stood in the corridor with nothing better to do than eye the Chief warily as he passed.

"I had a kid scheduled on the weights," Lucasian was saying. "We keep the place locked, so I had to let him in, set up the weights for the program he was on."

Terranova already knew that and asked no questions. When they got to a door near the end of the corridor, Lucasian took out a heavy key ring and unlocked it. He flipped on the lights as he stepped through the door into what looked like a small storage area.

Terranova bent down to inspect the lock, which was a simple slip bolt that any kid could open with a stiff piece of paper. A button below the hasp disengaged the lock mechanism.

"Is this supposed to keep anyone out?" Terranova asked.

"I requisitioned a decent lock two years ago," Lucasian said sourly. "When it gets here I'll put it on."

He had said the same thing to the grand jury. In fact, he used almost exactly the same words.

Two steps took him across the storeroom floor to the door to the weight room itself. He pushed it open and stepped through.

Terranova followed with a vague sense that he was missing something. He was used to the sensation. It was simply the way one part of his brain warned the other parts to slow down and be careful, to take nothing for granted. Over the years he had learned not to worry about these vague feelings of uneasiness. Sooner or later it always became clear to him exactly what he had missed, and that was the time to go back for the lost pieces. The mistake most detectives made, he had concluded from watching them work, was to put too much stock in thoroughness when in fact it was never possible to be thorough. Not in this job, anyway. Thoroughness was a myth that pressured you into thinking you could ask all the right questions the first time around and then seduced you into believing, once you had asked every question you could think of, that you had asked them all.

The walls of the room where Terranova joined Lucasian were covered with tile. There were no windows and no doors other the one he had come through. The Chief's eyes ran down the blank row of machines, their bare, angular joints highlighting the stark functionlessness of their design. Mechanical versions of Sisyphus' rock, they were machines that consumed energy merely for the sake of consuming energy, the antithesis of every other machine ever invented. Terranova had no interest in them and little interest in what the gym teacher was saying.

"He was here between the fourth and fifth machines," Lucasian said, moving down the row to show him the place. "Timothy Warren was kneeling down next to the bench and I could see there was a girl lying down on it. I guess she was dead already but I didn't know that. It never occurred to me. He yelled at me to get out even before I came through the door."

Terranova could have said the next sentence for him, quoting from the grand jury minutes of his testimony: *I was afraid he'd hurt her and I thought I'd better get help.* But he had heard enough.

"Is there another way to get in here?" he asked, breaking in before Lucasian could go on.

The gym teacher looked at him a long time before answering, as though he didn't understand why he wasn't allowed to finish his narrative.

"Not really," he said at last.

"What does that mean?"

"It means there's a door but you can't use it."

Terranova looked but couldn't see a door. "Show me," he said.

"Look," Lucasian said, "these two got in here like everybody else does. They slip the lock. They smoke dope, they get laid, I don't know what the hell they do. I'm chasing kids out all the time. I'll show you my letters. Either put on a real lock or let the kids use the facility. Because if it was in use, this kind of shit wouldn't be going on. I got tired of writing letters so this is the way it is."

"I understand that," Terranova said. "Can I see the other door."

Without a word, Lucasian squeezed past him through the doorway back into the storage room. Shelves were stacked with a jumble of unsorted towels, nets and sweatsuits, the floor littered with rubber cones and soft, underinflated balls. A heavy wrestling mat hung from hooks on the far wall, held in place by a length of rope that fed through a pulley device.

Lucasian undid the knot and released the rope, which hissed through the pulley as the mat crumpled to the floor. Behind it was a door with an empty socket where the knob should have been.

The crumpled mat shifted under Terranova's feet as he stepped forward to inspect the door. The hole for the doorknob was filled with plaster.

"Part of this used to be the gym teacher's office," Lucasian explained. "When we got the money for the weight room, somebody figured out this was the only place it could go and everything else had to move around."

"What's on the other side?"

"Girls' toilet. That's why we plastered up the hole."

Terranova pushed on the door. It didn't move.

"You didn't mention this to the grand jury," he said.

"I wouldn't have mentioned it to you except you asked. Don't tell me you've got to see the other side."

That was exactly what Terranova had in mind. It meant evacuating the girls' locker room, which took almost twenty minutes. When the girls' gym teacher came out to announce that the coast was clear, Lucasian led the Chief past the girls' lockers, through the still wet shower room and into an area that contained nothing but a dozen toilets with no stalls. The plumbing ran along the wall behind them, presumably to save the expense of sinking it into the floor.

"The door," Lucasian said, pointing. "I told you it doesn't open."

The door was right behind the toilets, secured with a sturdy padlock.

"Who's got the key?"

"No one," Lucasian said. "Maybe the contractor if he's still alive."

Terranova thanked him for the tour and asked to have a look at the dead girl's locker. The girls' gym teacher looked up the locker number and the lock combination for him. Ophelia's gym clothes were there, along with some books, but not the panties. The Chief closed the locker and thanked them without asking any questions, because he wasn't prepared yet to tell anyone what he had been looking for.

"If you guys ever got some spare time," Lucasian said, "what you ought to investigate is where the goddamn money goes. We paid to have that thing walled over. All we got was the lock."

JUST trying to keep the kids' minds off the window and the street kept Steven busy all morning. For once he was glad his classroom was at the back of the building looking down over garbage-strewn alleyways and blighted tenements instead of the police vans lining the avenue. In fact, he wouldn't even have known the police were still there if it weren't for the grapevine of whispers dispensing an uninterrupted supply of fresh, hot rumors and reports. Every time the bell rang marking the end of a class, his students rushed to the halls to find vantage points at the stairwell windows or in empty classrooms on the avenue side.

For the first three periods of the morning Steven did everything in his power to keep his students' minds focused on their routine work, as if through sheer diligence he could turn this into a normal day. His own mind, meanwhile, churned with a profusion of images as he seized on any familiar experience to which he could relate the atmosphere of electric distraction that crackled around him. He thought of news footage from Syria or Lebanon, documentaries about the children of Ireland, films he had seen and remembered from Berkeley, Kent State and Chicago in his childhood. Ireland especially stuck in his mind, children filing to school along soldier-lined streets. But as fast as they came to his mind, the images dissolved like reflections in a rippled pool. There were no tanks in the Bronx and wouldn't be.

This was the difference that kept coming back to him, as clear as the lesson in a Sunday sermon, urging calmness and order and responsibility, as though if he could only keep their attention focused narrowly enough on sentence fragments and run-ons in the seventh grade, on participles in the eighth, on last night's chapter of Edith Wharton in nine, the riot sticks wouldn't be used, the cops and their commanders would all go away.

For most of the morning Steven stuck to his pedagogical guns like the last soldier at the pass. When his eighth-graders came in, tiny Jamal Horton, whose sharply chiseled features reminded Steven of a quick, attentive squirrel, slapped Steven's hand, congratulating him for his performance in the lobby that morning.

Nothing would have pleased Steven more than to share the recollection with Jamal and the rest of them, to let the jokes come, giving free rein to their tumbling narratives. Instead, he forced himself to fall back on dignity, pulling away from the boy.

"That was so we could get up here and get to work, Jamal," he said, pompous and stiff, hating himself for the way he made the sensitive, bright-eyed boy skulk off to his seat.

As they drifted slowly toward their seats, the other children whispered and spoke aloud, comparing notes on what they heard from one source or another, what some of them had seen with their own eyes. Steven's eyes, though, stayed on Jamal, following him to his desk where the boy dropped heavily into his seat and slammed his grammar book down with an explosively dramatic thud.

"Again, Jamal. Only this time with less emphasis," Steven said curtly, wishing the words back even before he said them but powerless to resist this maddening and incomprehensible compulsion to play out his own bad faith as if it were a role assigned to him.

Jamal glared at him for a long moment, then raised the book an inch or two off the desk and lowered it with insolent delicacy, as carefully as if he were placing the last card on a house of cards. He looked up at Steven to see if he were satisfied and Steven turned away, hiding his knotted emotions in a quick series of orders intended to quiet the rest of the class and shoo them to their desks. He hurried to the door and closed it after pulling the last of the stragglers in from the hall.

When the class finally fell silent he turned to the blackboard and printed *I N G* in large block letters, to begin his discussion of participles. Behind him, a low voice he recognized as Bobby Ward's muttered something about the students arrested with Mr. Hinden being released from jail. He heard the whisper repeated over and over, crossing the classroom like a breeze scudding through an open window, and suddenly he turned from the blackboard and let his eyes flow over the faces in front of him. He realized he had no business trying to each English grammar when there were so many things happening to the world these children lived in.

Christ, how could he have been so foolish? How could he have assumed for a minute that his dry and airless world of participles and participial phrases mattered more than the dread and uncertainties waiting for them on the street wearing blue uniforms and carrying sticks? That was what they needed to know about, and he himself, Steven Hillyer from Litchfield, Connecticut, had run the gauntlet with them only a few hours before. Perhaps he had something he could tell them about it, perhaps had an answer or two for their questions, a frayed end of the truth they could wrap around their fears and doubts. They were kids, for God's sake, two of them had died upstairs just this week, three of them had been taken away in a police car just this morning, and Steven was writing *I N G* on the blackboard so he could teach them how to change a verb into an adjective.

"Did you have something to tell us, Bobby?" he asked, setting down the chalk and easing into the discussion.

Bobby Ward was a short, husky boy with a bookish look behind his owlish glasses. He read at fourth-grade level and would have been in remedial English classes except for a scheduling conflict that kept him on the regular track, where he followed class discussions with the forlorn patience of a child in the company of grown-ups telling stories he didn't understand about people he didn't know.

"I didn't say anything," he muttered into his chest.

"You were talking about the three boys who were arrested this morning, weren't you?" Steven asked.

Bobby straightened up in his seat and eyed his teacher guardedly. The question surprised him because he knew that he shouldn't have been talking in class and didn't understand now why he was being asked about what he'd said. He could only assume what he always assumed, that there must be a reason he didn't understand. Perhaps a warier child might have suspected a trick or a trap, but Bobby Ward's mind didn't work that way. His life on the whole had been filled with enough misfortune to make paranoia superfluous as a working hypothesis.

He nodded his head.

"Did you hear something about them, Bobby?"

"I heard they got out."

"You mean they were released?"

"Yeah."

"Where did you hear this?"

Bobby shrugged his shoulders and focused all his attention on his stubby hands.

"Did anyone else hear this?" Steven asked.

Maria Onofrio raised her hand. Steven called her name and she stood up because she always stood when she addressed the class. She said that a boy who had been outside heard one of the reporters telling it to another one. Some of the children thought the boys had been arrested for attacking the police, others thought it was drugs.

There hadn't been any attack, Steven was able to tell them. He knew that one of the boys was found with a knife and that the same might be true of the others.

For a few more minutes they swapped stories, learning a lesson, Steven hoped, about how one truth contradicts another, about the insubstantiality of complex events, which turn out, under the microscope of discussion, to be made up of tiny molecules of fact and perception. For a while they pretended they were reporters, interviewing each other, trying to decide what could be included in their stories, what needed confirmation, what had to be left out.

Then Lloyd Elijah, who always sat sideways in his seat to suggest that he wasn't really part of the class, ready from moment to moment to move for the door, changed the terms of the debate. "It's all bullshit," he muttered after listening in silence for ten or fifteen minutes.

Steven knew what was coming. He had been expecting it since he let them discuss the police. If you are going to let reality into the classroom, you had damn well better let it all the way in.

"What's bullshit?" he asked.

"Who they popped, what for, what they done."

"You don't think what's happening outside matters?"

"I don't think," Lloyd said, mimicking Steven's intonation, "any of this jerkoff discussion matters."

"Then what does?"

Lloyd was up out of his seat, pacing away from Steven toward the back of the room. He was pencil thin, the tallest boy in class, and his flailing gestures when he spoke couldn't possibly have been contained in the narrow space between his desk and the next. He sat through many classes as torpid as if he were hibernating, giving little or no indication that he even heard, let alone understood, what was going on. At other times he was so animated the open area at the back of the room had come to be known as Lloyd's stage. At another school, a teacher might have looked for an explanation for such erratic behavior. At La Guardia Junior High the explanation always came in little plastic ampules.

"They're doing a number on us," Lloyd announced, wheeling dramatically when he reached the back of the room.

He was a year or two older than anyone else in the eighth grade and when he was in the mood to be bothered at all with his little classmates, he openly courted their adulation.

All through the room the kids waited to hear why. Steven said nothing.

"First they come in and they blow away Timothy and Ophelia. Blew them away, just like that. Now they're looking to do a number on everyone else."

Maria Onofrio interrupted to protest that the police hadn't killed Ophelia James.

"Everybody knows that, girl. That's what I'm telling you. It don't make sense," Lloyd snapped back, intolerant of criticism at the best of times, utterly unwilling to accept it from a Puerto Rican girl. "They blew his head off 'cause they was in such a hurry to save the life of a dead girl? Get real."

"The TV said they didn't know she was dead," Jamal Horton piped up, conscious of the risks.

A chorus of assent from at least half the class gave Lloyd Elijah a challenge.

From the front of the room, Steven watched and waited, pleased with himself and with them. They were getting into it now, give and take, argument and counterargument. This was what English classes were supposed to do.

"And you believe that?" Lloyd shot back, ignoring the others, taking dead aim on Jamal.

"Why not?" Jamal said.

"Because somebody's fucking lying. How's that, Jamal?" he sneered, drawing the boy's name out into a singsong taunt.

The discussion was getting a little out of hand, needed a shove to get it back in the right direction. "We don't know that, Lloyd," Steven objected from the front of the room, adding his own authority to the mix.

Lloyd wheeled on him and his eyes blazed with an anger that had nothing to do with being interrupted or contradicted or even shown up in front of the others.

"*We* don't," he said. "But you do, Mr. Hillyer. You was right there when it happened."

"I was there," Steven said, shaken by the reminder.

"Then how come they killed Timothy?"

"I don't know."

"And what are they doing in here now?"

"They're outside," Steven said. "It's some kind of security precaution. I don't think there are any police in the building."

"Think again, Mr. Hillyer."

"Do you know that?"

"I do," Jamal said.

Everyone turned to look at him.

"A big fat cop," Jamal said. "The police chief or something."

"Where did you hear this, Jamal?" Steven asked.

"I didn't hear it. I walked him upstairs."

A buzz went through the classroom. "You got that, Mr. Hillyer?" Lloyd Elijah challenged from the back of the room. "The cops are back. What are they gonna do this time?"

"I don't know," Steven confessed.

Lloyd Elijah cocked his head to the side and nodded. It was the gesture of an old man, tired and resigned.

"Right," he said. "Everybody's lying to us but Mr. Hillyer. And the only reason he ain't lying is 'cause he don't know shit."

ABERNATHY'S was an old restaurant in a frame house that claimed to antedate the Revolutionary War. There were three entrances and it was possible to get in and out without going through the main dining room, which made it one of the few public places where people who couldn't be seen meeting each other could meet. The client list was highly selective, mostly political, although in recent years there had been a moderate and disturbing influx of business people. Without exception, the waiters were black men in their fifties or older who moved slowly, serving the meals with that almost extinct mixture of officiousness and familiarity that suggested nothing so much as family servants whose tenure stretched back through long-forgotten generations.

Philip Boorstin made a point of being the first to arrive and had to wait half an hour for the Commissioner. He spent the time, as he had spent the latter part of the morning, on the phone to his network of contacts in the Police Department, most of them deputy chiefs or higher whose tenures of office went back before Simon Pound and whose loyalties were to City Hall, where their real chances lay, rather than to the temporary incumbent in the Commissioner's office. By the time Simon Pound slipped into his seat and unfolded his napkin on his lap, Boorstin knew as much about the siege of La Guardia Junior High as the Commissioner did. They had very little to talk about in the twenty minutes Artemis Reach kept them waiting so they talked about the restaurant.

Reach entered the small room wearing a sulfurous smile and sat down abruptly with crisp nods toward the deputy mayor and the Police Commissioner that permitted him to avoid shaking the Commissioner's hand. "All right," he began, "let's hear what you gentlemen have to say."

Commissioner Pound had nothing to say and no intention of saying it. He leaned slightly back in his chair, savoring the insult of Reach's entrance with a look of intractable smugness that could only indicate that he felt himself to be above such snubs. This left the deputy mayor a twofold task, only half of which involved appeasing Artemis Reach. It was also going to be necessary to wipe that grin off the Police Commissioner's face.

"I came to you a few days ago, Mr. Reach," Boorstin began, "to ask for your cooperation in keeping a potentially volatile situation under control. I can't tell you how much Mayor Ehrlich and I appreciate the statesmanlike way you've handled the matter."

To Boorstin's left, Commissioner Pound's jaw dropped. By his lights, the one thing more dangerous than an arrogant demagogue was an arrogant black demagogue, and the only things more disruptive of law and order than even the worst black demagogues were the liberal politicians who abased themselves in front of them. Boorstin had either forgotten or chosen to forget Reach's provocative statements to the *Post*.

Reach, on the other hand, wasn't moved one way or the other by Boorstin's flattery. He correctly assumed that its purpose was to discomfort the Commissioner, which he took as a good sign of a conciliatory attitude. But it was only a sign. Bullshit by itself meant nothing to him. He gave the slightest mandarin nod, inviting Boorstin to proceed.

In a few quick sentences, Boorstin summarized the morning's events.

"The problem as I see it," he said at the end, "is that it's difficult enough to operate a public school system under any circumstances and doubly difficult when the schools are made to look bad by being cast in such an unflattering light. Does that seem a reasonable proposition to you, Commissioner?"

"Reasonable but irrelevant," Pound drawled. "My men didn't put those knives in those children's hands."

"Perhaps the students only wanted to protect themselves," Reach shot back.

"From what?"

"From the police. From the men who blew that poor child's head away the other day."

Boorstin silenced them both as though they were squabbling children. As a practical matter of efficient administration, he said, it was necessary that the conduct of business at La Guardia Junior High *seem* normal so that it could return to *being* normal. "I'm not asking you to agree with that assessment, gentlemen, I'm telling you that's the fact. Now what will it take to reestablish an appearance of normality at La Guardia, Mr. Reach?"

Reach was ready with his answer. "Get my principal out of jail," he said.

"I'm sure there's no problem with that, is there, Commissioner?" Boorstin asked.

It was a concession Pound was free to grant for the simple reason that he wasn't free to withhold it. If the police didn't drop the charges against Hinden, the district attorney would. "There's no problem with that," he said, smiling benignly.

"That's progress," Boorstin said, although all three men knew it wasn't.

It was still Reach's move and he complained that it wasn't possible to run a school with the police camped outside it.

"I can't in all conscience do anything about that," Pound answered without a trace of hesitation.

They argued it back and forth, with neither Boorstin nor Reach winning an inch of concession from the Commissioner, who was unwilling to publicly second-guess his Borough Commander. The police would be removed, he insisted, only when steps had been taken within the school to assure the safety of the faculty and the law-abiding portion of the student body.

Reach leaped to his feet, white with rage. "You want me to publicly admit that the situation inside that school is out of control?" he shouted. "You're not getting it!"

The Commissioner didn't move a muscle, barely raised his eyes. "When the need for protection has been removed, the protection will be removed," he said.

"We'll both be rotting in hell before this kind of blackmail makes me change one damn thing in the way that school is run."

Reach leaned forward with both palms on the table. The glassware tinkled like chimes in the silence. At last the Commissioner said, "Perhaps so. But in that case the police will remain."

"Maybe those cops of yours don't have enough to do," Reach snarled. "Believe me, Commissioner, it isn't hard to imagine a situation where they'd be kept busy enough in the Bronx."

"That's enough of that," Boorstin said quickly, but Reach literally pushed him aside to keep his sight lines open to the Commissioner.

"I don't make idle threats, Mr. Pound," he said. "The people of the Bronx are fed up with your gestapo methods."

"The people of the Bronx will obey the law or face the consequences," Pound answered with Delphic calm.

"What law? There's no law in the Bronx. Police officers kill a boy with impunity within the confines of a public school and then they harass the entire student body. Is that law? I can assure you school will not open on Monday while that sort of lawlessness prevails."

This was Reach's trump card, his nuclear arsenal, his doomsday machine. Thousands of angry children turned loose on the streets were like so many bottles of gasoline, and Artemis Reach held the fuses and matches in his hand. The danger was so obvious, the man so uncontrollable, that the threat rarely had to be made explicit. Yet it was always there, latent behind everything he said, occasionally trotted out for effect. Someday, Boorstin promised himself, he would call Reach's bluff. Destruction would be high, there were sure to be riots, but in the end the fallout would probably destroy Artemis Reach along with the mayor. There was something grimly satisfying about the prospect because it meant that Armageddon was a game two could play.

Boorstin said nothing, waiting until the Commissioner responded to Reach's threat.

"The security force remains," Pound said, lowering his voice exactly in proportion as Reach raised his. The two men glared at each other in obstinate silence.

"What about the detectives?" Boorstin asked at last.

For an instant it was as though two men who thought they were alone suddenly discovered a spy in the drapery. Both the Commissioner and the Chairman turned to stare at him as though they didn't know who he was. The Commissioner understood at once what he meant and his narrow lips trembled with suppressed rage. Reach waited to hear what would come next. If the student body was Artemis Reach's trump card, the detectives were Boorstin's, and he played it now.

"If they were disciplined," he said, "that might go a long way toward establishing police accountability."

Behind Simon Pound's expressionless eyes, a multitude of calculations were taking place. First, that a man capable of proposing what Philip Boorstin had just proposed was capable of anything. Second, that if this were so, the Police Department was going to have to give somewhere. So far, Pound had stood firm on protecting the office of the Borough Commander. He would have liked to protect the detectives as well but in reality they were more expendable.

"That's out of my hands," he said. "The grand jury has already made its determination."

"I know that," Boorstin said. "The Internal Affairs Division hasn't."

EIGHT years ago, Steven Hillyer had been one of only three members of his Teachers College class to be offered jobs by Community Board Sixty-one. The other two were black. At Teachers College the three of them had formed the core of an idealistic faction dedicated to the proposition that teachers could do more to reduce the injustice of American society than any other social agents. They borrowed their theory of human development from the writings of Erik Erikson and their sense of the teacher's calling from Robert Coles. Their hero, or one of their heroes, was Artemis Reach, who had recently seized control of one of the most intractable community school boards in the city and immediately initiated a long-overdue program of curriculum innovations and personnel transfers.

Simply the fact that half a dozen of Steven's classmates had applied for jobs at Sixty-one was the clearest possible indication of how thoroughly Artemis Reach had changed the perception of the schools under his control. For the first ten years of decentralization, while schools throughout the city cleaned house, those under Community Board Sixty-one went backward, their faculties and staffs quickly coming to consist almost entirely of exiles from more desirable assignments, and virtually all assignments were more desirable. Artemis Reach turned all this around. "Our schools have become halfway houses for those suffering from alcoholism, burnout or plain documented incompetence," he announced in one of his most often quoted speeches. "And it's the wrong half. Give me the ones halfway back and we'll take them. If they're halfway gone, they can't come to the Bronx."

As the only white teacher accepted at Sixty-one that year, Steven had every reason to feel that his career had been launched with a significant victory. As soon as preparations started for the opening of the school year in September, Will Fenton and Jeffrey Hills, the two black teachers who had come to La Guardia from Teachers College with him, began working on him to move into the school community as they had done. But Steven, who was living in an East Side walk-up on the edge of Spanish Harlem, was ready with an ideological justification for continuing to live in Manhattan. The Board wouldn't have hired a white man from a suburban background unless it believed in the value of adding an outside viewpoint to the local mix. Community control, Steven argued, would never work if autonomy were confused with provincialism.

In the intense and occasionally heated debates over even such inconsequential issues, Steven experienced both the beauty and the challenge of being young and committed. One had reasons for everything one did, even if they weren't necessarily the real reasons. Steven saw himself as a crusader, not a missionary.

Through his first five years at La Guardia, his confidence in the future of the educational revolution tempered his disappointment with the grim and relentless reality of everyday life, teaching aggressive and often hostile adolescents who didn't know how to be taught. Gradually, though, it wore at him as it wore at the others. Jeffrey Hills threw in the towel in the middle of the fifth year, quitting without notice one Monday morning by simply phoning in word that he wouldn't be back. When Steven went to look for him after school, his apartment had already been emptied.

A week later Will Fenton, who was close to Hills and badly demoralized by his departure, asked for a meeting with the principal and gave notice that he wouldn't be returning in the fall.

Steven felt abandoned, not merely because they left but because of the way they left. They had all been lying to each other, minimizing their disappointments, magnifying their small victories, telling each other it was working at least a little bit like the way they thought it would. In another week or month or semester or year, they told each other, they would start to see the difference. No one so much as hinted at the possibility of quitting, perhaps because they knew that, like a bad marriage, it would be over in a moment once it became clear there was a way out.

Only his anger at Hills's and Fenton's treachery brought Steven back to La Guardia for the sixth year even though he knew it wasn't enough of a reason to be there. For a while he deluded himself into believing that spite and stubbornness could accomplish what idealism could not. He was proud of himself for refusing to quit despite his lack of faith in his ability to make a difference. A year passed, and another. The last of the hopes with which he had begun teaching gradually wore away like the soft rock a river grinds into a canyon. Although there were other dedicated teachers at La Guardia—almost three-quarters of the faculty had been brought in since Artemis Reach seized control of the Board— the school's tone seemed to be set by the small clique of holdovers who lived a garrison existence within its walls, dealing with no one but themselves, bitterly going through the motions of what had once been careers.

How was he any different? Steven began to wonder. Because he cared? Hell, most of the people around him cared. It didn't seem to Steven that caring mattered anywhere near as much as he had thought it would, or even that it mattered at all. He hadn't a single shred of evidence that would allow him to believe his ideals made any difference at all in the lives of the students who passed through his classes. In the classroom next to his, Dennis Dougherty taught English by giving the same reading assignments he had given every year for a quarter of a century, returning essays without a mark on them except for a letter grade in the upper right-hand corner of the first page, and publicly counting the days until his retirement. What did his students fail to learn that Steven's students knew?

Still, Steven kept trying, clinging to practices he had established in his first years at La Guardia when he still believed in what he was doing. He ate lunch in his classroom every day and let the kids know they had a standing invitation to come in and talk. Every few weeks he reminded them again that he was there. *If you have any problems with any of the work, anything you want to talk about, grab yourself a sandwich and drop by.*

He ended up spending a lot of lunch hours alone, hunched over a square of waxed paper that caught the drippings from a chicken or tuna salad sandwich so adulterated with watery mayonnaise that it seemed to run through the bread like soup. Of course the door was open, so that anyone passing in the hall could see the sacrifice he made and the thanks he got. That wasn't why he left it open, but on the days no one came it at least served to dramatize his situation. He felt almost exactly the way he used to feel as a child when he sulked alone in his room while his mother failed to notice and his father made a point of ignoring it.

Once Dennis Dougherty poked his head in to ask Steven what the hell he was doing in an empty room at lunchtime. But it wasn't even possible to begin explaining to a man who lavished his best intellectual efforts on strategies for minimizing contact with what he called "the dwarfs." It would be like trying to explain the ecstasy of martyrdom to an unredeemed pagan. In fact it was so precisely like that that it cost Steven a few sleepless nights questioning his own motives.

Not that all of his sacrifices were wasted. At least twice a week, sometimes even more often, students would accept his invitation at least to the extent of asking a simple question and quickly fleeing. They didn't get the homework or didn't understand why a quiz answer had been marked wrong. They weren't profound questions, they weren't the openings for soul-searching discussions. But they were a form of contact, perhaps better than nothing.

Or perhaps not. Even though these encounters took place in the same classroom where he met his classes every day, the kids were so unused to finding themselves alone with a teacher that they acted as skittish as toddlers on the first day of school, as disoriented by the sight of Mr. Hillyer applying himself to his sandwich as they would have been if they had stepped through the door to find him on the toilet. In their minds, a private encounter with a teacher, unless it was disciplinary, violated one of the unspoken rules of distance that defined the space at school, making it hard for them to know, in even the most literal sense, where they stood. And so they held back just one tentative step inside the door, like the ducks on the ponds of Steven's childhood, requiring the gentlest coaxing before they would be ready to eat from his hand.

Some of those who tried it once didn't come back a second time, dropping their questions at his feet and retreating quickly back to the perimeters of a relationship they understood. But others returned often, like Maria Onofrio, a pedantic, bookish child with a sharp but narrow mind and an almost unnaturally clear sense of the road ahead, marked by signs listing the mileage: two more years to high school, five to college, nine to law school, eleven to an office on Stuyvesant Boulevard where she would fight the slum lords who collected exorbitant rents for heatless apartments with cracked windows like the one where she did her homework in the wintertime, taking off her mittens only when she had to write.

Like tiny Jamal Horton, whose fast mouth and quirky opinions livened up most classroom discussions even though, as he admitted to Steven one lunch hour, he never read any of the assignments for the simple reason that he couldn't read. Thinking the boy was being provocative, Steven opened a book at random, slapped it down in front of Jamal and demanded that he read. He listened in shock and horror as the bright-eyed star of Steven's eighth-grade class lettered out each word with arduous and heartbreaking difficulty, sweat standing on his brow, the chipmunk chatter of his high-pitched voice slowed to a pathetic stammer. For seven years, like an escaped convict, Jamal had hidden the guilty secret of his illiteracy. When Steven tried to talk him into remedial classes, even offered to tutor him himself, the boy shied away, so practiced in his defenses that they had become a way of life. *I'm doing fine*, Jamal said, fleeing from the room. He stayed away for two weeks and when he returned it was understood by both of them that the subject was out of bounds.

There were others as well, each with his own poignant story, each with her own shopping list of needs. Steven helped them with their English, settled feuds, read and corrected history papers before they were turned in, sometimes even went over their math with them. Yet never once, as he looked back, had they opened up their lives to him, talked about their families or their homes except in the small clues he now and then gleaned from a sentence in an essay or a stray comment in class. If they were closer to him than to any of the other teachers, still he was a teacher, he was the school, he was a white man, an Anglo, he wasn't from the Bronx. There could be warmth and closeness and sometimes even real friendship, but Steven despaired of there ever being trust.

After the provocative discussion of the police presence at La Guardia that started in his eighth-grade class and continued with the seventh graders who followed, Steven was reasonably certain that at least three or four kids would come back to continue the talk at lunch. But Lloyd Elijah's biting taunt echoed in his mind and he felt suddenly overwhelmed by an awareness of how little he knew. *Everybody's lying to us but Mr. Hillyer. And the only reason he ain't lying is 'cause he don't know shit.*

Why did he know so little about what had happened? Had he been hiding from it? Didn't he owe it to the kids to have some answers? Or to himself? He didn't even know why he was there when it happened. He assumed, at the time, that Rita Torres came to get him because he was so close to Timothy. But he didn't even know that for a fact. Had Timothy asked for him? Was Ophelia dead already when he did?

The questions were all familiar, because he had been asking himself all of them ever since it happened. Now he felt an urgent need to get some answers, to come to terms with events in which he had already played a critical role.

For a moment, as the bell rang ending the last period before lunch, he tried to tell himself it was important that he stay in his room, that he be there, waiting and available, for any children who came in. But what could he say to them, except to admit that Lloyd was right? Until he could answer some of his own questions, he couldn't answer theirs.

Before the bell had even finished ringing, he had stacked his text and grade books, deposited them in the bottom drawer of his file cabinet and thumbed in the lock. He hurried into the corridor and hesitated a moment. As a compromise for any of the children who might come looking for him, he left the classroom door unlocked so that at least they would have a room where they could talk with one another. A school regulation required faculty to lock all unsupervised rooms, but he knew he wouldn't have been able to leave if it meant locking them out.

He walked quickly to the stairs, moving almost at a run, absently tossing back greetings to a few teachers and students who dropped perfunctory hellos in his way. Normally the stairwells at La Guardia were reserved for couples. At lunch hour every day the stairs were cluttered with fondling lovers and would-be lovers, the girls seated on the steps, the boys posturing before them on the landings, crotches at eye level, promoting their coming attractions. All year round there seemed to be a perpetual dampness that suggested passion in the trapped, still air, even though, for the most part, a kiss or a grope was as far as it went, for the stairwells were methodically patrolled. Still, once in a while a teacher, by doubling back to break his normal routine, might stumble on a case of actual fornication. Today, though, the rites of teenage lust were all on hold as a large fraction of the student body clustered at the stairwell windows like a herd at a watering hole, straining for a glimpse of the troops laying siege to the school.

Steven raced up to the fifth floor, taking the steps two at a time. He asked a kid outside the gym where he might find Mr. Lucasian but got no answer other than a shrug. Since Lucasian had found Timothy, he could tell Steven what, if anything, the boy said.

"I think he went downstairs with the cop," a second kid said.

Where downstairs, he wondered. The office? It wouldn't do any good looking for him there. If Lucasian was still with the police he wouldn't be able to talk and probably wouldn't want to in any case. He had been tense enough at the grand jury, cold and distant. Another visit from the police wasn't going to make him any more accessible.

Steven turned and hurried back down the stairs, racing all the way to the second floor. He threaded through the knot of boys gathered at the double doors leading into the cafeteria drinking milk and lemonade from cardboard cartons.

He stopped just inside the door and looked around for Rita Torres, who usually ate with a few other Hispanic teachers at a corner table. She wasn't there. His eyes floated down the line of teachers and students queued in front of the steam table and he saw her, a splash of color like sunshine in a room as dank as the gray steam that rose in shapeless clouds from under the hot trays. She was wearing a yellow print blouse with a red bandanna tied at her throat, cool and hot at the same time, the intense shock of her dark hair framing a face that scowled with concentration as she studied the lackluster choices in front of her. For a moment Steven stood still, watching her with the calm and deliberate secretiveness of a man alone on a quiet street at dusk unexpectedly presented with a beautiful woman on the opposite side of a carelessly drawn curtain. Rita was in fact that beautiful.

Skirting the line, he moved in behind her, greeting her with a simple "Hi" that turned her head with a crinkled smile of surprise.

"Oh," she said. "Hi."

She and Steven rarely spoke, on Rita's part simply because she had little to do with anyone on the La Guardia faculty other than the Hispanics, on Steven's part for more complicated reasons having to do with his shyness and the way she looked. For as long as he could remember, he had never been able to approach any girl or woman who really excited him except at an oblique angle, signing up for the yearbook committee because she was on it, running for class office, teaming with her on a class project. All his life he had gone to proms and dances and movies with plain and boring girls who didn't in the least interest him while he waited for the subtle chemistry of workaday friendship and common endeavors between himself and the Rita Torreses of his life to strike the spark that would carry them straight from where they were to passion.

"Could I talk with you a minute?" he blurted quickly.

Rita's eyes wondered perceptibly what this might be about, but she said "Sure" and asked him if he wasn't having something to eat. He said he wasn't.

She passed up the various options for a hot lunch and chose a salad instead, pale greens covered with a white dressing as shiny as mayonnaise. While they waited for the line ahead to clear enough to let her get at the coffee urn, she offered him a few of the standard jokes about cafeteria food and he answered in kind. She had a pleasant laugh, more lighthearted and girlish than he expected.

"You ought to at least have a cup of coffee," she said as she filled her own cup, but he declined.

"Nothing?" she asked, motherly.

"Nothing," he said.

They found an unoccupied table off to one side of the room. The moment he sat down opposite her, he realized how conspicuous he looked sitting there with nothing in front of him, as though he were advertising the fact that something other than lunch was going on between them. He couldn't tell whether anyone around them had noticed but suspected that Rita had urged him to get *something*, probably with this in mind.

Resisting an impulse to hurry back for a cup of coffee, he plunged straight to the reason he was there.

"I never asked you," he said. "Why did you come and get me?"

He had thought her eyes were black but when she looked straight at him he saw flecks of color, rich amber and green, like reflections of firelight. Her gaze was steady and her eyes held his long enough to make him want to look away. Digging her fork into her salad, stabbing at the greens as if she were looking for something buried under them, Rita finally broke the contact. When she looked up her expression was guarded and distant.

"I went over all of it a million times with the police and the grand jury," she said. "Didn't you?"

He nodded.

"Then why would you want to go over it again?" she asked with such intensity that for a moment all the answers he had ready at hand seemed inadequate.

"Because I have to know," he said simply.

She studied him a long time without answering, and when she spoke, her voice was measured and cold. "I got you because I thought you could help Timothy," she said. "It seemed like the right thing to do at the time."

With a suddenness that caught him completely unprepared, she picked up her plate and got to her feet, turning to go. He didn't understand the contempt in her voice, the urgency of her need to be rid of him. Did she blame him for failing to save the lives of those two children?

He lunged across the table and caught her wrist, then pulled his hand back as she wheeled to glare at him. Offended and angry, her eyes insisted that he had no right to touch her, demanded that he release her at once.

"I meant who told you? How did you find out?" he blurted. "Did Timothy say anything? That's all I want to know."

"I don't care what you need to know or want to know," she said, her voice sharp and low, cutting like a blade. "I'm sure it's different where you come from. Up here ugly things happen. We learn not to dwell on them."

He watched her leave, his mind as close to blank as it had ever been. When he got back to his room the door was closed but not locked.

Lloyd Elijah was slumped unconscious at a desk by the window, a broken ampule of crack in front of him.

H A L Garson, just back from lunch, was unlocking his room when Steven rushed into the corridor, shouted to him that he had an OD in his room and then raced back inside. Garson started for the stairs to get help just as a dozen students in the hall started for Steven's room, attracted by the alarm.

Garson got only three steps when he realized that in another thirty seconds Hillyer was going to have a crowd control problem to go with his OD and that any one of these kids could carry a message downstairs far faster than he could. He caught the next boy flying past him, turned him around so their noses were practically touching and issued a series of precise orders. Go to the nurse's office and tell her there is a medical emergency in Mr. Hillyer's room, go to the principal's office and tell the assistant principal the same thing, don't tell them anything else and don't tell anyone else anything. He asked the boy if he understood and sent him on his way, then reversed field and hurried into Hillyer's room.

By the time Garson got through Steven's door, the dozen kids were two dozen. He didn't bother throwing them out because that would have kept him busy all afternoon and it would have been a losing battle in any case. He threaded through them, shoving them generally back as he made his way toward the corner of the room where Hillyer was kneeling over one of the students giving him CPR. When he got close enough he recognized the kid as Lloyd Elijah, without surprise and with no particular emotion. There wasn't a teacher on the fourth floor who hadn't at one time or another found Lloyd nodding in a corner, stupefied on drugs.

After a few seconds Hillyer stopped pumping at the kid's chest and sat upright, struggling to catch his own breath.

"No go?" Garson asked.

"He's breathing," Steven panted. "It stops and starts. Is someone getting the nurse?"

The boy had been breathing shallowly when Steven first found him but a few seconds later he gave a shuddering wheeze and then everything stopped, breath and heartbeat and the flutter of his eyelids. Twice Steven got him going again, and twice his heart and his lungs stopped. This was the third time. It was like trying to kick over a motor on a winter day, and Steven kept hoping that one of these times it would catch and keep running.

"She's on the way," Garson said. "What happened?"

"I found him like this."

"Found him?" Garson echoed hollowly.

He knew all about Steven's lunchtime gab sessions with the students and for a few days had actually considered starting such a practice himself. But in the end he decided it wasn't his style. In general, Steven and Garson had very little to do with each other, each essentially a loner manning a distant outpost, coming to this place from opposite directions. Hillyer struck Garson, in any case, as a bit too much of a saint for his tastes.

Only a saint could be such an asshole as to let himself forget for even a minute who these kids were. Too many of them were never more than an eyeblink away from the next fix. An open door to an empty room was like an invitation to an orgy, guaranteed to get them popping, snorting or shooting whatever chemicals they used to keep their pathetic lives at bay.

As his quick eyes took in the scene, Garson immediately noticed the broken crack ampule on the desk. He checked the kids all around him to see who else had seen it, but most of them were staring at Lloyd Elijah, whose skin was the color of dry leaves, whose chest rose and fell in such shallow undulations that it was scarcely possible to tell from looking at him that he was breathing at all. A few of the students were looking curiously about, studying the artwork on the walls like tourists in a museum, as though the familiar room had suddenly become a new place for them now that someone lay near death on the floor. None of them seemed to be looking at Garson and he didn't really care if they were because Bronx kids learn to keep their mouths shut even before they learn to talk. He leaned on the desk in a way that looked almost natural, letting the palm of his hand settle over the ampule, then folded his fingers under it. When he took his hand away, the tiny piece of evidence was gone and with it all the complications it could bring.

He turned to Steven, to tell him what he had done, but before he could do or say anything there was a bustle at the door and Mrs. Higgins, the school nurse, pushed her way in. She was a small but forceful black woman in her sixties who cleared a path for herself with a string of barking commands that mowed the kids out of her way like a scythe.

"You were with him and he passed out," Garson whispered urgently. "Let it go at that."

Steven looked up at him, questioning, then glanced to the desk, where the broken ampule told the story of a room left unattended. Only it wasn't there.

He looked to Garson, who nodded a confirmation. Steven's guts tightened with panic and his eyes flew to Mrs. Higgins, hurrying toward him. Behind her, two uniformed cops had come into the room and now stood in the doorway, radiating authority. Before Steven realized what was happening, Mrs. Higgins was pushing him aside, kneeling over the boy. Any second now the cops would be standing over him, demanding to know what had happened.

For a moment Steven felt knotted and confused, wishing he could tell Garson to put the thing back, wishing at the same time that he had thought to put it in his pocket himself before Garson had to do it for him.

Across the room, a signal of some sort seemed to pass between the two cops and then one of them stepped forward to take charge of the kids, herding them into a corner of the room away from where the boy was lying on the floor. The other moved toward the victim with long, heavy strides.

"Are you the nurse?" he asked, looking down at Mrs. Higgins, who was wearing a white uniform and the kind of cap only nurses her age still wore.

Her eyes ran the length of him, from his blue pants to his blue tunic to the blue cap on his head. "Are you a cop?" she asked.

The exchange snapped Steven's attention back from his own problem and he had to bite his lip to keep from laughing.

The cop flushed red but had no intention of tangling with her. "Awright," he grumbled sullenly, "we've got a medical team on the way up. Now which one of you wants to tell me what happened?"

He was looking at Garson and Steven.

"There's not much to tell," Steven said. The measured calmness in his voice surprised him, steadied his pounding pulse. "We were talking and then he just passed out."

It was done. It had been easier than he expected. He didn't look around to see Garson's reaction but he could imagine it. *Good morning, Hillyer. Welcome to the real world.*

The cop had a notebook in his hand. He flipped back a page and began taking down information, starting with Steven's name and Lloyd's. All his questions about the boy were in the past tense, as though he were already dead, but in fact Lloyd's eyes were open by the time the Police Emergency Services medical team made it up to the fourth floor. After another half hour he was able to walk out of the room on his own feet, his arms draped over the shoulders of two medics. They told Steven they were taking the boy to a hospital for observation.

And that was the end of it. The cop never questioned Steven's version of the incident. He had no reason to.

LEWIS Hinden and Artemis Reach arrived at La Guardia Junior High at exactly the same time, Hinden in the backseat of a police car. Reporters, summoned back to the school by news that Hinden had been released, converged on their vehicles even before they could get out, but both men brushed them aside, huddling together for a whispered conference behind Reach's car. The Chairman wanted to know if the students had been released and was informed that they hadn't been. He asked if Hinden was prepared to make a statement.

"I'll defer to you on that, Artemis," Hinden said, readily supplying the response he assumed was expected of him.

"For Christ's sake, Lewis, show a little backbone," Reach hissed back. "It's your school they're camped outside. You're the one that got arrested."

"Yes, sir," Hinden quickly agreed. "Is there anything in particular you think I should say?"

Reach had already turned and was making his way toward the reporters, whose microphones jabbed forward like so many fixed bayonets. "Just the cops and niggers stuff," he said over his shoulder. "Let's go."

He ignored the shouted questions, raising both hands in a sort of pontifical gesture for silence, announcing simply that he had nothing to say at this time and had come to assure himself that the police weren't interfering with educational processes within the jurisdiction of Community School Board Sixty-one.

He heard reporters asking for his comments on the grand jury's decision not to indict the officers involved in the deaths of the two La Guardia students, asking if he had spoken with Mayor Ehrlich or the Police Commissioner, asking if he had played any role in Hinden's release.

"I told you, I'm simply here as an observer," Reach repeated. "Until I've had a chance to evaluate the situation, I've got nothing to say."

"Could you just tell us what you're going to say after you evaluate it, Mr. Reach?" a young reporter shouted from the back of the pack, saying aloud what the others were all thinking. To anyone with experience on the New York political beat, the notion that Artemis Reach needed time to evaluate a situation was absurd, and the possibility that he had nothing to say was downright inconceivable.

Reach joined in the laughter. "I imagine I'm going to be outraged," he said, deftly making himself part of the joke instead of the butt of it.

The press loved him, as they always had, not simply because he was good copy but even more because he invariably treated them with the respect they imagined they deserved. They had made him, and he not only knew it but acted as if he knew it.

"But for the moment," he went on, "I'm simply pleased that the principal of this junior high school has been delivered from bondage."

Reach gestured toward Hinden, who stepped obediently forward to answer questions. Dutifully, the reporters aimed their microphones at Hinden, who was ready with glib and boring answers for everything they asked. He assured them there were no problems within La Guardia's walls that couldn't be handled by school staff without police intervention.

Someone asked Hinden how he squared that claim with the fact that the police rescue unit had been called inside barely an hour earlier to deal with a student OD.

None of the other reporters seemed to have been aware of the incident and an excited mutter of journalistic jealousy ran through the crowd. Hinden barely batted an eyelash. His chronic inability to recognize the implications of events in this case prevented him from getting flustered. He was just beginning to say that no school in the city, or any other city for that matter, was drug-free when Reach stepped in front of him to claim the microphones before any of Hinden's inanities actually made the afternoon papers.

"This is the first I'm hearing about it, Charlie," Reach said, addressing the newspaperman across the microphones. "This is exactly why the cops have no business dragging Lewis Hinden out of the school where he's needed to deal with emergencies like this. If there's an opportunity for a statement later, you'll have one. Right now the health of that child comes first."

Grabbing Hinden by the arm, Reach virtually yanked him toward the school like a mother dragging a balky first-grader after her.

The cops at the door must have been given new orders because they scattered as if the cavalry were riding down on them, adroitly getting themselves far enough to either side to be out of frame for the news cameras. There had been plenty of pictures on the morning news that looked like Mississippi; there weren't going to be any more.

In a moment the Chairman and the principal found themselves in the school foyer, Hinden wearing that slightly pained and bewildered look that habitually crossed his face whenever he found himself inside the junior high school he presumably ruled. In his own childhood, children stayed in their classrooms and the hallways were as empty as if the building had been evacuated. At La Guardia students wandered around at all hours and Hinden had never been able to find out why.

Artemis Reach was already heading for the corridor off the main foyer that led to the principal's office. For a moment nothing connected, and then Hinden realized that he was the principal and that it behooved him to arrive at his own office along with the Chairman. His shoes slipping on the polished floor, he jogged along after Reach, catching up with him at the far end of the foyer.

"Two hundred goddamn school days a year, and some asshole has to wait till the cops and every newspaper in town are outside to pop all his fuses," Reach muttered under his breath.

It struck Hinden that the student hadn't *picked* this day or any other to give himself an overdose, but he had more sense than to point it out. Besides, he didn't get the chance. The sound of footsteps from the main staircase stopped them in their tracks and turned them around.

A tall, slender black boy stumbled down the stairs like a badly beaten fighter leaving the ring on the shoulders of his seconds, who in this case wore the insignia of the Police Department's Emergency Services division. Mrs. Higgins was only a step behind them, accompanied by more uniformed officers and one of Hinden's teachers.

With Hinden on his heels, Reach hurried back across the foyer to intercept the odd procession as it came to the bottom of the stairs. "I'm the Chairman of the school board and this is the principal," Reach announced in his most oratorical style. "Where are you taking this boy?"

"Just taking him in for observation," one of the Emergency Services officers said. "Looked kind of like an OD but he's regained consciousness."

The cop was a black kid with a pencil mustache that looked as if it had taken him a month to grow. If he knew who Artemis Reach was from television or the newspapers, he gave no sign of it. Reach jumped on him like a tiger on meat.

"Unless you've got a medical degree, son, I wouldn't go around saying what it looked like if I were you. Now what do you say we get him to the nurse's office where this lady can have a look at him."

The cop swallowed hard to keep himself from giving an answer he'd be sorry for. "He ought to be in a hospital, sir," he said, in exactly the tone of voice he had been trained to use.

"He's not unconscious, for God's sake. You walked him downstairs to keep him moving, isn't that right?"

"Sir, we can't be responsible . . ."

"Of course not," Reach exploded. "I'm the Chairman and that makes me responsible. How the hell are you going to keep him moving if you stick him in the back of an ambulance?"

The cop looked across the pale and unconcerned face of Lloyd Elijah to his partner, who didn't have any suggestions to offer.

Mrs. Higgins said, "Let me just check him out," and that settled it. The cops let her show them to the nurse's office, which turned out to be scarcely larger than a walk-in closet, with a cluttered metal desk taking up half the space. The walls were covered with insipid posters urging beholders to say no to drugs and yes to vegetables. There was a poster demonstrating the Heimlich maneuver, another from Planned Parenthood and a third soliciting contributions to fight sickle-cell anemia, all of them competing for the scarce wall space, overlapping each other, some of them in danger of disappearing completely under placards for newer and more urgent causes. It seemed possible, if one peeled off enough layers of them, that there would be war-bond posters underneath, mixed in perhaps with warnings about polio and diphtheria.

Reach and Hinden watched as the procession moved through the office into a small treatment room with an examining table and a vintage couch on which generations of moaning adolescents had sweated out fevers, stanched bloody noses and experienced the first seismic jolts of labor pains. Except for the police medical team supporting the boy, the cops had all managed to disappear along the way. Steven stayed by the boy's side as the cops helped him up onto the table.

Artemis Reach pushed his way in with the others, shoving the officers aside to stand over the boy, studying him severely for what seemed like a long time. Steven, who was only a few feet away, felt his eyes lock on the Chairman's face, which wore a look of such concentrated intensity that the possibility of a volcanic eruption of rage seemed imminent. His dark face framed by the black beard could have been chiseled out of a single piece of ebony. All the life in it was contained in his jet-black eyes, glaring down at Lloyd Elijah like glowing coals.

Even the boy, groggy as he was, sensed the avalanche of wrath pouring down on him and squirmed on the table as though he wanted to get back on his feet. Reach placed a hand on his chest, holding him in place with two fingers pressed to his ribs. There was no warmth or helpfulness in the contact.

"How are you feeling, son?" Reach demanded. His voice was low but filled the room, like the quiet rolling of a large drum.

"I'm fine, sir," the boy answered with a trace of a stammer in a voice that hardly seemed to be his own. For Steven, who had experienced Lloyd Elijah's icy insolence for two years, there was something frightening and unnatural in the transformation. Lloyd was a kid who knew neither fear nor respect, yet he sounded afraid.

"Passed out, did you?" Reach went on.

"Yes, sir."

"Do you think you can stand up now?"

He raised his hand and the boy wavered for an instant, as though one of the guy wires supporting him had just been cut.

Mrs. Higgins' hands shot forward to steady him. "I don't know as he ought to be getting up, Mr. Reach," she said, softening the defiance with her gentle southern accent.

"Well you just take your hands away, Mrs. Higgins, and let's see how he does," Reach said, gentleness answering gentleness.

The old woman held her breath, fearful that the boy would topple, but she did as she was told.

Lloyd steadied, like a pendulum subsiding. He looked up at Artemis Reach with an oddly childish grin.

"That's fine, son," Reach said. "Just sit there a minute like that and then we'll see if we can't get you up and about."

"He's supposed to go to the hospital," Steven said, surprising himself. He feared that Lloyd might go into arrest again any minute, but Artemis Reach, in his eagerness to have the boy on his feet, didn't seem to care.

Reach whirled on him. "You're who?" he demanded.

"Hillyer, sir. Lloyd is in my class."

If the name meant anything to the Chairman, he didn't show it. "He'll get hospitalization if he needs it, Mr. Hillyer," he snapped coldly.

"It's a precaution," Steven shot back stubbornly. "He almost died."

Reach's eyes were locked on Steven. "Hinden," he barked at the principal behind him.

Hinden had remained in the doorway, where there was still a bit of air to breathe. The closeness inside the room made his nerves tighten and his stomach float in his abdomen, so that he had to close his eyes to prevent himself from becoming ill. He opened them when he heard his name. "Yes, sir," he managed to say.

"Get the name of a good doctor. Make this boy an appointment for after school."

Hinden used the opportunity to hurry off, pretending he had been told to make the call at once. Steven wanted to call him back, to tell him not to let this happen, but he didn't dare and knew that Hinden wouldn't have dared either.

Reach for his part didn't take his eyes off Steven, but when he spoke it was to Lloyd. "There are a hundred reporters outside who want to put your picture on the news tonight if you're carried out of here. There are a hundred cops out there just dying to give you a record as a drug offender. Are those the chances you want to take, son?"

"No, sir," Lloyd said.

"Then get on your feet."

Steven tensed as the boy pointed his toes toward the floor and then, supporting himself with his hands, let himself slide off the examining table. He seemed almost to flow over the edge of it, spilling slowly like thick syrup. His feet settled onto the gray floor and he hesitated there a moment, took stock of his senses and then stood free from the table. The beginnings of smile played at the corners of his mouth but then, just as he seemed about to announce that he was fine, his eyes rolled upward in his head and he swayed precariously like a slender tree in a storm.

Steven lunged forward, grabbing for the boy's arm, but Artemis Reach got there first. Only he didn't grab Lloyd, he grabbed Steven, a long, powerful arm thrusting straight across Steven's chest, his fingers biting with startling sharpness into the muscles of Steven's shoulder.

Steven whirled toward him and looked up into the scowling black face. For an instant he felt in some kind of danger and wondered why the police didn't do anything, but the moment passed and Reach said, "He's all right. Give him a chance."

"The hell he is," Steven shot back.

"I'm okay, I'm okay," he heard Lloyd's voice saying, soft and distant, from across a tidal wave of nausea. The boy was standing steadily now, the color coming back to his skin as though he were a picture on a television set and someone was playing with the dials.

"Sure you are," Reach said to him, but he didn't release the pressure on Steven's shoulder.

Steven could feel the anger welling up inside him. Damn them if they wanted to play these ghetto macho games, tougher than drugs, above the fallibilities of their own hearts and brains. Every blood vessel in the boy's skull might burst at any second—and what? He went down fighting? He gave it his best shot? Is that what this would be about? It was the code Reach lived by, the code the boy lived by. Then let them have it and let them die by it if that was what they wanted.

He twisted violently away from the pressure on his shoulder, pulling free of Reach's grip, panting with rage. Reach slowly turned from him and looked at the boy.

"There you go," Reach said. "Walk him around a little, Mrs. Higgins. He's going to be just fine."

She let Lloyd lean on her and they moved slowly for the door. Steven watched them pass through it, heard their shuffling steps across the office floor. He felt a hand on his shoulder again and whirled to face Artemis Reach.

His shoulder still throbbed where Reach's fingers had squeezed down to the bone, but Reach himself wore a bland smile almost otherworldly in its chilling serenity.

"I appreciate your concern, Hillyer," the Chairman said. "And we all appreciate what you tried to do for the Warren boy. You understand my position, don't you?"

Steven looked at him in shock. Was he being contrite? Or seductive? If this was the famous Artemis Reach charm, Steven wanted no part of it. "Are you asking for my approval, Mr. Reach?" he asked.

Reach's black eyes sparkled and his face split into a wide grin.

"Your approval, Hillyer?" he laughed. "I wouldn't even know what to do with it."

CHIEF Terranova stabbed at the elevator button with lethal intent but the doors took forever to close. He never walked the two floors between his office and the Commissioner's. The veins at his throat still pulsed with anger at the news that had been waiting for him when he got back to his office. Internal Affairs hadn't signed off on the two detectives from the Bronx shooting. Even with the grand jury verdict in, the *investigation* was going to continue.

He knew how the Department worked. The investigation would continue for as long as it took. Someone wanted these guys jacked up.

The moment he stormed off the elevator, the Commissioner's secretary looked up and told him, even before he could ask, that the P.C. wasn't in. "He had a luncheon appointment. Should I tell him you're looking for him?"

"Tell *me*," Terranova said. "Call me the minute he gets in."

Luncheon, he thought bitterly as he waited for the elevator to make its way back up. It was a prissy word for a damn witches' Sabbath where they cooked up nasty recipes for solving their own problems with other people's blood. His people. No one had to spell out for him the nauseating details of the deal that made Detectives Vincent Donadio and James Franks the fall guys in a political game neither of them had been invited to play. He could see Deputy Mayor Boorstin's thumbprints all over the place, could smell the P.C.'s candied breath.

Guess what? It wasn't going to work. Their first mistake was not inviting enough people to their luncheon. Terranova should have been there to remind them that before they started messing over Albert Terranova's detectives, they should have considered the fact that New York City's detectives had a chief.

Reaching his office, he stopped at the door and beckoned Lieutenant Brucks, his secretary, to follow him inside. The lieutenant, who sat at attention even when no one was around, sprang to his feet and marched with the precise, rapid steps of an overwound toy to the office door, where he waited for his boss to step aside before entering.

"Yes, sir," he asked.

"This is to everyone in the squad," Terranova barked, leveling a stubby forefinger at the lieutenant's eyes as though he were personally responsible for everything that had gone wrong in living memory. "I want work-ups on everyone involved in the Warren-James homicides. That's everyone. Students, teachers, straight up to the Board of Education. Victims, witnesses, their families. Is that clear?"

"Yes, sir. I'll get the orders out now."

Brucks started for the door, squirting sideways past the Chief, who filled three-quarters of the doorway. The telephone on his desk was ringing on an inside line.

"Brucks," the Chief called before the lieutenant could field the phone call.

"Yes, sir," Brucks said, turning at the desk. "Preliminary reports on your desk in the morning. Is that all, sir?" That meant Saturday morning, but the Chief didn't go by the calendar. The men in his squad accumulated massive overtime.

"Close enough. I want Williams now. And if that's the P.C.'s office, tell him I'm on the way up."

Within seconds, the Chief was joined at the elevator by Detective Hartley Williams, a broad-shouldered, big-bellied man who had a growling South Carolina accent despite having been born and raised in Brooklyn. Williams had been the first detective Terranova named to his squad when he took office. An intimidating presence, Williams was rightly regarded as the number one man in the three-thousand-man Detective Bureau. The elevator came and they rode upstairs together, discussing the James girl.

"That girl died a virgin," the Chief said. "Does it strike you as likely she'd whip off her underwear and go meet a guy in a locked room?"

"Maybe she wasn't planning to stay a virgin," Williams suggested.

That was possible. But the school corridors were never empty and Terranova couldn't picture her brazen enough to walk past a couple dozen staring eyes into that room.

"There's a back way into that room," he said. "The door's locked and there's no key. Maybe the plate comes off, maybe they force it. Take someone from Forensics and check it out."

Williams promised to get right on it. When the elevator door opened Commissioner Pound was waiting in the reception area wearing the all-purpose smile he used for greeting foreign dignitaries. "Don't bother telling me we've got to talk, Al," he said. "I've already cleared time for it."

"A little late, isn't it?" Terranova shot back. "I already got word you're lifting their shields."

The Commissioner held up a hand for peace and turned the gesture into a kind of wave, beckoning Terranova into his office. He eased the door closed and gestured toward the bar. "Help yourself, Al," he said.

"That's what I intend to do, sir," Terranova said, electing to misunderstand. "Help my men, too, if I can."

"I understand it doesn't look pretty. I realize you have to stand up for your men. Frankly, I admire that in a chief."

"I don't really give a shit, sir."

"Al, I'm being tolerant because there may be some toes stepped on here. Don't abuse that tolerance."

"It's the furthest thing from my mind, Commissioner," Terranova said, letting that stand as an apology. "I just wanted to know what the deal was."

"There was no deal."

"But you are lifting their shields."

"Pending investigation. If the shooting turns out to have been justified, you can rest assured they'll be reinstated."

Terranova smiled but there was little warmth in it. "I'll be sure to tell them you said that, Commissioner. It will mean a lot to them," he said, turning for the door.

Simon Pound watched him go, a finger poised in the air as he debated with himself whether to say anything further. He scarcely knew Terranova at all, in the sense one knows the strengths and weaknesses of the men one commands, where one can and cannot count on them. All he knew of Terranova was a reputation, and it wasn't a reputation calculated to make a police commissioner comfortable. Under the circumstances, it seemed wiser to say something now than to wish later that he had.

"Al," he said, stopping Terranova at the door. "I wouldn't tell them anything if I were you. They'll be notified in due course."

"I've always leaned toward the personal touch, Commissioner," Terranova answered, letting his words carry the weight of insolence while his tone stayed level as a plank, without so much as a trace of irony.

"It's advice, Al. Sometimes it's not a good idea to pick up sticky things."

It was advice that had been repeated to Terranova over and over ever since his earliest successes in the job began to carry him toward command, advice embodied in those tawdry laws of survival that were the only things that ever made him ashamed of being a cop. The moment a cop gets in trouble other cops move away, even his partners putting distance between themselves and him with the same brutal self-interest that tells a moose or antelope to walk away from old or weakened members of the herd with the smell of death already on them.

The correct assumption to work on was that Internal Affairs would notify Donadio and Franks of the disposition of their case in its own time. For the Chief of Detectives to put himself in the middle of the process, delivering the message personally, was unheard of and could be taken to imply a lack of confidence in the normal running of the machine.

Damn right it could. That's exactly what it implied. If anyone asked, Terranova would be more than ready to explain it to them.

His driver was waiting for him with the car. Using the siren to beat the Friday afternoon traffic, already thickening toward sclerosis, he made it to the Willis Avenue Bridge in barely twenty minutes. They crossed to the other side and Terranova slumped lower in his seat, pried the refrigerator door open with his foot and pulled out a milkshake as the grim and defeated landscape of the Bronx rolled past his window.

He was out of the car before his driver could come around to open the door. "Hour, hour and a half," he said, propelling his bulk with his usual quickness toward the high, arching station-house doors.

Inside, he heard a buzz of whispers at his unannounced arrival as he hurried to the stairs. It was strange that he could walk long distances at a blistering pace that left younger, trimmer men panting, but always found himself breathless at the top of a staircase. He had to stop for fully a minute, gulping in hot lungfuls of air before the heaving of his chest subsided. He smoothed the hair at his temples with his hands and walked into the detectives' muster room, exactly in all essential details like the muster rooms in other precincts where he had spent the best and most productive years of his life. As he entered the room his small eyes moved from desk to desk, meeting the eyes of the men, half a dozen of them, jackets off, weapons in evidence as they fielded phone calls and pecked at typewriters loaded with color-coded report forms. He wished he was still one of them with far more passion and earnestness than even the most ambitious of them could ever wish to change places with him. In a hierarchy like the Police Department everyone aspired to command even though those who had it knew that command sucked.

Lieutenant Commander Klemmer stepped out of his office as if on cue, having just been notified by the sergeant downstairs that the Chief was on the way up. "This is a surprise," he said. "You should have told me you were coming."

Terranova said only, "We have to talk, Paul."

Klemmer stepped aside and gestured him into the office. At the doorway Terranova hesitated, said softly, "I want Donadio and Franks, too."

Among the eyes that followed the Chief and the Lieutenant Commander to the office door, none watched them with more intensity than those of the two detectives who knew they were the subjects of the Chief's visit. Klemmer gestured to the men with a forefinger and they hurried from behind their desks.

Terranova quickly inventoried the two detectives as they entered. Donadio was smaller than he had expected; the picture in his mind had been of a sturdy, dark-haired Italian who worked out regularly, young and slightly dim, the new breed out of the movies. Donadio didn't look like that at all. His clothes looked as if they had been worn a day too long and he had a lean and wiry body with only the muscles God gave him.

Franks was even more of a surprise, close-cropped hair, a perfectly drawn mustache, broad in the chest and shoulders, slim at the waist, a black cop who would have fit in at Headquarters or even City Hall. He returned the Chief's gaze steadily, as if he were taking the opportunity to make assessments of his own, almost daring Terranova to wonder how he measured up to the detective's expectations, or even what those expectations might be. Over the past ninety-six hours the Chief had become so involved in the lives of these two men, had reacted so intensely and personally to the decisions made about them, that he hadn't realized until this moment that he had never so much as set eyes on either of them.

"You wanted to see us?" Donadio asked, with a suggestion of challenge in his voice. It struck Terranova that he was probably his kind of cop, an old-fashioned detective who didn't take shit from anyone, even the bosses.

Klemmer said only, "Chief Terranova, Detectives Franks and Donadio. The Chief wants to talk to the three of us."

Terranova invited them to sit down but they both declined with muttered replies. Perhaps they did it to be difficult. They had only to look at the Chief to know he wouldn't be comfortable on his feet, especially after hurrying up a long flight of stairs. Or maybe they didn't care one way or the other, just wanted to have the meeting over with as quickly as possible.

"In a shooting case," Terranova began, shifting his weight until he felt balanced evenly on both legs, "the Department always conducts its own inquiry independent of the civilian investigation."

He knew they knew that, but he had to start somewhere. Their impassive faces told him to skip past the bullshit and tell them what he had come to say.

"We're lifting your shields," he said. "That's not final, but that's where it is right now."

For a moment no one spoke. Then Klemmer said, "Jesus Christ," coming up out of his chair.

Donadio said, "Where the fuck's this coming from? No one even talked to me. Anyone talk to you, Jim?"

Franks was staring at Chief Terranova, staring actually at the part of the room he was in, his eyes boring in, looking straight through him. If there had been an eye chart on the wall behind the Chief, Franks would have been able to read it. "No one," he said without taking his eyes off Terranova.

"Then what the fuck are we talking about?" Donadio demanded.

"You'll be interviewed," Terranova said. "This is a temporary suspension pending . . ."

"What the fuck's pending?" Donadio shouted. "It's a bullshit bag job, you know it, I know it."

Klemmer stepped right in front of him. "Watch it, Vince," he said sharply.

"Or what?" Donadio shot back, pushing past him to face Terranova again. "You used to be a cop, didn't you? You know a bag job when you see one, don't you?"

"Would it matter if I said yes?" Terranova asked.

"Not in the least," Donadio sneered. "If you'll excuse us, Chief, we've just been fucked. Unless there's some rule we gotta listen to you tell us we weren't, we're getting out of here."

He stormed to the door, yanked it open and turned to his partner. "Coming?" he asked.

"You go ahead," Franks said in that quiet, even voice that never changed.

Donadio slammed the door on his way out.

"He flies off the handle sometimes," Klemmer said. "He's a good man."

"You don't have to tell me that, Paul," Terranova said and turned to Franks. "You're getting a bad break on this one," he said. "I'll do everything I can."

Franks looked at him as if he didn't much believe him or didn't much care. "Has it been announced yet?" he asked.

Terranova shook his head. "No, not yet," he said.

"Is there any chance you can hold it off?" Franks asked.

It wasn't much to ask. "Till tomorrow. I think so," Terranova said.

"No, just till later tonight," Franks said. "We're having some people to dinner. I'd appreciate it if you could keep it off the evening news."

VICTORIA James smoothed her skirt and blouse and called that she was on her way. The knock came again, two firm but polite raps on the frail wood of the door, which was so thin that if anyone knocked too hard they would put their hand right through it.

She glanced around the room to make sure it was as straight as her skirt and blouse, then reached for the door and unlocked it. She was as nervous as a schoolgirl. Not over seeing Dr. Carlisle, heaven knew. He was as good as family, she had known him that long. But he was bringing a stranger and strangers always made her skittish.

The breath rushed out of her in a kind of gasp the moment she opened the door and saw the person standing next to the doctor. He was a black man so incredibly tall she couldn't even guess his height. To her all tall men were giants. But this one *was* a giant, taller by a head than Mr. Dalrymple at work, who was tall enough for people to remark on it all the time.

It wasn't just the man's height that took her breath away. He was without any question the best-looking man she had ever seen in her life. He was clean-shaven and his hair was short and neat. His skin, as smooth as a boy's, was the color of that pretty, light wood that makes the best-looking furniture. His lovely smile seemed to say that even though he looked as if he just stepped out of a magazine, he didn't think of himself as anything special.

Victoria James hadn't the slightest doubt that indeed he was something special. Yes indeed. It didn't even matter who he was. She knew just looking at him that this man was going to be a help to her as surely as if he were an angel of the Lord coming to her the way they came to people in the Bible to help them in their times of trouble.

"Victoria, this is Tal Chambers," she heard Dr. Carlisle say. Then he said, "Mrs. Victoria James. May we come in, Victoria?"

Oh heavens, she thought. *I must look like an idiot standing here.*

"Of course," she said quickly, flustered, her hands flitting about the way they always did when she wasn't quite sure what she was supposed to do. "Yes, please. Come right in."

As she stepped back from the door to let them in, the tall man said, "I'm sorry about your daughter, Mrs. James."

His name had just run away from her. Dr. Carlisle had said it only a second ago and already she didn't remember. Yes she did. It was Tal something. Chambers, she recollected just in the nick of time. "I believe you are, Mr. Chambers," she said. "That's a kind and Christian thought. If you'd care to sit down, I'll just fix us something to drink and I'll join you straightaway."

She gestured toward the chintz couch in the tiny living room they were standing in the moment they stepped through the front door. Victoria had bought that couch for five dollars down on the day she decided, eight and a half months pregnant with Ophelia, that she could not live at her husband's mother's house one single day longer and found this apartment. It was new then, the fabric so bright and cheerful that it seemed to fill the room with the brilliance of its colors, making her think every time she looked at it that it was a sign that this little apartment was going to be a real home.

It had been home for almost fourteen years now, thanks to the good Lord who provided and no thanks at all to Herman James, who then and ever was about as ready to take on the burdens of a husband and a daddy as he was to sprout wings and fly. Two weeks after Ophelia was born he went running back to his mother, complaining that the baby's little bird-like cries wouldn't let him sleep at night, which was nothing but an excuse because he more than made up for it in the daytime.

And now the couch is still here, Victoria thought as she set a plastic pitcher of iced tea on a tray and three glasses around it. It isn't bright anymore, but it did its job, didn't it, outlasting everything.

Tal Chambers got to his feet as Mrs. James came out of the kitchen and offered to take the tray from her, but she put it down on a bureau. She filled the glasses and handed them around before she sat down to listen to what Dr. Carlisle and Mr. Chambers had to say.

The doctor took a sip of the tea, and since there was nowhere for him to put the glass down, he held it cradled on his knee. "I've had a talk with the medical examiner, Victoria, and he was kind enough to let me see his report. I can absolutely assure you there are no indications that your daughter was sexually molested in any way," he said.

Victoria closed her eyes and offered a prayer of thanks.

On the couch opposite her, Tal looked away so as not to intrude and his eyes fell on the small shrine in the corner of the room. A silver-framed picture of the Virgin in pale colors that suggested a wan and wistful serenity stood on a tiny pine table covered with a fine lacy cloth so white it almost sparkled. For some reason it captured and held his attention so steadily that he had to pry his mind off it, snapping his head around when he realized that Mrs. James was speaking.

"I knew that had to be," she was saying. "I knew those things I heard on the radio couldn't be true."

"You can rest your mind about that," Tal said.

She looked straight at him, her small features focused and intent. With her quick nervousness she had reminded him when he first walked in of a small, wary bird, but now it seemed he saw a touch of the hawk in her, keen and concentrated. And why shouldn't she be a hawk as well? They needed that, too, these small, wary women who fought back against a world their men surrendered to. There was a shrine like Mrs. James's in Tal's own mother's house, only there the picture was of Jesus soaring triumphant at the Resurrection, in His eyes the look of just such a bird.

Mrs. James was telling him that she had called Dr. Carlisle the moment she heard the radio broadcast because he was the kind of doctor a person could count on for the truth. She didn't know what part Mr. Chambers had played in this but she was grateful for it. As she said this she blinked back a thought and her eyes darted to Dr. Carlisle, a sparrow again, the moment of the hawk vanishing utterly.

"He couldn't know that without examining her, could he?" she asked.

Dr. Carlisle shook his head.

"Examined her like that?" she asked.

Dr. Carlisle knew what she meant. "Yes, he would have to," he said softly.

She sucked in her lips, suppressing a shudder. "She'd never been ex-amined like that," she said, aching with the awareness of her little girl, too tender and young by far for these things, dying with the purity of a child only to lose it after she was dead.

Then Mr. Chambers, speaking so softly his voice was like a ripple on the surface of the silence, urged her to be patient and strong because the radio and the television and the newspapers were still going to talk and write about Ophelia and reporters were going to come and ask her ques-tions, but she would be better off not talking to them at all, even on the telephone.

She heard the warning in his voice more than the reassurance, felt herself tensing from the center of her body outward, her stomach knotting, her muscles straining against each other to hold themselves ready.

"Why would they be asking questions?" she demanded sharply, like an accusation.

Mr. Chambers leaned forward on the couch. "Mrs. James," he said, "the reason all these questions came up was because some of your daughter's clothing was missing."

She cocked her head with a blank look of incomprehension. How could they lose the child's clothing? What did it matter if they did?

Dr. Carlisle reached into his breast pocket and took out a piece of paper. He handed it to her and said, "This is the list of her clothing when they examined her at the medical examiner's office. She wasn't wearing panties."

Victoria James's eyes swam in her head as she tried to read the paper, but the letters danced in front of her like blackflies swirling in the air. She could feel her confusion focusing itself, heating up, turning to anger. Was this how they were helping her? This wasn't help, it was a test, a test from the Lord to measure how much pain she could take, first taking away her girl and then piling one thing on another, the radio in the morning and the doctors stripping her little girl naked to look at her and now this stranger testing whether she would believe that the little girl she brought up was prancing around in that sink of a school with her pants off.

"That's a lie," she said, dropping the doctor's paper to her feet as she stood up. "A damn lie."

Tal Chambers and Dr. Carlisle were on their feet as fast as she was, both of them towering over her in the small space between the chintz couch and the chair. She took a step backward and then another, to get away from them, thinking that sometimes the devil sends messengers like this and sometimes God sends them as a test the way an angel of the Lord told Abraham to butcher his little boy.

Now she was a different bird, loud and fierce and terrible, her small sharp beak thrust forward as she flew at their eyes, attacking mindlessly, driving them from her nest. "Don't come back with those lies," she squawked, "don't you come back to my house with those lies!" driving them out the door.

She pulled it closed and snapped the lock. And then she lay her head on the door frame and wondered if it could be true. Surely it couldn't.

Surely it could. For who was so high they could say with certainty they could never fall?

No one was so high.

The devil set traps for little girls, set them right there in the space between their legs, drawing them toward him with every step they took.

* * *

C O M I N G out of the subway a block from his mother's apartment, Steven paused for breath and realized that Broadway was as airless as the subway tunnels under it. The sidewalk was crowded with a mix of people so unlikely that it looked like one of those amusing scenes from a movie studio where extras from westerns and musicals and outer space are all having lunch together. There were the elderly Jews, little men with caved-in chests and big bellies, shuffling beside their shapeless wives in floral dresses, the last remnants of the Upper West Side's old guard. There were the black hustlers so shameless they would try to peddle a blank video-tape, a pair of sandals or a fountain pen on the sidewalk in front of the very store they stole it out of. It wasn't even dark yet and a frail hooker, so painfully skinny it seemed she would break if anyone touched her hard, was already working the street, offering thin-lipped blow jobs, quick and cheap, crouched in the backseat of a taxi.

Around the prostitute, as though in a different world, mothers pushed strollers loaded with groceries while their displaced children bobbed alongside, protesting shrilly. Men drifted out of the corner market, their arms wrapped around paper bags bulging with grapes and lettuce, a quart of milk, a couple pints of Häagen-Dazs, their black leather briefcases dangling from their clasped hands. The sunken-eyed hooker's presence seemed to mock them all, flaunting her depravity in the midst of the normal people hurrying home, staking her claim to a share of the business. *We sell what we have to sell*, she seemed to say. *That's how it's always been, couscous or compact disks, pizza or pussy. Damaged goods, marked down.*

Two or three beggars worked the block, one by the newsstand, one at each corner. *Spare some change. A quarter, anything. Feed the homeless, feed the homeless.* The neighborhood had always had its winos and derelicts, spilling onto the streets from the single-room welfare apartments on the side streets between West End Avenue and Riverside Drive, aggressively begging for the next drink. But these people were different, lacking the alcoholics' bitterness and intensity, their voices soft and coaxing, their faces full of sorrow and indifference, as though they had all the time in the world. They thanked you even when you gave them nothing, wished you a good day, offered God's blessings. In just the past few years they had multiplied tenfold, twentyfold, turning the street into a third-world casbah, declaring on every corner how garishly everything had gone wrong, hundreds of them, thousands if you walked far enough, impossible to ignore and impossible to satisfy.

Steven dug some change out of his pocket and slipped it into the hand of the man on the corner. "God bless you," the man said, "I know He will," leaving Steven to wonder, as he turned the corner, how such faith was possible.

On his way down the hill toward his mother's apartment, Steven stopped abruptly halfway down the block. He had moved in with his mother when his apartment was trashed, accepting it as a defeat like a child brought home after running away. But tonight the prospect of dinner and a long evening in the still, close air of her apartment was more than he wanted to deal with. It was Friday night and the thought suddenly hit him that there was a basketball game at school. He hadn't been able to find Lucasian all afternoon but Lucasian would be there. If he had remembered the game before he left school he would have saved himself a long subway ride back to the Bronx.

Still, it was a small price to pay for putting Lloyd Elijah's taunt behind him.

He turned around and hurried back to Broadway, where the man to whom he had given the quarter started to ask him again but recognized him and waved him past, as though the street were his theater and Steven had his ticket stub in hand. There was something touching in the gesture, which seemed to suggest that the possibility of connection wasn't completely out of the question.

He bounded back down the subway steps and dropped a token in the turnstile. He could hear a train pulling in below him and raced down the flight of stairs to the platform level, catching a glimpse of the downtown express just as its doors began to close. A black kid in the first car saw him running for the train and held the door. Steven thanked him as he slid through and found a seat.

By the time he got back to La Guardia it was after six o'clock. The game had probably started already.

He wondered if the police would still be there but didn't have to wonder long, for he saw them as soon as he rounded the corner. The massive deployment of the morning had been cut back to only about a dozen cops in riot gear, lounging pointlessly now as though they were on leave. No one seemed to be in command. A police van was parked at the curb, waiting either to take the troops away when the school finally closed or to transport possible prisoners.

No one moved to detain or question Steven as he made his way to the front door, his eyes rigidly ahead, intent on ignoring the cops if they were willing to let that happen. Apparently they were.

A black family entered ahead of him, mother and father and two little girls who must have had an older brother on one of the teams. Each of the parents was steering one of the girls, a hand firmly in the middle of her back, as though they would have drifted off if left to their own devices. They disappeared through the door half a dozen paces ahead of Steven.

Basketball games at La Guardia were never well attended, largely because the school had a long history of listless, mediocre teams. During his first few years at the school Steven attended games regularly and even made a point of mentioning them in class, congratulating his students on a good game whenever possible. He thought he could build school spirit but gave up the effort when one of the players asked him to stop embarrassing him in front of the class. Steven hadn't been to a game in at least two years.

By the time he reached the fourth-floor landing he could hear an occasional cheer drifting down the staircase from the gym. A moment later he could make out the voices of parents calling their sons' names and the rhythmic stamping of children's feet pounding the planks of the wooden bleachers that lined one side of the court. There was a certain sadness to the sound as well as the sight that greeted Steven when he stepped into the gym. A few scattered clusters of parents and brothers and sisters were trying forlornly to make themselves into a crowd.

The scoreboard hadn't worked in years but it was easy to tell that the game wasn't going well for La Guardia. From the far side of the court Lucasian scolded the kids loudly, yelled at them to quit standing around, sent in substitutions every time the ball changed hands. "You're in a game, you're in a game," he'd shout. "C'mon, let's see a little movement."

Steven waited just inside the door. After a minute or two Lucasian noticed him and Steven nodded a greeting across the floor, but the gym teacher looked away with an expression that could have been displeasure but may have been merely distracted indifference. A few minutes later, when Lucasian glanced back in his direction, Steven tried to signal that he wanted to talk to him but Lucasian looked away again as though he didn't understand.

Steven drifted over to the bleachers and asked one of the parents how much time was left in the period.

"Only just started," the man said.

Steven watched a few minutes more, but there were so many fouls and other time-outs that it began to feel as if the period would never end. Restless, he wandered back into the corridor and drifted toward the weight room as though there were something drawing him to it. Behind him, the uneven hammering of a basketball dribbled raggedly down the floor punctuated the hum of voices from the gym and the hollow sound of his own footsteps.

His heart quickened as he neared the door, then stopped abruptly when he realized it was open. Only an inch or so, but open.

He stepped to the door and pushed it back enough to look inside. There was no one there, just the jumble of old towels, mats and equipment he remembered vividly from the other time. And directly opposite him, on the other side of the storeroom, the door to the weight room itself. He stepped toward it, barely daring to ask himself what it would feel like to look at those tiled walls again.

As he reached for the doorknob he saw it turn, and an instant later he was chest to chest with a man nearly a head taller than himself. He took a quick step backward, startled and momentarily afraid. He had to remind himself that there were a hundred people only a few dozen yards away.

The tall black man seemed to be surprised, too, because he fell back a pace, just as Steven did, each of them thrown off balance by the other with an almost comic literalness.

For a moment neither knew what to say. And then they both tried to speak at once.

"You're not supposed to be . . ."

"Look, I was only . . ."

They stopped, each deferring to the other, and then they both laughed uneasily at their discomfiture. That was when Steven realized he was talking to Tal Chambers, the only hero La Guardia had ever produced.

"You kind of caught me by surprise," Chambers said.

Steven was sure that Chambers's surprise was nothing compared to his own.

"My name's Steven Hillyer. I teach English here," he said, offering his hand. "You're Tal Chambers, aren't you?"

Chambers nodded. "Hillyer," he said. "Then you're the guy who was here when it happened. I've been meaning to talk to you."

Yes, that was who Steven was, or at least who he had become. The guy who was there when it happened. And Chambers was the guy whose name the room bore, lettered in bronze on a plaque just inside the door. In an odd way their identities were linked by that small dark cube of space Chambers had just come out of.

"This place is kind of special to me," Chambers said as they stepped across the storage room and into the corridor. "I was hoping you could tell me what happened."

You asked the wrong person, Steven thought with more than a trace of irony. But before he could say anything, a shout from the direction of the gym spun them both around.

"Hold it! Hold it right there, Hillyer!" Barry Lucasian screamed from the gym doorway as he charged across the basketball court and down the corridor. Behind him, about a dozen boys in shorts poured out of the gym in pursuit, bench warmers from both teams eager to see what all the excitement was about.

"Awright, Hillyer, what the hell's going on here?" Lucasian shouted, racing the length of the hall as if afraid his quarry would try to get away. As he got closer and realized there were two men at the weight room door, he slowed his pace to a rapid walk. When he was still a dozen feet away he stopped short.

"Tal?" he said, part surprise and part sheer incredulity. It certainly wasn't a question, though it sounded like one. He had known Chambers for years.

Some of the young basketball players surged in around Chambers, filling the space. His name was being whispered all around.

"I'm sorry, Barry. This is all my fault," Chambers said.

"You're with him?" Lucasian asked, directing the question at Chambers as though Steven were an uninvited guest.

"We just ran into each other," Chambers said. "I wanted to have a look at the place, that's all. Whatdya say we get back to the game."

But Lucasian wasn't ready for that. "What about you?" he said sharply, turning to Steven.

"A few things I wanted to talk about," Steven said. "Now's not the right time."

"I know what you want to talk about," Lucasian snarled. "You were looking for me all day, weren't you?"

"I was," Steven said. "I had a couple questions about what happened."

"Where the hell do you get questions?" Lucasian exploded. "I've had cops and grand juries and cops again. Now I gotta answer an English teacher?"

"Take it easy, Barry," Chambers started to say, stepping between them. But Lucasian reached past him to jab a finger into Steven's chest.

"Listen to me, Hillyer," he said. "That fucked-up poet of yours messed up in my facility and I'm taking the heat for it. I've had it up to here with questions. Now what do you want to know?"

"If you want to talk, let's talk after the game," Steven said, keeping the indignation out of his voice because of the kids hanging on every word between them.

"Don't tell me what's the right time. This is the only time you're getting. Now what's the question? How they got in there?"

"That's one of them," Steven said.

"How'd you get in, Tal?" Lucasian asked.

Chambers shrugged. "I didn't want to bother you," he said. "I slipped the lock."

"There's your answer, Hillyer. Next question."

Steven wasn't sure what the next question was. A dozen things raced through his mind but the one he asked was, "Did Timothy ask for me? Did he say he wanted to talk to me?"

"He didn't mention your goddamn name. Is that it?"

It wasn't, but they couldn't go on like this in front of the kids.

"That's it," Steven said.

"Damn right," Lucasian snapped. "The sooner this thing goes away, the better for all of us. If you want to make trouble, Hillyer, I can make some too."

He turned abruptly to face the kids. "What do you say we show Tal Chambers we still play basketball at this school," he said.

He slapped Chambers on the back and together they started for the gym, the players clustering around them. Chambers draped his arms over the shoulders of the two boys nearest to him and said, "We had some pretty good teams here in my day. Barry tells me we still do."

The two boys beamed. One of them asked him if he knew Walt Frazier and Chambers said he had played against him.

Tal paused at the door to the gym and glanced back at Steven, waiting, forgotten in the corridor, but he went inside without saying anything. From the brightly lit gym Steven could hear the referee's whistle and the staccato drumming of the ball, the squeak of sneakers on the wood floor.

D o n a d i o was already gone when Franks came out of the Lieutenant Commander's office. There were only two detectives left in the squad room, all the others having discovered a witness to something whose statement needed clarification, a complainant who had to be questioned again, a sudden hunch on the whereabouts of a suspect. Neither of the detectives who remained in the office so much as looked at Franks as he walked to his desk and packed his file on the Warren-James killings into his briefcase. He picked up the phone and dialed his home.

"I'm getting out early," Franks said. "Anything you want me to pick up?"

He jotted a few things on a pad and then said, "Okay, I'll see you in a while." Then he said, "Yeah, I love you too."

He stuffed the shopping list in his pocket, picked up his briefcase and started for the door. Normally he would have said something to the men on his way out, but if they didn't have the balls to say anything to him, he wasn't going to let them off the hook that easily. The worst thing about cops, even those who weren't afraid of anything, was that they were afraid of each other.

He managed to keep his mind almost totally blank the whole way home. On the Henry Hudson Parkway he turned on the radio to learn if Terranova had been able to keep his promise, but there was a song playing about a man whose wife didn't love him anymore and Franks didn't have the patience to wait for the news or find another station.

He clicked off the radio and drove in cocooned silence, the windows rolled tight, the monotonous drone of his own tires on the pavement the only sound he was aware of. The highway wound down to a comfortable two lanes, with traffic lights every mile or so at intersections that led off into pretty villages where there were grassy football fields behind the schools and the public libraries were in little brick houses with flags flying in front. Perfect little villages where the kids rode their bikes to school every morning.

Jim Franks swallowed back a thought and locked his mind on the traffic, not wanting to reflect on the life he was giving little Jimmy, buying him a pretty world where he could pedal to school as free as a child could be, because that thought would bring him to La Guardia Junior High and then he wouldn't know how to make himself stop thinking.

He eased off the road at the Dobbs Ferry exit, stopping halfway up the hill in front of the grocery. It called itself a specialty shop because of the fifty-pound barrels of coffee beans and the boxes of tasteless English crackers, but whatever it called itself, it was still a grocery store. In Dobbs Ferry, at least this side of it, from the foot of the hill on through to the other side of town, one could no more shop at a grocery store than one could have one's shirt pressed by someone who wasn't a French cleaner. He bypassed the shopping baskets stacked inside the door and took the list out of his pocket. A dozen French rolls, a small wheel of Brie and a box of paper napkins. It took him only a minute and he presented his purchases at the counter. A black man was still a novelty here, but they all knew Jim Franks and accepted him calmly. The fact that he was a detective gave him, in fact, a somewhat glamorous aura, a dash of spice in a social mixture that tended toward the bland.

Lenny was in the kitchen when he got home, the children nowhere in sight. She was chopping scallions at the counter, the knife making a rapid rattling sound so quick and efficient it seemed to be made by a machine. She looked up, tossing her head to fling her hair back, and asked him if he remembered to stop at the market.

The shopping bag was at his chest, carried in front of him the way one carries a baby, which meant her question was rhetorical. He never understood why she couldn't simply say what she meant. "Were they out of Brie?" Or, "Were you able to get everything?" Instead, she had to ask a question to which no answer other than the bag so obviously in his arms was necessary. The indirection of it annoyed him more than it should have, so he didn't answer at all and said instead, "I'm going to take a shower. What time are they coming?"

She stopped chopping and used the back of the knife to wipe the scallions from the board into a small bowl. "I told everybody seven-thirty," she said, "but the Brownmillers won't be able to be here before eight."

Before going upstairs he stopped in the den. Jimmy was watching cartoons, so he stayed a minute to watch with him, but they were those mindless and joyless cartoons where the characters' jaws went up and down like hinges when they talked and nothing really funny ever happened. After a minute he said, "Hi."

Jimmy said, "Hi, Dad," without taking his eyes off the television.

"You know we're having company for dinner, don't you?"

The boy grunted an affirmative.

"What are you going to do?"

"Hide out, I guess."

It seemed like a good idea. Jim smiled. The boy was only eight but he had a pithy way of making his points. "Did you eat?" Jim asked.

"Mom said you'd go to McDonald's for me."

That seemed like a good idea, too. McDonald's and badly drawn cartoons, the life they had raised their children to. "Think about what you want while I take a shower," he said. "Do you know where your sisters are?"

"Around I guess," Jimmy said.

Jim switched his briefcase from one hand to the other and went upstairs. Laura and Susan, it turned out, were both asleep in their room, which was certainly out of character. Even the baby, Laura, who was three now, hardly ever napped anymore, and certainly not this late in the day, so he knew they would be up pretty soon and good for the rest of the evening. They must have been bored silly, with their mother tied up in the kitchen, to have fallen asleep at all.

He put his briefcase on the dresser in his bedroom and crossed to the closet to put his gun on the top shelf where he always kept it, out of the children's reach. Then he remembered that he didn't have his gun anymore because he had left it in his desk. He knew he would be asked to turn it in and was surprised he hadn't been asked already. The only reason he could see was that neither Klemmer nor the Chief of Detectives had the balls to bring up the subject. He was glad he had thought to leave it at the station because in the morning, when someone called and ordered him to bring it in, he'd be able to tell them it was in his desk.

He wondered if Donadio had done the same thing. Probably. Vince wouldn't give any of them the satisfaction of watching him surrender his weapon.

Franks got undressed and walked naked into the bathroom, stopping for a second to look at himself in the full-length mirror in the small dressing room between the master bedroom and the master bath. Sometimes he liked what he saw, because he had a trim athletic body, which was one of the few things he was vain about. But this wasn't one of those times. His shoulders looked hunched, and even straightening his back didn't help because it made him feel as if he were posing to conceal a reality it was too late to hide. His dangling genitals looked comical in the reflection, as though they were an afterthought. Women's bodies, he realized, were much more carefully planned.

He lathered and rinsed quickly under the shower and had just begun shampooing his hair when the bathroom door opened and Susan's piping voice asked, "Daddy?"

"What is it, honey?" he asked back.

"Jimmy said you were going to McDonald's for him."

"Mm-hmm."

She didn't answer. He said, "Suzie?" and heard the muffled, unintelligible response of a sobbing child.

He parted the curtains and saw his little girl staring at him with her tiny fist jammed into her mouth. "What is it, honey?" he asked.

She blubbered a bit and managed to say, "I want McDonald's too."

"Of course. I'll get you whatever you want. You know that," he said.

"Jimmy said you were going for him," she pouted.

"Well I'm going for whoever likes little square pieces of chicken." She took her hand away from her mouth. "And gloppy chocolate milkshakes." Her eyes began to sparkle but her mouth was still wrinkled. "And french fries. And co-oo-oo-*kies*," he said, finally winning the smile. "Who would that be?"

She looked down the way she always did when he teased her and said "Me" in a very small voice.

"That's right," he said. "And Laura. And Jimmy." He turned off the water and stepped out of the shower, reaching a towel from the rack. He was conscious of her eyes on him, staring at his penis as though hypnotized by the movement of it as he dried himself. Neither he nor Lenny had ever made an issue of nudity in the family, but at the moment it felt like an issue or at least something he didn't want to deal with, so he quickly covered himself. "Why don't you be the waitress and get your sister's order," he suggested, sending her away.

Lenny was in the bedroom when he came out. "Everything that's supposed to be cold is in the fridge and everything that's supposed to be hot is in the oven," she said. "Are you finished with the bathroom?"

"Finished," he said.

She stopped undressing to look at him closely. She hadn't looked at him since he came home. "You didn't shave," she said. The shadow over his cheeks gave his face a look of feltlike softness that she found appealing, but he always shaved in the evening for company.

He took a shirt from the drawer and stripped out the paper without answering. She reached back to unhook her bra, then stepped out of her skirt, but he could see she was still thinking about it. "Is something the matter?" she asked, cocking her head.

"They suspended me," he said. "How's that for the matter?"

The words took her breath away, stunning her in a way that made it hard for her to know what to say or even what she was feeling, whether it was more hurt or outrage. "How can they do that?" she said at last, moving to him.

"They can and they did," he said, as though he were indifferent to it or above it, the tough guy who could take whatever they dished out without flinching.

She put her arms around him, but even though she was naked except for the small bright red panties, the warmth of her body against him felt neither comforting nor erotic. He loved her and she was beautiful, but he had never been able to use love as a drug the way some men did. When there was trouble, nothing helped.

He squirmed away from her and slid his shirt over his shoulders.

"Why don't we cancel tonight," she said. "I can still get everyone on the phone."

"You don't have to do that," he shrugged.

"I know I don't *have to.*"

"It'll give us something to do."

"Is that what you want?"

He shrugged again. "I asked them to hold off the announcement. I don't need a living room full of people feeling sorry for me."

She thought she understood what he was saying. "If that's what you want," she said. "But we can get out of it with just a few phone calls."

"The kids want me to go to McDonald's," he said, a slight edge to his voice, as though he were telling her how little dinner or canceling dinner mattered. "I think I'll run by the video store and rent them a tape."

"Maybe you'd better do that first," she said. "Before everything worth seeing is gone."

Just like that, and they were back to the details of running a family, his world falling apart while attention focused on rationalizing the errands.

ON HIS way downstairs from the gym, Steven stopped to get Rita Torres's phone number from the faculty directory in his desk. He was surprised to see that she lived in Spanish Harlem, only about a dozen blocks from his apartment, and took it as a good sign. This time he wasn't going to let her say she didn't want to talk about it. The fact that he had learned less than nothing from Lucasian left him oddly energized, intent on pursuing it further.

He took the train back to Manhattan, hurried up the stairs at the Ninety-sixth Street station and looked around for a phone booth. There were two pay phones on the corner, shielded by plastic hoods. The handset had been ripped out of one of the telephones and the second one gave no dial tone when he lifted the receiver. He slammed it down in disgust.

"You gonna be long, amigo?" a guttural voice growled at him in heavily accented English.

"What?"

He turned and found himself facing a young Puerto Rican in Cuban-style fatigues, his face dotted with the makings of a beard. "The phone," he explained. "You gonna be long?"

Steven wasn't sure what he meant or why it mattered. "It doesn't work," he said, looking down the avenue for another phone.

Without a word, the young commando reached past Steven to pluck down the receiver, tightened the earpiece with a few quick turns and held the instrument in front of Steven's face. "It works," he said. "Keep it quick, right?"

Steven put the phone to his ear. There was a dial tone now, which Steven acknowledged with a quizzical expression as he turned his back on the young man to put in a quarter and dial his number.

"Two minutes, amigo," his benefactor growled from behind. "Then I gotta cut you off."

The phone rang three times and a woman's voice answered in Spanish. "Rita Torres, please," Steven said.

"*Momento*. Who is this?"

Steven gave his name. There was no response but he heard the clatter of the phone being set down. There were no background voices at the other end of the line and he couldn't hear Rita's name being called. In fact it was so quiet he began to think he had been hung up on. The seconds passed slowly, bringing his lease on the telephone closer and closer to expiring.

Finally a woman's voice said hello. He had no idea what kind of place he had called. It could have been a rooming house with a phone in the hallway, or it could have been her home.

"I wanted to speak to Rita Torres," he said, a bit sternly.

"Steven?"

He hadn't recognized her voice. On the telephone it seemed deeper than he remembered it, older somehow.

"Right," he said. "I was thinking we kind of got our wires crossed in the cafeteria this afternoon." He had gone over a lot of ways to begin this conversation, and this wasn't one of them.

"Look, I'm sorry about that," she said. There seemed to be a bit of a laugh in her voice. "Sometimes I get a little crazy."

"No, no, you were probably right," he broke in quickly. "I thought maybe it might be a good idea if we could talk about it a little."

"About the shooting?"

"Not about that so much," he said, conscious of the evasion. It was a touchy area. He didn't really know what he wanted to talk about, just that he wanted to talk to her. "Just about, I don't know, the whole thing I guess."

"I suppose so," she said.

For a moment neither of them spoke. Then he said, "The thing is I've only got the phone for another minute and I've . . ."

"You've only got what?"

"The phone. I'll explain about that when I see you."

"When you what?"

Clearly they weren't understanding one another. He took a mental step backward and tried again.

"Look, I'm in a phone booth. I'm only a few blocks away."

"Do you want to *meet* someplace?"

She said it in that tone people use when they try to guess the intention of foreigners who are using all the wrong words.

"I could come over there."

"You don't want to do that. Where are you?"

"Ninety-sixth and Lexington."

"Wait there," she said.

"I could walk over, it would only take . . ."

But she cut him off again. "Ten minutes," she said. "Don't run away."

The phone went dead in his hand. He felt he had been manipulated in some way he wasn't clear about and then it dawned on him that he had gotten exactly what he had wanted, so perhaps he had been the one doing the manipulating.

The Puerto Rican boy in the fatigues asked for the phone back and then unscrewed the earpiece before hanging it up.

Steven checked his watch and looked up Lexington Avenue where she would be coming from, thinking ahead to where he might take her for a drink or a cup of coffee, what he would say.

"What the hell is this, man?" the Puerto Rican said in his ear.

Steven glanced around with a look of incomprehension. His mind was already running through scenarios for the next few hours. He had hired a cleaning company to scrub the filth out of his apartment but they hadn't done anything to put the mess back in order. This meant that even if everything worked out, he had nowhere to take her afterwards.

"C'mon," the kid said sharply, gesturing with his thumb. Earlier there had been a kind of sardonic humor in his voice that wasn't there now.

"I'm meeting someone," Steven said, failing to pick up the signs.

"Yeah, well meet him somewhere else."

He sounded truculent but not necessarily menacing. Just because he knew how to fix the phone didn't mean he owned the street, and Steven bristled at being ordered about. "I'm not bothering you," he said.

"The fuck you're not."

"Look, I'm only going to be here a couple of minutes," Steven shot back, sharpening his own voice. He was at least a couple inches taller than the boy and a good deal heavier, although he didn't for a moment imagine he'd be any match for him in a fight. Not that it would come to that over standing on a street corner. It was ridiculous to think it would.

Still, ridiculous or not, Steven began to sense things moving in that direction. He would just as soon have walked away but a streak of stubbornness he didn't quite understand or recognize in himself kept him from doing so.

"You use the fuckin' phone, man, now get outta the fuckin' space."

The boy's voice was pitched higher than it had been. A man passing by glanced over, then quickened his pace. A woman hurried her daughter along.

"Take it easy. I'm not bothering you," Steven repeated, but already he was starting to inch backward.

There was a sharp click from somewhere, a sound Steven knew. At La

Guardia he had seen the knives come out often enough and had seen the results. He didn't look down for the blade but took a decisive step backward. Something hit him in the back and he realized it was the phone hood. The wings at either side hemmed him in and it was too late to say anything or even just to explain that he was leaving. His hands came up to ward off the blade (he had seen that, too, hands sliced down to the tendons, dangling like empty gloves) and all he could say was "All right, all right."

It was clear that he had to get out of there, even though the only way was toward the boy. Shutting down his mind to all thoughts the way you do when you dive into cold water, he lurched forward and to the side, the surprisingly sharp corner of the phone shell cracking into his shoulder, drawing a straight line across his back as he slithered sideways like a crab, keeping the boy in front of him. He lost his balance as he stumbled from the unexpected curb and a pain shot up from his knee, which seemed to lock on impact.

The kid, though, hadn't moved. He glared after Steven and then spat once and turned away, already resuming uncontested ownership of his telephone.

Steven gasped out a long breath and realized that he was panting like a dog in the summer. His back hurt where it had hit the phone hood and he was certain he must have cut himself on a rough edge. The pain was sharp, but he didn't feel any blood. He turned and started across to the north side of Ninety-sixth, where Rita would be coming from. Although his knee felt stiff at first, it was working normally again in a few seconds.

He looked up Lexington but didn't see her. She had said ten minutes and he wasn't sure how long it had been. Probably only a minute or two, although it felt longer. A lot longer. Time passes slowly when you are almost knifed, a rule of nature he hadn't fully understood before. After a few minutes a crosstown bus pulled in at the curb and a dozen people formed a queue and filed inside. The bus belched out a series of rude noises and lumbered off toward Central Park and the West Side. Steven checked his watch again, and when he looked up he saw Rita hurrying toward him, her hair flying behind her, accentuating each step. She was wearing jeans and a red blouse in some kind of rippled fabric. Her hair flowed with the motion of her body and she smiled when she saw him. They met halfway up the block.

"You didn't have to do this, you know," he said as soon as she was close enough to hear.

"It's very nice of me," she agreed with a light laugh. "Actually I wasn't doing anything anyway. Do you know where we're going?"

The difference between the biting anger of the way they had parted in the afternoon and the way she spoke and smiled now was enough to make his head spin, but it was a pleasant, even exhilarating sensation. He didn't have the least idea where they might go, so he shrugged, saying it depended on whether she wanted to get something to eat or just wanted a drink.

"There's a nice little place not too far if you don't mind walking," she said.

He said that would be fine and they turned around and started back uptown.

"This thing's really messed you up, hasn't it?" she said after they had walked a little way.

"Not really. In a way, I guess," he answered, not sure whether he was agreeing with her or not. A lot of things had happened since the killings—the grand jury, the burglary at his apartment, living with his mother again, and then everything at school this afternoon and evening, Lloyd Elijah, Artemis Reach, Barry Lucasian. Maybe it wasn't just the killings that preyed on his mind. Maybe the accumulated weight of all of it was getting to him. He hadn't thought before that he was messed up, although now that she put it that way it struck him as a fairly accurate description of his state of mind.

They reached 100th Street and she turned left toward Third Avenue. There didn't seem to be anything but tenements on both sides of the street, each with its stoop leading up to a tiny foyer lit by a bare bulb. Inside, the hall doors were all propped ajar, their hinges no doubt sprung. Ahead, the portion of Third Avenue he could see looked just as dark and empty, and he wondered where she could be taking him and why they had turned.

"What happened to your jacket?" she asked.

"My what?" he said and then remembered. "The oddest thing happened when I called you," he said, launching into an account of the young man who knew how to fix the pay phone and acted like he owned it.

She interrupted him with a laugh. "Don't you know what that is?" she asked. "The drug dealers get their calls on the pay phones. They disconnect them like that so people don't tie up the line."

"I guess," he said. "Anyway, he didn't want me waiting in his office."

"He cut you?"

"He was thinking of it. I cut myself on the phone booth."

He thought he sounded rather impressively casual about it, but Rita said, "You ought to use a little common sense, really. Some of these guys are crazy. They all think they're going to die anyway."

Was it that simple? he wondered, looking over to see whether she really thought so or was just saying it as a kind of shorthand for something she didn't actually understand any better than he did. But she was looking straight ahead, her head back, her lips taut and thoughtful. She didn't seem to be aware of his eyes on her.

At the corner she turned again. The block consisted mostly of small stores hunkered behind steel shutters, but halfway down the block a splash of light spilled on the sidewalk from a small restaurant with its name lettered colorfully in the window in an involved, intricate script suggesting tangled vines. He only had a chance to make out the word *Caribe* before Rita led him through the door into a lively, crowded room.

A waitress in tight jeans led them to a table, where Steven let Rita order for him in Spanish without looking at the menu. The clientele was all young, both the men and women dressed mostly in sleeveless T-shirts, so that the overall impression was of a sea of bare arms. The room was bright and cheerful, decorated in cool pastels that exuded a sense of unmistakable hopefulness, as though the owners, whom one imagined to be as young and slender as their customers, knew some secret that hadn't yet penetrated the blighted streets outside.

Steven commented on the pleasantness of the restaurant and Rita filled him in on its history. A brother and sister had opened it only a few months ago, doing all the decorations themselves with the help of a few friends. There was no money for contractors and so they had done even the plumbing, the electrical work and the masonry themselves. The space had been a drugstore before that, so they had to install the entire kitchen, put up walls and a new ceiling, hang fixtures, following the instructions in do-it-yourself books as they taught themselves half a dozen trades.

"Were you one of the people who helped?" he asked, taking his clue from the tone of pride he detected in her voice.

"A little," she said. "On weekends. Listen, I can't get over how rude I was this afternoon. I'm not usually like that."

It took him a moment to register that she was talking about their meeting in the cafeteria. He dismissed her apology with a shrug as the waitress arrived with slices of lime pie and two mugs of scented coffee, an aroma of cinnamon and a spice he didn't recognize wafting up to him on the steam.

"There was an OD in my room this afternoon," he said when the waitress was gone.

Rita said she had heard. She asked who the boy was and tossed her head when he told her it was Lloyd Elijah. "He's got a lot of problems," she said.

They talked for a few minutes about Lloyd, about the police at the school and the atmosphere of grim fatalism that had been hovering in the air like a sharp, astringent smell since the deaths of Timothy Warren and Ophelia James. Then Steven surprised himself by saying, "There was one of those little crack vials on the desk. I got rid of it before the police saw it."

Her eyes went wide with surprise and her hand came across the table and rested on his, a startling intimacy that he hadn't in the least expected. He was glad he hadn't mentioned Hal Garson's role in any of it.

"Oh, Steven," she almost gasped. "Why would you do a thing like that?"

He had to stammer for an answer and managed something about having left the room open, wanting to keep it simple, having as few things as possible to answer for.

Her fingers threaded through his cupped hand with a warmth that was uncannily erotic and her eyes were locked on his.

"You are so naive," she said, gently, not mocking, as though he were something to marvel at, a grown man who still believed in Santa Claus or didn't know where babies came from. The closeness of the moment caught him off guard, almost embarrassed him, and he tried to distance himself from it.

"I don't think it's as complicated as that," he said. "No one's going to say anything."

"Of course they will," she said. "These kids are always getting in trouble. And that's how they get out of it. You really shouldn't trust them. Ever."

"You don't mean that."

"Steven," she said in a tone of strained patience that would have identified her to anyone listening as a schoolteacher, "it's not a major felony but it could be a lot of trouble. Besides, if you're going to do something like that, you don't sit down in a restaurant and tell someone you hardly even know about it."

Now it was his turn to laugh. He turned his hand so that it returned the grasp of hers and said, "You mean I shouldn't trust you either?"

"Yes," she said. "That's exactly what I mean. There's no reason you should."

He was startled by the intensity in her eyes, which flashed darkly as though she meant for him to take her warning seriously. The distance across the table between them suddenly had grown impossibly wide.

Without thinking, he took his hand from hers. He was sorry at once but didn't know how to repair the damage.

When she spoke again her voice seemed to come to him from a considerable distance.

"What was it you wanted to know this afternoon?" she asked.

For a moment he had trouble remembering. But then he asked, "Who told you what happened?"

She hesitated before answering, and in that moment the distance between them shrank back to what it had been only a moment before, as though she had been carried back toward him on an invisible wave.

"Charlie Wain," she said and nodded, confirming the fact to herself.

Charlie was the boy guarding the door when Steven and Rita arrived on the fifth floor.

"Not Lucasian?" Steven asked.

"Barry went for the police. Charlie came and got me."

"Why you?"

She laughed lightly. "I think he has a crush on me," she said. "Or maybe I was just the first teacher he saw."

Steven nodded, considering the scenario, trying to picture the sequence in his mind. If Lucasian and Charlie Wain both ran for help, then no one had been with Timothy and Ophelia from that first moment until Steven arrived.

"Why?" Rita asked. "What are you thinking?"

"I just wondered what anyone saw. Whether Ophelia was alive. What they were doing."

"What did Barry say?"

He looked at her quizzically. She had a knack, it seemed, of being always half a thought ahead of him.

"How did you know I asked him?"

She laughed again, that light laugh that seemed to suggest she thought he was being foolish. "He would be the one to ask," she said. "He was there."

Steven told her about going to the school, and about Lucasian's outburst when he was questioned about it.

"Maybe he's got a point," she said. "What happened happened. Does it really matter why?"

He thought it did, and tried to explain. He didn't understand what could have driven Timothy to kill the girl. If he knew whether or not Ophelia was still alive when Lucasian and Charlie Wain first found them, then maybe he could start to put it together in his own mind. Much of the questioning, from the police and at the grand jury, had focused on whether she was alive when the police finally got there, because the issue for them was what the cops did. The issue for Steven was Timothy.

Until the assistant district attorney read him some of Timothy's poems in front of the grand jury, he hadn't even known, for example, that Timothy had any relationship at all with Ophelia James. It was such an unlikely pairing, a pained and angry boy filled with more bitterness than he could handle, a quiet, friendless girl, shy, withdrawn and deeply religious. What would Timothy have wanted with her? Or she with him? He remembered her from seventh grade, when she had been in his English class, dressed in plaid skirts and blouses buttoned to the neck, like the uniforms of parochial school girls. She was timid around boys, blushed and stammered in class at the slightest hint of anything that touched on sex or sexuality or even just the passions that drove the unreal characters in the fiction they read to fight or cheat, to assert themselves or to run away from home. He couldn't imagine that another year could have changed her into someone who wouldn't hide from a boy like Timothy Warren as desperately as if he had been the devil himself.

"Maybe they didn't have anything to do with each other," Rita suggested. "Maybe he just grabbed her."

Steven shook his head and told her about Timothy's poem, quoting it to her, surprised to find that he remembered all of it.

> *Forty ways, Ophelia,*
> *Like streets belonging to a foreign gang,*
> *Hostile streets,*
> *Forty, O,*
> *Down into your Manhattan,*
> *The parts we never see or touch,*
> *Is that the way you want it, O?*

"My God," she said when he was finished. "He was in love with her, wasn't he?"

Steven only nodded. He had thought the same thing.

"Are there other poems about her?" she asked.

He didn't know. He asked her if she thought Charlie Wain would talk to him about what he had seen.

"He might. Let's ask him," she said, signaling the waitress for a check.

THEY could as well have been on the moon, Steven felt, looking around at an area so arid, pocked and cratered that it seemed to have little in common with the geography of earth. Then they looked at each other with matching expressions of resignation and bewilderment, as though the subway had shunted them to a siding in another part of the universe. The few cars parked at the curb seemed to have been left there to decay. In another month or so, maybe a week, maybe by morning, they would have melted down to ground level, dissolving into the oily puddles that stood around them. *The mountains and hills laid low,* Steven thought, overwhelmed with the wide vista of catastrophic erosion that stretched around him in every direction. He almost asked Rita if she had taken them to the wrong subway stop.

They walked in silence without seeing any signs of life except the darting, furtive play of headlights coasting through an intersection a long block ahead. But the moment they rounded a corner, the stark vacancy of the side street erupted all at once into the dense syncopation of a living city. Scores of people, kids and old men, lounged purposelessly on parked cars, leaned with chronic indolence against graffiti-stained storefronts, or crouched at the curbs passing paper-bagged bottles among themselves.

Steven looked to Rita, whose eyes scanned the faces with as much assurance as if she had entered a familiar room. "Do you think you'll be able to find him?" he asked.

"I grew up on streets like this," she said.

She headed directly for a cluster of teenagers in front of a fried-chicken store and asked if any of them had seen Charlie Wain.

A heavy black girl with a pie-shaped face said, "He was here couple minutes ago," and a boy asked, "What are you doin' here, Miss Torres?"

Steven recognized a few of the kids from school, though none were in his classes. They recognized him as well, greeting him with a medley of well-intentioned gibes. *Charlie forget his homework, Mr. Hillyer? Howdya like the neighborhood, Mr. Hillyer? Next time you oughta take her to a movie, Mr. Hillyer.*

Rita singled out a Puerto Rican girl and spoke to her in Spanish. The girl's answers came back either angry or annoyed, but it sounded to Steven as if she was answering Rita's questions. After a few minutes Rita thanked her and led Steven quickly away.

"There's a basketball game at the playground on Tremont," she explained. "He might be there."

After ten minutes of walking past gutted tenements, they could see the playground ahead of them, a cloud of dirty yellow light hanging over a square of black asphalt surrounded by a decrepit Cyclone fence. In New

York City almost all playgrounds are fenced, some of them locked at night to keep the children out at hours the Parks Department doesn't countenance. Gaping holes in these fences can go unrepaired for years, and sometimes whole sections of fence are missing entirely, but the ritual of locking and unlocking the gates goes on just the same. The Tremont Avenue playground was a perfect example. Although long sections of fence lay useless on the ground, the gate was secured for the evening by padlock and chain. Behind it, two full teams of children drove the length of the court for lay-ups into the netless baskets.

Steven and Rita slipped into the playground and looked around. He could see at once that Charlie Wain wasn't one of the players. Although he didn't know the boy well and had never had him in class, a picture of the hulking, awkward youngster, well over six feet tall, dark as night, was etched in his mind from the morning Timothy Warren died, a one-man guard barring all comers from the weight room door. Steven could still hear the low rumble of his voice—*I didn't let no one in, Miss Torres*—dense and obedient and eager to please.

Deep in the shadows behind the spectators, where the lights directed at the basketball court didn't reach, Steven could barely make out the shapes of three boys huddled together in the darkness. After a minute or two they split up, two of them melting into obscurity on the other side of the fence, shoulders hunched, hands thrust deep in windbreaker pockets. The third boy started toward the court. He was tall and heavy.

Steven nudged Rita, gesturing with his head.

At the same moment the boy stopped and appeared to look directly at them, hesitated for only a flicker of indecision, then turned and walked quickly away, moving with a shambling bearlike stride that rocked his broad shoulders from side to side.

"Isn't that him?" Steven whispered urgently, starting to move already.

"I think so," she said, "maybe," her voice unsure. But she was right with him.

The boy was moving much faster than he appeared to be, so Steven had to jog to keep up with him, Rita trotting beside him, the slap of their feet on the pavement loud even against the machine-gun rattle of the dribbled basketball, the pounding gallop of the players' shoes.

Ahead of them, the tall boy vanished through a hole in the fence without so much as a backward glance.

Steven and Rita reached the spot a few seconds later and stepped through. It was as though someone had thrown a switch, plunging them into darkness. The lights in the playground seemed a long way behind them. As near as Steven could tell, they were in a broken field of some sort, the footing uneven, like a rock-strewn beach. Clumps of low, scrubby weeds licked at their ankles. There was no sign of the boy.

Steven stopped to listen, catching Rita's hand to stop her next to him. She was only a foot away and he could see no more of her than an outline against the playground lights. He thought if they stopped moving they would be able to hear the boy's footsteps, but they heard nothing except the insistent staccato of the game over a deep rumble that must have come from an expressway somewhere in the distance.

Ahead of them, a shape darted through the night, visible for only an instant as it flickered across the pinpoint street lamp on a distant block like a bird blotting stars.

"There he is," Steven called, and they set out running, lurching over the scarred terrain. Buildings had stood here once, perhaps a school, all that remained of it now the broken stones under their feet and the dense, willful weeds that asserted their primacy amidst the rubble.

How he and Rita kept their footing he didn't know. Once or twice he felt her stumble at his side, but each time she caught herself and kept pace. The end of the lot loomed nearer and nearer, a dark street that held no particular promise. A low row of bricks, all that remained of a foundation, caught his ankles and sent him crashing to the sidewalk, where he hit hard, sliding on his palms as he fought to keep his face above the pavement. The grit worked into his skin like needles, sending a searing shock of pain all the way up to his shoulders. Warned by his fall, Rita jumped the obstacle and stopped near where he lay.

He rolled onto his back and looked up to see her scanning the street, first one way, then the other. He started to tell her he was okay but she spoke before he did, calling Charlie's name into the night.

"Is he there?" Steven asked, getting to his feet and gingerly rubbing his palms together to work out the loose dirt.

"I think so," she said. "There."

She pointed toward the doorway to a building across the street. Perhaps there was someone standing there, pressed back against the closed door, a dark shape against the shadows. Perhaps not. He couldn't tell.

"Charlie! It's me! Miss Torres!" she called. "I want to talk to you."

In the silence that followed, Steven kept his eyes fastened on the doorway, his ears straining to pick up a response. He wondered whether there was anyone in any of the tenements across the way who heard her call.

"Charlie!" she called again. "It's Miss Torres!"

Across the way something moved. A figure stepped from the doorway and started across the street. Steven was sure it was the boy they had been chasing.

In a minute Charlie Wain was moving toward them with a kind of hangdog shuffle. "Didn't know it was you, Miss Torres," he mumbled in a tone that in a pinch might pass for apology. He was wearing a long gray topcoat that dangled from his shoulders like a serape.

Steven said nothing and Rita didn't ask the boy who he thought they might have been.

"Mr. Hillyer has a few things he wants to ask you, Charlie," she said. From her tone she could have been talking about an English quiz.

Charlie said, "Yeah I guess" and gestured to Steven with a vague waggle of his left hand. A loose bracelet of white gold caught the light of the street lamp, glowing dully.

"The day Timothy was killed, Charlie," Steven began, "could you tell me what happened."

"I don't know."

"I don't mean with the cops. I mean from the beginning."

"Hey," the boy said, more or less helplessly. He looked to Rita.

"Please," she said, but Charlie Wain only took in a breath and nodded his head. If he was going to help, it wouldn't be by volunteering anything.

"You were with Mr. Lucasian, weren't you?" Steven prompted, trying to help the boy get started.

"I guess."

"And he took you up to the weight room?"

"*Took* me?"

"You went up there with him? To the fifth floor?"

"C'mon, what the fuck's this about?" Charlie asked sharply, directing his annoyance at Rita. "What do you want to mix me up in this shit for?"

"You won't get mixed up in anything, Charlie," she reassured him. "It's just for Mr. Hillyer."

Charlie shuffled his feet and looked away.

"He was there," she said. "You remember that. He went in and tried to help Timothy. Tell him whatever you know about what happened."

The boy studied her a moment, turning thoughts slowly in his mind. The thin membrane of his patience had been stretched to the point of transparency. Steven could see it about to snap.

"I didn't have to come back here y'know," Charlie said.

"But you did," Steven said. "Miss Torres appreciates that and so do I."

The boy nodded and then said bluntly, "I didn't go up there with no one."

Steven glanced to Rita. She had told him otherwise. She looked as puzzled as he did.

"Then what were you doing on the fifth floor?" Steven asked.

"He got me on weights. Football, right? It's bullshit."

"What's bullshit?"

"I'm gonna play football? Get real."

"So you went up there to work out on the weights?"

"That's what I'm telling you."

"Okay, fine, that's helpful, Charlie," Steven said, trying to work the edge back out of the boy's voice. "You just went up there to work out by yourself."

Charlie shook his head. "It's locked, dig. Some bullshit from a couple years ago. So I wait up there so the dude can let me in."

"Mr. Lucasian?"

"Uhnnnh. A couple minutes and he ain't there yet. I figure I try the door and it's open. And that's when I seen them."

"You went in by yourself?"

Did he ask for me? Steven had asked Lucasian. *He didn't mention your goddamn name,* Lucasian had said, only to hurt. He wasn't even in the room. It was Charlie Wain. And now Charlie turned to Rita with a look of exasperation. "I gotta tell this guy everything twice?" he asked.

"Please, Charlie," she said.

"Yeah yeah," Charlie mumbled and turned back to Steven. "So you wanna know what they's doing? Like the girl, she's on the bench, see, she's laying out on the bench. Man, like I know this school is weird but I don't expect no chick laying out on no bench."

"Where's Timothy?"

"He's like on top of her."

"He's lying on top of her?"

"You got the picture. I don't know if he's humping her or what. And I go kinda *huh* and he looks up at me."

Steven's head was spinning. That wasn't what he wanted to hear. The newspapers at first said Ophelia hadn't been molested, but then this morning there was a story suggesting she might have been. He thought he knew Timothy, and when he thought of the boy's dark and passionate intensity, it was never as simple or brutal as the picture Charlie Wain was painting now.

"What about her? What was Ophelia doing?" he asked, his voice hollow.

"I'm not looking at her, Mr. Hillyer. That's the truth. I'm just backing out of there."

"Did he say anything? Did either of them?"

"Something I guess. Could've."

"Which one of them?"

"Him, I guess. I don't know. Said anything it's like *Charlie get outta here*, but I couldn't say. Could be he didn't say nothing."

"It's important, Charlie. What did he say?"

"That's what I'm telling you. Timothy goes *stuff it* and I'm outta there. I mean I don't have no fucking tape recorder. Nobody tells me there's gonna be a quiz. He don't say *stuff it* exactly. It's like I say *Timothy, what do you be doing here?* and he says *Get out get out get out*, like that."

"What about Ophelia? Was she alive, Charlie?"

"What the fuck's he doing on top of her if she ain't alive? Jesus."

"I mean did she say anything, did she move, did she make any sounds?"

"I'm telling you what I seen. I don't know fuckall who's moving, who's what."

"Did he threaten her? Did he say he'd hurt her?"

"I'm telling you what he said."

"So you left?"

"Better believe it. And that's when he shows up."

"Mr. Lucasian."

"Is someone stupid around here? Right. He's there when I come out and I tell him, so he's going for the cops and I go downstairs to find Miss Torres here."

For a moment no one spoke. The boy's account didn't mesh with any of the pictures in Steven's mind or with what Lucasian had told him only a few hours before. He had come to the Bronx because he wanted to hear that Ophelia James was conscious and moving, because he wanted her to have said something, or Timothy, something he could play back over and over like a tape, an image he could scan in his mind like a photograph until he understood why they were there together in the weight room and what might have happened that brought Timothy Warren to the point where he snapped her neck.

In the silence, Charlie Wain waited for another question, bouncing impatiently on the balls of his feet, already in motion to somewhere else.

Nothing was clear to Steven anymore, not even the things he thought he knew. Too numb and confused even to begin sorting it out yet, he said only, "All right, Charlie, I really appreciate this. Thanks."

"Yeah right," the boy mumbled in response. He stepped between Rita and Steven and lumbered up the street.

Steven felt the pressure of Rita's hand on his arm and turned to face her.

"Was he any help?" she asked.

"I don't know what's help and what isn't anymore," he said.

Then, before she could say anything, the question he had been meaning to ask Charlie all along, the most important question of all, suddenly jumped to the front of his mind and he turned and called Charlie's name.

The boy stopped and turned to face them. His shoulders were hunched and his arms, dangling loosely by his sides, looked oddly long.

"Were they friends?" Steven called down the street. "Was Ophelia Timothy's girlfriend?"

The word seemed to hang in the air, incongruous on that ruined street. It echoed like something from childhood, like tinkling wind chimes, and should have been surrounded by high-pitched teasing giggles. Who had girlfriends anymore? He was talking, after all, about two children who were dead.

"Hey," Charlie called back, evasive and noncommittal. He took a few more steps before he vanished into the night that filled the space between two feeble lamps.

W H I L E they waited for the train, Rita took each of his hands in turn and inspected it closely in a motherly way that embarrassed Steven enough to make him pull away. He told her she reminded him of Snow White checking to see if the dwarfs had washed for dinner.

"And you remind me of Grumpy," she laughed. "What makes me think there's no iodine or bandages at your place?"

"Wrong," he said.

"There is?" She didn't sound as if she believed it.

He shook his head. "There's not even a place."

Telling her that he didn't have an apartment hurt even more than the miscellaneous pains in his hands, knees and shoulders. He was sure that if he asked her she would come home with him, or if not sure at least comfortable enough with the possibility that he would have been willing to risk asking. After what they had just been through he felt a sense of communion with her that she must have felt as well. But there wasn't a damn thing he could do about it for the simple but humiliating reason that he was staying with his mother.

He explained on the subway ride back downtown how that state of affairs came about, telling her the story of his gutted apartment and the two detectives with their dim threats, hoping that she would share his outrage.

"And you just *left* it like that?" she asked in a voice that didn't convey either sympathy or commiseration.

"I didn't leave it like *that*," he answered defensively. "I mean I got some cleaners to come in and clean the shit out."

"Well, that was very resourceful."

"Look, everything I owned was ruined. What was I supposed to do?"

"Go home to your mother, I guess."

"What the hell's your problem?" he shot back angrily. He had gone home because he needed a place to stay. It had nothing to do with his mother.

She held up her hands for peace. "No problem," she said. "I seem to have hit a nerve."

"You didn't hit a nerve."

"You mean you're always like this?"

"All right. I'm a grown man and I ran home to my mother. Is that what you want me to say?"

"I'm sorry. No, I don't want you to say anything, all right?" But she leaned back in the seat, looking away from him.

"No problem," he said, mimicking.

For a minute or two they didn't even look at each other, each of them studying the nearly empty subway car. Then she said, "You're right. I've never had my apartment broken into. It must be awful."

He turned to look at her. Her hair had drifted down low over her eyes and she looked very young and distant and self-contained. He nodded a confirmation.

"Anyway," she said, "I live with my mother too."

She pouted in a small and fragile way that hid the beginnings of a smile. He smiled back. "And you're giving me such a hard time?" he asked lightly.

"Well it does kind of present a problem, doesn't it," she said.

His nerves jumped under his skin and he could feel his face flush. He was certain he understood what she was saying and felt a sudden rush of desperation not to let the moment get away from him.

"They did clean it up," he said, grabbing at the first solution that presented itself. "I mean it's still a mess but at least . . ." He couldn't find the words to finish what he was trying to say.

"There's no shit on the floor."

"Exactly."

"I don't think so, Steven," she said, shaking her head in a way that looked weary and filled with regret. "I appreciate the thought but it wouldn't be very nice."

He nodded his agreement but inside he felt knotted with that churned and bitter taste of rejection. He felt like a gawky adolescent with nothing to say in his own defense after a crude and badly timed grope. They rode the train in silence the rest of the way back to Manhattan, Steven holding his damaged hands with fingers splayed like the veins of a leaf. His palms itched and burned at the same time, a kind of poison-ivy feel. If he tried to move his fingers even slightly, the pain reminded him not to. "Maybe we can go somewhere and talk," he suggested, trying for an offhand tone he couldn't quite manage.

"Do something about your hands or they'll get infected," she said. "Then we can go to the park."

She waited on the street while he went into an old German restaurant that looked as if it might have a passably sanitary men's room. It took him almost ten minutes of scraping at his palms with his nails under running water to work the grit out from under the skin. When he came out, Rita was talking with a man in Spanish but got rid of him as soon as she saw Steven.

"These guys are amazing," she said. "If you tell them you're not a hooker they think you'll fuck them for nothing. Let's go."

They walked down Eighty-sixth Street to the East River and wandered through the park until they found a pleasant spot on the stone breakwater just south of Gracie Mansion, the mayor's residence. On the far side of the river, lights from tenements and the waterfront danced like stars in the sky while farther downriver the lights of the bridge spun off like pinwheels of fireworks. For a while they stood by the parapet listening to the water lapping darkly against the stones beneath them. He put his arm around her and she let her head drift to his shoulder.

"I don't know what I should do," he said at last, his tone thoughtful but distant.

She pulled away from him, turning to face him, choosing to misunderstand. He had meant to share his doubts with her, but instead she seemed offended that his mind was so far from this moment with her. "There's nothing to do, Steven," she said sharply. "If you didn't understand that before, you ought to understand it now."

"Now?" he asked. "Nothing's clearer now."

"It's not?" she shot back angrily. "Why did we just go up to the Bronx and chase down Charlie Wain if you won't listen to what he tells you?"

"What the hell did he tell me?"

"That Timothy was on top of that girl. What does that sound like to you?"

"It sounds like it doesn't make sense," he answered quickly, his indignation matching hers. "Timothy had problems, but raping girls wasn't one of them. And what was she doing there? Ophelia wasn't a girl who sneaks up to the fifth floor to get laid."

"Maybe she wanted to be, Steven. Maybe she got tired of being a little girl. It happens."

And then, alone with him, she changed her mind and Timothy killed her. It was possible, but it didn't sound right to Steven, because it wasn't what he wanted to believe about either of the dead children.

"All right," he said softly, grudgingly conceding the possibility. "But what about Lucasian?"

"What are you talking about?"

"He was in the room with them, he said so. Charlie said he wasn't."

For a moment she said nothing, and then, when she spoke, her voice was gentle and understanding, the anger drained out of it.

"I know it's hard to accept," she said. "It was all so ugly and you don't want it to be ugly."

"No," he confessed. "I don't."

"Then don't look at it. Look at me," she said.

Her hand touched his face.

"We're here. Now. We're not in the Bronx. Let it go."

"I can't. I don't even understand why you'd want me to."

She answered with a light kiss, her lips at first just brushing his. And then she pulled herself to him with a force and urgency that almost took his breath away. His mouth and nostrils filled with the taste of her mouth, a fresh and piquant taste of lime and mint tumbled with the faint intoxicating scent of crushed wildflowers like a kaleidoscope of pale blues, pale greens, pale yellows. His hand groped at the back of her neck, tangling in the intricate blackness of her hair, which seemed to coil around him like a marvelously sprung trap.

For an instant he felt frightened and inadequate, as though his own sexuality were something tame and manageable and mundane measured against the force of her passion. He knew that she could overwhelm him if she cared to and if he let her, but he fought against it, struggling for control of the moment. His fingers clawed at the roots of her hair, his hand pulled her ass into him, grinding her loins into his so that he could be sure she understood. In the end it was Rita who surrendered, twisting free of him and stepping back as far as his hands allowed.

For a moment then they stood at something short of arm's length, as though the passions of the last few breathless seconds had been some sort of a contest.

"Let it go," Rita said at last, a touch of sternness, or perhaps just resignation, in her voice.

He nodded his acquiescence with a wan smile and she answered with another kiss.

"Why don't you get that apartment of yours cleaned up," she said, and laughed like a young girl.

SATURDAY

T H E traffic stretched in front of him like a wounded snake. *Traf-fuck* Vince Donadio called it. On a Saturday morning it had no business being like this. He lowered his head to the steering wheel and rubbed at his forehead, trying to get the circulation going. His right foot had dandled on the brake so long he had lost all sense of where it was except that the car wasn't moving. Which either meant it was on the brake or he was out of gas.

Talk about hitting the nail on the head. Had anyone ever been more out of gas than Vincent J. Donadio, about-to-be former first-grade detective in the New York City Police Department, presently under suspension because his partner shot a spade headcase with connections to City Hall? He was so out of gas it showed.

"What?"

His head snapped around and he looked blankly at the girl next to him on the front seat. *Shit. He must have been talking out loud.*

"What did you say?" she asked, taking his look for a question.

"Nothing," he said.

"You said something. I heard you say something."

"Just talking to myself."

"Great," she said.

She was twenty-two years old, tops, and already she had the bitch act down perfect. *Great.* That was all she said but she could turn one word into a whole discussion.

"I was just thinking how fucked up this city is," he said.

"You can pull up," she said, gesturing at the car ahead, which had rolled forward two or three feet.

"Right. We wouldn't want to stay here when we've got a chance to be there," Donadio said, easing his foot off the brake for a second or two.

"Look," she said, "don't take it out on me."

There wasn't any point continuing the discussion, so he kept quiet with his eyes on the road, as though he were driving. The George Washington Bridge hung at the far end of the highway, three miles away by actual measure, twenty minutes by subway, forty-five at a hard, steady walk, a whole fucking morning and afternoon at the rate they were going. He noticed how many of the cars around him were in worse shape than his, which was a four-year-old Plymouth. There were VW bugs with bumpers and doors different colors from the bodies and old Dodges that were held together by the rust, little Jap cars so nondescript they had names that didn't even mean anything in Japanese, let alone English.

Here he was, a guy living on a cop's salary with alimony and child support to pay, and still he had a better car than three-quarters of the people in the city. If that didn't tell you how fucked up this city was, nothing did.

If more examples were needed, he had a ton of them. How's this for starters? A healthy Italian male in the prime of his life, who lives alone in a slum tenement apartment you wouldn't wish on the homeless, drives out to the suburbs, to Dobbs Ferry no less, to see his spade partner. Is that crazy or what?

And see him why? Because the two of them are going down the tubes together and the one who didn't even do the shooting had this crazy idea in his head that they had to make plans for fighting back.

Donadio reached across and let his hand rest quietly on the girl's thigh. She was wearing shorts and her skin felt cool and smooth.

She didn't say anything to let him know she knew his hand was there but that was okay. The old guinea magic was working anyway. He looked across at her and saw she was gazing straight ahead, more or less absently. That was her style. She'd ignore him for a while, then she'd look at him, then she'd kind of sigh and everything would be back to normal. Her name was Marla (*marla femina,* he sometimes said) and she had been dating him for three months, living with him for two. The feel of her soft, cool thigh made his head spin.

Or maybe it was the Jack Daniel's. In any case it was spinning and he couldn't remember if it had been spinning before he touched her. It seemed vaguely that it had, but he was willing to give her the credit.

Her shorts were some kind of silky fabric, very thin and light, and she wore these tiny bikini panties under them that were so small he didn't know why she bothered. If the shorts had been loose he would have slid his hand under them but they wrapped around her thighs like bandages. He did the next best thing and let his hand glide along the fabric, over the tops of her thighs like pedaling up to the top of a hill and then coasting down the other side—Whee!—and coming to a rest where his fingertips could actually feel through almost nonexistent fabric the complicated contours of her complicated pussy.

"Vince," she said.

He didn't say anything so she took his hand away, picking it up by the wrist like it was a dead animal she didn't want to touch.

"What's the matter with you?" he asked.

"Are you crazy? What do you think you're doing?"

"What do *you* think I'm doing?"

"It doesn't matter what I *think* you're doing," she said petulantly, breaking the string. "You're not doing it."

"Why not?"

"In the middle of the highway? C'mon, Vince."

"We're in the car."

"What does that matter?"

"It doesn't *matter*. You said we were in the middle of the highway. I thought I should point out we happen to be inside a car."

"Yeah, with windows all around it," she said.

The traffic rolled forward half a dozen yards. Donadio kept his foot on the brake, ignoring it. "You think the whole world's got nothing better to do than look at your pussy?"

Oops, he thought. *Wrong thing to say. Of course she thought that. Every woman in the world thought that. And most of the time they were right.*

"I just don't like fooling around where people can see," she answered, pouting.

"No one can see."

"Yes they can."

"Look in the cars," he said. "How many crotches do you see?"

She looked around and saw that he was right but she was too stubborn to give up. "They can see from trucks," she said.

The car behind him honked the horn. He was supposed to close up the space between himself and the car ahead. Like hell.

"There are no trucks," he said. "There's no trucks allowed on the West Side Highway."

"There are too trucks."

"Don't tell me. I'm a cop. I know the law here."

The driver behind tooted again. Donadio gave him the finger.

"Are you saying that's not a truck?" she asked. She pointed straight ahead.

Damn. It *was* a truck. A fucking yellow Hertz rental as big as a house just ten cars ahead. He had been looking at it for hours. He just wasn't thinking.

The bastard in back was leaning on the horn now. There were fifteen yards of empty pavement in front of Donadio and there seemed to be some urgent reason why he should cover them with his car.

He grabbed the door handle and yanked it back hard, flinging the door open.

"What are you *doing*?" she asked.

"I'm getting out of the fucking car," he said. "What does it look like I'm doing?"

He slammed the door behind him and lurched as if the pavement were bucking. Somehow he managed to keep his balance. It was just the heat outside, he figured, the heat coming off the pavement, after getting up so fast after sitting so long. He had to hold on to the roof of the car but he was sure he'd be okay in a minute and he was.

He stared at the driver of the car behind him. "What kind of sound do you think that horn's gonna make coming out of your ass?" he demanded in his most authoritative voice. The driver was a tiny Pakistani who could just barely see over the steering wheel. What in the name of God possessed a man like that to blow his horn in the first place? It was amazing what traffic did to people. Anyway, he looked scared now, cranking up his window as fast as he could.

Good. Let him sit there without air. Detective Vince Donadio had other fish to fry.

He turned around and aimed himself toward the yellow rental truck that didn't belong on the West Side Highway. He was conscious of not walking straight and tried to correct for it but nothing he did worked, so he just let himself weave forward, making a kind of half-assed joke of it. He imagined people in all the cars were discussing him, knowledgeably informing each other that he was drunk. This was probably true because he had been drinking all night, but it wasn't really any of their fucking business.

"You," he barked, zeroing in on Hertz's yellow truck.

Hertz had been watching him in the rearview mirror. The window was open. "Are you talking to me?" Hertz said. He looked to be a pretty big guy, two hundred, maybe two-twenty. But he didn't especially look like he wanted a fight.

"You bet I am," Donadio said. "Did you see any of the signs that say 'No commercial vehicles'?"

"I didn't notice them," Hertz said.

The man was being deliberately provocative, but Donadio kept his voice calm and professional. "There are no commercial vehicles permitted on this highway," he said.

"I'll keep that in mind."

"A truck is a commercial vehicle."

"I said I'll keep it in mind," Hertz said. "Now why don't you get back in your car, pal?"

"Because there's no fucking trucks on this highway," Donadio snapped, losing the professionalism completely.

The man was out on the pavement so fast it was like the truck had an ejection seat.

"Are you a cop?" he demanded, face to face with Donadio.

"Yeah."

"Then write me a summons and get out of here," Hertz challenged.

It was in fact the reason why Donadio had gone over to the truck. But it struck him for the first time that his suspension made any such action awkward. Plus the fact that he didn't have a summons book with him. He took an unsteady step backward, trying to think of a way out that wouldn't make him look like more of an asshole than he looked like already.

"That's all right," he said. "I just wanted you to know."

He was backing up, which wasn't natural for a born fighter like Vince Donadio. He veered slightly and bumped into the truck.

"Let me see something," Hertz said, moving after him.

"It's awright, forget it," Donadio said.

"I got my daughter with me," Hertz said.

Donadio glanced over. There *was* a little girl in the passenger seat. Donadio just had time to wonder what the hell that mattered when Hertz came right back at him with the explanation.

"You come right up to my window talking filth and you say you're a cop. I want to see something," Hertz said.

Hertz was holding a shield in his hand. His name, it turned out, wasn't Hertz but August Schultze and he was a patrol sergeant in the Seventeenth Precinct.

T H E curtains were drawn, the apartment dark as Tal Chambers let himself in with his key and silently closed the door behind him. It was the middle of the morning but L.D. was still asleep, curled under the dappled green sheets like a kittenish child, her back curved protectively around, her legs tucked up. One arm rested on top of the sheet, a splash of soft brown innocence that an artist would have dashed in with a single fugitive stroke suggesting without openly naming the coiled sexuality she hid so well in her sleep, a fire banked under ashes.

Tal looked at her for a long time, marveling, before he slowly unbuttoned his shirt and peeled it back, then stepped out of his shoes, snapped back the buckle on his belt and slid his zipper down, the hissing of the metal louder than he wanted it. She sighed in response and seemed to settle into the mattress without perceptibly moving. In five seconds he was naked, hard now, his own breath shallow and eager, the thought of his own nakedness in front of her exciting him while he carefully kept all images and even the awareness of her body out of his conscious mind. He concentrated instead on seeing her as she was, languid and indifferent, as curled and cuddled as a child, putting off for as long as possible the moment when she would stretch out those long legs, loll her head back on the pillow as she straightened her back and came alive, the transformation so sudden and overwhelming it was like a fantasy.

There had been a girl in Portland when he was still playing ball who swore that foreplay was the ruin of sex. Nothing excited her so much as springing on him at odd, distracted moments, when he was on the telephone, mixing a drink or reading the paper. She would unzip his fly and pull his cock out with the quick stealth of a purse-snatcher, diving for it like a heron, stuffing her mouth with the soft and folded lump, her eyes almost crossing as she watched it unfold from between her lips, backing out as it grew.

At the time Tal hadn't understood her fascination with soft cocks, but it wasn't the sort of practice a man discourages with questions. When he met L.D. he began to understand. There was a jolting thrill from the sudden eruption of sexuality that all his experiences with the sweaty heat of seduction couldn't match. For as long as he could remember, the women he found exciting were ripe and taut. He used to imagine them crossing and uncrossing their legs, exciting themselves under their clothes, buying time with a pulsing flexing of the right muscles until all the fragrant passions were ready to be let loose. He could spot them in an instant even in a crowded room (even, his teammates used to say, from the basketball court).

That was the game he played in those days, a game of pledges and promises. To reach an understanding with a woman like that, to bask for an hour or an evening, the longer the better, in the relentless fragrance of her tense waiting, that was what it was all about, the reason every man in the world would have wanted, at least for the moment, to be Tal

Chambers. It was, he used to say, like waiting for a pie to come out of the oven, a pie that always tasted better for the waiting.

His relationship with L.D. started the same way. He met her at one of those receptions Congressman Kellem staged about once a month to announce the formation of a new commission or committee or panel to change the face of the Bronx for the better. This one had something to do with athletic programs for teenagers in the congressman's district and Tal had been named to the committee, along with two retired Yankee infielders and a pair of defensive backs from the Giants who lived and played their games in New Jersey. None of them had been briefed on what the program entailed so L.D. spent the evening moving among the athletes like a hummingbird in a flower bed, darting in the moment a reporter approached, answering the questions as though all these well-paid black jocks were so many ventriloquist's dummies, and then gliding off to put words into the mouth of the next committee member.

If any woman ever had that aura of ready sexuality, L. D. Woods had it. Christ, did she have it. The brains of every black man in the room, and most of the white men, raced to keep up with his loins, running a high-speed data search through every line that had ever worked to get a set of hips like those where they were meant to be. By the time Tal Chambers intercepted her in mid-flight, four of the athletes had already phoned home to lie to their wives about an old friend they had run into and would be going out with for drinks. Tal looked so deep into her eyes that he felt he knew everything there was to know about her and said with a laugh, "If you survive this, do you think we could have a drink?"

"I'd like that very much," she said in a husky voice that made his nerves tingle. He could smell the pie in the oven, blueberries swollen with heat and ready to explode.

Toward morning, when they finally fell asleep in her bedroom, he was more sore and satisfied than any woman had ever made him. He thought he knew passion and thought he knew lust, but L. D. Woods had caught him between her tight, powerful legs and wrung him out like a dishcloth. Metaphors raced through his mind. She was fire, she was lightning, she was a white-water river, a runaway train. She was every one of those things. But in the morning, after he showered and shaved and returned to the bedroom to find her still asleep, she turned out to be so much more.

She had been sleeping that morning exactly as she slept now, her silky hair gleaming like a jet-dark aura around her face, her body curled and gentle, so soft and innocent he would have sworn that neither he nor anyone else had ever touched her or ever would. He moved to the bed, drawn by an intensely chaste and wrenching yearning for the simple touch of her skin, half expecting to see his hand pass through her like smoke in a bubble, ready to feel her vanish on his tongue like cotton candy.

He had stroked her cheek as if she were his own child, then lay beside her and waited as long as he could before letting his hand slide along the sheet until his fingers brushed the dense down of her pussy and everything changed in one thrilling and violent instant that turned sleep into passion the way a magician turns silk handkerchiefs into doves.

Now he slid into her bed practicing the same discipline, his mind clear and far away so that when it happened it would happen like thunder on a bright day. And it did because it always did, a sudden surging shock of her uncoiling limbs, and then he was inside her, pulling her toward him harder and harder until it seemed the pressure of her thighs against his would fuse them into one perfect and self-complete entity, cock and cunt locked to each other so that nothing else would ever be needed. They kissed till it hurt, made love until there were no part of each other they hadn't delved. He lay on his side and drew a line with his fingertip in the gleaming between her breasts and down the rich even plain of her belly, as dark and lovely as plowed earth after rain. She sighed twice to even her breathing and then laughed easily as his fingertip drew intricate patterns on her skin.

"Don't you want to ask me what happened last night?" he said.

L.D. knew he had gone with Dr. Carlisle to see the dead girl's mother and had expected him to call or come by afterward. He didn't, and now she said nothing, letting him tell her about it in his own time.

Tal started by talking about the pale furniture and the shrine in the corner of the room like the one in his mother's house. He tried to describe Mrs. James but fell short, sensing even as he talked that he was leaving out the most important things because he didn't know yet what they were.

"I wish to hell I knew what happened to her daughter," Tal said thoughtfully, a stark image in his mind of Victoria James at the door as she showed them out, her eyes flashing with confused indignation.

L. D. Woods touched her long, delicate fingers to his temple and traced an arch across his brow. *Yes, yes, Tal Chambers, I understand,* her fingers said. *The woman is righteous and fears God, and so you want to bring her the truth.*

For L. D. Woods though, it wasn't simply a question of truth. She had spent the better part of her adult life chairing committees that nobody knew existed, writing memos on issues nobody cared about, biding her time as Congressman Kellem's caddy, as a foot soldier in Artemis Reach's army. Enough was enough.

Once in a lifetime an issue presents itself that people care about, and when it does, you have to be ready. Ophelia James was that kind of issue, or could become one, a little girl from a home like the one Tal described, who went to school in the morning and never came back, whose death no one understood or cared to understand. Yet that child's death had been enough to get a deputy mayor racing to the Bronx to make sure City Hall didn't suffer for it, enough to induce Artemis Reach to play ball with the deputy mayor so that he wouldn't suffer for it either.

We'll see, she thought. She had known since the day Philip Boorstin came calling on the Board that something was peculiar but she hadn't known what. Tal made her see it, with his sad and compassionate account of a small, angry, outraged woman. It was this woman L.D. had to think about, this woman she had to help. Artemis Reach was protecting himself and Boorstin was protecting the mayor. But no one had thought to protect little Ophelia James and no one was protecting her mother now. L.D. accepted the role and accepted it gladly.

In gratitude to Tal, who had brought it to her as a gift, she drew his head to her breast and held it there, feeling the warmth of his skin against hers, the gentle tickle of his hair.

Most men take from a woman, whether it's love or sex or something in between. But Tal Chambers had just given her something and she wanted to pay him back.

"WHAT have we got?" Chief Terranova growled as he stepped off the elevator.

Lieutenant Brucks looked up from the memo he was reading and saluted laconically as he slid to his feet. A small stack of manila folders on the corner of his desk jumped obediently into his hand and he held them out for the Chief.

No matter what time Terranova came to work in the morning, weekdays, weekends, or holidays, Brucks was at his desk, just as he was still there when Terranova left each night. Terranova told him once he was like the light in a refrigerator, which everyone knew went out when the door closed even though no one had ever seen it happen. The lieutenant took it as a compliment, which it was.

In his office, Terranova tossed the files down with an explosive slap, then shuffled around behind the desk and settled in before leafing through them to see what kind of job his men had done.

There was nothing on either Donadio or Franks, which was no surprise. It would take time to go through their jackets. He settled for reading the files in the order they were presented.

The report on the top of the pile concerned the mother of the dead girl, Victoria James. She had no criminal record and seemed to have raised the child herself. She had held the same job with the Transit Authority for twelve years and was self-supporting with no record of welfare or ADC payments except for a ten-month period thirteen years ago when her daughter would have been an infant.

The report on the daughter took up even fewer typewritten lines because there was virtually no information on file. She had no record with juvenile authorities, got honor-roll grades and was a member of half a dozen church groups. Murder victims, Terranova had noticed a long time ago, fell into two groups. Either they were total skels the world was better off without, or they came just inches short of sainthood. For some reason, no one bothered killing ordinary sinners.

The dead girl's father at least made more interesting reading. Herman James had done minor time on a variety of charges of the type usually associated with numbers running. He also had been charged with rape on three separate occasions, all by the same woman, all of the complaints reduced to assault by the complainant and then bargained down to illegal entry so the judge could sentence him to time served. It was a familiar pattern that usually showed up in a file when a man paid a call on his lady after she kicked him out and changed the locks. It didn't take twenty-plus years of police experience to read into these few notes the life story of a small-time loser who passes his existence on this planet without ever catching a break or deserving one.

Terranova tossed down the file with an impatient grunt and levered himself up from his chair. He looked in the refrigerator but didn't like anything he saw there. What the hell. Life can't be all puff pastry. He made do with a cold chicken breast and a plastic container of noodle salad, which he carried back to his desk with a vivid sense that he deserved better.

Snorting like a rhinoceros, he dropped the paper plate with the chicken and the container of salad on his blotter, then stabbed at the chicken with a fork as he reached for the next report on the pile and scanned it quickly. He immediately felt his chest tighten with annoyance. What the hell was this? One page on Timothy Warren? The kid was in the middle of every-thing, a chronic fuckup who had been giving everyone fits for years. The file should have been an inch thick. Instead, Terranova found himself looking at a few notes on a three-year-old arrest for creating a disturbance in a schoolyard, and even that had no follow-up because the arresting officer apparently signed off on the case when the boy was sent to a Bronx hospital for psychiatric evaluation. There was nothing indicating the result of that evaluation, even though there should have been, and there were no reports on other incidents, even though the testimony presented to the grand jury made it abundantly clear that Timothy Warren got into trouble on a regular basis.

Terranova pressed the intercom and asked Brucks to see if Williams was around the office. He glared down at the rest of the reports on his desk with a look that came close to incinerating the paper. Even when there was a good reason for it, there was no excuse for shoddy detective work. Was that a contradiction? *Very well, then I contradict myself,* Terranova thought. *I am large, I contain multitudes.*

He rammed the uneaten half of the chicken breast into the plastic container of noodle salad and slung it at the wastebasket violently enough to send the basket tottering. Then he stormed back to the refrigerator, determined to find something he liked. This time a plate of cold pasta appealed to him in a way it hadn't a few minutes earlier. He took a milkshake from the freezer and put them both in the microwave, the milkshake for just a few seconds to thaw it enough to get a straw in, the pasta a few seconds longer to take the chill off. Pasta was better cold than reheated, but not ice-box cold.

Williams was in his office before he finished the pasta.

"This is what you give me?" Terranova barked by way of a greeting. He held up the Warren report with two fingers.

"When was I going to get more? You sent me up to the school," Williams reminded him.

Terranova was a fair man, but even fair men don't like being wrong. "How about when you got back?" he said. "And why don't I see a report about the school?"

Williams stepped up to the desk and riffled through the stack of reports, pulling out the one he wanted and presenting it with a bit of a flourish.

Terranova didn't like the sarcasm of the gesture but smiled in spite of himself. "Get yourself something while I read it," he growled, the offer of food as close as he cared to come to an apology.

Williams hesitated a moment as though trying to make up his mind whether he wanted to end up looking like the Chief. " 'Sawright," he muttered, waving off the offer and dropping heavily into the chair facing his boss's desk. It took Terranova only a few seconds to read the single-sheet report.

"You're sure of this?" he asked.

Williams nodded glumly. "It was a nice idea but it won't wash," he said. "The lock is good and none of the gym teachers has got the key. We checked the plate on the door and on the wall. They're bolted in, everything tight, no scratches on the bolts. We even checked the door hinges."

"And there's no other way in?"

"No, sir."

Terranova shook his head and tossed the report onto the desk. He would have liked it better if the kids were sneaking into the weight room somehow, because the corridor seemed too public a way for them to meet each other secretly. But facts were facts and he had learned not to argue with them.

"Okay, fine," he said, putting the question out of his mind. Besides, it didn't matter anyway, other than the aesthetics of getting it right. Detective Franks had seen to that, eliminating the need for trying Ophelia James's killer.

"We did come up with one thing you might want to file away somewhere," Williams said. "The English teacher, Hillyer, the one who testified in the grand jury."

The one whose testimony almost got Franks and Donadio indicted, Terranova thought. He looked up, interested.

"He came this close to having his second stiff of the week. A kid nearly OD'ed on him."

Terranova shrugged. "Goes with the turf," he said.

"That's what I thought. Except get this. The kid didn't nod off in class. It was lunch time, apparently Hillyer and the kid were alone in the room."

The phone rang. Terranova put his hand on the receiver but didn't pick it up. "What have we got on this guy?" he asked.

"The English teacher? No record, if that's what you mean."

Terranova hated having to explain himself. "No, that's not what I mean," he snapped. "He's got at best a funny way of teaching. See what you can find out."

He picked up the phone and listened for a moment without saying anything. Then he slammed the phone down and pushed himself back from the desk in what looked like a ferocious state of mind.

"Some kind of problem, Chief?" Williams asked, even though he knew his boss well enough not to expect an answer.

He didn't get one.

Terranova stared down at the empty plate on his blotter with an expression of distaste. "If I don't cut this shit out I'm going to be in serious trouble," he mumbled, partly to himself and partly to Williams. When things were going well he never felt heavy, and in fact managed at times even to take pride in his bulk, the way a sumo wrestler might. When things got fucked up, he disgusted himself.

He made a sweeping gesture toward the desk with the back of his hand as though he were sweeping everything to the floor. "I just gave you something to do," he told Williams. "What are you sitting here for?"

Twenty minutes later Chief Terranova's car pulled to a stop outside the Seventeenth Precinct station house on West Fifty-third Street, a four-story stone structure nestled between an elegant brick town house and a thirty-story stack of luxury condominiums. Terranova gestured for the driver to wait and hurried inside, glancing at the desk area as he made his way to the stairs. The sergeant behind the desk looked up as laconically as a doorman, which is in fact what he was, and went back to reading the book open on the blotter in front of him. There was no other activity downstairs, no other sign of life. Terranova had never worked in any of the East Side precincts and wondered how anyone could stand it.

The only people in the detectives' squad room were a tall and thick-chested blond man in a plaid flannel work shirt and a chunky teenage girl who might have been his daughter from the way the set of her thin-lipped mouth matched his. In a corner by the coffeepot, head down and deliberately inconspicuous, sat Vince Donadio. He looked up as Terranova's footsteps echoed across the floor and nodded his head but it wasn't a greeting. Terranova chose to ignore him and continued on to the captain's door.

Behind him, he heard someone come into the room and glanced back to see a dramatically cantilevered lady in short shorts. She made straight for Donadio, her heels clicking sharply on the bare floor, the naked length of her legs brazen and provocative in the otherwise featureless room. "Jeez, Vince," she said, much too loudly. "Doesn't anyone ever clean the ladies' room around here?"

The captain got to his feet as Terranova stepped into his office.

"What are we looking at here, Summers?" Terranova asked without preamble.

Quickly, in clipped, bureaucratic phrases, Captain Gerald Summers presented the situation as though he were filing a report. A bland and undramatic man who undoubtedly had risen to command as effortlessly and as unremarkably as smoke rises in a chimney, Summers was in his forties but looked a good ten years younger. There was no wear on his face. He never referred to Donadio as other than Detective Donadio or to Schultze as other than Sergeant Schultze. When he was finished, Terranova asked him if anyone had been hurt.

"Hurt?" Summers asked, as though it weren't an English word.

"Did they have a fight? Did your man get hit?"

Summers seemed almost dumbfounded by the question. "There were no blows," he said.

"Then what the fuck are we talking about?" Terranova barked in outrage. Unless his man had a broken jaw, or at least a chipped tooth, the incident should have been disposed of at the precinct level. You don't let a beef like this go any higher.

But Summers was a tightass and obviously didn't see it that way. "Detective Donadio has been suspended from the police force," he began with a tone of tolerant condescension. "He identified himself as a police officer. He was intoxicated. And he used abusive language in the presence of Sergeant Schultze's teenage daughter."

"Do you mind if I talk with him?" Terranova asked.

"Which one?" Summers asked, simply because he didn't understand.

Terranova bristled at the question. "What does it matter which one? I can talk to anyone I damn please, can't I, *Captain?*" he asked, emphasizing the difference between them in rank.

"Yes, sir. Of course," Summers answered quickly.

"Good. Then I'll start with Donadio."

Terranova turned around and walked out of the office, leaving the door open behind him so that Captain Summers was stuck with the choice of following him or not, closing the door or not. Men like Summers, he figured, were all protocol. Such choices were difficult for them.

Donadio was still seated at the table near the coffeepot with the girl in the shorts sitting next to him. Their heads were bent close together but they didn't seem to be talking. Donadio looked up as Terranova loomed over him.

"You seem to have a drinking problem," Terranova said.

Donadio smiled archly. By this time he was stone-cold sober but there was a crookedness to his grin as though he counted on still enjoying the indulgences customarily granted to the drunk. "*I* was drinking," he said. "*He* had the problem."

With a finger held discreetly close to his chest he pointed in Schultze's direction.

"You identified yourself as a cop?"

"Twelve years in the job," Donadio said. "You identify yourself that way."

That was true. Terranova would go to his grave thinking of himself as a cop no matter how many years earlier he had turned in his shield and gun. He didn't like the game Donadio was playing, mordant and sniveling and angling for pity. When it came right down to it, he didn't like Donadio. But the man's failings were the failings of a cop. Terranova had concluded a long time ago all good cops, whether they were Italian or black or whatever, were Irish underneath, tough but sentimental, strong men who could cry.

"I'll take care of this," the Chief said. "You'd better get out of here."

Donadio pushed himself to his feet and the girl in the shorts sprang up beside him. The shorts clung to her crotch. "This is Marla," Donadio said. "And this is the Chief of Detectives."

She held out her hand but Terranova saw no point in taking it. "Aren't you married?" he asked Donadio, ignoring her to the best of his ability.

"Past tense," Donadio said. "I suppose I'm supposed to thank you."

"Not especially," the Chief said. "Just try to stay out of trouble long enough to let someone do you some good."

"I'll give it my best shot," Donadio grinned. "How long do you think that will be?"

Terranova gestured for him to get out in lieu of an answer, but the moment Donadio and the girl started for the door, Schultze was up from the table like a shot, moving to intercept.

"Where do you think you're going?" he demanded, positioning himself in front of Donadio.

Donadio glanced back to the Chief with a wide-eyed look. "Is he kidding? You haven't squared it with them?" he asked in a tone of wondering disbelief.

"Just get out of here," Terranova answered. And to Schultze he said, "Detective Donadio is leaving under my orders."

Captain Summers was out of his office by this time, standing next to his sergeant. "There are serious allegations pending against this man," the captain said.

"There are no allegations," Terranova corrected.

He despised men like Summers although, God knew, the Department probably needed them. For that matter it needed murderers and rapists, muggers and stickup men or they'd all be outside directing traffic. It showed how little need counted for. If either Summers or Schultze had been different sorts, Terranova might have been tempted to explain. Instead he said simply, "Don't buck me on this, Captain."

The captain started to protest but Terranova cut him off. "People who buck me generally get hurt," he said. "I don't think this is worth getting hurt over."

* * *

THE cop standing at the door when Evelyn Hillyer opened it didn't offer any explanation for his presence. He asked if she were Evelyn Hillyer, then asked, "Is Steven Hillyer your son?"

"Yes."

"Do you know where we could find him, ma'am?"

"I'm Steven Hillyer," Steven said, moving into the entrance foyer.

"The Chief of Detectives has some questions he'd like to ask you, Mr. Hillyer. If you'll just come with me."

Steven and his mother looked at each other, her look asking him the same question he asked the officer. "What's this about?"

"I'm sorry, sir, I was just asked to pick you up."

It didn't seem reasonable to expect someone to walk out with a stranger with no more explanation than that, but the officer stood so solidly in the doorway it was obvious he wasn't going to go away and couldn't be argued with.

"Just let me get my coat," Steven said, half expecting the cop to follow him to his room.

The cop didn't but his mother did, racing along a step behind him.

"I'm sure it's just about what happened at school," he said, grabbing a jacket and hurrying back to the front door.

"Are you in some kind of trouble?" she asked, her voice doubtful as well as breathless from keeping up with him.

As a matter of fact he was sure he was in trouble. He couldn't imagine why the police would come for him unless someone had told them about the crack vial that had been taken off the desk where Lloyd Elijah passed out. But he had no intention of telling his mother any of this.

"Of course not," he snapped. "I told you, it's about what happened."

He was driven downtown in the backseat of a police car, the cop as uncommunicative as a statue, leaving Steven free to brood about his predicament. They could probably charge him with obstructing justice if they wanted to, and judging from the way the two detectives who came to his apartment on the night of the burglary felt about him, there was a fairly good chance they would want to. He considered asking whether he could talk to a lawyer but decided against it for the time being.

At Headquarters, Steven was kept waiting with no more explanation than the fact that the Chief was "out." When a half hour had passed, he considered announcing that he couldn't wait any longer, but the lieutenant behind the desk looked unapproachable. He had just decided to give the

Chief another fifteen minutes when he heard the elevator doors opening behind him. He turned to see the bulk of an immense man filling the space.

Like every reasonably astute New Yorker, Steven knew what Chief of Detectives Albert Terranova looked like. He had seen him countless times on the news. In political cartoons he was portrayed as a blimplike figure with a heavy Easter Island head perched on top of a shamelessly mountainous body. But the small scale of television screens and newspaper pages led one to dismiss the images as scurrilous exaggerations, like Nixon's nose. In the flesh, it turned out, the man looked more unnaturally bulky than even the unkindest cartoonists had ever dared to suggest. It wasn't surprising that he hesitated a moment before stepping off the elevator, as though he had to be sure the door was fully open before attempting to step through. It would be impossible for a man of his size to come into any room without turning his entrance into drama.

"Hillyer," he said. "I'll be with you in a minute. Send Williams in."

Clearly the first statement was addressed to Steven and the second to the lieutenant at the desk, but Chief Terranova uttered them both as though he were reading from a list. He stepped through an unmarked office door, which closed behind him.

A moment later a tall black man in shirtsleeves emerged from an office and strode briskly toward the Chief's door, his path taking him right past Steven. His eyes, which seemed to have no whites, measured Steven with cold efficiency and then he disappeared into Terranova's office.

Expecting to be called in any minute, Steven studied the *Police Gazette* lithographs on the wall. A few minutes passed and he realized he wanted to go to the bathroom. He turned to ask, only to find the lieutenant on his feet. "If you'll come this way, Mr. Hillyer," he said, opening the office door.

The police, Steven thought wryly, probably had some device for monitoring the state of a visitor's kidneys.

Inside, he found Terranova seated behind a heavy walnut desk, with Williams standing over his shoulder looking down at some kind of report the Chief held in his hand. The detective wore a revolver in a holster at his waist.

"Sit down, Mr. Hillyer," Terranova said, not looking up but raising a hand to gesture as though he were directing traffic. His plump fingers appeared to lack joints.

Steven sat in the only chair facing the desk, feeling the way he imagined some of his own students felt when he made them wait after class. In fact he often kept them waiting, just as Terranova was doing, while he reread his notes on the paper or test he wanted to see them about. He promised himself not to do that anymore.

Finally the Chief let the paper settle to his desk and looked up. "You teach at La Guardia, that's right," he said.

It wasn't a question but Steven answered it anyway.

"English?"

"Seventh and eighth grades. Yes, sir."

Terranova smiled. He seemed to have very small, square teeth. "That was always my favorite subject," he said. "I don't suppose anyone reads *Silas Marner* anymore?"

"They might somewhere," Steven said. "It wouldn't go over too well at La Guardia."

"No relevance, I suppose," the Chief said, with an odd grunting sound almost like a sigh. "In my day the kids adjusted to the books. Now the books have to adjust to the kids."

Terranova's wry observation disarmed Steven more than he wanted to be disarmed, for he hadn't expected anything like it from a cop.

"Before we can teach a book we have to get them to read it," Steven said, conscious that he was making excuses.

"I suppose," Terranova said, but it was clear he had already lost interest in the subject. He leaned back in his chair and said, "Detective Williams and I are trying to get some kind of handle on what you're about, Mr. Hillyer."

"What I'm *about*?"

"You were very close to the dead boy, weren't you?"

"I thought I was. Yes, sir."

"And you testified at some length to the grand jury."

Steven had been told that grand jury minutes were strictly confidential, but he had no doubt at all that transcripts circulated freely to interested parties. No question had been put to him, so he said nothing.

Neither did Terranova. But Williams, who had moved to the window, looked back into the room and said, "You're havin' a kind of rough week, wouldn't you say?"

"I'm not sure what you mean," Steven said. He genuinely didn't know what the detective was getting at, but his answer sounded evasive even to his own ears.

"A boy and girl you taught killed, another boy that almost died in your room yesterday," Williams drawled. "I call that a rough week."

Steven could feel himself tensing. He had missed his chance to tell them what had happened in his room and now they were bringing it up first. Whatever he said wouldn't sound the same, so he simply said, "Yes."

"That boy have a history of drugs?"

"Which one?"

"The boy that passed out yesterday. That's what I just asked you about, Mr. Hillyer."

It was all Steven could do to keep from standing up. "You mentioned two boys, not one. That's why I asked," he shot back angrily.

"Is there some reason you're not answering the question, Mr. Hillyer?"

"What question?"

"Did that boy have a history of drugs?"

"I think he did, yes."

"Where did he get his drugs? Do you know that?"

"I have no idea."

"Well, where did he get the drugs he used yesterday?"

"I told you, I don't have any idea."

"You were with him, weren't you?"

Steven's head was spinning. The huge man sat behind his desk impassively judging the cross-examination going on in front of him while the detective stood over him, firing questions, clearly accusing him of something. Of what? Supplying Lloyd Elijah with the crack that almost killed him? It was ridiculous and they should have known that. He was a teacher. But he knew already how hard it would be to convince them it was ridiculous. He was already trapped in his own lie.

"No, as a matter of fact I wasn't," Steven said, his fingers knotting in front of him as he tensed for the detective's response.

"You weren't with him when he passed out?"

"I went down to the cafeteria. He was unconscious when I got back. There was one of those crack ampules on the desk."

There. He had said it.

"There was?" Williams asked.

"Someone must have picked it up. When I looked a little later it was gone."

"You didn't mention this to the police," Williams said.

"I wasn't even thinking," Steven lied again, feeling oddly more comfortable with this version than with the one little bit of truth he had given them. "I was worried about Lloyd, it was all very confusing."

Williams had been bending in close to him but now straightened to his full height and leaned back against the wall between two windows.

"I suppose you were confused when you told the officer you were with him when he passed out," he said very softly.

"I said that because we're not supposed to leave our rooms unlocked," Steven said. "I didn't want to get in trouble."

Williams didn't even bother responding. He turned his head to look out the window over the rooftops of lower Manhattan with the bottom of the harbor shimmering brightly in the distance. For what seemed like a very long time no one said anything and then the Chief leaned back in his chair and said, "Let me ask you a couple questions about the other boy, Mr. Hillyer."

"Timothy?" Steven asked stupidly. Of course the man meant Timothy.

"That's right, Timothy Warren. What was he into, Mr. Hillyer?"

The detective was still looking out the window, as though this line of questioning held little interest for him. Terranova, however, was studying Steven with cold, measuring eyes.

"I don't know that he was into anything," Steven said.

"Everyone's into something," Terranova said, in a tone that suggested he was making a witty or at least an interesting observation about human nature. He smiled slightly, waiting, to give Steven a chance to appreciate the comment, and then said, "Was he into drugs, too?"

"I didn't think so. I never saw any sign of it," Steven said.

Terranova nodded, perhaps accepting the answer. "What about a boy named Charlie Wain?" he asked.

Steven felt a cold trickle of sweat run down his sides. His face felt hot and his brow was sweaty. He was sure that Terranova had noted it already, registering it somewhere behind those mocking steel-gray eyes.

"What about him?" Steven asked, managing to keep his voice under control. Had the police been following him? They must have been. Why? He felt confused and frightened, the way he had felt when those two detectives came to his apartment the night of the burglary and made their sneering threats. And this man was the *Chief* of Detectives. He wanted to get up and leave but didn't know how. In fact it took all the concentration he could muster just to keep his mind on what Chief Terranova was saying.

"Does he deal drugs?"

"I don't know."

"But you know him?"

"I know who he is. He's not my student."

Williams moved away from the window and was at the side of the desk now, only a few feet away, his legs braced wide apart, his holstered revolver at about Steven's eye level. "But you went to see him last night," he said. "In the Bronx."

Behind his desk, Chief Terranova raised both palms like a teacher who has just let two squabbling children try to work out their differences and now has to step in. "Why don't you tell us about that, Mr. Hillyer?" he said.

"Look, I don't know what this is all about," Steven blurted out, jumping to his feet. "And I'm not sure I want to talk about it. I went to see a student. Is there anything wrong with that?"

"I thought he wasn't your student," Williams said, even though Steven had addressed himself to the Chief.

"Nobody said there's anything wrong with it," Terranova said. "Why don't you want to tell us about it?"

"Because I had my apartment broken into, damn it!" Steven shouted, giving in at last to the outrage he had felt since that night. "They ruined everything, they shit on the walls and then two cops showed up."

Terranova glanced down to his desk and back up quickly. "That would be Mullaney and West," he said.

So he knew about that too. There didn't seem to be anything he didn't know.

Steven jabbed a finger at whatever it was Terranova had read. "Does it say they threatened me? Does it have that down there too?" he demanded.

"What kind of threats?"

"I don't remember the words. They suggested it happened because of the way I testified in the grand jury. They suggested it could happen again."

Terranova studied him closely for what seemed a long time. "I'll look into it, Mr. Hillyer," he said. "You have my assurance on that. Now why don't you tell me why you went to see Charlie Wain last night?"

Steven doubted that he could explain. "I . . . I don't know if it will make much sense," he said, conscious that he was stammering.

Terranova tossed his head as though that didn't matter, inviting him to go on.

"Ever since Timothy was killed, I've been thinking about it a lot. I heard that Charlie Wain was the one who found Timothy and Ophelia in the weight room. I wanted to ask him about it."

"You're *investigating* this, Mr. Hillyer?" Terranova said. There was a tone that may have been derision in his voice, but Steven couldn't tell whether it was because he believed him or because he didn't.

"No, I'm not investigating anything," Steven said. "I just wanted to find out what happened."

"And did you?"

"No."

Terranova smiled again and his hand moved the papers on his desk. "I don't have any more questions for Mr. Hillyer," he said abruptly, catching Steven by surprise. "What about you, Hartley?"

Williams merely shook his head.

Steven looked from Terranova to Williams and then back again, scarcely sure he had heard right. He was positive they would stop him if he started to leave, but neither one of them said anything so he turned and walked to the door, sensing their eyes on his back.

He rode down in the elevator as confused and troubled as he had ever been. They talked to him as if he were a criminal, they probably suspected him of trafficking in drugs. In fact he was sure the only reason they had sent him away was that they'd already made up their minds they wouldn't believe anything else he said. It was his own fault, too, chasing around Bronx slums in the middle of the night.

Anyway, what did it matter? He still wanted to know what happened between Timothy Warren and Ophelia James in those last few minutes before they died. But knowing wouldn't change anything. Timothy was dead and the girl was dead. The last chapter was already written.

Except that there was no hope of understanding the ending without understanding how it began. This is what he told his classes with each new book they read. The last chapter always lies hidden in the first.

LENNY Franks was working in the garden when she heard a car pull up. It sounded as if it had stopped right in front of the house, and she went around to see.

In fact there was a car, with a man and a woman getting out. The woman was wearing shorts cut so high they looked indecent and a halter top. She had teased blond hair. The man waved to Lenny, skirted around the walk and started up the driveway toward her, with the girl following a few steps behind. She looked like something from a cable TV movie, all eye makeup, bosom and legs.

"Jim in?" he asked.

"Vince?" Lenny asked in return. Until that moment she hadn't recognized her husband's partner. She had met him only once, at a party for the whole squad almost two years ago. He had been drunk and was with an eighteen-year-old girl. All the other men brought their wives. He wasn't her husband's partner at the time, and she also remembered not being thrilled when Jim told her a few months later that he was going to be teamed with Donadio.

"Good memory," he said, giving her a very boyish, charming smile. "This is Marla. Lenny Franks. Where's Jim?"

Jim was in the backyard doing repairs on a swing set he had put up last summer for the kids. One of the legs kept working itself into the soft ground, throwing the whole thing off balance. Over the past couple of weekends he had disassembled it, dug out four broad holes and filled them with cement to a few inches below the ground line, setting metal receptacles for the legs into the cement before it hardened. The best thing would have been to put the whole thing on a platform but he didn't want to cut up the lawn that much. As long as he was careful to make sure the four anchors were level, he was confident this would work. Jimmy was working beside him, handing over bolts and wrenches as required.

"Jim, look who's here," Lenny called, ushering Donadio and the girl into the backyard.

Franks did a masterful job of making their appearance seem like a pleasant surprise, although in fact the last thing he wanted was to be reminded of the job. He had thought after the dinner party last night that he wouldn't be able to sleep but in fact he slept well, and in the morning he was able to put everything but the weekend completely out of his mind. He had always had the kind of intensity of will and self-discipline that allowed him to seal off chambers in his mind like the bulkheads in a submarine, locked firm against even the most intense pressure.

Donadio said some nice things about the yard and the house and what a good looking kid Jimmy was and then he said, "Jim, we gotta talk about this thing."

Franks wasn't so sure they had anything to talk about. "I'll tell you what," he proposed. "I promised the kids I'd get this done. Give me a hand, it shouldn't take more than an hour and then we can talk."

Donadio agreed, although even the simplest tool was a mystery to him. He had grown up in a world where nothing ever got fixed.

Jimmy, meanwhile, looked at his father with soulful, hooded eyes.

"That all right with you, pal?" Jim asked him.

"Yeah, sure," the boy said, but he went into the house to see what was on television.

While the two men worked, Lenny didn't get off so easily. Marla hung by her shoulder asking questions about everything she was doing and marveling at the answers. Even a simple thing like loosening the soil around the roots of a shrub struck her as incomprehensible, as though there had to be some magic involved in a human being actually being able to divine what a plant wanted. When she couldn't stand it anymore, Lenny invited the girl into the house for some iced tea.

Donadio had four beers before the work on the swing set was finished. By that time it was late in the afternoon, and Jim managed to get Lenny off to the side to ask her if they had any steaks they could put on the grill because there was no choice but to invite them for dinner.

Like a good soldier, Lenny offered to run into town and pick up something at the butcher. She invited Marla to come along but the girl said she had already spent enough time in a car to last her a month.

When Lenny got back, she found Donadio, her husband and her son throwing a football around the backyard. The barbecue was already smoking. She also found Marla in the kitchen with Susan and Laura teaching the five-year-old tricks she could do with her hair while three-year-old Laura watched openmouthed. Along the way she had found the means to make herself a gin and tonic.

In another minute Marla would have them putting on blue eye shadow, Lenny thought, inviting Marla to give her a hand with dinner and making sure that her tone didn't leave the girl any choice.

There were hot dogs and hamburgers for the kids along with the steaks for the grown-ups, salad, garlic bread and chips. It was getting cool and Lenny suggested that they eat indoors. The children could eat at the picnic table outside.

The kids, who had already developed crushes on their guests, didn't go for the idea at all.

"Do we have to?" from Susan.

"Yes."

"We'll freeze," from Jimmy.

"Then put on a sweater."

"I thought you're a football player," Donadio said. "You have any idea how cold it gets in the football season?"

Grumbling, the kids went along with the plan, but even so nothing got talked about over dinner because Donadio was too much of the old school to talk about anything that mattered with the women around. Jim Franks could read Lenny's irritation in her eyes and in the grim set of her mouth. He turned to his partner and asked him what it was he wanted to talk about.

Lenny doubted it would do any good, but it was the kind of gesture she loved him for.

Donadio shrugged the suggestion aside with a story about his father, who never wanted to talk about anything over dinner because he was eating and then wouldn't talk about it after dinner because he was tired and then died when Donadio was thirteen after having successfully avoided all the discussions with his kids that can drive a father crazy. "If I ever have kids," Donadio concluded, "that's gonna be the rule. Let's save it till I'm dead."

In fact he had two children but rarely saw them.

When they finished eating, Lenny left the dishes on the table and moved to the living room along with everyone else. When it was time to send the kids up to their baths and bed, she let Jim do it. She met Donadio's glare with an incandescent smile as Jim headed off to take care of the children. "I'll bet you'd like something to drink," she suggested with wickedly insolent cheerfulness. "And how about you, Marla? Another gin and tonic?"

When Jim returned, Donadio mentioned how nice the neighborhood looked and suggested they take a walk.

"If you want to talk," Jim said, "let's talk. But let's do it in front of my wife."

This was a bitter pill for Donadio to swallow, but what choice did he have? A lot of the younger guys went around saying they discussed everything with their wives, and some of them probably did, up to a point. But these were mostly the college types, they probably gave it up after a couple of years, and in any case they sure as hell weren't black. His luck to get in a jam and find himself with a black yuppie for a partner. And anyway, who was it who got them jammed up in the first place? Donadio hadn't shot anyone.

"Awright," he said at last, glancing over to Marla as though he wished she didn't exist. "If I knew this was going to be a family discussion I would've come up here myself. But that's my problem, right?"

Marla studied her fingernails, as though she had been left to wait in the car.

"I've been thinking about what happened," Donadio began. "I don't think we ought to just take this lying down."

"I'm not lying down, Vince," Franks said. "There's nothing we can do."

Donadio was ready for that answer. "You know what this is about, don't you?" he challenged. "It's a bag job. It's some kind of deal to go after us."

"Maybe."

"No, no, no. No maybe." Donadio was up from his seat, waving off the idea with impatient gestures. "If it wasn't a bag job, how come they didn't lift our shields back on day one?"

"I've asked myself that."

"There you go. You see what I'm saying. We've got to fight this thing, Jim."

"Fight what? An investigation? Until it's finished there's nothing we can do."

Donadio's agitation was growing with each response. "That's perfect," he said, storming about the room. "We wait till they stick it up our asses and then we do something."

"Do what?"

"I don't know. I'm not up to there yet. First we make up our minds to fight them. Then we figure out how."

Franks got to his feet and shook his head slowly. "I don't need more trouble than I'm in," he said.

"Then you're going down, partner. You and your barbecue and your whole suburban life-style."

He jabbed a finger at Franks's chest and Franks slapped it away.

Donadio stepped away, going over to pull Marla from her chair. He turned to face his partner.

"You heard it here, Jimbo," he said. "They're looking for someone to take the heat for their fucked-up system. It's not going to be this dumb guinea."

Marla tried to thank Jim and Lenny for dinner but Donadio hurried her out the door.

Two nights at his mother's apartment had been enough. Steven felt as relieved to be going back to his own apartment as when he first moved out just before his junior year in college. This time, though, there was an element of dread mixed with his other emotions. He had no idea what he would find when he opened the door, what evidence the cleaners had left behind to remind him of the defilement of everything he owned.

Before he could get in he had to track down the super to get the key to the new lock Steven had asked him to install, and then he had to pay an extra twenty dollars over the seventy-five he had already given the man to cover the cost. The super blamed the additional cost on the locksmith and promised to bring around a receipt as soon as he located it, but Steven didn't expect he'd ever see it. In fact he was reasonably sure there wasn't a locksmith at all.

Still, ninety-five dollars wasn't out of line for a good lock these days. He handed over the money, collected his key and started upstairs. On the landing between the second and third floors, his blood began to run faster and the suitcase he carried felt so heavy he set it down for a moment to catch his breath. The suitcase, he realized, wasn't the problem so much as his dread of the wreckage on the other side of his apartment door. Since he was going to have to face it sooner or later, sooner was, if not preferable, at least no worse. He hurried up the remaining stairs.

The key was badly cut and had to be worked carefully into the lock and then worked even more carefully around, sticking at half a dozen different points before it finally turned freely to release the bolt. He swung the door back and braced himself for the shock he expected when he turned on the lights. But he didn't need lights because the blinds had been taken down and the fading daylight spilled into the space with an even and shadowless radiance, like moonlight, lacking depth and definition.

The carpets had been removed, the floors swept and scrubbed clean. His belongings, those that were salvageable, were gathered in the center of the room, the furniture huddled together as if in a warehouse, the accessories either lying on the couch or piled in neat stacks along with his books.

He stepped over the threshold and closed the door behind him, sealing himself in with the work ahead. In just the minute he had been inside, the room seemed to have grown perceptibly dimmer, so he plugged in a floor lamp and turned it on, stretching out the cord to position the light in the middle of the room. It gratified him that the lamp was unbroken and working. *I only am escaped alone*, it seemed to say, an electric Ishmael that had somehow managed to survive the wreck.

A quick check of the bedroom told him that the box spring had survived but the mattress, beyond salvage, had been discarded by the cleaners. The kitchen he found still intact, since the thieves hadn't touched it. But there wasn't a speck of food anywhere, because he had specifically told the cleaners to save none of it. The empty refrigerator stood open and unplugged.

He filled four ice trays with water, set them in the freezer, then closed the door and plugged in the refrigerator. It started to hum as if warming up to go somewhere.

Back in the living room, he attacked the stacks of books by sliding them along the floor to the open space between the clustered furniture and the windows, then disassembling the piles into smaller and more manageable stacks. The fact of the matter was that over the past year or so his library had grown increasingly disorganized, with new books jammed into available spaces regardless of where they should have gone and old books put back anywhere. This was a chance to set things to rights.

It was a slow process. So many of the books were torn, ripped straight down the spines, that he was kept on the move from stack to stack, matching covers with contents, front halves with backs, and loose signatures with any other parts he could find. As he worked, the savage industriousness of the thieves came home to him almost as a fresh shock. It was hard to imagine the dogged malice that kept them at the bookshelves for as long as it must have taken to do so much damage.

The longer he worked, the more he came to know where he could lay his hands on any particular book or part of a book. In a few hours he was darting about like a fly, sliding a dozen volumes aside to get to one that was buried under them, reaching here for the pages to complete his tattered Yeats, there for Crane or the other half of Hopkins. Now and then he paused long enough to search out a few verses that leaped to his mind with the poet's name, as though he had to remind himself that they were still just as he remembered them, like Frost on a road not taken or Hopkins on ruined trees,

> *All felled, felled, are all felled;*
> *Of a fresh and following folded rank*
> *Not spared, not one.*

A knock at the door dashed the rhythm of poetry and process, pulling him up short.

Barefoot and shirtless, sweating from the pace he had worked himself up to, Steven wiped a dusty hand across his forehead and stalked for the door.

Rita stood on the other side of the doorway, her head cocked quizzically, looking almost as surprised to see him as he was her. He realized how disheveled he must be. She held a large brown bag in both arms.

"Let me see how bad it looks," she said.

She stepped past him and scanned the room, her lips pursed analytically. "You're certainly making progress," she concluded with a lightly mocking laugh as she moved closer to inspect the two feet of shelves holding neatly ordered books.

"You would do it differently?" he asked, moving in behind her.

"I would have started with the kitchen," she said, thrusting the paper bag at his bare midsection as she turned to face him.

"What's this?"

"You have to eat, don't you?" she said.

He opened the bag enough to see what looked like an odd assortment of groceries.

She followed him to the kitchen, where he began to unpack half a dozen pita breads and a loaf of rye, white paper parcels of pastrami and prosciutto and two different kinds of ham, a jar of honeyed mustard. Rita had also bought rings of freshly sliced pineapple in a clear plastic container, a couple of pints of ice cream, a string of figs, a bag of potato chips, a bottle of gin and two plastic tumblers.

"I didn't know what you liked," she said as she watched him unpack.

"Oh yes you do," he said, and this time when he took her in his arms to kiss her, neither of them was surprised. Her mouth had that same spiced taste so vivid from last night that he could feel again the slow night wind brushing her hair against his face. Her fingers kneaded the muscles of his back as his lips slid from hers to find her throat, the hollow of her shoulder, the firm coolness of her neck scented from her hair. She arched away from him, inviting him to her breasts while her fingertips drew tangled lines like ivy on his chest.

Delicately, teasing himself with his caution, he worked the buttons of her blouse, peeling the fabric back only enough at first to expose the black lace of her bra and the hollow between her breasts that gleamed with opalescent whiteness under a light brushing of sweat. His fingers jumped to the next two buttons, fumbling now in their haste.

She took his hands in hers and placed them on her breasts, pressing them to her, the warmth of her, the soft perfection of her bosom filling the spaces between his fingers and rioting in his brain, his own voice floating up to him as though from another room, murmuring praise.

She slipped her blouse from her shoulders and it disappeared somewhere behind her. When she reached between his hands to work the clasp of her brassiere he released her just long enough to let the tracings of black lace slip away, floating into the void around her as languid as a falling leaf.

He let his eyes caress her, wandering from the calm curve of her shoulders to the arching fullness of her breasts, her nipples like bright coins. He could feel the pull of her beauty drawing him closer, like steel to a magnet. And as he tasted the softness of her body, he heard the murmuring hiss of cloth on skin, a sound like surf that seemed to draw him deeper and deeper into the shadows below her breasts, down to be drowned in the downed warmth of her belly, farther and farther into her fathomable depths, darker and dreamier into a buried universe of soft and moving shapes and shadows, textures and fragrances.

From the surface so far above him he knew he would never reach it, the sound of her voice, wordless, rose and fell, a cadenced, crooning moan as compelling and hypnotic as the sway of her loins, his lips and tongue prowling the tide-tugged grottoes of her flesh. Her hands pressed him into place, pulling him into her, closer and closer until he couldn't breathe except to breathe her, her voice pleading and urgent, urging, urging, Steven, Steven, even as her hips flung with violent, seismic tremors.

And then her fingers knotted in his hair and pulled him free, her eyes gazing down into his.

He stood and kissed her as roughly as he had ever kissed a woman, hungry and imperative, mingling the tastes of breath and cunt, tongue fighting tongue, his fingers biting into her shoulders, spine and butt while hers spun spells to free him from the prison of his clothes. Then, God, her hands were on him and, Christ, her flesh like flame and still her hands guiding him gliding into the heart and center and depth of her until the writhing riding rhythm of her hips ended everything.

They fell apart from each other, leaning back against whatever they could find to hold themselves upright, muttering banalities before they began collecting their scattered clothes. For a few moments, until they were dressed, it was as though neither one of them could quite acknowledge what had happened, as though even tenderness would have been an intrusion. When Rita asked Steven if he wanted a sandwich, it was the first intelligible thing either of them said.

"I talked to Barry," she said when they sat down to eat.

Her casual, almost offhand tone didn't blunt the surprise. "What?" he asked, sharp and displeased. He had managed, in just the few minutes with her, to put all the rest of his life out of his mind.

"Well," she said, meeting his objection with a smile, "you said he wouldn't talk to you. And you did want to know, didn't you?"

"Are you two friends?" he asked. He wasn't sure what sort of man she'd be interested in, but he was certain it wouldn't be Lucasian.

"Not really," she said. "Anyway, he's not as bad a character as you think. He was very apologetic about the way he jumped all over you last night."

Steven wasn't impressed. "Did he straighten out why his story and Charlie's aren't the same?"

"It's not really sinister, Steven," she said. "It happened just the way Charlie told you last night. Only Charlie can't stand cops. He's been in trouble a hundred times and I think he deals drugs. When the cops came, he begged Barry to leave him out of it and that's what Barry did. Maybe it wasn't the smartest move, but he's a pretty decent guy."

That made a certain amount of sense, especially the way Rita told it. Some teachers would do things like that for their students, although Steven doubted that Barry Lucasian was one of them.

"That's it?" he asked.

She nodded and smiled. "Aren't you glad I asked? Now do you think you can forget about it?"

He wasn't sure but didn't say so. They talked about other things while they ate, and then Rita began arranging the furniture while Steven went back to the books. When the ice in the ice trays showed the first signs of freezing they went out together for tonic and limes at an all-night bodega on Lexington Avenue and started on the gin, then made love again toward morning, this time on the bare box spring in the bedroom. The narrow slice of sky above the brownstones across the street was already going to gray when they finally fell asleep.

In Steven's dream, Timothy Warren perched like a genie, cross-legged on the desk in the Chief of Detectives' office, reciting stray verses from cummings in his piping, high-pitched voice.

> *her*
> *flesh*
> *Came*
> *at*
>
> *meassandca V*
>   *ingint*
>   *oA*
> *chute*

Baring his even teeth in a mocking grin, Timothy asked, "Don't you get it, Mr. Hillyer?" taunting Steven with the sparkling, insolent brightness of his perfect assurance. "Maybe you oughta try again?"

Swinging on arms impossibly long, he vaulted himself off the desktop, landing with magical lightness on his feet, which seemed to come untangled as he hung in the air.

>   *i will be*
> *M o ving in the Street of her*
>
> *bodyfee l inga ro undMe the traffic of*
> *lovely;muscles*

Laughing, Timothy clasped his hands behind his back and strode the length of the room with long, elaborate strides, stopping abruptly at the door to pull a crumpled envelope from the pocket of his jeans.

"I'm teaching you things, Mr. Hillyer," he said, exposing the dark intensity that always lay beneath his rare moments of playfulness. "There's answers in the poetry, man, it's all there, was is and will be. Pussy's got only questions, Mr. H. You want to know, you ask. Tropin', not gropin'. Read 'em and weep."

He laughed and a flash of silent light took his head off, rolled it on the floor, tumbling antically to Steven's feet, where it was a balled wad of paper when Steven bent to pick it up. He was in his classroom at La Guardia, probing at loose edges, prying the compact mass into a flat sheet veined with wrinkles. Faint, scarcely darker than the cracks in the paper, four verses from cummings were copied out in a jagged illegible scrawl. But even without being able to read it, Steven knew what it said.

> (i do not know what it is about you that closes
> and opens;only something in me understands
> the voice of your eyes is deeper than all roses)
> nobody,not even the rain,has such small hands

When Steven looked up Timothy was gone, and when he looked back to the page again it was blank.

DONADIO'S car made a screeching sound that could be heard from one end of Linden Lane to the other as it whipped a U-turn and raced away. In his living room, Jim Franks could only shake his head and gather up the empty and half-empty glasses. He could imagine the Michaelsons next door parting their drapes to see who made the noise. Kids, they'd probably figure. Kids were a problem in Dobbs Ferry, seventeen- and eighteen-year-olds with their own cars, racing the curved streets for the hell of it.

At least they'd never guess it was Jim and Lenny Franks's guests.

Guest? Hell, he was Jim's partner. In Dobbs Ferry a partner was someone you owned a business with. When Grady Townes was short of cash, he took in a partner. Al Henschell left his accounting firm and opened his own office with two partners. Greg Toland was negotiating to buy his partners out. These were the things people talked about over cocktails and dinners, the stories the men told about themselves when they shared the drama of their everyday lives, helping themselves to chips and a salsa dip while watching Sunday afternoon football.

A partner wasn't someone who was assigned to you and became, whether you liked it or not, whether you liked him or not, the most important human being in your life, a man you rode with, ate with, sat with in a parked car on endless stakeouts, the man who protected your ass the way you protected his. No, that wasn't a definition of partnership Dobbs Ferry would have understood.

They wouldn't have understood having for your partner a jerk from Brooklyn who fueled himself on beer and bourbon and made noises with his car like a teenager. And least of all they wouldn't have understood that when you fire your gun into the head of a fifteen-year-old boy, you take your partner down with you. You didn't have to like Donadio to know he was getting a rotten deal.

Realities like these couldn't survive the trip up the parkway from the city. Standing at the foot of the stairs, listening to the artificial laughter that drifted down from the bedroom television, Jim marveled at how well he had managed to keep all that at bay. Until tonight anyway.

It was no fluke that all of Jim's and Lenny's friends were white, the husbands all professionals who tacitly agreed to accord professional status to James Franks's career as a detective. If the criteria were that he carried a briefcase and wore a suit to work, then he qualified. Certainly this was Lenny's version of it, and it mattered a great deal to her that they fit in in the suburbs. Jim, on the other hand, knew that he was just a cop.

That paradox was the clearest proof, if any were needed, that what you were hadn't the slightest connection with what you were supposed to be. A few weeks earlier he had seen a black comic on television who got big laughs talking about black names that all sound like things you buy at a drugstore. There's a son named Advil, twin daughters Murine and Visine, and a wife named Cloret. Jim didn't find the routine funny, and in fact walked out of the room mortified. His two brothers were named William and Joseph and his sister was Susan. Their father owned a Ford dealership in New Jersey, new cars, not a junkyard, and sent all four of his children to college, where they learned all over again what they had always been taught at home, that the most damaging stereotypes are the ones that are true. Lenny's name, on the other hand, was Linette, and she grew up on Morningside Heights with a mother who played the numbers every day.

And yet it was Jim who quit college to put on a uniform, Lenny who bit her lip and waited with strained patience for the day he made the Detective Bureau so he could go to work dressed like a normal person.

The Tolands, to cite only one example, had been friends for a year before they learned that Jim was a cop.

Lenny finished cleaning up in the kitchen while Jim went out back to put the grill to order and straighten the yard. He came back in carrying more empty glasses, which he deposited by the dishwasher. Lenny hadn't said a word about Donadio's visit and he knew she wouldn't, but that left them with little to talk about. He said he was going upstairs to look in on the kids.

He found them in the master bedroom, all three of them lying on their elbows on the bed, feet waggling in the air, eyes locked on the television. If they changed channels they could see a story about their father on the news, but thank God they were too young to watch the news. Jimmy for sure would hear about it Monday at school, which meant he would have to be told something before that. Tomorrow would be time enough.

Jim's own father had already seen the story, but Jim was out when he called and Lenny told him the suspension was a technicality and it would all work out. His brothers would come by on Sunday, ostensibly to give support, wondering without ever saying so how anything different could have been expected when a man who had every imaginable choice open to him elected instead to live and make his living in such an ugly and violent world.

"Company's gone," he said. "Time for bed."

"Next commercial," Jimmy countered.

"Now."

In two seconds the boy was out of the room like a sprinter from the blocks, leaving his sisters to toddle after him. Susan clicked the TV off with the remote.

"Is that how you leave the bed?" Jim asked.

The baby made her escape while Susan smoothed at the covers with small hands, not changing anything. "That's better," he said, and she hurried away.

Jim waited till her footsteps faded and then he closed the bedroom door. He stepped into the closet and took his off-duty gun off the back shelf, where he kept it in one of Lenny's shoe boxes. It was a nine-shot automatic with a square shape, an unfriendly feel compared to the familiarly curving lines of his service revolver. Maybe, though, this was and had been all along the proper weapon for his hand, a gray steel extension of himself.

He held it in the palm of his hand and studied it the way a boy might mull a stone found in a stream, feeling the shape of it, hefting the weight. He slid his finger into the trigger guard and raised the gun, sighting down his right arm into the dark at the back of the closet. The space was narrow and his wife's dresses brushed his shoulders from both sides, filling some back portion of his mind with the remembered smell of her body even while the rest of his consciousness had all it could handle just trying to come to terms with why he was standing in a closet aiming a loaded weapon.

He noticed his hand was shaking and lowered the gun, but he didn't put it back in the shoe box. Instead, he put it on the shelf where he usually kept his service revolver and closed the closet door. He hurried back to the kitchen, urgently needing the sight of his wife's face. The man in the closet with the loaded gun was someone he neither knew nor trusted, as troubling as the stranger who shot and killed Timothy Warren.

MONDAY

A̲ᴛ ʟᴇᴀsᴛ a hundred screaming parents were massed outside La Guardia Junior High on Monday morning, protesting the presence of the police. *Police the Police, Not the Children*, their banners said. And *Keep Timothy Warren's Killers Away From Our Kids*.

While they heckled the cops and demonstrated for the news cameras, the police sent more and more reinforcements until the contingent was double what it had been on Friday. Half of them were detailed to keep the parents across the street from the school while the other half herded the kids to the door and frisked them as they went in. On Friday it had begun to seem possible that the situation would settle into a grim standoff, with the cops outside the school becoming simply one more fact of life the children accepted as reality. But the weekend somehow hardened attitudes on both sides. The tension was, if anything, even higher than on the first day.

Steven pitched in with about a dozen other teachers working the sidewalk, keeping the kids from getting themselves in trouble, cajoling them out of confrontations with the cops. Still, four students were arrested, all of them for fighting with the police. One of his own students, Jamal Horton, was one of them.

In addition, Felix Figueroa, a fastidious history teacher in his late fifties, was gashed on the scalp when he tried to get between a phalanx of riot cops and a knot of angry students. Kids collected in the hallway outside the nurse's office, refusing to leave until Mr. Figueroa came out for a hero's greeting and an escort upstairs to his homeroom.

The sidewalk wasn't cleared of children until well after nine o'clock, eliminating first period entirely. And even when everyone was finally inside, there wasn't a teacher in the school capable of competing against the shouts and chants of the demonstrators drifting up from the street. Teaching was out of the question. Kids with radios kept them on all morning, tuned to a Harlem station that broadcast constant bulletins from La Guardia.

Jamal Horton didn't return to school until just before lunch and then he went straight to his English class. He was greeted like a soldier returning from the wars, and in a way he seemed like one. An irrepressible kid, he struck Steven as unusually tense, sullen and withdrawn. Normally he thrived on attention and was a born performer, but while everyone barraged him with questions, he seemed uncharacteristically reluctant to talk.

"Just bullshit," he said. "They drag us down to the station and they stick us in a room. They drag us back here."

The kids wanted to know if he was questioned, if he was booked, what he was charged with, whether he really kicked a cop in the groin, which was the prevailing rumor about what he had done to get himself arrested.

"I didn't kick no one," Jamal said, "maybe an elbow," getting a laugh.

He smiled wanly at the response and Steven stepped in to rescue him from further questioning. "All right, let's get back to what we were talking about," he said. "I think Jamal's already given us the high points."

There were groans of protest but it didn't matter because the bell rang, ending the period and sending everyone scattering for lunch. "Jamal, can I see you a minute?" Steven called as the children hurried from the room.

Jamal's shoulders hunched in a dramatized posture of impatience but he waited right in the aisle where he was standing while everyone else filed out. Steven joined him there and sat on the nearest desk, putting himself eye to eye with the boy.

"Are you all right?" he asked.

"Sure, why not?" Jamal answered with an indifferent shrug.

"Did they give you a hard time?"

"They didn't give me nothing, c'mon," Jamal said. "If I don't get downstairs, there ain't gonna be shit left in the cafeteria."

"When did you ever eat lunch?"

"Yeah, well I'm hungry. Do you mind?"

There was a coldness in the boy's voice, an evasion just short of hostility, that Steven had never heard there before. He didn't think he had done anything to anger the boy but didn't feel right about asking.

"No, go ahead," he said, adding, as Jamal started for the door, "I'm here if you feel like talking."

Jamal stopped long enough to shrug. "Why would I want to do that?" he muttered. There was no mistaking the bitterness in his voice.

"I don't know. I don't know what happened," Steven said. "But I thought we were friends."

"Yeah, I thought so too," Jamal snapped back sharply. He turned away and hurried off without an explanation.

Baffled, even hurt, Steven hesitated a moment and then started after him. He was halfway to the door when Barry Lucasian stepped into the room. "You got a minute?" he asked.

"Actually . . ." Steven began.

"Only take a minute," Lucasian cut him off.

It was probably too late to catch Jamal anyway. Now that Timothy was dead, there wasn't another student Steven was closer to than Jamal, and the boy's inexplicable anger made him feel oddly lonely and isolated. But for the moment there was nothing he could do about it, no way after all to get through to a child who doesn't want to talk. Jamal, he told himself, would let him know what the problem was when he was ready.

"Sure," he said to Lucasian. "What's up?"

"I guess I was a little out of line Friday night," the gym teacher said. "That's all. I just wanted to tell you that."

"No problem," Steven said. "Tough day all around, I guess." He had never much liked the man and didn't need his apology now.

Lucasian, though, remained awkwardly just inside the doorway. "Rita said you were kind of upset," he said.

"I'm not crazy about being threatened, that's all," Steven said. "I got over it."

Lucasian managed an odd smile. "I was afraid you took it that way," he said. "It's just, y'know, everybody's been coming at me."

Steven said he did know, there were no hard feelings, and Lucasian finally left. The thought passed through Steven's mind that the world had lurched crazily the moment Timothy Warren was shot to death, and now every day less and less made sense. Jamal's anger at him for no good reason and Barry Lucasian trying to be nice were small things but they added to his sense of being in a world that had gone askew. If no one else had the answer, maybe Timothy did.

As soon as school was over Steven took a crosstown bus to the district attorney's office in a granite-faced but otherwise featureless annex to the courthouse. The security officer's desk on the ground floor was unmanned. Steven waited five minutes by the placard advising him to secure a pass and then gave up and headed for the bank of elevators, where a passenger getting off informed him that the district attorney was on the sixth floor. He soon found himself at the edge of a vast warren of rabbit-hutch offices created by a maze of chest-high partitions.

Traffic moved at double time through the aisles, and none of the young lawyers flying by expressed the least interest in helping a stranger. The women, Steven noticed, were for the most part slender, though few were pretty, and they all wore straight skirts and severe blouses like girls'-school uniforms. The men were in suits that hung badly, as though all the young lawyers had either lost or gained a great deal of weight since they bought them. Steven finally stepped directly in front of a woman who would have charged right past him if he had given her the chance.

"I'm looking for Jonathan Felder," he said.

"I wouldn't know," she said. "Are you sure you have the right office?"

"No, I'm not. That's why I'm asking."

She tilted her head back to look at him from another angle, trying to decide if he was being impudent.

"He's a district attorney," Steven said before she could make up her mind.

"*Assistant* district attorney," she corrected. "Why don't you have a pass?"

"No one downstairs to give me one."

For some reason this answer seemed to satisfy her. "Felder?" she said. "What bureau is he in?"

Steven didn't know what bureaus there were. "I don't know," he said. "He questioned me in the grand jury."

"In regard to what?"

"A boy who was killed."

"That would be homicide. Fifth floor," she said. "Take the stairs."

A few minutes later he stepped into Felder's office. "I don't know if you remember me, Mr. Felder," he began, but Felder cut him off immediately.

"Steven Hillyer, right? What can I do for you, Mr. Hillyer?"

Late in the afternoon the young lawyer's cratered skin and bad shave looked much worse than they had in the morning when Steven testified. His jacket was off, hanging on a hat-rack peg just inside his cubbyhole, and with it he seemed to have shed the air of pedantic formality he wore in the grand jury room. On the other hand, he seemed if anything even more tense.

Steven had decided on the way over that it would be best to come across as a humble supplicant, shy, pedantic, diffident and unthreatening. But he hadn't counted on facing a man who seemed so sweaty and vulnerable. It was going to be easier than he thought. "I guess you've heard about all that's going on at La Guardia," he began, just to open a conversational channel.

"The police you mean?" Felder asked. He motioned for Steven to sit down.

"The police are just half of it," Steven countered. "We've got a rather volatile student body. They're pretty upset about the whole thing."

"I can imagine."

Steven doubted that he could and suggested as much with a toss of his head. "The faculty, the administration, we're all working hard to head off incidents."

He smiled for no reason at all.

Felder smiled back but otherwise looked as though he were losing the thread of the conversation. He had been standing to this point but now he sank into the seat behind his desk. "Is there some way I can help?"

"Frankly I think there is," Steven said, leaning forward in his chair, his hands on Felder's desk. "One of the things we keep hearing is that the students are upset that nothing has been done for Timothy or Ophelia. We had a faculty meeting this afternoon and what we came up with was a memorial tribute in the *Guardian*."

Felder cocked his head quizzically.

"The school literary magazine," Steven explained. "As the faculty adviser I've been delegated to talk to you about it."

He bent quickly to unclasp his briefcase and pulled out a copy of the *La Guardia Guardian*. The magazine, six pages of mimeographed poetry, essays and stories, hadn't been published in four years but Steven was hoping that Felder wouldn't notice the date on the cover. He handed it to Felder, who feigned enough interest to leaf through it, then looked up at Steven. "Didn't you say you were the faculty adviser on this thing?"

"That's right."

"It says here the faculty adviser is Arthur Ward."

Steven was out of his seat and by the man's side in an instant. He flipped back to the cover page. "This is an old issue," he said, pointing to the date. "Ward retired about four years ago."

He left out the fact that the *La Guardia Guardian* retired with him.

"There's a very nice poem in there about the subways," he added quickly. "You really ought to read it."

He flipped a couple of pages and handed the magazine back, then folded his arms, giving Felder no choice but to study a column of greeting card doggerel about "Treasures that can be found/Buried underground."

"The student who wrote that is in high school now," Steven said brightly, taking the magazine back. "We hear she'll be going on to college."

"That's very nice," Felder said. "Let me get this straight. You want me to write something?"

The idea never would have occurred to Steven in a thousand years, and it seemed almost cruel to take advantage of Felder's vanity. On the other hand, the opening was too good to pass up.

"Well, that's one part of it," he said. "Something on the criminal justice system, put it in perspective, how it proceeds on a case like this."

Felder nodded as though he understood.

"Nothing negative about Timothy of course," Steven added.

"No, of course not. I think I could manage that, Mr. Hillyer. You said that was only one part?"

"Yes. We also want to publish some of Timothy's poetry. There was so much in the papers about his writing poetry, it gave him a kind of posthumous celebrity. La Guardia's Dylan Thomas, if you know what I mean. We thought a couple pages of the poems—something tasteful. They're not all inflammatory, you know. Some of them are quite lovely."

Felder had read the notebooks looking for ammunition and hadn't paid much attention to the milder stuff, but he remembered it was there and was willing to take an English teacher's word on its loveliness. He nodded thoughtfully and agreed that it seemed like a good idea.

"I'm sure you must think we're very naive," Steven said, sounding as naive as he could manage.

"Not at all. You deal with these kids every day."

"Exactly. And what we're hoping for is a kind of final tribute that will let us put this whole thing behind us on at least a slightly positive note."

Felder nodded vigorously. "You know, most of what we hear about the public schools tends to be rather negative," he said, obviously beginning a speech. "I mean the public in general, but also especially in this office. We hear about the crimes, the brutality, those kinds of things, so the picture we get may be somewhat distorted. This strikes me as a very creative, sensitive approach. It's nice to know there are teachers working in that direction, Mr. Hillyer."

"Then you agree? You'll help us out?"

"I'll do everything I can. What do you think? About five hundred, seven hundred words?"

"Five hundred would be fine," Steven agreed. "And with the poetry too?"

"I beg your pardon?"

"The poetry. Timothy Warren's poetry. You have no objection to our publishing that, do you?"

"No, of course not. But that's hardly up to me, is it?"

"I'm afraid it very much is," Steven said, smiling graciously. "You have the notebooks."

Felder sank back in his chair as though someone had just pushed him over. "You want me to give you the notebooks?"

Steven kept the simplest smile plastered on his face. "I don't actually need the notebooks," he said. "A Xerox would be fine."

Felder brightened noticeably. "Let me see if there's any problem with that," he said.

He shot out of the office and was gone almost five minutes. Steven let his eyes wander around the dreary little office while he waited. On a bookshelf set against the partition wall he spotted the coiled wire of Timothy's spiral-bound notebook poking from a stack of papers as though it had been buried alive there and had clawed its way out. The temptation to take it from the shelf was almost overwhelming.

When Felder came back he was accompanied by an even younger assistant. "No problem, Mr. Hillyer," he said. "We'll have your copies in a minute."

He handed the notebook to the assistant, who hurried off to the Xerox machine.

Steven pumped Felder's hand with the heartiness of a salesman. "The students are really going to appreciate this," he said. "I'll be sure to put in a note thanking you for your cooperation."

"Actually," Felder said, freeing his hand from Steven's grip, "the less said about this the better."

Steven kept his briefcase on his lap on the subway ride home, resisting the temptation to open it and begin reading.

Whatever else Timothy Warren was, he was a poet. And a poet, Steven believed and hoped, explained himself in his poetry.

L. D. W o o d s swung the cab door closed and pulled her coat around her even though it wasn't cold. The street was lined with dingy two-story buildings housing shabby hit-or-miss stores, the kinds of businesses that might support you only if you opened at six, closed at midnight and didn't hire any help. These, she thought, sighing with resignation, were her constituents, or would be if she had a constituency. People who worked like hell to stay even. And most of them couldn't manage even that. Two out of every three storefronts on the block were boarded up, and the ones that survived looked blighted and nasty, with dirty windows and letters missing from their signs.

She didn't get out in the streets often enough, she reminded herself as she headed for the subway. In Congressman Kellem's office it was seductively easy to ignore all the things out there that never came through the doors. Downstairs, the line of sullen people queued for tokens looked at her sourly as she moved past them toward the booth. "It's all right, I'm not getting tokens," she explained. She stopped at the side of the booth and checked her watch. It was exactly four o'clock.

Two minutes later the door to the booth opened and a small black woman stepped out, pulling on a coat.

"Mrs. James?"

The woman looked at her.

"My name is L. D. Woods. I'm with Community Board Sixty-one," L.D. said. "Could I have a few minutes of your time?"

Victoria James paused with the door to the token booth still open behind her, looking up at L.D. as though she weren't quite sure that she was expected to answer. L.D.'s hair gleamed even in the pallid light of the subway station like the hair of the models in the shampoo placards on the train. It didn't look like an ordinary black woman's hair.

"I don't have no one at that school, miss," she said, turning away to pull the door closed. The lock clicked with a decisive sound.

"Please. It's important," L.D. said. She had expected reluctance, even hostility, and was determined to meet it with only a simple plea.

"That school had no use for my little girl when she was alive, Miss Woods," Mrs. James answered coldly. "How come you're interested in her now?"

Victoria thought she knew the answer because her ex-husband talked to her about this very subject just yesterday. He had come by in the morning, waiting on the landing like a peddler till she got home from church, the first time he had so much as showed his face in her life in going on three years. He told her she should sue the school and the city against what happened to Ophelia, sue them for plenty. He told her they'd come sucking around to offer her money and she'd be a fool to take it because there was a lot more to be had if she knew how to get it.

It took her half the day to get it through his head that she didn't have the heart for either him or his lawsuits, and they ended up marching around each other like chickens in a yard, scolding at each other exactly the way they used to when he came around on a regular basis. And now, the very next day, this lady shows up from the school board to talk with her, exactly the way he said they would.

"I understand why you feel that way," L.D. said softly, her voice deep and patient. "I don't disagree. Is there somewhere around here we could get a cup of coffee or something to eat?" L.D. fell in step beside Mrs. James as they made their way to the stairs.

Not where your kind eats, Victoria thought. "There's a lot of places," she said.

A light rain had started to fall just in the past few minutes. The two women stood side by side, Victoria's head scarcely reaching to L. D. Woods's shoulder. L.D. scanned the street.

"Is there somewhere in particular, somewhere you like to eat?" she asked.

"I eat at home."

The rain was so light you could scarcely feel it on your skin, but by the time they stepped inside the Chock Full o' Nuts on the corner across the boulevard, their coats were dusted with fine flecks of water like sugar on a cake. L.D. touched a hand to Mrs. James's elbow and led her to a booth in the window. The men at the counter swung all the way around to look at them as they passed, something that never happened to Victoria James.

"We don't really have to do this," Mrs. James said, hunched on the bench. Under the table her fingers knotted and unknotted.

L.D. opened her coat and let it slide off, draped on the back of the bench. Her dress was simpler than Victoria expected, high to her neck and plain. "I don't think you know what I wanted to talk to you about, do you, Mrs. James?" she said.

"About Ophelia."

"That's right."

It felt good to say her name. Just saying the name, for the split second it took to say it, made her feel like she still had a daughter.

"And you people want to offer me something so's I don't sue you."

L.D.'s eyes tightened and she waited a moment before speaking. She hadn't expected anything like that and wondered for a moment if the woman wasn't quite as simple as she seemed. "Has someone talked to you about this?" she asked.

"My husband," Victoria said.

A waitress hung over them, beaming cheerfulness from over her pale blue smock. "What can I get you ladies?" she wanted to know.

L.D. ordered coffee and asked if they had any kind of muffins. Victoria ordered soup because she didn't take coffee and because Gabriel Plummer, who worked with her, swore by their soup.

"I mean other than your husband. Someone from the Board?" Miss Woods asked as soon as the waitress went away.

"No, miss."

"I'd rather you called me Linda," L.D. said, although she hadn't used that name in years. "Are you planning to sue the Board?"

"No, miss."

"But you talked about it?"

"He did."

"*He* did," L.D. repeated softly, reassured. Her instincts had been right about Victoria James. Tal's instincts really. She could almost see the shrine he had talked about, with its pale Madonna, and felt certain, for the first time, that Mrs. James would hear her out.

The coffee and soup came, but not the muffin, and the waitress went away again. Under the table Victoria's fingers twisted together so tightly that her knuckles began to hurt. She made an effort to pull them apart but she couldn't keep them apart without losing the drift of what the lady was saying. Something about apologizing for something, about misleading her, but Victoria couldn't see where she had been misled. She made an effort to concentrate and heard Miss Woods saying that she hadn't actually come to see her as a member of the Board.

Victoria didn't know what that could mean. She began to spoon the soup to calm herself so she could concentrate on listening.

"I don't know how I can talk to you about this, Mrs. James," L.D. said. "I don't have children of my own and I can't begin to imagine the pain you're feeling. So if anything I say makes you uncomfortable, please tell me and I'll stop."

She had a sweet, soft voice and kindly eyes. Victoria wondered how old she was. "It's all right," she said. "Say your piece."

"We were all very shocked when your daughter was killed, Mrs. James," L.D. began. She looked down briefly, but then looked up again so their eyes met. "There were so many questions about how it happened. And why. And it seems to me no one has answered those questions."

"No," Victoria said. "They haven't."

"I can't speak for the rest of the Board," L.D. went on. She reached across the table and rested a hand on Victoria's fist clenched beside the steaming bowl of soup. "I've had the feeling they only wanted the questions to go away. Last night I couldn't sleep and I decided this morning that I had to talk to you."

L.D. stirred at her coffee and set the spoon in the saucer. It was the truth, every word of it, but she felt herself gripped by a sudden fear that Mrs. James wouldn't believe her. The woman said nothing, and nothing in her eyes said what she was thinking.

"I don't think the questions will ever go away, Mrs. James," L. D. said at last. "Not unless someone is made to answer them. The police say they're investigating but they're not. All they care about is their man. Somebody has to stand up for your daughter."

"My daughter's dead, miss."

"Yes. If you tell me you don't want to know why, if you tell me you don't want to know what happened, I'll go away. I think more than anything in the world you want to know."

Tears actually came to L.D.'s eyes, two small tears as tiny as stars in a black sky. She blinked and they vanished without falling, but not before Victoria James saw them and wondered who had given this woman the right to cry for her daughter. "What do you want?" she asked.

"I want you to ask them to tell you what happened, to find out and tell you. I want you to ask the mayor to investigate. I can't do that myself. No one will listen. They'll listen to you."

"Ask who?"

"The mayor, Mrs. James."

"I can't ask no mayor."

"I can help you. I can show you how to do it. I'll resign from the Board if I have to. Let me help you, please."

L.D.'s voice sounded so small and urgent she seemed to be the one who needed help. Victoria felt confused, and there was also another feeling she didn't understand at first and then recognized. She was frightened, almost the way she felt frightened that afternoon when the police came to her in the station and took her away without telling her anything.

"I don't know," Victoria said.

"I need you to trust me," L.D. said. "That's all. If you'll just trust me we'll do the right thing."

The moment she said the words, L.D. realized, with a clarity that was like bright light in a dark room, that this was exactly what she needed. In a way she wouldn't have understood before, she needed this sad and frightened woman to trust her.

THE BLIND BOY AND THE NIGGER
by Timothy Warren

I hate the blind boy and the way
His eyes slide from face to face
Stare at empty space and glide
About the room.
*   The way his fingers roam*
Along the plate, clutch
The handle of a spoon
And act as though he saw it.

He cannot see how much
His empty eyes look ugly;
Protruding, they pretend to be
Eyes but are not.
  Or the way his hand meets
Another's, purely by accident,
And he smiles and the colored boy
Across the table
Smiles, tricked by open eyes.
Your hands met, but why do you
Smile at him?
Do you want to be his friend?
Then go along with his lies,
Say a word or two, pretend
That he sees you smile; get
To know him better.
Meet him again for dinner
And look at his ugly eyes.
  I hate the way that negro
And the blind boy cross the street,
Pass together through crowds,
Or stop together to eat.
You should get along quite well,
You two, with your mutual lies.
I don't care what you tell
Each other, but I hate the ways
A blind boy's eyes
Pretend that they have sight,
And a nigger plays at being white.

* * *

God is a Gothic architect
Who created man and now spends his time
Designing steeples and windows
To put on churches.
  God is a chubby policeman
Who is always laughing
And never troubles anyone
But looks like he has authority.
  God is a toothless old Roman
Who hobbles down the Appian Way

And knows much more than he can ever say
In jabbering Latin.
   God is a bearded man
Who cannot see or hear
But knows when the wind is hot or cold.

       * * *

In every way you touch me
You are immortal.
For when I die
That part of you which is me
Dies also.

       * * *

I do not want to die
(Not because I shall not be
Nor because it is
Forever) but because
My uncle died
And my mother didn't.
Because her face was scarred
With agony and her mouth
Was ugly to look upon
While his black cheeks were smooth as wood
And the lids of his eyes were deeply closed.
Because no one had ever seen him
With his thick fraternal hands
Spread (as they were)
On his quiet breast.

       * * *

The world is made of
Two
Different types
Distinctly bred:
Deeply dead people
Do
What they are told and eat
What they are fed.
Deeply alive people
Who
Do not know that
They are deeply dead.

* * *

FATHER'S DAY
by Timothy Warren

Aspirin tablets lined in tins
Circumscribed his life: pain
Was a part of it. The rest
He could not think of.
    There was, of course, Virginia:
Who had left into the rain,
Taking, one night, the best part of his
        memory,
Bundled the boy in a blanket,
Boarded a train
Bound east for glory,
Left only a note
That said that she would write.
    That was the start:
How long had they been gone?—
No, that won't do. Think of
Something else, he said. How old's the boy?
I wasn't kidding, pal. Get off it. There's
Other things to think of. The water
In the glass began to clear.
    A postcard followed, said little,
That she would get in touch. How long ago?
The postmark said. How tall?
He turned it in his hand and set it down
To take two tablets from the tin.
    Salicylic acid can dissolve the brain.

* * *

I

am the moon before sunset

* * *

PROPHETS E AND C
by Timothy Warren

O Lord O, why does the child die,

Steven read, his pulse quickening at the appearance of the single letter Timothy had used in his poem for Ophelia James. He had read through the poetry like a scholar searching obscure glosses, blind to the anger and tenderness of it. Although the notebook was written in pencil, these weren't rough drafts. He knew that the poems had been carefully copied out in Timothy's precise, almost girlish handwriting, with no evidence of the meticulousness with which Timothy worked and reworked everything he did, deleting lines, replacing one phrase with another, eliminating adjectives, struggling for the sudden surprise of a cleaner image or an unexpected rhyme.

Sometimes Timothy used to catch Steven at lunch or between classes to ask him to choose between two versions of the same line, demanding to know what was different about them, why one worked, the other didn't.

Steven brushed away these memories, arching his back to stretch the stiffness out and helping himself to a sip of coffee, which had grown cold. Through the doorway to the kitchen he could see Rita grading papers at the table, an image of domesticity as disorienting as the clear-eyed ham gazing up from the plate in his favorite Magritte.

"Anything?" she asked, looking up to catch his eye on her.

He waved away the question with a waggle of his hand and forced his attention back to the sheaf of photocopies in front of him.

O Lord O, why does the child die,
Breath thickening to fever stillness
That routs the mother's sins.
Is this the thanks we get, she asks,
For boarding a prophet, sharing our meals
With him?
A prophet heals.
Heal then.
  And then, and then,
Daring the Lord to magic,
Demanding breath from death,
Life from lifelessness,
The prophet took his leave.

Father, father, why forsake me?
Bands of fifty in the hills.
Father, father, don't forsake me.
Prophet heals and prophet kills.

Daring the Lord again and always,
Tempting him to bring fire from water,
Fire that melted rock and flesh
To show the power of truth.
God, what a god, God.
But weren't there slayings in the sayings?
O yes it had to be.
   Tricks like these worked then,
   Brought the message home.

Father, father, why forsake me?
Fifty prophets in the caves.
Father, father, don't forsake me.
Crack of doom but doom that saves.

There was a story behind the poem but Steven couldn't make it come clear in his mind. "My God, my God, why hast thou forsaken me?" Jesus asked on the cross. But Jesus had twelve disciples, not fifty. And there was no miracle Steven could remember in which Jesus had saved a child or turned water into fire.

He reread the verses and then carried the sheaf of papers to the kitchen, setting it in front of Rita. "You've got more religion than I do," he said. "What do you make of this?"

She read while he measured out coffee for another pot and put on a kettle to boil. He sat at the table with her while the water dripped through the grounds.

"I don't know," she said. "Maybe he's the prophet. Maybe he knew he was going to kill someone. Or might."

The idea made Steven uncomfortable and he took the poems back. "No," he said. "There's a story in the Bible. I'm sure there is."

She smiled tolerantly and reached out to put a hand on his. "What are you looking for, Steven?" she asked.

"I don't know. Something."

"Because you had a dream?"

"Because he wrote poems about things that mattered to him. If there was something going on that led up to what happened, it might be in them."

He leafed back, picked out the poem titled "Father's Day" and handed it to her. "He showed me a draft of this one once, it was very different. He told me he was born in St. Louis and when he was two or three his mother walked out on his father and they came to New York."

She read it while he poured out two mugs of coffee and pulled a chair around to wait by her side until she finished. She shivered as she lay the page on the table.

"Did he ever hear from his father?" she asked.

"I don't think so."

"It's very sad, isn't it?"

The numb, aching sadness in the verses was there even if you didn't know what Timothy had told Steven. But knowing it, you understood that the poem was about Timothy's father longing for a lost son, the boy's loneliness projected across half a continent and beaming back as his father's longing for him.

"Yes," he agreed, "very sad," replacing the page in its proper sequence.

He started back to the living room, tensing under a growing conviction that there was a key to this poem about a prophet who saved a child and turned water to fire, just as the story about a child taken from his father in St. Louis was the key to "Father's Day." The lobby doorbell startled him out of his thoughts.

The intercom to the lobby rarely worked well enough for voices from downstairs to be intelligible. Steven asked and got a garbled answer that told him nothing. He pressed the buzzer and opened the apartment door. From behind him, Rita asked who it was.

"I don't know," he said.

The pages of Timothy's poetry were still in his hand so he stepped back inside to put them on his desk and then, on an impulse, set that afternoon's grammar quizzes on top of them. Rita asked if he were expecting anyone but he wasn't. She went with him to the door.

For an instant, neither of them recognized the black man who rounded the landing below and started up the last half flight. "Mr. Hillyer," he said.

Rita gasped, the recollection suddenly clear in her mind of this same man standing over her, of this same voice, deep and calm, telling her not to get in the way.

"I'd like to talk with you," the caller said. "It shouldn't take long."

Automatically, from years of peremptorily demanding interviews, his voice framed the request as a challenge although he meant none. His face looked leaner than Steven remembered, his eyes more hollow and distant, but there was no mistaking the man who shot Timothy Warren.

VINCE Donadio circled the streets of Brooklyn like a jet that hadn't been cleared for landing. Twice he drove past the converted warehouses on the waterfront that housed the Internal Affairs Division without stopping, but the third time a car pulled out, leaving an empty space that sucked him in.

For as long as he had been a cop, this place had been the focus of his most persistent nightmares, combining in one center of malevolence all the evil powers others attribute to the boss's office, the dentist's office, prison and hell. A summons to report forthwith to Internal Affairs told any cop his career was as good as over. No one went willingly.

Yet here he was, both feet inside the door, looking around with a cold, analytic eye as though he had been called in to redecorate the place. The door swung closed behind him with a sound that suggested that, as hard as it had been to walk in here, it would be that much harder to walk out.

He found himself in a waiting room where about a dozen men sat on straight-backed chairs with a stiffness reminiscent of the earlier stages of rigor mortis. If the problem had been how to put twelve men in thirty seats without anyone sitting nearer to anyone else than absolutely necessary, a computer couldn't have solved it any better than this collection of torpid drunks. Christ, they were a pathetic lot, every last one of them suffering the ravages of middle age like a disease. Their suits were varying shades of gray, their shirts the yellowed white of old teeth. Their faces were sad-eyed and soft, as jowly as a basset hound's, as shapeless as if they had been molded out of putty. There wasn't a fit man in the lot, nor a man Donadio's age, nor a man with whom he had anything in common even though every one of them was a cop.

The realization went through Donadio like a virus, chilling him from the inside out, his legs actually weakening with the knowledge that he just might be looking at himself twenty years in the future. *No*, he tried to tell himself, these guys were empty shells. Had any of them been men at his age?

Yeah, he answered. All of them.

He told the anemic lieutenant at the desk that he wanted to see someone about his case.

"Name and shield?" the lieutenant asked.

Donadio gave him the information.

"Case officer?"

"I don't know."

"You don't know who your case officer is?"

"My partner shot a kid. Does that help?"

The lieutenant's expression indicated that he understood why this man was in trouble. He had a bad attitude. He told Donadio to have a seat while he checked it out.

Donadio scanned the room, trying to decide where he could sit without disrupting the neat geometric arrangement. While he was still figuring that out, half a dozen new gray men came in, checked in with the desk officer, then found themselves seats without so much as looking around.

That settled it. Donadio aimed himself at the door, then turned to look over the landscape when he got there. "Any of you guys want a lift?" he called out cheerfully.

There were no takers.

In the parking lot he took a minute to consider his options and then headed for Police Headquarters in Manhattan, where his luck changed because Chief Terranova was in his office and didn't keep him waiting at all.

"What can I do for you?" the Chief asked.

His office was about the size of the squad room at the Three-nine. No wonder he was in. With an office like that, it didn't make sense to leave.

"I figured I'd offer my services," Donadio said.

It wasn't his style to be evasive but this was pure evasion. He wished he had thought of some other way to say it. In fact he hadn't even thought at all, on the way over, of what he would say, counting on the words to just come to him when he got there. They didn't.

The Chief's eyes narrowed until they weren't much more than pinholes in the wide expanse of his face. They reminded Donadio of potato eyes.

"Why don't you just get to the point, Donadio?" Terranova asked. Donadio had been hearing for years that this guy was a son of a bitch, and that struck him right now as a reasonable assessment.

"I want to cooperate with the investigation," Donadio said, blurting the words out like a confession.

An outsider might not have known what he meant, but to a veteran like Terranova *cooperate* meant only one thing. Stool pigeons cooperated. Informants. Rats. Weasels.

"You what?" the Chief demanded.

Donadio didn't care. The hard part was saying it and he had said it. It was like jumping off a bridge. Once you got in the air the rest was all downhill.

"I said I want to cooperate with the investigation."

JIM Franks stopped two feet below the landing, braced for the English teacher's hostility. He knew that in Hillyer's eyes he was simply a killer and hadn't expected to be welcomed.

"We've got nothing to talk about," Steven said from the landing.

"Listen, nobody sent me here," Franks pleaded. "I need some help."

"What kind of help?" Steven demanded, his tone guarded and suspicious.

Franks opened his coat, holding it away from him on both sides. "I'm not on the job," he said. "I don't have a badge or a gun. I just wanted to talk."

Steven had scarcely seen Detective Franks in the weight room that day. He had a clearer sense of the other cop. He remembered seeing the two of them come in and then wondering where the black one had gone until the moment of the gunshot, and even then he was aware only of a monstrous presence looming over one of the machines like a thunder cloud.

"Go ahead," he said, still cautious.

"I wanted to know about the boy," Franks said. "I just wanted to know something about him."

There didn't seem to be anything monstrous about the man now. His question didn't sound like a cop's question. There was a hollow, distant look in his eyes, possibly fear.

Steven hesitated, considering his options, but sending the man away no longer seemed one of them. "All right, come in," he said.

He stepped back to let Franks pass and the detective stepped up onto the landing.

"I'm Rita Torres," Rita said, and Franks nodded.

"Yes, I remember you, Miss Torres."

Inside the apartment, Franks quickly took in the scene, his practiced eyes scanning the living room, inventorying the space for anything it told him about the people who lived here. Although everything had been put back in its place, it was easy to tell that the furniture and all the objects in the room had been recently rearranged, as though Hillyer had just had the apartment painted. But there was no smell of paint. It was also clear that the woman didn't live with him.

Steven directed him to a chair, then sat facing him on the couch with Rita next to him. Franks held up a hand to preclude either of them questioning him about the reason for this visit. He wanted to begin it in his own way. They waited.

"I never shot anyone," he said. "I never even discharged my gun. Before this, I mean. I wanted you to know that."

He looked down at his fingers and then back up.

"I'm sure that doesn't matter to you, but . . ." he paused. "The only other thing I wanted to say was that I used to think a lot about the kinds of situations that might arise. It was always clear when I had to use my weapon and when I didn't. Do you understand what I'm trying to say?"

"No," Steven said. He had a vague sense that the man was defending himself but he couldn't follow the logic of the defense.

Franks nodded his head with an air of resignation. "You don't have anything to drink?" he asked. "A glass of water would be fine."

Rita started to her feet but Steven stopped her with a gesture. He asked whether she wanted anything as well and she shook her head.

Franks watched Steven go with an almost panicky awareness of how badly he was handling the situation. Every emotion he felt seemed new to him, as though a newborn baby were suddenly expected to cope with pain and anguish and mortality. It didn't seem fair, and yet he knew that he was paying the price for having so carefully structured his life to avoid those stumbling blocks of self-doubt and uncertainty that tripped up other men. When the structure collapsed he was left naked and unready to make his way out of the ruins.

Rita said nothing and in a moment Steven returned from the kitchen with a glass of water. Franks drank it down in a gulp, as if he were taking medicine.

"I think about the boy a lot," he said. "My son is eight. I heard that the boy wrote poetry. Someone told me he lived by himself. I'm trying to get some sense in my mind what he was like."

Steven said, "I don't think any of us knew."

Rita looked at him sharply. "Steven was very close to him, Mr. Franks. I don't think you can do yourself any good with these questions."

"No, no, I want to know," he said.

Steven began to tell him everything he knew about Timothy, starting with the few facts he knew about the boy's childhood from his arrival in New York with his mother, who abandoned him to the care of an uncle who died when Timothy was around twelve years old. At best Steven could only piece it together in disconnected fragments, but he thought Timothy's mother took him back at that point and then disappeared a year or so later, leaving him with the man with whom she had been living.

The boy had written a short story dealing with these incidents, but withdrew into hostile silence when Steven tried to question him about them, so it was difficult to tell which parts of the account were autobiographical and which were fiction. Steven assumed that most of it was true.

According to the story, the child's parting from his mother's abandoned lover was worked out as if they were two adults agreeing on a divorce, each conceding that he got in the other's way, each expressing a rather tender concern for the other's welfare. That part of the story, which read almost like a satire, was difficult to take at face value, but the bare fact of the separation was probably true, for when Timothy enrolled at La Guardia Junior High he had no fixed address but lived with a series of classmates, staying with one family and then another, never in one place for more than a few months at a time.

Steven didn't know whether the boy's difficulties with the law started then or went back to his grammar-school days. He was arrested for truancy two or three times, usually when he was in the process of relocating, and it was never clear whether he just stopped going to his home of the moment or was asked to leave. Most of the women who cared for him reported that they found him to be a likable boy, unusually gracious, unnaturally well mannered and uncannily bright for his age. But at the same time most of them said, without explaining, that they thought he was a bad influence on their sons. He was as nocturnal as a bat, up until all hours when he stayed in, often disappearing in the middle of the night and returning near dawn. A few of the mothers with whom Steven talked complained about his writing. He gave the impression that he was taking notes on them, judging them, and that they were going to appear in his stories and poems. It felt like living with a spy, they said. Steven himself had never seen any of Timothy's writings that reflected on any of the families he stayed with.

Before he finished seventh grade Timothy was arrested once for setting a fire and once for destroying equipment in a playground. Oddly enough, he was never sent to a reform school or even a foster home. Each time he was back in school within a day or two as if nothing had happened, and neither Steven nor any of the other teachers who began to be concerned about him were able to find out how he had engineered his release. It was conceivable, because of his constantly changing addresses, that the records from one incident never caught up with the next, so that he was always treated as a first offender. Steven assumed he simply talked his way out of trouble and, given his ability to charm practically everyone he met, it was a reasonable hypothesis.

Last year, when Timothy was in the eighth grade, he had told Steven that some of the boys were trying to kill him, but he wouldn't say why. He began to carry a straight razor for his own protection and made a point of letting everyone know he had it. It was then that Steven and a few of the other teachers began their efforts to get psychological counseling for him, but their petitions to get him into an outpatient program never received a response. Twice he was found hiding in school closets, insisting that he had fled there for safety when the kids who were looking to kill him started to close in. But since he refused to say who they were or why they wanted to kill him, Steven assumed the boy either suffered from paranoid fantasies or was exaggerating a threat made in the heat of an argument.

About a month after he started carrying the razor, Timothy surrendered it to Steven and said that he wouldn't need it anymore.

"You think you're going to be all right?" Steven asked.

"One way or the other," Timothy answered enigmatically. "If you got a problem taking this thing, I'll put it back in my pocket."

Steven took the razor and Timothy never permitted the subject to come up again. The next time Steven had any indication Timothy was armed was when he found him in the weight room holding a knife.

Jim Franks listened to Steven's narrative intently, without interruption, nodding his head from time to time as though certain parts of the story were familiar to him. On the other hand, Rita, who had known the boy and had taken an interest in him when he was alive, seemed shocked by Steven's account, almost all the details of which were new to her.

For what seemed a long time after Steven stopped talking neither Franks nor Rita spoke. Then Franks said, "And he never saw his mother?"

"He saw her," Steven said. "She'd show up once in a while, a couple times a year, that's all. She'd come to school and wait for him outside. She'd buy him dinner. And then she was gone again. He said he tried to follow her but he was never able to."

In its way, this seemed the saddest aspect of the story, for one immediately imagined the young boy's eyes scanning the street for his mother every day when he came out of school. Did he duck out of conversations with his friends and hurry to the street so as not to miss her? Did he linger in front of school in case she was late? What did he tell himself on the days beyond number when she didn't come? Why was such precious loyalty given to someone who had no right to it?

They talked in hushed voices about the loneliness a child might feel and the cruelty of those who seem unable to fathom it. "Then what happened?" Franks asked at last.

Steven shook his head. That was the question he had been asking for a week now, and he wasn't any closer to an answer than he'd been the first night he woke up with it clawing at his consciousness like a dream.

"The girl wasn't his girlfriend?"

"I don't think so. But there were references to her in some of the poems he wrote."

Franks asked if he could see them and Steven handed him the photocopied pages. The detective read for almost half an hour in silence, occasionally, his brow furrowed in concentration, leafing back to reread some verses in the light of something that came later. When he was finished he lowered the pages to his lap with a look that seemed to express both weariness and resignation.

"I'm not very good at this," he said. "I think most of it's over my head." He managed a wan smile as he reached out to hand the pages back.

Steven returned the smile. "I was kind of hoping for a little help," he said, explaining how he had been going over the poetry looking for something that might explain what brought Timothy and Ophelia James together on the last day.

"Do you mind if we ask you a question?" Rita said.

She had been silent so long that Franks looked at her for an instant as if surprised to find her in the room.

"No, of course not," he said.

"Why would the police follow Steven?"

Steven was as startled by the question as Franks, who took a moment to think about it before even trying to answer.

"There's no reason," the detective said at last. "What makes you think they were following him?"

She told him about going to see Charlie Wain in the Bronx on Friday night and about Steven's interview with the Chief of Detectives on Saturday.

"I don't think either of you was followed," Franks said, getting to his feet. "You picked one of the busiest playgrounds in the Bronx for narcotics. My guess is you wound up in some undercover's report."

Franks extended his hand to Rita and then to Steven, neither of whom realized until he thanked them that he was leaving.

"I don't know if we were any help," Steven said at the door.

"Maybe you were," Franks answered. "I'm not sure what kind of help I wanted."

Rita was by Steven's side when he closed the door. "Do you trust him?" she asked.

All through Franks's visit Steven had felt in some ineffable way that he was talking and listening to someone as concerned as himself. He didn't carry the burden of guilt the detective bore for Timothy's death, and yet they seemed to share a common set of questions, a common assumption that there was something that defied understanding and wouldn't let them alone until they understood. Franks's last words at the door echoed Steven's own uncertainties. Yes, of course he trusted him, despite a hundred reasons not to.

Rita's distrust, on the other hand, seemed foreign to him, though he understood it came from a sensibility so different from his own that he wasn't quite sure how to deal with it. He paced back to his desk with a feeling of disquiet so profound it was a physical discomfort, a churning deep in his bowels that made him wish the whole last hour had never happened. If he didn't stop thinking about it, he knew it would call into question his whole relationship with Rita, and that was something he desperately didn't want questioned. He was willing to concede that she came from a background so predisposed to suspicion of the police that she couldn't see past it. He was willing to concede that their worlds were different. But weren't those differences at the heart and core of the reasons he loved her? Of course they were. Her eyes smoldered with a passion he knew no way of reaching except through her, her body carried him to places he would never see except through her. The difference was in the scent of her breath and the taste of her mouth, in the way he imagined her (her night-black hair frosted with plaster dust) as she helped her friends make a restaurant out of an abandoned drugstore.

You mean I shouldn't trust you either? he had asked in the restaurant.

That's exactly what I mean, she had said. *There's no reason you should.*

He gathered the poems Franks had left on the coffee table and carried them back to his desk, where he sorted through them again until he found his place in the troublesome poem he had been reading when the doorbell rang.

"Maybe I'd better go," Rita said.

He looked at her questioningly, trying to see in her eyes how much of his thoughts she had read.

"I'd like you to stay," he said.

She tossed her head. "Tomorrow might be better. You seem very far away."

"I am," he said. "That's why I'd like you here."

"Your string to the mouth of the cave?"

"Something like that."

"Come to bed when you're ready," she said, laughing lightly as she turned to the bedroom, her fingers already working the buttons of her blouse.

A couple of hours later, the sound of the telephone pulled Steven up out of a deep sleep. He reached for it in the dark and mumbled a hello.

The voice at the other end didn't sound familiar. "Listen to this," it said. "First Kings, chapter seventeen."

"What?"

"I'm sorry. It's Jim Franks. Just listen a minute. 'And it came to pass after these things, that the son of the woman, the mistress of the house, fell sick. And his sickness was so sore, that there was no breath left in him. And she said unto the prophet, What have I to do with thee, O thou man of God? art thou come unto me to call my sin to remembrance, and to slay my son?' "

"Timothy's poem, the woman who boarded the prophet," Steven said, excited.

"Right. Elijah saves her son. The other story's Elijah, too. Mean anything to you?"

Of course it did. Names always meant something in Timothy's poems, and Lloyd Elijah was one of Timothy's friends.

"I don't know," Steven said, holding back this information until he had a little time to think about it. "What's the other story?"

"Elijah makes God bring fire out of water and the people all believe. They kill the false prophets. 'Slayings out of sayings.' Isn't that what the kid wrote? First Kings eighteen. Look it up."

Steven found his Bible as soon as he hung up the phone and read the passage over and over.

Then the fire of the Lord fell, and consumed the burnt sacrifice, and the wood, and the stones, and the dust, and licked up the water that was in the trench. And when all the people saw it, they fell on their faces: and they said, The Lord, he is the God; the Lord, he is the God. And Elijah said unto them, Take the prophets of Baal; let not one of them escape. And they took them; and Elijah brought them down to the brook Kishon, and slew then there.

This was the fire from water in Timothy's poem, *fire that melted rock and flesh to show the power of truth.*

Tricks like these worked then, Timothy wrote. *Brought the message home.*
But what was the message?

TUESDAY

L . D . W O O D S took a backward step and cocked her head to survey Victoria James from scalp to shoes. Her appearance should suggest humility but not poverty, grief but not prostration. No one would sympathize with her loss if she looked like a woman who had nothing to lose, and no one would be moved to support her fight if she looked as if she had no fight in her. L.D. didn't like what she saw. Dresses had a way of riding strangely on Victoria's shoulders, one of which was higher than the other. She made her try on another dress, but it too looked all right only as long as Victoria didn't move. Once she so much as raised an arm, she began to look bunchy and rumpled, like a sharecropper's daughter in her Sunday best.

"Do you have a suit?" L.D. asked. A press conference was a major occasion for a woman like Victoria James. A suit wouldn't be overstating it.

L.D. opened the closet door to look for herself and found something with possibilities toward the back.

"I'll look a sight, Miss Woods," Victoria protested. "I haven't worn that in years."

But L.D. cajoled her into trying it on, and then studied the result judiciously before announcing that it was perfect. The narrow cut of the jacket looked old and austere in a way that suggested a kind of careworn stoicism Victoria would be able to carry off with considerable dignity.

Victoria was willing to take her word for it but looked in the mirror anyway, trying to see herself through Miss Woods's eyes. She wasn't having an easy time understanding what Miss Woods wanted of her. Things were happening too fast, and she didn't trust her own judgment enough to keep track of it all, let alone to raise questions. In her own eyes she looked pallid, small and ineffectual. The image that came back to her from the mirror filled her with a quiet dread that she would be caught out pretending to be something she wasn't. Even reminding herself that it was her own clothes she was wearing didn't help. They didn't feel like her own clothes, any more than her apartment felt like her own, or any of the decisions she had made.

"Are you sure this is all right?" she asked, turning away from the mirror. But Miss Woods had left the bedroom. Victoria found her in the living room, rearranging some of the furniture, pushing the pieces back to the walls. It made the place look like the waiting room at a doctor's office.

"There'll be about twenty people," Miss Woods explained. "Did you say something?"

"No, miss," Victoria said, accepting her costume for no other reason, really, than that the moment for asking about it seemed to have passed. "Is there anything you want me to do?"

L.D. stopped what she was doing long enough to fix Victoria's hovering nervousness with a reassuring smile. "I want you to take a deep breath, try to relax," she said. "If you're too nervous to sit down, maybe you could make us both a cup of tea."

A knock at the door froze Victoria as she started for the kitchen, but she didn't move to answer it, dimly conscious that it wouldn't be the right thing to do even though she was in her own house. "Are they here?" she asked, suddenly frightened.

L.D. checked her watch as she started for the door. "I'm sure it's Dr. Carlisle," she said. "No one's supposed to be here for another half hour."

Half an hour wasn't very much time. But Victoria couldn't tell whether realizing this made her feel better or worse.

In the kitchen she fussed over the tea while Dr. Carlisle and Miss Woods sat at the table going over some of the things Dr. Carlisle planned to say. She tried not to listen, and even the things she heard sounded as if they were about something else, not her little girl. She was glad that she had something to do and glad that Dr. Carlisle was going to do the talking, but even trying to concentrate on the simple things her hands were doing didn't settle her mind. The rattle of the teacups in their saucers as she carried them to the table mortified her. She felt even worse when Miss Woods, noticing her nervousness with a kind of pitying look, sprang up to offer her a seat at the tiny table that only had room for two.

The only place the table fit was in the corner by the window, with both chairs on the same side like a counter in a diner. It wasn't a kitchen you were supposed to eat in, but if she hadn't got that table and jammed it in there, Ophelia wouldn't have been able to use the table in the living room to do her homework.

"No, please. I couldn't sit anyways," she said, pulling her thoughts back to the woman standing in front of her, making the effort to stop thinking about things she could never change.

Dr. Carlisle got up from the table, too, holding his teacup with his hands cocked in front of him in a way that made Victoria think of rich white folks on TV, even though she couldn't imagine why something like that would pop into her head.

They wandered back to the living room like three children looking for ways to kill time on a rainy day, but a knock at the door rescued them from the tension of waiting.

L.D. asked the doctor to wait with Victoria in the bedroom while she answered the door. She didn't open it until the bedroom door was closed.

"Why are we in here?" Victoria asked, her nervousness turning to alarm as she realized that the conference was happening now, actually happening, and she had never really had the chance to sit down by herself and figure out in her own way and at her own pace whether it was a right and just and Christian thing to do and how it could do her little girl any good, who might be better off with everything just forgotten.

"Miss Woods doesn't want them asking you a lot of questions until they're all here," he explained.

"Are they going to ask me a lot of questions?"

"Miss Woods and I will answer most of them," he said.

She looked at him as if he were someone she had never seen before. "You're not a Christian man, are you?" she asked, surprising herself even more than she surprised him with the question.

He thought a moment before answering, and then smiled and said, "Christ teaches us to accept suffering. A doctor can't do that."

From beyond the door she could hear men's voices and once in a while, mixed in with them, Miss Woods's voice, but she couldn't make out anything they were saying. It had never struck her before that a doctor couldn't be Christian because sickness and disease were a part of God's plan for us, but it made sense the way he said it. It didn't make him a bad man, but it did seem to say he wasn't the man she had thought he was for so many years. She remembered the first time she had gone to see him, when her husband was gone and her baby wouldn't sleep. She was so tired it was all she could do to fix the child her bottle. He was the only doctor she had ever seen and he was very comforting.

The voices outside the bedroom door multiplied until it sounded like a party, and then it got very quiet and Miss Woods came to the door and asked both of them to come out. Miss Woods stopped Victoria to straighten her jacket on her shoulders and said, "Don't let the cameras and microphones scare you. These are good people and they want to help." She smiled in that very pretty way she had and then they walked out together.

The shock almost knocked Victoria from her feet and she had to reach a hand out to the wall to steady herself. Although she was coming out of her own bedroom, she felt as if she were somewhere else the second she passed to the other side of the door. The glare of bright lights hit her with the impact of a strong wind, and it took her eyes a moment before they could sort anything out. There probably weren't more than the twenty or so people Miss Woods had said there would be, but they looked like a legion. The lights on their cameras made it impossible to tell how many of them there were or even how crowded the room was, because she couldn't see past them to the other wall.

She felt as though she had been tricked, and wanted to go back into the bedroom and close the door until they all went away. But Miss Woods was holding her elbow and she found herself moving into their midst without even being aware that she was walking at all. She almost fell, and would have except that Miss Woods caught one arm and a young man jumped forward and caught the other and said "Watch your step, ma'am," as he helped her over the tangle of cables that wound ahead of her and ended in a bouquet of microphones bristling like long-stalked lilies on the table where Ophelia did her homework. The thought flashed through her mind that in a little while these people would all go and leave a mess behind.

"I appreciate your coming here, ladies and gentlemen," Dr. Carlisle was saying, bending at the waist to talk into the microphones. "I'd like you to meet Mrs. Victoria James." Victoria nodded, and the doctor continued. "I'm Winston Carlisle and I've been Mrs. James's family physician for about thirteen years. Her physician and her daughter's, which is why it was suggested to me that I might be the right person to speak for them now."

"Whose suggestion was that, doctor?" someone asked from somewhere in the middle of the lights.

Victoria tried to see where the voice came from but couldn't. It was like talking to people on the other side of a wall.

"I'd just like to make my statement if I could and then Mrs. James and I will be glad to answer all of your questions," Dr. Carlisle said. "Can these things be adjusted so I don't have to bend down?"

Another voice said, "We're picking you up just fine, sir."

Dr. Carlisle resumed his speech, standing straighter now.

"You all know that Mrs. James's daughter Ophelia James was killed at

La Guardia Junior High last week. Unfortunately, you don't know much more about it than that, I don't either, and nobody seems to. The reason I feel particularly outraged is not just at the death of this child but at the fact that no one seems to care how or why it happened."

He talked on and on, but it was hard for Victoria to follow what he was saying. His voice rose and fell in the familiar rhythm of anger and denunciation she recognized as that of a preacher, but the meaning of his actual words was lost in a kind of general flow of emotion. If she closed her eyes it was almost like being in church, with familiar voices ringing out hard and familiar truths. Before she knew it, the doctor had stopped speaking and the voices of the multitude answered with a chorus of shouted questions, their voices sharp and querulous after his, which was both deep and sweet.

"What about the grand jury, Dr. Carlisle?"

"Are you bringing an action against the city, Mrs. James?"

"Are you saying Commissioner Pound deliberately misled the press, Dr. Carlisle?"

"Are you talking about a cover-up here?"

"Are you saying the Warren kid didn't kill her?"

Carlisle held up his hands for silence. "One at a time, please," he said. "Someone asked about the grand jury. I don't know if the grand jury process was subverted or tampered with in any way. The problem is that the grand jury had a very limited question before it. They only addressed themselves to whether or not Detective Franks was justified in the shooting death of Timothy Warren. And that's got nothing at all to do with the mess at a public school of this city where a God-fearing little girl goes to school in the morning and doesn't come home that night. That's the question I want answered."

"You said you wanted a special prosecutor appointed. Does this mean you don't trust the police, the district attorney's office, who?"

"The police have already shown us what their priorities are. They're looking after their own."

"What are you hoping to find out, Dr. Carlisle?"

"What happened. Why it happened. What anybody's doing to make sure it won't happen again."

"Was the girl molested or wasn't she?"

"She was not."

"Why would Commissioner Pound suggest she was?"

"You'll have to ask him that."

"Does Artemis Reach support this demand for an investigation?"

"I'm hoping he will."

"Are you going to sue the city, Mrs. James?"

"Mrs. James isn't suing anyone. We just want answers."

"Is that right, Mrs. James?"

"I answered that question. Anyone else?"

"Can't she talk for herself."

"Yes, I can talk for myself," Victoria said. Her voice sounded choked, as if someone was squeezing her throat, but she couldn't abide letting that man suggest she was feebleminded without giving him some kind of answer.

"I'm not suing anyone. That won't bring my little girl back. I just want to know what kind of schools they're running. Who's supposed to be looking after these children? My Ophelia gets dragged off and . . . and nobody knows how. She was my little girl and I want to know how that happens. I want to know what happened to her. That's what they owe me and that's what I want to get."

For a moment no one spoke, and the reporters seemed to look at one another and at their notebooks and at the floor. Victoria wasn't sure if she had said the wrong thing, but she had to get it off her chest and she was glad she had. She looked for Miss Woods, to see what she thought, but couldn't see her at first.

Then someone asked a question about Ophelia, about what kind of student she had been, and someone else asked if Victoria had a picture of Ophelia they could put in the paper and what kind of activities she was in at school. Victoria told them about Ophelia singing in the church choir and in the choir at school. Out of the corner of her eye she spotted Miss Woods watching from the side of the room, and she seemed to be smiling, pleased with the way it was going, so Victoria felt good about it, too, and thought that after all she'd done the right thing speaking up like that.

STEVEN prowled the hallway outside his homeroom like a bird of prey, determined to find Lloyd Elijah the minute he came in. He'd arrived at school about an hour early, when the building was barely coming awake. Even the police outside seemed listless and indifferent. A sergeant waved him in with a perfunctory nod while his men sipped coffee from Styrofoam cups.

Gradually, the deserted corridor began coming to life, echoing first with the slogging footsteps of the teaching staff, the earliest arrivals moving slowest. As the school day approached, the pace quickened, students filtering in along with late-arriving faculty, peeling their coats as they hurried to their rooms.

Jamal Horton, who did morning duty running errands for the office, passed by with an armload of bulletins to be distributed to all the fourth-floor teachers.

"What's this one about?" Steven asked lightly as Jamal handed him his copy. The boy could read at least well enough to get the gist of the bulletin if he tried, and usually he did because he liked to know what was going on.

This time, though, he hurried past Steven without answering. Whatever Jamal had been upset about yesterday was obviously still bothering him.

"Hold it, Jamal," Steven called after him, hurrying to catch up. The boy looked up at him indifferently. "All right," Steven said. "What's your problem?"

"Who said I got a problem?"

"What did you mean yesterday, you *thought* we were friends?"

"You said that," Jamal protested with stubborn evasion. "I agreed with you."

"Did I do something that upset you?"

Steven didn't think he would get an answer. The walls kids put up can be impenetrable, more even than those of adults. Except for hiding, he thought, they have no defenses, and so they have to get good at hiding.

"Look, it ain't like we're *pals* or something," Jamal snapped back bitterly, sneering the word. "You got your friends, I got mine, so don't push it. You're just one of my teachers, that's all. I got lots of 'em."

He turned and bolted down the corridor, refusing to hear Steven call his name, flying past the other teachers in the hallway without even slowing to give them their memos.

Steven watched him go, pained. Oddly, he felt closer to Jamal than any of the other children except Timothy. Could two kids have been more different, he wondered, the one intense, articulate, old and wise and bitter, the other so lively, childlike and open—open, at least, until yesterday. He had lost Timothy and now he feared he was losing Jamal to some bitterness he didn't understand. It left him very much alone.

The chatter of voices rose quickly, until soon the hallway was filled with sound, a rising stream of noise that flowed into all the spaces and bounced back off the walls, an almost palpable wave of energy. Simple conversation became impossible as children greeted each other with outdoor shouts. A few of the teachers glanced curiously at Steven, positioned strategically in the middle of the tide, eyes scanning the students. Except for a perfunctory exchange of inaudible hellos, no one said anything to him. The first bell had already sounded when he finally saw Lloyd Elijah.

Steven pushed through the students and caught up with the boy just as he reached his homeroom door.

"I've got to talk to you," Steven said.

"Sure, whatever. I've got to get in."

The boy started to step through the door but Steven caught his arm. "All right. When?"

Lloyd shifted uneasily on his feet. Children were filing in around them, moving slantwise to give the two of them as wide a berth as possible in the narrow doorway. From inside the room Steven could hear Dennis Dougherty's voice growling over and over, with no change of tone, no sign of impatience, *Get in your seats, c'mon, c'mon, get in your seats, get in those seats.*

"Later. I'll see," Lloyd said. "What's this about?"

"Timothy Warren."

The boy pulled away. "Get out of my face, Mr. Hillyer."

"Lloyd, will you take your seat," Mr. Dougherty said, only a few paces away. His wrinkled hand reached for the door to close it but stopped when he saw Steven. "I didn't know it was you, Hillyer," he said. "You need a minute?"

"That's all right. We'll finish this at lunch, Lloyd," Steven said.

Lloyd answered with an indifferent shrug and slipped into the room. "Once more into the breach," Dougherty muttered as a pleasantry, swinging the door toward Steven.

Steven's own homeroom students were busy chasing each other about the room when he came in. Even those not involved in the game were gathered in playful clusters as far as possible from their own desks. He waited in the doorway, letting the quickly whispered word of his arrival bring them to order. Every teacher he ever had had told his class that he expected his students to behave in his absence exactly as if he were there, and Steven took a smug pride in never once having said it. A teacher who truly believed that kids wouldn't go crazy when the teacher left the room was the victim of a certifiable delusion.

He glanced down at the bulletin Jamal had put in his hand. "It has come to our attention," it began. The assistant principal sent out four or five bulletins every week, all of them dealing with matters that had come or been called to her attention. Steven waved the bulletin over his head as he made his way to the front of the class.

"I'm open for guesses. What's come to their attention?" he asked.

Hands shot up all over the room as the children hurried to their seats.

"Raoul."

"Hanging out in the stairs."

"Not even close. Laverne."

"Cutting classes."

"Raoul was closer. Will."

"Hanging out somewhere else."

There was a chorus of boos.

"That's cheating. You've got to take a real guess."

"On the roof."

"You had your chance. Alfredo."

"The cafeteria."

"You're in a rut. All right, I'll read it to you. 'It has come to our attention . . .' "

The words were greeted with a series of mocking cheers.

" 'That cigarette smoking has been going on in the girls' rest rooms on the third, fourth and fifth floors.' "

The first-period bell rang as the children all groaned and hissed their disapproval.

"I was late, it's my fault, now we'll never know what's going to happen. For those of you who want to study it in detail, it will be posted on the wall. For the time being I suggest you girls do your smoking in the boys' room."

Laughing and adding their own jokes to his, the children gathered their books and headed out for their first-period classes. For a moment he was alone in the room, their light laughter hanging in the room after them like a delicate fragrance. His own first-period students began to straggle in with their paperback copies of Richard Wright and their notebooks under their arms. The thought crossed his mind that he had made a mistake telling Lloyd what he wanted to talk to him about. Lloyd would avoid him the rest of the day.

He put it out of his mind while he taught, but when his fourth-period class came in, Lloyd Elijah wasn't with them. Steven wrote out a note, folded it in half and looked around for someone to give it to. Normally it would be Jamal but today he didn't feel right about that. On the other hand, he reminded himself at once, he wasn't going to ratify the boy's anger. Nothing had changed on his part.

"Take this down to the secretary, get an answer and bring it back," he said, handing Jamal the folded slip.

Jamal disappeared as quickly as if he had been an illusion.

He was back before the class was ten minutes into its discussion of *Lord of the Flies*. Maria Onofrio didn't like the way the book started because the author didn't explain why all these children had been on a plane together without any adults.

Jamal slipped the note onto Steven's desk and took his seat, his hand already in the air.

"Jamal."

"Maybe if the writer don't tell us what they're doing there it's 'cause he don't want us to know."

Steven studied him a minute, looking for a message in the response. "That's a good point," he said at last. "Anyone, why do you think a writer would do that?"

He unfolded the note while Carmello Ortiz suggested that maybe it was a surprise the writer was saving for later.

According to the note, Lloyd had gym and two shop classes in the annex next door after lunch. On a warm, bright day like today gym would probably be out in the park. The best time to catch him would be right before lunch, when he might try to slip in and out of his homeroom.

"That's good, Carmello. It's something we'll have to watch for," he said. "Could there be another reason?"

He led them around to the possibility that they weren't told where the boys were coming from because the author didn't want them to know, was telling them it wasn't important.

Two minutes before the end of his last morning class Steven told his students he was dismissing them early and asked them to stay out of the halls until the bell rang. He waited outside Dougherty's room and went in the moment he heard the bell, threading through the students hurrying out.

"Which one is Elijah's desk?" he asked.

Dougherty pointed. "Why? What's up?"

"Nothing really," Steven said.

"That little prick giving you trouble?"

"No more than usual."

The kids from Dougherty's homeroom were coming in and depositing their books, then heading off for lunch. Steven divided his attention between the door and Lloyd's desk, and got what he was waiting for when a boy named Boyd Burrows dropped off his own things and then lifted the lid of Lloyd's desk to put in his books for the morning and take out his notebook for shop.

Steven was at his side in a second. "Where is he?" he asked.

Boyd looked up, startled. He was a broad-shouldered black boy with a flat face and small, suspicious eyes. "Who?" he said, already set to tough it out.

"Don't give me that."

"I don't know. He just asked me to drop his stuff off."

"He cut English. I didn't report it. Do you want me to?"

The boy didn't answer.

"Give me the notebook."

Boyd studied his antagonist for a moment and let the beginnings of a sneer flicker on his lips as he decided not to resist. He handed Steven the notebook. It wasn't his problem.

"Now where were you taking it?"

"He's in the damn stairs. What's the big deal?"

"No big deal," Steven said.

Lloyd Elijah shook his head and blew a breath toward the ceiling when he saw Steven come through the door into the stairwell. "Are you crazy or what?" he snarled.

"Why don't you talk to me? Make up your own mind?"

"The dude's dead, Mr. Hillyer. I figured you'd know that."

"I saved your life Friday, Lloyd. Does it count for anything?"

Steven hadn't wanted to say that unless he had to, but Lloyd's resistance was so strong he didn't feel he had a choice.

The boy dropped his eyes and jammed his hands deep into his pockets. He paced away across the narrow landing.

"Look," he said, "if I tell you there's nothing to talk about will that square it? Me and Timothy, we weren't even tight."

"Come on into my room, Lloyd."

A steady stream of children moved through the door from the hallway, taking the two of them in with quick glances before hurrying down to the cafeteria. Steven could hear the high giggle of girlish laughter from a landing down below.

"Not here, man," Lloyd said.

"No. In my room. Let's go."

Lloyd shook his head, decisive. "After school."

"Is this a trick, Lloyd?"

"I gotta see someone, that's all."

Something told Steven he had the boy now, and it was a mistake to let him get away. But he was afraid Lloyd wouldn't talk to him here or anywhere else unless he showed at least a measure of trust. "All right," he said. "You tell me where."

"I got shop in the annex. Metal shop. Meet me there."

"You'll be there?"

"Hey, you saved my life, right," Lloyd said.

He slipped down the stairs like smoke drifting away.

* * *

IF THERE was one thing Philip Boorstin hated more than being out-smarted, it was being outsmarted twice. It wasn't just his reputation that hurt, though God knew that hurt plenty. And it wasn't just ego, although Christ only knew why people were always putting ego down, as though it wasn't the spring that kept the whole watch ticking. Boorstin knew that he had got where he was by promising he could keep Junius Ehrlich a step ahead of everyone who was supposed to be a step behind, and so far he had always delivered. Always.

That was the trouble with infallibility, he reflected with some bitterness as he waited in the airport lounge. A winning record wasn't good enough. You had to win them all. Like Russian roulette.

From where he stood he could read the headline on the copy of the *Post* a man in one of the chairs was reading. "Cover-up in School Slayings," it said. Inside there were two articles inspired by Victoria James's press conference and a sidebar about her daughter. "Dead Girl's Mom Wants Special Prosecutor." An editorial supported her demand as well as the demands of the parent protesters outside the school for the second morning this week.

Bullshit, bullshit and more bullshit. The parents at La Guardia Junior High, at least the parents of the decent kids, were probably thrilled to have a little police protection. Cops in the corridors wouldn't have been a bad idea, but at least outside was better than nothing. And what did the dead girl's mom think a special prosecutor could investigate?

Boorstin thought he knew who was behind it all. Artemis Reach. He put the woman up to the press conference, he was behind the leaderless demonstrators. It was no more likely that those people had organized themselves than that L. D. Woods, who was a great-looking lady but not a player, had dreamed up the press conference all by herself.

The more he thought about it, the angrier Boorstin became. That bastard Reach had looked him in the eye on Friday afternoon and prom-ised to keep quiet on the issue, to let it die the way the shock of any killing dies in a city that has seventeen hundred killings a year. The problem was that promises didn't mean a thing to sons of bitches like Artemis Reach.

The other person he blamed was himself, for trusting Reach in the first place.

Just last night Boorstin had assured the mayor that the situation was under control. Which it had been, in the sense that the demonstration had been orderly. He had said the same thing again this morning when the mayor called from Phoenix. Two minutes after he hung up the phone he learned that Victoria James had spent her morning entertaining a couple dozen reporters in her living room trying to make trouble out of an incident that by rights should have been buried a week ago. The whole thing was set up so swiftly and secretly that City Hall didn't even know about it until it was over and a bunch of reporters showed up to ask him if the mayor was considering appointing a special prosecutor.

There were no reporters at the airport now only because Mayor Ehrlich hadn't announced his arrival plans. Otherwise he would have had to answer questions before he had a chance to find out what Boorstin had gotten him into.

Junius Ehrlich was the first one off the plane, but he stopped the instant he stepped through the door from the jetway, his squat, broad-shouldered body parked square in the middle of the doorway, forcing the rest of the passengers to pick their way, grumbling, around him.

"Awright," he growled. "What the hell has been going on?"

His tie was down, his jacket rumpled. He always arrived everywhere looking as if they had asked him to fix the plane. Boorstin half expected him to say, *Sorry I'm late, we had some engine trouble, I had to put in a new set of plugs.*

"How much did they tell you?" Boorstin answered evasively. "Let's get away from here."

He had counted on breaking the news to the mayor in his own way, forgetting that nowadays there were telephones on airplanes.

The mayor fixed him with a beady look suggesting that what he really wanted, if he could have had his way, was to stand right there and not move an inch until Boorstin gave him some straight answers about how much trouble this was going to be. The only reason he kept slick little Jews like Boorstin around was because they knew how to take care of things. But you had to watch them every step of the way, because they always took care of themselves first. He knew it would have suited Boorstin perfectly to keep quiet until they were in the backseat of the limo, where he could lean back against the cushions and explain away a series of fuckups as if it was all one brilliant strategic move after the next. When a fixer like Philip Boorstin shits in the stew he tells you it's an old family recipe for shit stew.

But Ehrlich couldn't stand his ground in the middle of the airport with everybody around him already starting to whisper, *That's the mayor, isn't it? Honey, look, isn't that the mayor?*

"Where do you want me to start?" Boorstin said as they walked. "I take it you've been briefed."

"I'll tell you who briefed me," Ehrlich shot back. "That twerp from CBS—he was on the plane—he briefed me pretty good. And that cunt from NBC. They're asking me questions I don't have one fucking answer for. How the hell do you think that looks?"

"What did you tell them?" Boorstin asked.

He knew it was the wrong thing to say before the words were out of his mouth.

"Never mind what I told them. You tell me."

"Friday I had everything worked out with Reach and the P.C. Yesterday they start with the demonstrations and this morning there's a press conference."

That didn't square with what the mayor had been told. "Reach had a press conference?" he asked.

"He didn't call it himself."

"Who did?"

"L. D. Woods."

"The one who works for Kellem?"

"Yeah, her."

Ehrlich shook his head, thinking that one over. "God, what a piece," he said.

Boorstin couldn't resist a small laugh. "The sky's falling and you're thinking about a piece of ass," he said.

"I'm not thinking about her ass," the mayor said. "Although if I was . . ."

He left the sentence unfinished, trailing off into recollections of the last time he'd seen L. D. Woods.

By this time they were outside the terminal. The mayor's driver opened the car door, stepping back almost with a bow. It struck Boorstin again how lucky they were that no one knew what flight the mayor had been on. If the press had been waiting for him at the airport it would have been a disaster.

"Let me get this straight," Ehrlich said, leaning back practically against the door so he could look Boorstin in the face. "These people want a special prosecutor for what?"

"Who knows."

"The kid killed the kid, right? That's not changing. And the cop killed him. We're taking care of that, aren't we?"

"Internal Affairs. Yeah."

"Do we want to send it back to the grand jury?"

"It would look like a cave-in," Boorstin said. "It would look like a fix."

Ehrlich nodded. "Then there's nothing to investigate, right?"

Boorstin shrugged. "The way the thing was handled, whatever's in back of it. That's what they want investigated. Do you want that investigated?"

"I think they'd find your fingerprints all over it, Philip," the mayor said, with a low sound that was almost a chuckle. In the darkened backseat of the car, with its shaded windows, it was impossible to see the expression on his face.

"My fingerprints are your fingerprints, Your Honor," Boorstin reminded him. "Anyway, the bottom line is it's a race thing. If it was a white kid we'd have all the answers."

"Would we?"

"Hell no. But nobody would be asking. A white kid cracks a girl's neck and then gets blown away, he doesn't get to be a martyr."

Ehrlich made a snuffling sound that may or may not have meant anything. "What about this demonstration?" he said. "What do they want?"

"They want the cops gone."

"Any reason we can't give them that?"

"Commissioner Pound, that's all."

"He can be handled. Any reason we should?"

"Artemis Reach. He can make a lot of noise if we don't give him what he wants."

"I thought you worked out a deal with him."

"I did. Friday."

"Then that settles it. Fuck him."

The mayor turned to look out the window, checking out the steel peaks of the city rising in the distance.

The suddenness and the finality of his decision took Boorstin's breath away. The basis of Boorstin's political vision was keeping people happy. Not necessarily giving them what they wanted, but at least keeping them happy, a meticulous process of trading, adjusting and accommodating. The mayor's principles were a lot simpler. *Fuck him.*

Boorstin was sorry he hadn't thought of it himself.

THE building next to La Guardia Junior High had been a factory until it went out of business in the early sixties, when everything in the Bronx started going out of business. It remained empty for almost twenty years, windows broken, floors collapsed, turning as old buildings do into tracery shells of themselves that come to seem so fragile even their walls begin to look transparent. In the mid-eighties the city seized the property for back taxes and turned it over to School Board Sixty-one to house the state-of-the-art shop program Artemis Reach insisted on as one of his top priorities. Before Reach resurrected it, the shop department at La Guardia consisted of a few elderly teachers giving outdated instructions on archaic equipment that might have taught the kids a hobby but certainly not a trade. Among educators everywhere, but especially in the ghetto, trade schools were in disrepute, scorned as an adjunct of a tracking system that sent white kids on to college and black kids out to work.

Artemis Reach changed that. Part of his genius was that he could take an old idea and make it sound new by focusing on the aspects that used to work. He convinced parents in the Bronx that their children were being cheated by academic programs that only contributed to the dropout rate. "If your children want a college education, then we're going to prepare them for it," he said. "But, damn it, if they want training for a decent job, don't let this city get away with not giving it to them." The shop annex was one of his proudest accomplishments and the most visible monument to his leadership.

Even when Steven hurried into the building at ten minutes after three, he was met by a jumble of conflicting noises that carried a cheerfully industrious message. He paused to listen a moment, sorting out the sounds of hammers and forges and engines, wondering ruefully if anything useful ever got made in an English class. He knew that in just the three minutes it had taken him to get here, the classroom building where he worked had emptied like a punctured balloon. This place sounded as if it still had hours to go before it settled into silence for the night.

He asked directions to the metal shop and was pointed toward the back of the building. The shop itself turned out to be a high-ceilinged space almost the size of a gymnasium. The machinery, presses of some sort—Steven knew next to nothing about such things—hunkered like squat monsters around the edges of the room while the work tables gleamed with the cold cleanliness of an operating room. To one side of the room three boys in white shop coats, safety visors covering their faces, bent over a high-speed saw that screamed terribly as its needlelike blade worked its way through a metal slab. An instructor stood behind them.

Lloyd Elijah didn't seem to be there but the visors and coats made it impossible for Steven to be sure. The instructor was a thick-bodied man with a wide, flat face who wore his hair in a nineteen-fifties-style brush cut. Steven had seen him at faculty meetings without ever knowing who he was. He raised his safety goggles, setting them on his forehead, as Steven approached.

"Help you?" he asked.

"I'm looking for Lloyd Elijah. He told me to meet him here."

"Uh-uh."

"You mean he's not here?"

The screech of the saw cut out sharply, running down octave after octave until it died in a strangled whimper. The instructor glanced at the three boys and Steven's eyes followed his. As they peeled back their visors, Steven saw that the tallest of them was Charlie Wain. He didn't know the other two.

Wain gestured with a movement of his head and the instructor said, "That's right," and walked away.

"This is the right class, isn't it?" Steven called after him. "Is this his last-period class?"

The man didn't stop, but pushed through a door, which swung closed behind him. The building had fallen silent, and Steven could hear the instructor's footsteps hurrying away.

"What are you doing, Mr. Hillyer?" Charlie asked.

There wasn't any doubt in Steven's mind that Wain had sent the instructor away. A knot of fear tightened in his gut. He tried to tell himself he was wrong but couldn't make it convincing. "I'm looking for Lloyd," he said.

"Well, Lloyd ain't here."

"I see that."

He started to turn but Charlie moved in front of him. The knot inside him got tighter.

"You come up to see me with a bunch of questions," the boy said. "I answered them. Say we let it go right there."

"I haven't asked you any more questions," Steven answered defiantly. Whatever this was going to come to, it would come to. Backing down now wouldn't help.

Wain moved half a step closer but Steven held his ground. He could feel the boy's breath on his face. "Now you be after Lloyd," the boy said. "He don't like this shit either."

"Let him tell me that."

"He ain't here. That's telling you."

"And he asked you to give me this message?"

"I'm giving it, that's all. You could have got hurt up there on Tremont Ave, Mr. Hillyer. Them streets ain't safe."

"What are you afraid of, Charlie?"

"Bullshit."

"What do you call it? You threaten me because I want to talk to Lloyd. What are you afraid Lloyd might say?"

"I ain't threatened you, man."

Steven saw the fist flash forward, but it came too fast for him to avoid, catching him just above the belt, a searing pain followed almost at once by a wave of nausea that left him gasping for air as he slumped forward, holding himself. He was dimly aware that one of the other boys had hit him, not Charlie.

"Now that's a threat, asshole," Wain said, grabbing Steven's shoulders and pulling him upright.

Steven's body moaned a protest. It felt ripped inside, and the only way to hold it together was to stay bent over. But Wain wouldn't let him.

"You understand the difference, Mr. Hillyer? You fuck with me, I fuck back."

Steven couldn't answer him. Sweat beaded on his forehead like water seeping from a squeezed sponge. He could feel the pressure of the table edge at the back of his thighs as Charlie pushed him back against it. The thought of that needle saw and the sound it had made raced through Steven's mind like the fire on a fast fuse.

For what seemed like a long time no one moved. Steven's nerves stretched to the breaking point as he tensed for the click of the switch, the sound of the saw leaping to life just behind him. But it didn't come.

"What I'm afraid of is you might get hurt, Mr. Hillyer," Charlie Wain said, taking his hands off Steven's shoulders and letting him sag forward. Steven heard them walk away, but he stayed doubled over for a long time, holding in the pain with his hands.

Slowly, as the nausea came under control and the pain subsided to an aching cramp, he forced himself to stand upright and move toward the door. The first few steps hurt more than he thought they would but he was able to keep moving. The possibility crossed his mind that something was ruptured, and he was afraid that if he stopped he wouldn't get moving again. It might be hours before he was found.

It hardly seemed possible to Steven that anyone could do so much damage with one punch, but the surprise probably had something to do with that. If he had seen it coming, maybe he would have taken it better.

In the corridor, he leaned against the wall for a minute, letting its coolness settle the pain and calm him before he headed for the street, where the remnants of the police contingent still loitered by the vehicles waiting to take them away. Instinctively he turned away from them, making an effort to hold himself erect and walk steadily until he was around the corner. Nothing could have spoken more vividly of how complicated his life had become over the past eight days. Under any normal set of circumstances, a man who has just been beaten up ought to feel some relief at finding a cop around. Steven felt none. With a kind of feral instinct that was entirely new to him, he sensed that the police weren't on his side in any of this and that the best thing he could do was to get away from them before anyone started asking questions.

He was able to find a seat when the subway came, and he kept his eyes closed almost all the way back to Manhattan. He dozed off in the swaying car, his head drowsing back against the window, lulled by the rhythmic pounding of the rails. He came awake suddenly, for an instant thinking he was going to school, and jumped to his feet, certain he had missed his stop. But the sharp stab of pain when he moved filled in the muddled spaces in his memory. The train braked hard into a station that turned out to be his stop, and Steven plodded upstairs and walked slowly home.

He let himself in the downstairs door and rang the bell with one hand while he jabbed the key at the foyer lock. He pushed the door closed behind him and started up the stairs just as the buzzer released the lock again. Good. Rita was there. At least he wouldn't be alone.

She was waiting at the top of the stairs.

"What did he say?" she asked, and then saw what he looked like and gasped. "Steven, what happened?"

He didn't even start to tell her about it until he was sitting on the couch. Rita sat next to him.

"He wasn't there," he said.

She didn't say anything, even though she had guessed that Lloyd wouldn't be there when he told her he was going to meet the boy.

"I got your friend Charlie Wain instead," Steven said, and went on to tell her as much as he could remember about what had happened.

When he finished, she said only, "Let me get you a drink." When she came back from the kitchen she found him on the phone.

"If you could call him at home and ask him to call Steven Hillyer I'd appreciate it," he said and gave his number.

She handed him the glass of gin and tonic but sat across from him in the soft chair.

"Who did you call?" she asked.

"Franks."

He didn't have the detective's number, so he had to call the Thirty-ninth Precinct. He hated leaving his name, but there was no other way. The officer he talked to said he would pass on the message.

Rita stood up and walked away. Her fingers played for a moment with some papers on his desk, and then she turned to face him. "Charlie Wain is a crack dealer," she said. "What just happened to you has got nothing to do with Timothy. It's got nothing to do with anything you care about."

"Do you know that?"

"I saw what was going on in that playground."

"Maybe."

"Steven," she said in a tone of strained patience, "an English teacher who doesn't even know why a kid on Ninety-sixth and Lex puts the pay phones out of order is no match for these people."

"I'm not trying to match anyone."

"You're going to get hurt."

The phone rang.

"You're wrong there," he said. "I already did."

It was Jim Franks, and Steven told him everything that had happened.

"I'm not a cop anymore," Franks said. "You know there's not much I can do."

Steven hadn't expected this answer, but he wasn't surprised. "I just thought I'd tell you," he said.

In bed that night he lay awake listening to Rita's even breathing until the slow and stately rhythm of it, like surf gentling on a quiet beach, grew insistently in his mind into a firm and pulsing beat. He drifted toward sleep while the rhythm he heard shifted subtly into swaying anapests that seemed to spiral him dreamily away from himself. And then the words came, over and over:

> *Father, father, why forsake me?*
> *Bands of fifty in the hills.*
> *Father, father, don't forsake me.*
> *Prophet heals and prophet kills.*

smothering his mind like a blanket, lulling as rain on a windowpane,

> *Father, father, why forsake me?*
> *Fifty prophets in the caves.*
> *Father, father, don't forsake me.*
> *Crack of doom but doom that saves.*

WEDNESDAY

T H E rest of the day, after the press conference, was downtime as far as L. D. Woods was concerned. She hid out in her office all afternoon, taking no calls, letting the reactions develop on their own, like inoculations that had to be given time to take. She figured that the messages from the mayor's office, the district attorney's office and Chairman Reach all meant the same thing. They wanted to know what it would take to make Mrs. James and her charges go away. If L.D. talked to them, the negotiating process would start at once. She was better off making them wait at least until Wednesday morning.

She sent an intern on the staff for the afternoon papers, and was encouraged by everything she read. *Newsday* called the grand jury inquiry inadequate and gave a guarded endorsement to Mrs. James's call for a fuller investigation. The *Post* was leaning the same way, and accompanied its account of the press conference with a sympathetic profile of Ophelia and her mother based on an interview with the pastor of their church. Both papers linked the press conference to the demonstrations outside the school, creating the impression of extensive unrest.

Late Tuesday afternoon Congressman Kellem knocked on her door and let himself in. An old-fashioned man, honest and somewhat doddery, he had always had an awkwardly paternal attitude toward L.D., the same attitude he had toward his constituents. He sat down opposite her desk, settling in, leaning forward. It was a sign he wanted to talk.

"Tell me something," he said. "Do you know what you're doing?"

She thought she did.

"Is there really something to this?" he asked.

"I think so."

He thought this over. "You don't think I should be doing anything?" he asked.

The thought of doing anything terrified him. He had been in Congress since the district was Jewish, and he survived now thanks to a patronage network that assured that the Democratic party would renominate him every two years. His part of the bargain included making no waves.

"No," she said, "it's not really your kind of issue."

He seemed relieved to hear it.

"It's yours?" he asked.

She said that it was and he pushed himself up heavily from the chair and shuffled to the door.

"I'm an old man, L.D.," he said. "You're young. You have to be careful what enemies you make."

He left without explaining, but he didn't have to. She knew he meant he wouldn't be a problem for her, but that didn't matter because he couldn't have been if he wanted to. It was also a warning. She assumed he was referring to Artemis Reach.

When she got home to her apartment in Chelsea early that evening, the doorman told her two reporters had been by and left their cards. One was a woman from the *Times,* the other a man for the local NBC affiliate. She slipped the cards into her pocket and instructed the doorman to tell any other callers she was out.

"Even Mr. Chambers, ma'am?"

"No," she said. "Send Mr. Chambers up."

She dropped her briefcase on the bed and played back her phone messages. Two of them were from the reporters who had come to the apartment, there were a few hang-ups, a few calls from other journalists and one from a staffer in Congressman Kellem's office who liked to pester her at home with meaningless questions because he couldn't get up the nerve to come on to her in the office. At the end of the tape there was a message from Tal.

"That lady's had enough shit in her life without you using her to launch your career. I hope it works out fine."

That was all.

What an arrogant, insufferable message, she thought. Tal had this righteous streak in him. He would have done something quietly, behind the scenes, to help Victoria James, the way he had persuaded someone to make a phone call to a friend who called a friend who got him the coroner's report. How far would that approach have gotten him? Nowhere. Her way was better. *Using* Victoria? Using people was when you didn't care what happened to them. L.D. cared.

She rewound the machine without taking down any of the numbers and reset it to answer on the first ring. Then she took a bath, letting the hot water and the scented oil worked on her skin and her mind. Tomorrow things were going to start happening, she told herself. Tonight she wanted to put it all on a shelf.

After the bath she didn't feel like making herself anything to eat, so she settled for a bag of cheese-flavored popcorn she had bought for Tal and a glass of Evian, carrying them to the couch, along with the Anne Tyler novel she had been promising herself she'd read for months. She felt as if she was in college again.

Within minutes she was lost in the life of a woman she'd never met and wouldn't have found interesting if she had, caught up in a set of quiet passions so deeply buried under the layers of a listless marriage that they hardly seemed to be passions at all. Most of the story unfolded in a car, and already L.D. could feel herself hypnotized by the slow movement through space and the memories of long drives in the littered backseat of her father's Pontiac as it wandered through familiar turns. When the woman left her husband at a gas station in the middle of nowhere, L.D. realized she was crying and put the book down.

It wasn't like her to cry over a book, or anything else for that matter. It was ridiculous. She felt lonely, though she was the least lonely person in the world and there were very few things in her life she cared to rebuke herself for. She had never felt more firmly in control.

For some reason, though, she couldn't argue the feeling away this time. Annoyed and angry, she flung herself off the couch as decisively as if she had somewhere to go and marched to the bathroom, where she blew her nose and dried her eyes and took stock of herself in the mirror. *Damn you, Tal Chambers*, she thought. *What's your interest in all of this anyway? That stupid room with the plaque with your name on it? Are your reasons any better than mine?*

As her eyes searched her face in the glass, she told herself she wasn't exploiting Victoria James. Even if he thought she was, was that any reason to leave a message like that? And did it matter what he said?

Yes, obviously it did, or she wouldn't have been crying in an empty apartment over a woman who wasn't real in a story that wasn't true. The answer surprised her, but once she recognized what she was dealing with she knew at once what she should do about it. If Tal imagined he had reasons not to call her, then she would call him. She believed in pride, but not the kind that got between her and what she wanted.

She dialed his number and reminded herself while the phone rang that all these things were simple if only you kept them simple. *I want you to make love to me*, she would say. They could talk things over afterward, if there was still anything to talk over.

His machine answered the phone and she hung up without leaving a message.

She didn't think she could get her mind back into the book, and the half-eaten bag of popcorn on the floor next to the couch looked like a bad joke. Going out on the tiny balcony off her living room, she watched the city for a while, a weltering grid of lights as random and unpatterned as the stars. Yes, she had been thinking of herself and her career when she went to meet Victoria James in the subway station. So what? She was also thinking about Mrs. James, helping her, protecting her. She cared about this frail and frightened woman, had cared even before she met her. Wasn't that enough?

Angry at being forced to defend her motives, she stormed from the balcony, jammed the book back on the shelf in the living room and dumped the remnants of the popcorn in the kitchen trash. She turned off all the lights and went to bed, emptying herself of thought. Although she expected to have trouble falling asleep, the next thing she was aware of was the jangling of the telephone and her own voice announcing that she wasn't in. She groped for the phone in the darkness and put it to her ear.

"I'm here," she said, her voice husky with sleep. "Sorry, I forgot to turn it off."

"Miss Woods?"

She sat up sharply and tried to blink herself awake. The familiar outlines of her room came slowly into focus.

"Yes?"

"I'm real sorry to trouble you, Miss Woods. I didn't know who to call."

"Victoria?"

"Yes, miss. My husband's here and I can't make him go."

She was whispering, which gave her thin, reedy voice an unfamiliar timbre. The man must have been in another room and she couldn't afford to be overheard.

"Is he hurting you, Victoria?" L.D. asked urgently. "Is he threatening you?"

"Please," Victoria whispered. "I can't talk. Please."

L.D. heard a click as Victoria's phone lowered onto its cradle and then the line went dead.

Her feet were on the floor in an instant, and she managed to shed her nightgown while she dialed Tal's number. This time he answered.

"Tal, it's L.D.," she said. "Can you get here right away?"

"Are you all right?" His voice was sharp with alarm.

"I'm fine," she reassured him. "Don't park. I'll be downstairs."

She hung up the phone and dressed quickly, jeans and a shirt, then grabbed her coat and purse and hurried to the lobby to wait. It wouldn't take him more than a few minutes to get there. She hadn't even thought to check the time or put on her watch, but the night doorman, who had been sleeping upright on the bench between the outer and inner lobby doors, told her it was a little after three and then settled back to sleep. While she waited for Tal she played back Victoria's call in her mind, trying to gauge how frightened the woman was, how much danger she might be in. There was no way to tell.

She saw Tal's black Jaguar come around the corner and moved to the curb as he pulled up.

"What's wrong?" he asked even before she was in.

"Victoria James just called," she said. "Her husband showed up and she can't get rid of him."

The Jag jumped from the curb and made a left against the light to circle the block and head north.

"Did she call the police?" Tal asked.

"No."

"Did you?"

She thought that one over before answering. "Do you think we should?" she asked.

"Depends on the game plan, doesn't it?"

He didn't glance over to check her reaction. They were moving very fast up Sixth Avenue and he kept his eyes on the road.

"I didn't call them because I called you," she answered brittlely.

His voice came back softly musing, as if he were talking to himself. "Domestic disturbance. Not very good for the image. Of course if he knifes her you've got one hell of a martyr."

"You bastard," she said.

He finally looked at her. He knew she felt his eyes on her but she refused to acknowledge them in any way, staring resolutely ahead. In profile, her face stern, her lips firm and tight, she looked about as beautiful as it was possible to look. He admitted this to himself, but still didn't like what he saw.

They turned east, heading for the highway.

"What did she sound like?" he asked at last, breaking the silence.

"Worried I guess," she said. "Scared."

"Which?"

"Worried."

He considered a moment and said, "We'll be there in ten minutes."

Since there was almost no traffic, Tal was able to ignore all the lights and get them to the FDR Drive in minutes. The Jag sped north at close to ninety, weaving in and out among slower cars that randomly dotted all three lanes, Chambers handling the car with such ease that it was almost impossible to realize how simple it would have been to get killed. Still, the speed gave them a good excuse for not talking, and L.D. kept her head turned away from him, watching the East River fly by in a blur. Sooner than she would have thought possible they were wrenching through a maze of rutted Bronx streets that looked as lifeless and desolate as the buildings that flanked them like canyon walls. He pulled to a lurching stop in front of Victoria James's apartment building.

"Shit," Tal said with a glance back at the Jag as they hurried for the front door. In this neighborhood the car could be picked clean inside of twenty minutes.

Despite what passed for a lock, the lobby door opened easily with a few twists of the knob. There was an elevator but it smelled bad and was slower than walking, so they charged up the stairs to the fourth floor. Tal knocked loudly and opened the door. L.D. followed him in.

"How we doing?" Tal said from the doorway, his voice calm and uncannily cheerful. He had learned a long time ago that a man who fills the door frame when he steps into a room doesn't have to talk tough.

Herman James, who had learned almost nothing in an even longer stretch of time, said, "What the fuck?"

James looked to be nearly twice the size of his ex-wife, no more than five eight or nine in height but squarely built with broad, sloping shoulders and heavy arms. His face was flat and badly shaved, and his watery eyes were flecked with red. He seemed to have had Victoria cornered by the window, but as he turned to face the interlopers at the door she darted away, hurrying toward the safety of the kitchen.

L.D. stepped past Tal and went to join her.

Tal said, "I think you better be going, Mr. James."

"Who the hell are you?" James asked, but there was little challenge in his voice, not enough to bother Tal. Tal's own mother was a single woman, and Tal had been dealing with men like Herman James since he was twelve. They were strong and violent enough to terrify women, but when a man faced them down you could smell their fear all the way across the room.

"Right now, Mr. James," he said, walking toward him.

A coat lay across the back of the couch, with a hat on the cushion nearby. Tal picked them up and held them out. The worn cloth of the coat felt greasy in his hand.

"Look, man," Herman James whined, "this here's between me and my wife."

"I can make this as hard for you as you want," Chambers said.

James snatched the clothes away and moved for the door, skirting around a chair to avoid passing near Chambers. He stopped halfway across the room, brave again. "You just tell her . . ." he started to say.

"No, I'm telling you," Chambers cut him off. "You call her again, you come over here again, you can count on dealing with me."

In the kitchen, Victoria sat slumped at the table sobbing with shame while L.D. stood over her, slim, skilled hands massaging the tense, sinewy knots of muscle in the woman's tiny shoulders.

Victoria's wrists and arms had red marks where her ex-husband had grabbed her, and there was another mark at the side of her neck. Since he hadn't really been beating her, she said, she didn't think the police would come. Otherwise she wouldn't have called Miss Woods in the middle of the night. He used to show up once in a while when Ophelia was alive, but she was never afraid with the child there. She was always able to make him go. This time she knew he wasn't going and that's why she called. She apologized over and over, humiliated by her fear and her powerlessness.

L.D. comforted her as well as she could, and when the sobbing stopped she slipped into the chair next to her and laid a hand over Victoria's tangled fists.

"People are supposed to help each other," L.D. said earnestly. "There's nothing wrong with asking your friends for help."

Tal came in and told them James was gone.

Until that moment Victoria hadn't even thought about who the man Miss Woods had brought with her might be. She had fled the room so fast when Herman let go of her that she didn't even take the time to look. Now her eyes darted from Mr. Chambers to Miss Woods with that strangely birdlike rapidity Tal had found so curious the first time they'd met. Her expression posed a question that he answered before she could ask.

"Miss Woods and I are friends," he said.

Victoria made them tea and found some biscuits in the cupboard she could serve with it. They talked until the sky was fully light and she seemed to have regained her equanimity. Tal assured her that her ex-husband wouldn't be back but left his home and office numbers just in case. At the door, Victoria caught L.D.'s hands in hers. "Are you sure we done the right thing?" she asked.

"Victoria, we did the right thing," L.D. answered earnestly, putting as much conviction in her voice as in her words. "He didn't hurt you. Everything will be fine."

Mrs. James looked to Tal.

"I'm sure it will," he said, but his eyes didn't meet hers.

His car was still at the curb where he left it, untouched. If they had been looking for signs from heaven, that would have been a clear one. As it was, neither of them commented on it.

"Satisfied?" he asked when L.D. was seated next to him in the car.

"Ever since the girl died, her ex-husband has been coming around. He thinks there's money to be made out it," L.D. said. "This would have happened anyway."

"And at least this way she had us to call."

"Yes."

She leaned over to read the dashboard clock and said, "I don't think it makes much sense to go home. Do you think you could drop me at the office?"

He didn't start the engine. "Long Dark Woods," he said. "You know they call you that, don't you?"

"Yes."

"I always thought it was a reference to your legs."

"I'm sorry I'm not just a pair of legs, Tal."

"What's in this for you, Tiger Lady?"

"You know the answer to that."

"Champion of the People," he said. "And then you run for what? Kellem's seat in Congress? Reach's job on the Board?"

He made it sound like disloyalty. Men owned their jobs the way they owned their wives.

"Is that a problem?" she asked.

"No," he said. "No problem. What's in it for her?"

"Truth and justice," she said. "I can take the subway if you don't want to give me a ride."

He turned the key in the ignition and eased from the curb. Hell, he thought, what did he want in a woman anyway? Force and fire. Well then, ambition went with the package.

When he dropped her at the office, he told her he'd call her for dinner.

WITHOUT a badge in his pocket, things could get tricky, but Jim Franks wasn't going to worry about that. He didn't need the badge to identify himself as a cop, not after twelve years in the job. People read it in his face, and the way he walked on the street.

He started at Lloyd Elijah's home, although when a kid like that doesn't go to school he usually doesn't stay home either. A girl opened the door as far as the chain lock allowed. She looked to be about twenty and her face had that ravaged look, skin stretched tight, that marked a heroin addict as clearly as needle tracks.

"I'm Detective Franks," he said. "I'm looking for Lloyd Elijah."

"No," she said. "He ain't here."

"Mind if I come in?"

"I told you he ain't here."

"Then you won't mind answering a few questions," he said.

His shoe was wedged into the crack of the door, giving her no choice. He would have to let her close the door to take the chain off, but people always opened it again, as though their chance to lock the man out was gone for good once that foot got in.

The girl licked at her lips and mumbled an unintelligible assent so he let her close the door and listened to the sound of the chain sliding off. He eased the door back and stepped into the room, where the rank smell of overused air grabbed him like a pair of arms around his chest. The girl was barefooted and bare legged, in a thin print smock with a sweater over it. She had probably been pretty a couple of years ago, Franks thought with that mixture of anger and regret he always felt at one time or another every working day of his life.

"Where is he?" he asked.

She shrugged her shoulders and cocked her hips, resigned to waiting out the rest of his questions.

"But he does live here?"

She blew a breath toward the ceiling. *Look at this shithole,* it said. *Lives here. Right.*

"You're his sister?"

"Christ you're good at this," she said.

"Did he come home last night?"

"I wasn't paying attention."

"So you don't know what time he left this morning?"

"Not a clue."

"Do you mind if I look around?"

She waggled her hand, inviting him to help himself. He went through the motions but there wasn't anything he saw that he couldn't have described even before he'd stepped into the apartment.

There is a certain level of poverty and despair that leaches the identity out of people, leaving them only the stripped-down humanity of being merely human, the way penguins are penguins and cattle cattle. People got ground down until they weren't even people anymore, all of them so precisely alike that there wasn't a difference you could name and say this is her, this is him, this is the other one. It had happened already to Lloyd Elijah's sister, standing splay legged in front of him, meaninglessly defiant. She was every twenty-year-old junkie he had ever seen.

"Who lives here with you?" he asked when he finished his inspection.

She blew out another breath and said, "My mother."

"Where is she?"

The girl didn't answer, her attention wandering. In a few minutes it would be impossible to talk to her at all.

"I asked you where she is?" he said sharply, calling her back to this room, to this time.

"I don't know."

"Does she work?"

"Yeah."

"Where does she work?"

"I don't know."

"Think," he said. "Where does your mother work?"

Her brow wrinkled from the effort of concentration, and he knew even before she answered that whatever she said now would be all he'd get out of her. "Different places," she said at last. "She got a new job, that's all I know."

He left the apartment and tried his luck with a downstairs neighbor. He told her he had to get in touch with Mrs. Elijah because her son had been hurt on his way to school, and she gave him the name of a diner only a few blocks away. The trick was one he had been using for years and it always worked.

The diner turned out to be the only establishment on the block still in existence. One by one the stores around it had all been boarded up, and then one by one the boarding had been ripped out so the empty spaces could be stripped of plumbing and electric fixtures, wiring, pipes and any stray objects left behind when the businesses failed. Litter from the streets collected through the glassless windows. Tattered blankets on the floors suggested recent habitation.

He wasn't surprised that a restaurant in such a setting wouldn't have many customers. In fact there were none when Franks walked in. A black man in his sixties or older, his spine curved like a question mark, looked up from scraping the grill and followed the detective with his eyes. A stout woman seated at the end of the counter hurried around behind it, taking up the coffeepot and carrying it with her. She set a cup in front of him.

"Mrs. Elijah?" he asked.

The coffeepot hung poised above the cup. "Are you a cop?" she asked.

"Detective Franks. I'd like to ask you a few questions about your son Lloyd."

The old man moved away from the grill and settled in at the far end of the counter.

"Is Lloyd in some kind of trouble?" the woman asked, the edge in her voice suggesting that she wasn't used to trouble from Lloyd. He thought he could see a resemblance to her daughter in the eyes and mouth.

"No, ma'am," he said. "He didn't go to school today. I'm trying to find him."

"They don't send cops for that."

"It's about the homicide at the school, ma'am. We're trying to find out what happened."

"Lloyd didn't have nothing to do with that."

"That's right, ma'am. But we've got some questions about Timothy Warren. He was a friend of Timothy's, wasn't he?"

"God rest his soul," she said.

"Yes, ma'am."

He waited to see what she would say.

"You want some of this here coffee?" she asked.

"Please."

She filled his cup and returned the pot to the heater. When she came back she asked him how he had found her.

He told her he had been to her apartment.

"Cherisse told you where I'm working?" She sounded surprised.

"No, ma'am. One of your neighbors."

"But you seen Cherisse?"

He nodded. She thought a moment and then she said, " 'Tisn't like Lloyd to miss school. He's not like that one."

"Did he say anything? Last night or this morning. Anything that might indicate where he was going?"

She paused to think again, cocking her head and resting a stubby-fingered hand against her cheek in a way that looked so quaint and old-fashioned that Franks thought of his own grandmother. "Come to think of it," she said at last, "I don't think he come home last night at all."

He asked her a few more questions but she didn't know where her son might have spent the night, whom he might be with or where he might be now. She couldn't tell him much about Timothy Warren except that he had lived with them for about a month and a half and then had moved out, a month or so ago, when Cherisse came back.

Franks paid for the coffee and left. He stopped at a phone booth on his way to the car and called Dwight Matthews, a detective working out of a narcotics unit in the Thirty-sixth Precinct. Franks and Matthews had been partners for almost a year and a half and Jim thought he could trust him. "What's your day look like?" Franks said. "Any chance we could get together?"

"Shit, I just made some plans," Matthews said. "Wish you called earlier."

"Like before I got suspended?"

After a moment of hesitation on the other end of the line, Matthews said, "Awright, Jim. What do you want?"

"I'm interested in a kid named Lloyd Elijah, goes to school at La Guardia. I could use the names of some known associates."

"How much trouble can I get in?"

"None if you pull the file yourself," Franks said. "I wouldn't ask if I didn't need it."

"Give me your number," Matthews said, and Franks read him the number off the pay phone.

Matthews rang back in less than twenty minutes. "Is this guy still around?" Matthews asked.

"He was around yesterday."

"Dealing?"

"Just around. Why?"

"We got him as a small-time crack dealer. At least he hung around with the dealers. Then he dropped out of sight."

"No," Franks said. "He still goes to the school. I've got a man who saw him there Friday, saw him there yesterday."

The shrug at the other end of the line was almost audible. "Could be," Matthews said. "But he dropped out of the business."

On a hunch Franks asked, "When was this? Two and a half, three months ago?"

"Yeah, about then. You still want those names?"

According to Mrs. Elijah, two and a half months ago was when Timothy Warren had come to live with Lloyd.

Matthews read off half a dozen names of kids Lloyd Elijah hung with. Except for Charlie Wain, they meant nothing to Franks, but he hadn't expected that they would. Matthews said, "Look, I hope it works out okay with that problem you've got," and Franks said he was sure it would.

What Matthews didn't say, because it went without saying, was that he would appreciate not being called again. Friendship was good for a favor, but not more than one.

By this time it was after noon and Franks called La Guardia Junior High to leave a message for Steven Hillyer to call him. He gave the number at the phone booth and his first name. "It's important that I talk to him right away," he said. "I'd appreciate it if someone could take the message up now."

The voice was that of the same secretary he had spoken to earlier in the morning when he had called Hillyer to ask if Lloyd Elijah had shown up at school.

"I gave him the message myself," she said. "If he didn't call you back . . ."

"He called me back," Franks said. "Now I'm calling him back. I'm counting on you, babe. If you did it once you can do it again."

She laughed and promised to deliver the message. If she looked half as good as she sounded, she would make someone very happy.

Franks figured he'd give Hillyer half an hour to get back to him and then he'd start checking out the names Matthews gave him. He leaned against the phone booth and shifted his shoulders until he was comfortable. Waiting was something he was good at, and while he waited he thought about Lloyd Elijah's mother, who was so sure her son wouldn't turn out like her daughter, so confident he went to school every day, and then hadn't even noticed that he didn't come home for the night. He thought about the fact that Elijah stopped running with his crack-dealing friends at about the time Timothy Warren moved in with him, but he knew he had a long way to go before he could figure out what it meant.

The phone rang much sooner than he expected. It was beginning to look like a decent day.

Franks read Steven the list of names. "Do you know any of them?" he asked.

"Charlie Wain. He's the kid I told you about."

"I got that. Any of the others?"

"No."

"Kind of what I figured. I'll see what I can find out."

He started to hang up the phone, then put it back to his ear.

"Hillyer? You still there?"

"Yes."

"Did you know the Warren boy lived with Elijah for a while?"

"No."

"I didn't think so. I'll keep you posted."

The rest of the day was as unproductive as the morning had been promising. The process consisted of going from corner to corner, hangout to hangout. Pick a name on the list and start asking. Normally you got answers because no one wanted trouble with the man over where some dude might be. And normally the answers weren't worth shit, because it was just as easy to send a cop in the wrong direction as the right one. You threatened, you cajoled, and once in a while you shook someone up. Sooner or later you ended up in the same place as the kid you were looking for.

But every one of the kids on the list told him that Lloyd Elijah didn't run with them anymore. They hadn't seen him. Where would he go if he didn't go to school? They all shrugged. And then they all said the same thing. "I told you, man. We ain't tight."

The only one he couldn't talk to was Charlie Wain, for the same reason he hadn't left his name with the school secretary when he called Hillyer. Wain would recognize him. Wain had been at the weight room door when he and Donadio responded to the call. So he settled for following the boy after school and ended up watching him sell crack on a street corner as openly as if he had the franchise. Wain kept the drugs in a paper bag in a trash basket so if a cop showed up he had nothing on him. When it began to get dark, a girl who didn't look old enough to drive pulled up in a Buick at least as old as she was. She got out of the car and talked to Charlie. Then she took over at the trash basket and Charlie drove off in the Buick.

Franks watched the car bump down the street and decided against following him. It was late, he was hungry and Lenny would be holding dinner. He hadn't told her where he was going in the morning and didn't want to explain now.

On the drive home to Dobbs Ferry he added up the day's receipts. His father used to say you can't go broke making a small profit, and if that was true then the day was at least a push. He knew a few things he hadn't known in the morning.

One of them was that Lloyd Elijah wouldn't be easy to find.

B O O R S T I N rode up in the elevator without paying any attention to the sounds it was making or the way it spasmed at each floor, protesting about how high he wanted it to go. But, like *The Little Engine That Could,* it collected itself each time and kept going until at long last the doors inched back to let him out into the eighth-floor corridor.

He wondered whether another light bulb or two would have done more harm than good. Certainly you could see better. On the other hand, why? There were cracks in the plaster. The tile floor, which once, God help us, made this place a showplace, as elegant a business space as any in the Bronx, or even Manhattan, had been patched so many times the pattern of blacks and whites (faded blacks and dirty whites) was impossible to decipher. The ceilings were over ten feet high and he knew without even going into any of the offices that they were all large, because the building dated from the time when people still believed in large rooms.

He passed a door that said "Men" and figured he'd better use it, but it turned out to be locked. Since no one can be tough when he has to take a leak, and since he didn't want to show up for his meeting asking for a men's room key, he rang the bell at the orthodontist's office next to the men's room and waited to be buzzed in. *An orthodontist no less,* he said to himself. *So there are still Jews in the Bronx.* It was a joke, of course. There were thousands of Jews in the Bronx, hundreds of thousands. Otherwise Bert Kellem wouldn't still be in Congress and Philip Boorstin wouldn't be begging an orthodontist's receptionist for a men's room key on his way to Kellem's office.

The receptionist inspected him closely when he told her what he wanted, and he knew that if he hadn't been wearing a suit the answer would have been no. But she must have approved of what she saw because she handed the key over. "Don't forget to bring it back," she said.

The key was attached to a piece of laminated pasteboard the size of a dinner plate.

He relieved himself at the urinal and checked himself out in the mirror while he washed his hands. He wasn't a vain man, not in the least, but on the other hand this wasn't Kellem or some other flatulent politico he was going to meet. He still had a vivid memory of Linda Dawson Woods at the Board meeting, her eyes sparking fire as she berated him with statistics about inadequate social services in the Bronx. He still got jittery with the overwhelming sense of her body in even such a small gesture as flinging a report across the table at him. She was a lady who used every-thing she had, and she had it all.

He shook the water from his hands and with his fingers still damp smoothed the hair at his temples, which tended to curl more than he liked. He straightened his tie and then his shoulders, nodded his approval at his image in the mirror and marched from the bathroom ready to show Ms. L. D. Woods how the big boys played.

The congressman's office was a surprisingly active hive considering it wasn't an election year and nothing ever got done there. The staff, too, seemed much younger than Boorstin expected, boys and girls in jeans and shirtsleeves milling about with a refreshing air of purpose. Boorstin looked around for someone he could ask for directions to L. D. Woods's office and found himself looking right at the forehead of Congressman Kellem himself.

"Philip," the congressman boomed, as loud as if they were on opposite sides of the room. "What brings you up here?"

"A little business with one of your people," Boorstin said as his hand went up and down in Kellem's. "How are you doing, sir?"

"*Kinahura.*"

Kellem was a short, round man with a reasonably decent hairpiece on the top of his head.

"It's quite an operation you've got here, sir," Boorstin said. "I'm impressed."

Kellem looked around, pursing his lips and nodding with approval, a benign and not especially bright Santa showing off his elves to a visiting dignitary. "It's young people, Philip. They keep you young," he said. "You want to see L.D., right? I'll take you back there."

He took Boorstin's elbow and led him down a short corridor, where he knocked on an office door and opened it without waiting for a response.

L. D. Woods was standing behind her desk facing the window, the telephone at her ear. She turned as the door opened and held up a finger. At the Board meeting she had been seated at the opposite side of the table the whole time, but the parts he hadn't seen then were every bit as good as what he had. She was still wearing the jeans she'd slipped on to go rescue Mrs. James. Philip noticed they followed her hips like skin.

He waited with the congressman at the door until she hung up the telephone and came around from behind her desk.

"You know Philip Boorstin, L.D.," Kellem said.

"We've met," she said, offering her hand.

Her grip was unsurprisingly firm. Her eyes locked on Boorstin's as if she were prepared to test which one of them would look away first.

"Miss Woods," he said.

"I'll leave you two alone," the congressman said. "Be nice to him, L.D. He came all the way up from City Hall."

When the door closed Boorstin said, "I think that was supposed to be a joke."

"Not really," she said. "What did you want to talk to me about, Mr. Boorstin?"

The Square One game. As though she didn't know. He wasn't about to play it.

"Basically I'm a messenger here," he said. "So are you. The message is that this is a big city. People reach understandings and then they live by them. It's the only way it will work."

She motioned for him to sit and sat facing him, crossing her legs. "Did we have an understanding?" she asked.

"I did," he said. "It's in everyone's interest to make this thing at La Guardia go away."

"How is that in Mrs. James's interest?"

The answer was that Mrs. James wasn't a player. If you started from the fact that it was a big city, you quickly came to the conclusion that Victoria James's interests didn't count, or at least they didn't count for much. But he couldn't say that. "What is her interest?" he said instead.

"She made that clear yesterday. She wants to know what happened to her daughter."

"A psycho kid snapped her neck. What's the next question?"

"That's the only question, Mr. Boorstin. And that's only part of the answer. Is there some reason the mayor doesn't want the rest of it answered?"

He got to his feet and walked away from her, turning his back. He ran his fingers along the edge of a bookshelf, almost as though it were his office, then turned and said, "I didn't come here to negotiate, Miss Woods."

She didn't mind sitting when the man she was talking to stood. Most people do, and as a result someone like Boorstin enjoyed moving them around a room the way a good fighter moves his opponent around the ring. L. D. Woods simply stretched out her legs and leaned back in her chair. "Then why did you come?"

"Because I spent two hours with Artemis Reach Friday afternoon and we came to an understanding."

"What has that got to do with Victoria James?"

"What do you say we drop the bullshit and talk about this thing in a sensible way?"

"Whichever you're more comfortable with, Mr. Boorstin."

It was a damn good line and he gave her credit for it with a nod, smiling in spite of himself.

"That's very cute," he said. "But the bottom line is my boss doesn't like your boss going back on his word."

"Unless you mean Congressman Kellem, I don't have a boss, Mr. Boorstin."

"I mean Artemis Reach."

"I'm a member of the Board. He's Chairman. I don't work for him."

She was on her feet now.

"I know you're fronting for him on this, so I came to see you," he said. "Am I wasting my time?"

"I don't know what your time's worth, Mr. Boorstin. I think I'm wasting mine. I'm not fronting for anyone."

She walked toward the door and held it open, inviting him to leave. He closed it when he got there, shoving it out of her hand, and they faced each other, eye to eye.

"Let's not make any mistakes," he said. "You tell Mr. Reach if he goes back on his word on this, he's going to find himself boxed up in a very small part of the city."

"Mr. Reach has nothing to do with this," she said. "If you don't want to believe that now, you'll find out soon enough. Victoria James is not going away until someone tells her why her daughter died. Let's not make any mistakes about that, Mr. Boorstin."

When she opened the door this time, Boorstin left. They would tell him downtown that he was being naive, but he believed the lady. L.D. wasn't fronting for Reach, she was in this for herself, and that changed the equations all around. He didn't know yet how it changed them, but it wouldn't take him long to figure it out.

In the end it would come down to a choice between helping her out or burying her. Boorstin leaned toward helping. A responsible government had obligations to all of its citizens.

ON THE other side of the office door, L. D. Woods leaned back against the wall and let out a long, slow breath. Her hands were trembling and she tapped out a quick tattoo on the wall by her side to make something purposeful out of something she couldn't control. The meeting had been more of an ordeal than she expected, even though she'd handled tricky negotiations before, sometimes with heavier hitters than the arrogant deputy mayor.

She knew she could be as tough as any of them when the knives came out. But until today she had always worked with a set of clear instructions, carrying out someone else's agenda. Once she had faced down a construction union that threatened to stop work on an office building Bert Kellem had invested two years of arm-twisting to get for his district. On dozens of occasions she had gone head-to-head with black and Puerto Rican community groups because the congressman liked to put her out front with minorities, and she had taken on some of the most powerful Jewish Democrats in the Bronx because Kellem couldn't afford the risk of grappling with them himself. She always got what she wanted and never gave away more than the congressman was willing to give.

This was different. There was no one in back of her, no one to decide what losses were acceptable, what compromises were viable, where to draw the lines. Besides, she was on a collision course with Artemis Reach, which was like a yacht sailing into a freighter. Boorstin was only a warm-up.

On the whole, she told herself, it was a good experience. She hadn't flinched, and if she gave the impression of being an intractable woman, so much the better. She and Boorstin knew each other a little better, liked each other a little less and would be ready for the next round.

Just putting it in those terms calmed her down and focused her thinking. By the time she stepped away from the wall and let out a long breath to get the last of her nervousness out of her system, she was already considering her next move. She figured Boorstin would need a little time to put his ducks in order now that he knew he was dealing with L. D. Woods rather Artemis Reach. Twenty-four hours, she decided, was more than enough. After that Victoria James would be in front of the cameras again.

She reached for the phone and dialed the WNBC reporter who had been trying to reach her since yesterday. He wanted an interview and she countered by offering to let Mrs. James appear on the studio segment of the five o'clock news, where she would be questioned by the anchor-woman. The reporter called back in twenty minutes with his news director's approval and L.D. agreed to meet him for dinner to discuss what Mrs. James would be prepared to say.

She spent the rest of the afternoon working with Bert Kellem's staff of eager interns on a proposal for a program to give elderly people jobs in day-care centers. That was the congressman's specialty, the kind of something-for-everybody legislation that cost next to nothing and generated mountains of positive publicity. She had her work cut out for her there—drafting letters soliciting statements of support and news releases detailing the support as it came in.

As the afternoon wore on the staff began to dwindle. By five-thirty L.D. was alone in the office. She worked until she was able to reach Victoria James at six to tell her about the interview scheduled for the next day.

"Just me?" Victoria asked.

"She's a very good interviewer. She's not intimidating. And I'll go over all the questions with you tomorrow afternoon."

"Couldn't you be there?"

"I'll be right there. I'll only be a few feet away," L.D. reassured her.

But Victoria wanted her included in the interview so she could answer any of the questions if she had to.

"I'm meeting them tonight," L.D. told her. "If that's the way you want it, then that's the way it will have to be."

She called for a cab, left a message for Tal canceling their dinner plans but asking him to keep the rest of the night free. Then she locked up the office and hurried downstairs, figuring she just had time to get home and change before meeting the man from Channel Four. The street, which consisted mostly of old office buildings, emptied out quickly at five o'clock and by six was always deserted. She looked around for her taxi, which the dispatcher had promised in five minutes.

"Miss Woods."

A broad-chested black boy no more than fifteen or sixteen years old but well over six feet tall was standing right at her elbow. She hadn't even heard him come up.

"Yes?"

"Mr. Reach wants to talk with you," he said. "C'mon."

His took her arm but she pulled free, jolted by a sudden stab of alarm.

"I've got a dinner appointment. Tell him I'll get in touch with him tomorrow," she said, trying to convince herself that this was a normal conversation, that the boy's unexpected familiarity had been no more than that.

"Can't do that," he said, and though she tried to step away from him, his hand caught her arm in a grip that this time left no room for ambiguity.

"What the hell are you doing? Let go of me!" she shouted, trying to wrench free.

He shoved her toward a battered old Buick idling driver-side to the curb only a few feet away. "Don't give me no trouble," he said. "Get in the car."

"Let go of me!" she screamed, her eyes darting around for help. A couple halfway down the block walked on as though they hadn't heard.

She kicked at his shins and tried to pull away from him, but his hand clamped on her wrist like a powerful trap. With his free hand he yanked open the door. "C'mon," he growled, pushing her down into the car. "Slide over."

She was almost lying behind the wheel and righted herself, looking up to see him looming over her in the open door frame. As she started to slide across the torn upholstery, she grabbed for the shift lever and threw it in gear, stamping her foot on the gas.

The car lurched but didn't move. The engine stalled out with a shudder.

He reached in and shoved her hard enough to knock her sideways on the seat. Then he slid in behind the wheel, apparently indifferent to her attempted escape. "Brake was on," he noted laconically, releasing it and restarting the engine. "Stay cool. He just wants to talk."

There was nothing for L.D. to do but hope he was telling the truth, her emotions buffeting back and forth between fear and rage. Within a few minutes they were driving on unfamiliar streets, for she knew little about the Bronx beyond the boundaries of Congressman Kellem's district. Everything around her looked unutterably desolate, dashing her hopes, but on the other hand there was something almost reassuring in the cool ease with which the boy drove, holding the wheel loosely with his left hand, a white-gold bracelet dangling from his wrist, his right hand resting on the seat between them. He didn't say a word but glanced at her from time to time without turning his head.

They drove along a street that followed the perimeter of a large park. When he turned into the park her heart began pounding so loudly she was sure he could hear it. He drove down a narrow lane that was almost instantly swallowed up in thick trees. The thought of leaping from the car flashed through L.D.'s mind but she realized the futility of it almost at once. Even if she weren't hurt in the fall, he would catch her easily. Already the city streets seemed a long way behind her.

The car slowed and then stopped. "He's up there," the boy said, gesturing toward the windshield. "Go ahead."

She hadn't noticed the other car in the darkness, but now she recognized Artemis Reach's Lincoln, parked about twenty yards ahead of where they were stopped.

She reached for the door handle, looking over to the boy to make sure she understood what he wanted her to do. He offered no objection so she let herself out.

The top floors of a few tall apartment buildings were just barely visible over the tops of the trees. She couldn't find a sign of the city anywhere else she looked.

She walked toward the Lincoln and was able to make out Artemis Reach's silhouette in the front seat when she was a few feet away. Going around to the passenger side, she opened the door and slid onto the seat.

"Close the door."

His deep voice reverberated like a drumroll in the narrow space. She pulled the door closed.

His right hand flashed toward her with a stabbing motion. She flinched as the side of his fist hit against her chest, and she realized there was a sheet of paper in his hand.

"Read it," he said.

She took the paper and his hand went away. He reached for a switch on the dash and the overhead light came on, small and feeble, barely enough to read by.

With her hands trembling, her mind so confused she couldn't even begin to sort out what possible message she would see on the page, she unfolded the crumpled sheet and read it. It took a moment for her eyes to pick out the letters that lay across the page like shadows. When they did, she realized that she was reading her letter of resignation from Community Board Sixty-one.

"Sign it," he said when she stopped reading.

He handed her a ballpoint pen, clicking it into position.

She signed obediently and handed him the paper and pen. For some reason she wasn't afraid anymore.

He took them in silence and then turned the light off. "You had it all, bitch," he said. "What the fuck were you thinking?"

"I was thinking that someone ought to look into what happened," she said, finding strength in the firmness of her own voice.

He swung around to face her, his eyes flashing anger in the darkness, a long black finger jabbing at her face. "Then you come to me with those thoughts," he shouted shrilly. "Who the fuck do you think you are?"

"You were too busy making deals, Artemis."

He smiled bitterly. "You talked to Boorstin already? Is that right?"

"He said you and he had an understanding."

"Listen to me," he said softly. "I'm only saying this once. There's no investigation going to happen in my place unless I want it to."

"Then why don't you want it to? Are you afraid of something, Artemis?"

"I don't give a shit about your investigation," he said. "You want a special prosecutor, you want the fucking attorney general, then you come to me and I get them. You didn't do that. Now Artemis Reach doesn't hop on the bandwagon of some cunt he put on the Board in the first place."

"Well this cunt isn't on your Board anymore, Mr. Reach. You've got my letter of resignation."

She reached for the door.

"Charlie'll drive you back," he said.

"I'll walk."

"Think about this while you're walking, Woods," he said. "You got the looks and you got the job. You had the position on the Board and me on your side. Two of them are gone and I can fix it very easy that you'll be out of work and ugly. Don't fuck with me."

* * *

THE big car leaned through a series of turns, its siren screaming traffic out of the way, its cherry light spinning red flashes onto the black windows of glowering tenements. It lurched to a stop at the mouth of an alley. Two radio cars, angled in to form a V, barred the entrance to the alley.

Chief of Detectives Terranova pulled himself from the backseat of the car and settled his feet on the pavement. Hartley Williams was by his side before he could ask for him.

"This way, Chief," he said.

A rusted steel trash can between the corner of the building and the radio-car bumper narrowed the passage to only a foot or so. Williams reached down to roll it out of the way but the Chief waved him back impatiently and maneuvered his large body through the small space.

About a dozen uniformed police stood around in the alley with little to do other than keep clear of the detectives and forensics technicians already at work. Emergency Services had set up powerful lights bright enough to film a movie. From where Terranova stood, the far end of the alley disappeared in a blinding glare.

Detectives crouching to examine the ground and search for evidence stood as he passed, touching their foreheads as though to tip back non-existent hats, the last vestiges of an instinct to salute. *Chief*, they muttered, *How you doing, Chief?*

He acknowledged them with papal nods as he bore in on the pool of light. The alley, he could see now, ended in a brick wall just beyond the point where most of the men were gathered. Flashbulbs sparkled like fireflies as a police photographer recorded the scene.

As he approached the cloth-covered corpse that was the focal point of all the activity, the crowd of men around it parted as if on command. Terranova crouched like a catcher over the body, letting out an involuntary grunt as he lowered himself onto his haunches. He picked up a corner of the cloth and folded it back. The face of a teenage black boy looked up at him.

Williams crouched next to the Chief. "His name's Lloyd Elijah," he said. "Goes to La Guardia Junior High. I figured you'd want to see this yourself."

THURSDAY

T ERRANOVA sent Hartley Williams and Carl Green out on the street to track down Lloyd Elijah's known associates. He brought the rest of his squad with him when he walked into the principal's office at La Guardia Junior High the next morning, prepared to question every kid in the school if he had to. It took less than fifteen minutes with Lewis Hinden for him to realize that the principal knew very little about the students. "Who does?" he asked.

Amelia Armstrong, the assistant principal, was brought into the meeting. A stout black woman with gray hair and a tendency to lower her head in order to look over her glasses, she gave the impression of shrinking from any form of conversational contact. She had been at La Guardia Junior High for over a decade and seemed to find the school a mysterious environment that had been thoroughly mapped with statistics and reports but had never actually been explored. Despite her minimal contact with the natives, she was able to help Terranova and the army of detectives he brought with him put together a short list of Lloyd Elijah's friends, based largely on school records.

Terranova doubted that her list had much to do with the way the dead boy actually led his life. It didn't matter. It was a place to start, and all starting places were pretty much the same. Detective work was a matter of moving from one thing to the next, like feeling one's way out of a maze. In the end there was only one exit and sooner or later Terranova knew he would find it. "I'll need four offices," he said. "Unless you've got empty classrooms."

Hinden and Mrs. Armstrong huddled together for almost twenty minutes, apparently negotiating the space that could be made available. In the end they offered him an unused language lab on the second floor, an office in the main administrative suite shared by half a dozen paraprofessionals who could be sent home for the day, the guidance counselor's office and Mrs. Armstrong's office. She couldn't have looked more uncomfortable with the solution if she had been ordered to bivouac troops in her bedroom.

"And some kind of holding area," Terranova said, not even bothering to express his gratitude for her sacrifice. "I'll need somewhere to keep these kids after they're questioned."

"Holding area?" Hinden gasped, an image flashing through his mind of freedom marchers penned in makeshift compounds. "I want these children returned to their classrooms the moment you're finished with them."

"That's out of the question," Terranova answered bluntly.

Hinden stood stiffly in front of him. "I can't countenance that kind of disruption," he announced in a tone that suggested his unlimited confidence in the efficacy of polysyllables for overwhelming opposition.

Terranova snorted as he habitually did when he couldn't be bothered answering questions. Disrupting the educational process in a school that was producing more homicides than rocket scientists wasn't high on his list of concerns. What Lewis Hinden, in his three-piece suit, could or could not countenance was even lower. The fact of the matter was that he hadn't yet permitted the release of the dead boy's name, and he wasn't about to let the kids go back upstairs after they were questioned and tell everyone else what this was all about.

"We can take them all to the precinct if that's the way you want it," he said.

Hinden instructed Mrs. Armstrong to send out a memo canceling any activities scheduled for the small auditorium on the second floor, and then took the Chief on a tour of the facilities that would be made available to him while a secretary checked the list of students' names against the schedule cards in their files, adding the room numbers where they would be found. On his way out of Mrs. Armstrong's office, Terranova asked whether any of the students on the list were in Steven Hillyer's English class.

Hinden passed the list to Mrs. Armstrong, who scanned it, ran through a set of mental calculations and handed it back with the information that Moore, Brown and Means were all Hillyer's students.

"Start there," Terranova said, passing the list to a black detective named Doug Phelan.

"Where do we find this guy's class?" Phelan asked.

"Mr. Hillyer? He's on four, isn't he?"

"Four-oh-eight," Mrs. Armstrong replied.

A boy walking toward them suddenly reversed direction and hurried away. "Who was that?" Terranova asked. He thought it was the kid who had taken him upstairs to see the gym teacher last week.

Hinden didn't know.

"Oh, he's just distributing the memo about the auditorium," Mrs. Armstrong explained. "He has a learning disability."

If there was a connection between these two facts, Terranova didn't get it. Nor did he care. "Jamal something," he said. "Is his name on the list?"

"No."

"Put it on."

JAMAL caught his breath in the stairway and tried to think what he had to do. It wasn't getting any better, it was getting worse. Cops in the school now, and they were coming upstairs. The fat one was the guy he had taken upstairs to talk to Mr. Lucasian last week, and now there were a lot more.

He was confused, and he had trouble keeping his mind from racing when he got like that. Thoughts spun in his brain, jumbling together like two stations on the radio, as he tried to think why they were there, if he should warn Mr. Hillyer and if they were going to arrest his English teacher. No way. They're after kids, which he could tell just from the way they walked and talked and moved, like they got a kick out of it. And not the dealers like Charlie Wain either, because his type walked through all the shit like they were invisible, messing everybody up, and nothing ever touched them.

Jamal thought about Mr. Hillyer meeting Charlie Wain on Tremont Avenue and felt sick. Three kids had told him it happened, everybody at school knew. And some kids say there's teachers in back of it all, got to be, just like there's cops and politicians and people like that who are protected, because face it Charlie Wain can't add two sixes and get a twelve so he can't be putting all this together. There's got to be someone else. And here he almost let Mr. Hillyer talk him into getting tutored a couple of times, almost thought of asking him to do it, thinking all along *Mr. Hillyer he's tight with Timothy Warren* but then it turns out it's Charlie Wain he's meeting on Tremont Avenue.

Tears glistened in Jamal's eyes and he wiped at them with the back of his hand and wiped at his nose and then walked out into the corridor.

He wasn't going to tell anyone anything, wasn't going to warn anyone. He just went into his English class, looking down at his knees as he slid into his seat.

Maria Onofrio was standing up like a totem pole next to her desk, talking about something. Jamal could see her shoes and her socks in the aisle. And Mr. Hillyer was saying something but Jamal kept thinking he had to jump up and warn them that the cops were coming, only he couldn't do it. And then he heard Leon Wilkie say something that made everybody laugh and he tried to laugh too, like he was in on whatever they were talking about. But he knew there were cops coming up the stairs right now and he could have said something, only he didn't.

Then it was too late because the door swung wide and the laughter suddenly hung suspended in the air and everyone turned around to look. Except Jamal, because he was looking at Mr. Hillyer.

Two detectives, both black, moved into the classroom on the back end of a wave of silence that seemed to flow out from them like a form of radiation. The detectives wore gray suits, and their badges weren't on display, but no one could have mistaken them for anything other than cops.

Maria sank into her seat as though she had been ordered to. Aurelio Mannero and Bobby Ward, leaning across the aisle to slap each other's hands, froze in the middle of the gesture, then drifted away from each other by a kind of inertial pull. To Steven it seemed the only movement in the room was Jamal Horton's eyes, which darted from the cops to him and then back.

"Yes," Steven asked. "Can I help you?"

"I'm Detective Phelan, this is Detective Young," one of the men announced, a sturdy, authoritative man with close-cropped hair and a thick mustache. He drew a leather case from his pocket and flipped it open to show his badge, but there was a kind of truncated awkwardness to the gesture, as though he wasn't sure whether he was expected to show it to the whole class. "This is an English class? Hillyer, is that right?"

"Eighth-grade English. Yes."

Behind Phelan, his partner took out a folded sheet of paper, flipping it open with one hand. He was younger, not too many years out of school himself.

Phelan said, "We have reason to believe that some of these students have information relevant to a homicide investigation. We'd appreciate your cooperation. If your name is called, identify yourself and come with us."

"Byron Moore," Detective Young read from his list.

"Bullshit," Byron Moore shouted from his seat, getting to his feet and squaring his shoulders at them. "I ain't going nowhere." He was one of the older boys in the class, a muscular fifteen-year-old with a major reputation.

"Are you Byron Moore?" Phelan challenged.

Steven rushed from the front of the room, moving between desks until he stood next to Moore. "If you want these children to leave their classroom," he said, "they're at least entitled to an explanation."

"I told you what it's about. A homicide investigation. If your name is called, come downstairs with us," Phelan answered levelly.

"That's not an explanation."

The students followed the exchange with awed fascination. Standing up to a cop earned instant respect.

Phelan took a moment to consider what needed saying. There were a lot of kids to be questioned and once he started explaining, there would be no end to it. The order by itself was enough.

"Byron Moore," he repeated.

"I don't know nothing about no homicide," Moore said, pulling back from the hand Steven reached out.

"No one's accusing you of anything, Byron," Steven said. "They just want to ask you some questions."

He could sense the disappointment all around him. He had challenged the cops with a question but the minute they dropped an answer on him he backed down. At least that was the way it looked to the kids, and he didn't know any way to make it look different.

"We're just going downstairs, Mr. Moore," Phelan said.

Young said, "Step this way, please."

The boy looked around like a cornered animal. There was nowhere to go and everyone's eyes were on him, creating, whether it made sense or not, a kind of obligation he didn't know how to walk away from. He took a step backward and the cops moved too.

"Byron, think," Steven said, but it was already too late. The cops were moving in concert, Phelan, the one who did the talking, coming straight at him, the other one circling around to get at him from the side, the difference between his meaningless, reflexive action and their coordinated response settling the end of the confrontation as clearly as if it were a film they had all already seen.

"Fuck it, Byron, just go with them," one of the kids called, and others echoed him, trying to forestall the same certainty.

The boy was creeping steadily backward now, trying to keep both cops in sight.

"They just want you to go downstairs, Byron. I'll go with you if you want," Steven said, but the boy continued to back away from him.

All around him children began to scatter, sliding from their desks in front of Phelan and in front of Young, moving toward the edges of the room.

Phelan held his left hand out, in a kind of stop signal, moving steadily toward the boy with almost hypnotic deliberation. "We don't want trouble, son," he said. "Just come downstairs, we'll ask you some questions."

The left hand flashed out to catch the boy's hand, and as Byron flailed at it to knock it away, the second detective was suddenly on top of him. That fraction of a second of distraction was all it took for Young to spin the boy around and twist his arm behind his back with a wrenching force that quieted him instantly.

"You're not gonna give us any trouble are you, son?" Phelan asked.

Byron said nothing, his head lolling in almost a caricature of defeat.

"Why don't you go wait for us over there," Phelan suggested, releasing his grip on the boy and indicating a spot at the side of the room. Byron trudged off obediently.

Steven looked at him from the middle of the room, numbed for a moment by the awful virtuosity of the way they had managed to subdue Byron, not unaware of the restraint that prevented the confrontation from getting uglier.

The second detective had the sheet of paper in his hand again. "Lester Brown," he said.

Lester was at the side of the room where most of the kids had gathered. "Yeah, awright," he said, stepping forward.

"Jeremiah Means."

Jeremiah stepped forward and stood beside Lester.

"Jamal Horton."

"Present," Jamal called out in his piping voice, going for the laugh and getting it.

CHIEF Terranova waited in Mrs. Armstrong's office until the first group of students was brought down. He looked them over, directed his detectives to question them in the various rooms he had commandeered, and remained in the assistant principal's office with Phelan and Young to conduct the interrogation of Byron Moore himself.

"Have a seat, son," he said after Young closed the door. "We'd appreciate all the help you can give us. What's your name?"

"Byron Moore." He let his hands hang limply by his side but remained standing. A tough guy.

"We don't want to make any problems for you, Byron. We just want to talk," Terranova said. "I asked you to sit down."

"I don't have nothing to talk about."

"Maybe not," Terranova agreed, pacing around behind the boy. He rested his heavy hands on the back of a square metal-frame chair with a vinyl seat. "On the other hand you haven't heard our questions yet."

The chair came up an inch off the floor and flew forward, slamming into the back of the boy's legs with enough force to knock him into it. Terranova was standing over him before he'd even had a chance to realize he was sitting, the Chief's round, moonlike face hovering just before his eyes. "We'd like to know a little bit about Lloyd Elijah," he said.

The pain in his legs brought tears to the corners of Byron's eyes, bright spots that he blinked away defiantly. "What about him?" he asked.

Terranova questioned Byron for about five minutes, learning little, and then left him to Phelan and Young while he wandered into the next office to see how the detectives in there were doing with Jeremiah Means. He listened to the questioning without speaking, letting the presence of an unidentified stranger work as it always did in interrogations, distracting the subject and lowering his defenses. Not that it mattered. There was no defiance in this boy anyway, a scrawny, fidgety kid with a glittering line of sweat beading on his upper lip. He quickly gave them the names of half a dozen kids who knew Lloyd Elijah better than he did.

Lester Brown, who was being questioned in the guidance counselor's office, slumped low in his seat, insisting over and over that he hardly knew Lloyd Elijah at all.

"Then how come your name's on our list, Lester?" one of the detectives asked.

"I don't know."

"No reason, Lester? It just popped up on the list?"

"I got busted with him I guess."

"You *guess* you got busted with him?"

Lester dug his chin lower into his collarbone and didn't answer the question. They knew what he meant.

"What were you busted for, Lester?"

"Nothing . . . some kind of bullshit thing," the boy muttered.

"It had to do with drugs, didn't it?" the detective guessed.

Since Elijah didn't have a record, whatever he and Lester had been busted for together probably wouldn't show up under Lester's name either.

"Possession," the boy answered, his voice lowering almost to a whisper. "Misdemeanor possession. They said I wouldn't have a record, fucking liars."

"Nobody lied to you, Lester."

"How come you knew about it?"

"Because you just told me."

The boy looked sick. He asked if he could go to the bathroom and one of the detectives went with him. "When he gets back, ask him about Timothy Warren," Terranova suggested, and then moved on to check in on the little messenger with the learning disability being questioned upstairs in the language lab, which turned out to be a roomful of cubbyholes with earphones coming out of them. Terranova poked around at the equipment, trying to get the hang of it, while Jamal Horton met every question with a question of his own.

"Lloyd's got a drug problem, doesn't he?"

"You got him dealing, is that what it is?" Jamal asked.

"Nobody said dealing. Drug problem, that was the question, Jamal."

The interrogation was being conducted by Bert Elton, a short man in wire-rimmed glasses. He was Terranova's least intimidating detective.

"I kind of thought he had himself straightened out," Jamal said. "Have you guys got him locked up somewhere?"

"Why don't you let me ask the questions?"

"How can I answer them if I don't know what we're talking about?"

"Was he dealing?"

"Is that what somebody told you?"

"Yes or no?"

Jamal rolled his eyes and seemed to be running out of patience.

"I'm trying to tell you," he said. "He was out of that stuff. If he's back in, he's back in. Depends on what you hear, doesn't it?"

"I want to hear it from you."

"He might have got back into it, yeah."

"Who did he run with, Jamal?"

"He's dead, isn't he?"

He didn't know why he asked this, but he knew all of a sudden that Lloyd Elijah was dead, and it was his death they were investigating. It didn't matter whether they said yes or no or didn't answer him at all. They were here because Lloyd Elijah was dead.

"Just answer the question," the cop said.

But Jamal was lost somewhere in his own thoughts and actually held up a hand to keep the detective quiet while he tried to work this new information into the pattern of everything else he knew.

"Shit," he said at last, "he had himself straightened out, too, y'know that. Had himself straightened out and now he's dead."

Jamal was talking to himself. He didn't care whether they believed him about Lloyd or not. His voice seemed to come from very far away, and Terranova stepped forward to slip into the seat next to him.

"We didn't know that, Jamal," he said softly. "Tell us about it. How'd he get himself straightened out?"

The boy looked up at him but said nothing.

"You were his friend, weren't you?" Terranova asked.

"I'm everybody's friend."

It wasn't a boast. His voice was hollow with resignation.

"Were you Timothy Warren's friend, too, Jamal?"

Jamal's head bobbed slowly.

"And so was Lloyd, wasn't he?"

The boy's head hung to the side and his eyes were fixed on an empty part of the room.

Terranova waited a long time and then he put his hand on Jamal's knee and said, "We'll want to talk to you again, son. You can help us, you know that. Take your time."

The Chief lifted himself from the chair and shambled to the door. Elton went with him, looking for instructions.

"Stay with him," Terranova said. "Don't push, give him all the time he wants."

He left the room and went back to the assistant principal's office, where Phelan and Young were questioning a tall, truculent boy in a black turtleneck.

The moment the Chief opened the door, Phelan broke away from the interrogation and hurried across the room to meet him. They stepped out into the anteroom, closing the door behind them.

"Anything?" Terranova asked.

"Elijah wasn't in school yesterday," Phelan said. "And he cut out early the day before. His last class was metal shop and he left half an hour before it ended."

"Any reason?"

"Don't know. But how's this for interesting? Steven Hillyer went over to the shop looking for him."

Terranova blew out a stream of air in lieu of saying anything and paced away from the detective. Hillyer's name kept coming up in all the wrong places.

"You want to talk to him, Chief?" Phelan asked.

"Yeah."

Phelan had already started out when Terranova stopped him. It was still too soon to talk to Hillyer, he thought to himself. More pieces of the puzzle might fall in place if he waited. Hillyer wasn't going anywhere. "No," he said out loud, "let's stick to the kids for now."

Phelan shrugged, remembering the way Hillyer stood up to him in front of his class. He wouldn't have minded going back up to that room again to take Hillyer out of it.

"But the minute classes are over," Terranova added, "I want Hillyer's ass in this office."

As the day wore on, the initial anger at the appearance of detectives in the school and in the classrooms began to give way to sullen resentment and then numbed resignation. The scenario of the first raids, with cops marching into classrooms bearing the names of the children to be taken away, was repeated over and over in classroom after classroom until a dull and heavy dread overwhelmed the whole school. The sheer predictability of it somehow added to the despair, and even kids who boasted they were afraid of nothing began to be afraid.

In the hall between classes Steven compared observations with Rita and Hal Garson, and they each told the same story of fighting for the children's attention, struggling to keep the kids' eyes as well as their own off the doors. Above all, the growing awareness that the students who had been taken away didn't come back preyed on all their minds and turned the police operation into an incomprehensible horror.

"My God, we're whispering," Garson said at one point, and for a moment they all fell silent as though listening to hear if this was true. Around them the children moved from class to class so silently that even their footsteps seemed muffled. When Dennis Dougherty joined them to suggest a betting pool on when the classes would be completely empty, no one could quite manage those tolerant smiles with which they usually greeted his mordant observations.

Late in the afternoon, with no one able to say where they had heard it or where it began, word that Lloyd Elijah was dead began to spread through the school like fire in dry wood. By one account he was killed in a shoot-out with the police. Others reported that he was found dead in an alley, others that he died by his own hand. Steven didn't hear the rumor until just before the last period of the day, when Maria Onofrio walked up to him while he was talking with Rita and Garson. She stood slightly away from them in that posture of indefatigable patience that made it so easy to overlook her. When she noticed the girl, Rita said,

"Did you want to talk to us, Maria?" Only then did Steven realize she was there.

Maria took a timid half step forward. "I was wondering if Mr. Hillyer knew if it was true about Lloyd," she said, addressing herself to Rita because it was Rita who had asked the question.

"If what's true about Lloyd?" Steven asked.

"They're saying he was killed," she said, looking down at her own shoes.

Rita crossed herself and Garson muttered a curse under his breath. Steven's mind leaped back to the last time he had seen Lloyd, in the staircase at lunch on Tuesday. He wasn't in metal-shop class when Steven went looking for him, and Detective Franks looked for him all day Wednesday and never called back.

"Who's saying that?" Steven forced himself to ask, more to keep his thoughts from running away from him than because her answer mattered at all.

Until that moment Steven had assumed Franks hadn't called because he hadn't found Lloyd. But suddenly there were other possibilities. What, after all, did he know about Jim Franks? Nothing, nothing at all.

Except that he killed Timothy Warren. And then went looking for Lloyd Elijah because his name was in Timothy's poetry. The thought made him shudder.

He looked over to Rita and thought he could see in her eyes that she was thinking the same thing. She seemed to be holding her breath.

Maria said, "I don't know. A lot of the kids are saying it."

"These rumors start and they just keep going," Steven said, conscious that he was meeting her apprehension with nothing but a platitude. At the moment he didn't have more to offer. The bell rang, punctuating his confusion, and he heard Rita say something to Maria in Spanish.

"I'm going downstairs to see what I can find out," Steven said. "Can one of you cover my class?"

"I've got a study hall," Garson volunteered.

Steven muttered something about being back as soon as he could and ran to the stairs, racing down with his hand on the banister like a kid, holding himself in at the turns at each landing. He was out of breath and his head was spinning when he lurched out of the stairwell on the ground floor with the strangely dreamlike sensation of rushing through a door in one place and coming out somewhere else entirely. He seemed to be in a place he didn't know, even though everything around him was disconcertingly familiar. The strangers in dark suits moving back and forth between the offices with grimly official expressions on their otherwise expressionless faces had somehow transformed the space in their own image, making it theirs.

With the deliberate and measured stride of a man trying to appear inconspicuous, Steven marched to the assistant principal's office, thinking it was too bad the police had taken Jamal. He could have used him now, because Jamal always seemed to know what was going on at the school before anyone else. Did the police, he wondered, know this about Jamal? Was that why he was taken?

"Hold it. You can't go in there," a deep voice announced as he raised his hand to knock on Mrs. Armstrong's door.

A uniformed cop had materialized out of nowhere. A detective passing from one office to the next glanced over but kept going, satisfied that the thick-chested young patrolman had the situation under control.

"I'm a teacher here," Steven said.

The cop simply shook his head, conveying the message that such considerations didn't matter in the least. He said nothing.

"I have to see the assistant principal," Steven objected.

"I told you, no one's allowed in," the cop said, nettled at having his ruling questioned. "Anyway, he's not there."

"She," Steven corrected. "Do you know where she is?"

"All I know is I'm not supposed to let no one in."

His face settled into a look of impassivity that announced as clearly as a set of printed instructions that it would be pointless to discuss it with him further.

Steven turned away and walked to the next office. He reached for the doorknob and glanced back at the cop, who watched him indifferently, making no move to stop him. Apparently there were still parts of the school not under occupation.

The office belonged to an administrative assistant, but when Steven stepped in he found Mr. Hinden and Mrs. Armstrong there, a pair of deposed sovereigns waiting out their time in this administrative limbo. Mrs. Armstrong was sitting next to the desk reading a brochure. Hinden appeared to be pacing the floor but stopped and turned when the door opened. "Yes?" he asked in a decidedly petulant tone.

"The children are very upset and there are a lot of rumors going around," Steven said. "If there was anything we could tell them . . ."

"If there was anything we could tell them, don't you think we would have?" Hinden shot back.

"I wasn't implying a criticism, sir."

"Of course not. There's nothing to criticize. I can't even get in my own damn office."

"Yes, sir. The latest rumor is that Lloyd Elijah is dead."

If he couldn't get any information, at least he could get a response. Steven was hoping Hinden knew what was going on even if he wasn't permitted to say.

"Well I wouldn't take any part in rumors if I were you, Hillyer," the principal snapped.

"Is it true?"

"You already have my answer."

"I don't have anything," Steven said. "I've got twenty-five kids every hour who are getting more and more scared."

But in fact Steven did have his answer. Lloyd was dead.

"I can't help you," Hinden said.

Mrs. Armstrong said, "Don't you have a class now, Mr. Hillyer." It wasn't a question.

Steven hurried out of the office. The cop in the hallway wasn't in evidence but Steven was sure he was still around. It didn't matter. Ahead of him, just disappearing through the door to one of the other offices, he thought he saw the broad back of the detective who had questioned him at the Chief of Detectives' office on Saturday. He felt in a strange way like a spy who had infiltrated behind enemy lines. He walked quickly back to the stairs, taking them two at a time up to the fourth floor.

Hal Garson was pacing along the front of Steven's classroom, talking about social conditions in America between the end of the First World War and the Depression. He interrupted himself when Steven beckoned with a gesture, appointing one of the kids to supervise the discussion while he was gone. He met Steven in the hallway, pulling the door closed behind him.

"What did you find out?"

"I think it's true about Lloyd," Steven said. "But don't repeat that because I don't know. How are you doing in there?"

"They tried to tell me what you've been doing but I couldn't follow it. So I turned it into a history class."

Steven knew he was expected to say something grateful and friendly, but his mind wasn't working that way. "Do you mind taking the rest of the period?" he asked.

"Where are you going?"

"I'm not sure," Steven said. "Please, just do it for me, Hal."

Garson glanced at the door behind him. The high, shrill voices of the children, not out of control yet but working toward it, filtered through like light through frosted glass. "Sure," he said. "Anything you want me to tell them?"

"I don't *know* anything."

"I meant homework."

Steven's mind was so charged with all that was happening that it was difficult to remember that the normal routines of life still had to go on. He was grateful to Garson for having a grasp of that. "Tell them to read another chapter," he said. "And thanks."

"Hey," Garson said, shrugging it off. He opened the door and disappeared into the burst of hotly contesting voices that momentarily spilled out from the classroom.

Steven didn't even wait for the door to close. He paced back up the corridor to Rita's room and let himself in. A tall girl standing in the middle of the room paused in her recitation.

"Don't stop, Daphne. You're doing fine," Rita said, already moving to the door. The girl's voice resumed, something about Bigger Thomas and what his experience meant to young blacks in the Bronx today, her words hesitant and uncertain now as she searched her notes for where she had been before the interruption.

"I'll just be a minute, Daphne," Rita said from the door. "Look over your notes. And the rest of you better be ready to be called on next."

In the hall she said, "It's true, isn't it?"

"I think so."

Her hand took his wrist. "Steven, I'm scared," she said.

Her eyes glowed with a dark, cold light that seemed to come from deep inside, like the light in a jewel. He wanted to hold her and tell her that he was afraid, too, but neither was possible here. "You told that cop about Lloyd and now Lloyd's dead," she said.

He had been thinking exactly the same thing himself. There was a connection between Timothy's death and Lloyd's, but how could the connection be Jim Franks? It didn't make sense and he said so.

"Then tell me what does."

"I don't know."

He wanted to go but she held him as much by the fierce intensity of her eyes as the clutch of her fingers on his sleeve. "Please," she said.

He knew her mind was filled with vague fears about what might happen next, while his was still focused on what had happened already. Whether or not Franks had anything to do with Lloyd's death was almost beside the point. The reality was that Lloyd was dead now because Steven tried to question him about Timothy and Ophelia. There wasn't the slightest doubt in Steven's mind about that. He had wanted to know why they had died because he believed that knowing was important. And what had wanting to know got him? The death of another boy, but not one step closer to the truth.

He tried to tell himself he had come too far to turn back now, and yet he had come nowhere at all. He couldn't turn back, but the reason had nothing to do with truth at all. It had to do with fighting back. A child he loved had been killed and it didn't really matter why. What mattered was doing something about it. *The tygers of wrath are wiser than the horses of instruction.* He should have known this as early as the night he picked through the rubble of his belongings in a daze of outraged impotence. Blake knew it, tried to explain it to him that night, but he hadn't understood until now.

"I'm all right," he said. He waited until Rita was back in her classroom before he turned and hurried to the stairs.

''Y ES," the woman said, easing the door back.

Victoria James was much smaller than Steven had expected, enough so that he almost looked past her and then had to lower his eyes. The resemblance to her daughter was so strong it threw him into momentary confusion, as though the last ten days were all a nightmare and he was standing in a hallway talking to Ophelia.

"I'm Steven Hillyer," he said. "I'd like to talk to you if I could, Mrs. James."

The doorway stood open only a few inches but there was no chain lock. Only her slender arm barred his way. He wondered if she knew how unsafe it was, opening the door like that to a stranger. At the same time he thought of Ophelia the last time he saw her, curled like a kitten in Timothy's arms. The mother seemed to have inherited her daughter's vulnerability.

"I'm sorry," she said. "Do I know who you are?"

"I'm a teacher at La Guardia Junior High," he began, but she cut him off almost at once.

"Oh," she said. "*Mr.* Hillyer. I didn't place it when you said your Christian name."

He felt strangely gratified and flattered as she stepped back, inviting him in. It was over a year since he had been Ophelia's English teacher, and still her mother remembered his name. He imagined Ophelia telling her mother what was going on in her seventh-grade English class.

Following her into the small living room, he let his eyes wander over the worn surfaces, the pale colors. The room made him feel that he had been there before, the frayed and faded fabrics somehow as comfortable and familiar as one's own clothes. He realized with a sharp pang of regret that it was years since he had been in one of his students' homes. When he first came to La Guardia he visited with families often, searching out any plausible pretext for talking with the fathers and mothers about their sons and daughters. Lately he hadn't done it at all.

"Ophelia always said you were a good teacher," she said. "Can I get you a cup of tea?"

"Thank you," he said. "No. I wanted to tell you how sorry I am about what happened to Ophelia."

"That's kind of you," she answered softly, bowing her head for a moment and then inviting him with a gesture to sit. She sat opposite him, in an upholstered chair as shapeless as a bean bag, her hands folded neatly in her lap. For a moment neither of them spoke and then she said, "She was my only child, you know."

"Yes, ma'am," he said. He had known it only from the newspapers. Ophelia communicated almost nothing about her family in class or in the papers she wrote. "I'm sorry I didn't come sooner."

"Not at all," she answered with a sweet and reassuring smile. "This is very kind of you."

He didn't want another silence so he took a deep breath and jumped straight to the part of the conversation he had thought through on the long walk over. "I'm not quite sure how to say this, Mrs. James," he began. "I read the things you said in the newspapers the other day. I think you're right."

She cocked her head to one side, the way Ophelia used to do in class. She said nothing.

"I think there are a lot of things that haven't been explained about what happened," he said, and then added, "About why it happened I mean."

Her head straightened and her small eyes bore in on him. She wanted to believe he was offering her help, because Ophelia always said nice things about him. But she had to be careful. She wished she had Miss Woods with her because Miss Woods would tell her whether or not to talk to this man.

"Say your piece, Mr. Hillyer," she said, her voice surprisingly sharp.

"I wanted to know anything Ophelia might have told you about Timothy Warren," he said. "There was some connection between them. I hoped you could tell me what it was."

She was on her feet at once. "She was thirteen years old, Mr. Hillyer," Victoria announced, holding her head high. "She didn't have no truck with boys, none at all."

"She didn't talk about him? She didn't ever mention him?"

"How does this help my little girl? Bringing up this filth again?"

She was standing so close to him it was difficult for him to stand and even harder to remain seated. But he couldn't move. His pulse pounded with the realization that she did know things he didn't about her daughter's death. "I'm not bringing up anything," he pleaded. "I'm asking you."

"What do you know about my little girl?" she demanded, flinging the words at him like a challenge. "What sort of child was she, Mr. Hillyer?"

"I don't know how to answer that," he stammered, confused by her strange, erratic intensity. "She was very bright, Mrs. James. And she was quiet—very quiet."

She took his words almost as a rebuke, as though he were telling her how unquiet she was. She felt she might be losing her grip on herself, felt the unquiet in her own mind, something inside her head stirring her thoughts to a fast boil. "Was she a good girl, Mr. Hillyer? Just tell me that," she heard herself say.

"Yes," he said, not knowing what more he could say.

Her body hung before him like a puppet on a string, dancing slightly with a jerking, nervous tremor that ran from her shoulders down, and her hands jumped together in front of her, her fingers working themselves into a tight knot. She turned abruptly and walked away from him, and he was able to rise now and move after her.

"She was a very shy girl, Mrs. James," he said, standing over her shoulder. "Gentle and shy. She was a good girl."

It took a moment, but then he saw the tremor in her shoulders come under control, brought to stillness through an effort of will he could barely comprehend. She turned to face him, her eyes still burning with the effort it had taken.

"They say she didn't have no pants on," she said, almost hissing the words.

"Who says that?" he asked.

"You didn't know?"

He shook his head dumbly, baffled by her words and what they might mean. No underpants when she died? That seemed to be what she was saying. Had Timothy molested her? Did they meet as lovers? Was this what it was all about? Charlie Wain had said the same thing, or suggested it, but Steven hadn't accepted it then and didn't accept it now. He didn't want to believe it any more than Mrs. James did.

"Who says that?" he asked again, more urgently.

"I oughtn't have told you," she said. "I oughtn't be talking to you at all."

She started to move away from him, backward, as though afraid of him. She stepped through the kitchen door and he saw her reach for the telephone on the wall. He thought for a moment she was calling the police, and he stopped moving so that she wouldn't think he was pursuing her. "Oughtn't be talking at all," she repeated to herself as she dialed a number.

And then she said, "There's a man here from the school, Miss Woods. He's asking me questions about Ophelia."

R I T A saw the detective standing outside Steven's classroom when she came out of her own room at the end of last period. The man waited until the rush of students subsided to a trickle and then stepped in. Rita hurried to the doorway to see what was happening.

Once the detective walked through the door, he stopped in his tracks. "What the hell," he said. "You're not Hillyer."

Hal Garson was behind Steven's desk. He looked up at the cop with an expression of bland surprise. "That's right."

"This is Hillyer's room, isn't it?"

"Most of the time. Yes."

"What do you mean, most of the time?"

"When he's here it's his room. He's not here now."

The detective stiffened, reacting to the flippancy in Garson's voice. "Where is he?" he demanded.

"I don't know. He had to leave and he asked me to take his last class."

Rita hurried out of the doorway before either of the men saw her. She took the stairs up to the gym, threading past students on their way down, and found Barry Lucasian on the gym floor folding the wrestling mat. A student was helping him.

"That's all right, I'll take care of it," Lucasian said as Rita crossed the wooden floor to him. She waited until the student was gone and said, "The police are here about Lloyd Elijah."

"I know," he said. "That's what all the kids are saying. Want to give me a hand with this?"

He stepped across to the far side of the mat and picked up a corner. Rita picked up the corner on her side.

"Steven left school when he found out," she said as they paced the length of the mat, folding it back over itself. "Hal Garson took over his class."

"Where did he go?"

"I don't know."

"What did Garson say?"

"He's with the police. I don't think he knows."

Lucasian didn't say anything until he had bent down and hefted the heavy mat onto his shoulder. "It'll be all right," he said, his voice flat and expressionless, not in the least reassuring.

She followed him to the equipment room and helped him hang the mat on its hooks and hoist it up so it hung evenly, covering the sealed doorway to the girls' shower.

"C'mon, don't look so worried," he said, laughing as if he were trying to humor her out of her concern. "Nothing's going to happen. Let me know if you hear from him."

Downstairs, the students being held after their interrogations had all been released and Chief Terranova was meeting with his squad in the assistant principal's office when Detective Phelan walked in with Hal Garson.

"Phelan, that isn't Hillyer," the Chief barked, scowling unpleasantly at the black teacher.

"Tell me about it," Phelan said. "His name's Garson. He says Hillyer asked him to take over his class."

Terranova stepped away from the other cops and approached Garson. "You're a teacher here?" he demanded.

"That's right. Hillyer had to leave and he asked me to take over his class."

"Is there something amusing in this, Mr. Garson?"

Garson's grin grew a shade broader. "Only that I say that to my students all the time," he said. "I never realized how pompous it sounded before."

A few of the cops looked down at their shoes, but the Chief of Detectives didn't seem amused. "Do you remember what Hillyer said about where he was going?" he asked.

"He didn't say."

"And you didn't ask?"

"No."

"What time did he leave?"

"Just before last period."

"And when did he tell you he was going to leave?"

"That was when he told me."

"And you don't know where he went?"

"That's right."

"And you wouldn't tell me if you did."

Garson shrugged.

"You don't like cops, do you?" the Chief asked.

"I have an uncle who was a cop."

"Get him out of here," Terranova said.

It was as much prompting as Garson needed. He left the room before Phelan could escort him out, pulling the door behind him.

Terranova turned at once to the detectives clustered on the other side of the office. "Hartley," he said, "you've got Hillyer's address?"

Hartley Williams had been out in the field all day and had just caught up with the rest of the squad a few minutes ago. "I think he's staying at his mother's," he said.

"Take Carl and get over there. If he's not there, wait. He's got an apartment, doesn't he?"

"Yes, sir."

"You and Walsh cover it," he said to Phelan. "Whatever time that little prick shows up, I want him downtown."

PHILIP Boorstin was a troubleshooter by trade, which meant he expected trouble and a certain amount of shooting. What he didn't expect was to get hit. Punched in the face as if there were no better way to work things out than a common brawl.

Christ Almighty.

Luckily he saw the blow coming soon enough to duck, so it caught him on the left temple just next to his eye socket. If he had been hit in the jaw, which was what Reach had aimed for, Philip was reasonably certain he would have been knocked unconscious. As it was, he only fell back against the corner of his desk while Rachel screamed "Stop it" two or three times, even though there was nothing to stop since Artemis Reach gave no indication of intending to hit him again.

Boorstin could feel the area around his eye turning blue. "Are you finished?" he asked.

"You fucking snake," Reach snarled back.

"Rachel, you can go now," Boorstin said, mustering that air of total imperturbability that had always been his strong suit. "Mr. Reach and I have some things to talk about."

He probed at the bruise with a fingertip while Rachel studied him closely, apparently trying to divine some hidden message in his words, such as a request to phone for the police. She didn't even consider the possibility that he simply wanted her to leave.

"Rachel," he repeated, waving his hand impatiently when she still hadn't moved from the doorway.

With a look of resignation she backed out of the office and pulled the door closed, leaving Boorstin free to concentrate his full attention on the lunatic in front of him.

"What I've got to do is make up my mind whether to charge you with assault," he said. "You can help me out by telling me what this is all about."

Reach jabbed a finger right at Boorstin's face. "You fuck with me, I fuck with you. That's all," he said.

"And you don't think a man your age should have outgrown this kind of schoolyard shit?"

"No."

"How did I fuck with you?"

"We had an understanding, Boorstin. Just because that cunt comes on television . . ."

"Hold it," Boorstin jumped in. "If you mean your lady friend and her request for a special prosecutor, no one's doing anything about that."

"No?" Reach challenged. "What do you call all the cops up at La Guardia?"

"We never said we'd take them away. You know that."

"Not the ones outside, damn it. The ones inside. Don't play games with me, hymie."

Boorstin hadn't heard anything about police going into the school. This wasn't the best way for a deputy mayor to learn about new developments. "There are police *in* the school?" was all he was able to say.

"You're telling me you didn't know?"

"That's exactly what I'm telling you. Now aren't you sorry you hit me?"

He grinned at Reach in a way that seemed to make bygones bygones. In fact, it was a delicate situation, touch and go, and his flippancy was only a cover for the process he always called *lining up the ducks*. Mayor Ehrlich claimed not to care one way or the other about Artemis Reach, but that was only because the mayor never understood how tenuous was his own hold on the electorate. Artemis Reach's hostility could cost Junius Ehrlich far more votes than Junius Ehrlich could ever get for himself. Boorstin was sure that long after Junius Ehrlich had disappeared from the political scene, Artemis Reach would still be a force to reckon with. In a kind of vision, Boorstin could actually see the chunky mayor fading away like a special-effects ghost, done in by a junior-high-school mess. But Artemis Reach was still there, black and powerful. If

Philip didn't want to disappear with the mayor, it behooved him to make nice.

Besides, there was a matter of principle here, and when principles pointed Boorstin in the direction he wanted to go he was never above relying on them. It was one thing to say *fuck him* because it looked as if Reach had gone back on his promise when L. D. Woods and the dead girl's mother held their press conference. But it was clear now that Reach had had nothing to do with that. If the cops were opening it up again, they had to be put back in line. Police commissioners, like mayors, come and go, but men like Reach just keep coming.

Boorstin punched a button on the speaker phone and tapped out the Commissioner's number. All he got was a deputy who either knew nothing about operations in the Bronx or had been instructed to say he knew nothing. He said that the Commissioner was expected back early in the afternoon.

"But you can get in touch with him, can't you?" Boorstin asked.

"He's not in the office now, sir," the deputy's toneless voice droned wearily. "I'll give him the message as soon as he gets in."

"Are you trying to tell me the Commissioner of the whole goddamned Police Department cannot be reached?"

"No, sir. I'm telling you I'll give him the message as soon as he comes in."

"Do you understand who I am?" Boorstin snapped. (It was easy to see why punching people was such an attractive alternative. The trouble was that the people Boorstin wanted to punch usually weren't within reach.) "I am the deputy mayor. I am calling on behalf of the mayor. And I am instructing you to get in touch with Commissioner Pound this instant by whatever means you have at your disposal and instruct him to call me at my office at once. Is that clear?"

"Yes, sir."

Boorstin clicked off the phone and threw up his hands. Reach dropped back into a chair like a man staking out the most comfortable seat in the room for an evening in front of the television. "That's it?" he asked.

Boorstin shrugged. "He'll call back."

"Why can't you do anything?"

"Because I don't know what cops are in there or why." This seemed to make sense even to Reach. "Besides, I can't give orders to the police," Boorstin added for good measure.

The P.C. didn't call back for more than half an hour. When he did, he professed to know no more about the police operation at La Guardia Junior High than Boorstin or Reach.

"Whatever it is," Boorstin said, "it's not going to be worth the fallout. I'd put a stop to it right now if I were you."

"I'm not in the office," Simon Pound said in one of his typical non sequiturs. "I'll put out some feelers. Meet me at my office in about an hour."

"With all due respect, feelers aren't going to do it, Commissioner," Boorstin said, more for Reach's benefit than because he thought it would do any good. The P.C. wasn't about to interfere with an ongoing operation until he knew what it was about.

Rachel got them both coffee and they talked until it was time to ride over to Headquarters, keeping mostly to safe topics. By the time they arrived at the Commissioner's office they were pretty much in synch on what they wanted.

The Commissioner, of course, wasn't in, but the deputy let them wait in his office because a deputy mayor couldn't be expected to wait in a waiting room. They availed themselves of the deputy's offer of bourbon and water.

"Did you ever consider running for office?" Boorstin asked, watching the ice cubes dance in his drink.

"The school board is an elected office," Reach reminded him.

"I meant citywide."

"Why should I?"

"Power," Boorstin suggested. "Get things done."

"If I was the mayor," Reach said, "all it would mean is I'd have to worry about some crazy nigger like me."

The door opened and the Commissioner let himself in, smiling benignly at the sight of a Jewish liberal and a black demagogue enjoying his liquor in his office. "Don't bother to get up, gentlemen," he said, but of course they did. He moved around behind his desk, forcing them to leave the sitting area and come to him. He sat down and they pulled up chairs facing him. Then he tapped his fingertips together before speaking.

"There are indeed police at La Guardia Junior High, Mr. Boorstin," he began. "They've gone there to question students in connection with a homicide investigation."

"We know all about the homicide," Boorstin objected wearily, wondering why Pound was going over ground already covered.

"I'm afraid you don't, gentlemen," Pound smiled. "This is a new homicide."

It struck Boorstin that Simon Pound was one of very few men on the face of the earth who could find pleasure in the contemplation of a new homicide. "What new homicide?" he asked.

"A La Guardia student."

Clearly, Pound was enjoying this conversation. He must have been tickled pink when the feelers he put out sent back word of fresh depredations in Artemis Reach's domain. No doubt Pound felt invulnerable, because there wasn't much Boorstin could do about a legitimate investigation.

Reach, though, wasn't about to surrender so docilely. "This boy wasn't killed in the school, was he?" he asked, getting to his feet.

"No, sir. In an alley."

"Then why the hell is a public school filled with cops?"

"Because a student's associates tend to be in school, Mr. Reach. Even in the Bronx. If that's where they are, that's where the police go to question them."

"Bullshit."

Pound only shrugged.

"In the first place, we're not talking about a couple of detectives. We're talking about a dozen men," Reach said loudly, beginning a speech. In fact, Terranova had brought less than twelve men to the school, but the difference wasn't worth quibbling about. "In the second place," the Chairman went on, "they're not questioning anybody's *associates*, they're questioning everybody. They put a dragnet through the whole school, they're rounding up kids left and right, and they're holding them incommunicado after they finish grilling them. That sounds like disruption. It doesn't sound a whole hell of a lot like a homicide investigation."

Pound said nothing for so long that Boorstin finally asked, "Is this true, Simon?"

"I don't see how it could be," the Commissioner answered quickly. But his face had turned parchment white.

"Yes or no? Is any of it true?"

"I assume the investigation is being conducted properly."

"If you don't know how lame that sounds," Reach said, "then you're even more of an asshole than I thought."

"Who's running it?" Boorstin asked, sticking to the pragmatic.

"Chief Terranova."

"Why don't we get him up here?"

Pound rang Terranova's extension without even answering the question. He asked for the Chief and then he said, "Reach out for him. Tell him I want him to contact my office forthwith."

He hung up the phone and reported lugubriously that the Chief of Detectives was "in the field."

"You bet your ass he is," Reach grinned wolfishly. "If neither one of due consideration for the educational process. Do you understand me, Chief Terranova?"

"No, sir. I don't believe I do."

There was no doubt in Simon Pound's mind that the man was trying to be exasperating. He didn't care. Personally, he wouldn't have minded if Terranova padlocked the whole building, but personal considerations didn't enter into it. Regardless of whether or not Terranova's action could be justified as an investigative method, the Chief of Detectives should have known better than to take such a sensitive action without clearing it upstairs, where of course it wouldn't have been cleared. From a moron like Borough Commander Dwayne Norland, who had started the whole mess in the first place, it was almost excusable. From Terranova it amounted to insubordination. Commissioner Pound couldn't think of a single reason to put up with it.

"What I mean is that neither you nor your detectives are to go back into that school without my specific authorization," he said, giving himself the uncharacteristic satisfaction of raising his voice. "And before I give such authorization I will need the names of the detectives who will be setting foot on school property, the names of the individuals they will be questioning and the reason for such interrogations. Now have I made myself clear?"

From his seat on the couch, Boorstin was so acutely conscious of having just witnessed the finest moment of Simon Pound's life that he felt like applauding. He had just watched a small man harpoon a whale, and while he knew that, simply as creature to creature, the puny biped was no match for the monster, he knew just as certainly that the whale could wind up as candle wax.

At the window, Reach sighed with relief but otherwise kept his reaction to himself.

Meanwhile, the whale in question blinked his small eyes as though noting the presence of the harpoon in his flesh and steered straight for the boat. "If we could have a word, Commissioner," he said, moving between Boorstin and Reach to the Commissioner's desk, leaving the two of them bobbing in his wake. He gestured with his thumb toward the wet bar in the corner of the office and banked that way, apparently intending the Commissioner to follow him there so they could talk out of the hearing of Boorstin and Reach.

As the Commissioner moved to join him, Terranova glanced back at Boorstin and then Reach, catching them in an uneasy exchange of looks. *You had your fun*, he thought. *Now sweat.*

you can get this shit stopped and leave my school alone, I guarantee you more trouble than you can handle."

"It's being worked on," Boorstin tried to reassure him. "As soon as we've got Terranova here, we'll get to the bottom of it."

The minutes turned into half an hour. Commissioner Pound tried the phone again and was told that the Chief's office had been unable to get through to him.

"Send someone," Boorstin suggested.

The Commissioner placed another call and hung up the phone with a look of utter defeat. "There's no one to send," he said. "He's got the whole squad with him."

"Simon," Boorstin said in a tone normally reserved for conversations with the implacably dense, "you command every police officer in this city. Please don't tell me you can't find a cop when you need one."

"It's a fucking farce," Reach groaned, literally throwing his hands up in the air, and then pacing back and forth in front of the windows overlooking all of lower Manhattan. He looked to Boorstin like a man on the verge of violence.

It was well after four o'clock before the Commissioner's deputy finally rang through to say that Chief Terranova had arrived.

"Did you want to see me, sir?" Terranova asked as he came through the door, quickly taking in the fact that the P.C. was behind his desk, Artemis Reach was looking out the window and Philip Boorstin was sitting on the opposite side of the office thumbing through a magazine. Clearly they were not currently on speaking terms.

"You've been at La Guardia Junior High?" the Commissioner asked.

"Yes, sir."

"How many men did you have with you?"

"Ten."

The P.C. glanced over at Reach and nodded his head, conceding that at least this part of Reach's account was substantially accurate. His eyes went back to Terranova. "Who authorized you to go into that school?" he asked.

"It's a public building, sir," Terranova answered coolly. "We don't need authorization to go into it."

"Well you do now, sir," Pound snapped, flinging the words at Terranova like so many darts. He had been waiting for hours for someone to get tough with, and now he had his chance.

"I beg your pardon."

"The Police Department is not in the business of disrupting education: services. Whatever investigation you're conducting will be carried on wit

"I understand what you're saying, Commissioner," he said out loud, keeping his voice low. "I just thought you should know, out of the hearing of those civilians, that if you or any other political appointee interferes with a criminal investigation, I would have no choice but to resign. Think it over."

He turned away and lumbered from the room without even giving his boss a chance to respond. He waited until he got into the reception area with the door closed behind him before he permitted himself a smile, then waited until he got downstairs to his own office and thawed a chocolate shake in his microwave before he wiped the smile off his face long enough to slurp the whole shake down at once.

He was smiling because he had just made things simple for Commissioner Pound by giving him a choice between fucking with Artemis Reach and fucking with Albert Terranova. It would take a certain amount of bravado for Simon Pound to stand up to Reach, but he could do it if he had to. Bravado mixed with a sort of cold-blooded cunning seemed to be among the Commissioner's assets. On the other hand, it would take balls to stand up to Chief Terranova, and Simon Pound didn't have them. He had appointed Terranova Chief of Detectives, even though he hated his guts, because he didn't have the balls not to. Nothing had changed since then because it never did. If balls grew on trees, no one would carry a gun.

L. D. WOODS sat facing Steven across the narrow space of Victoria James's living room, her legs exquisitely crossed, questioning him about the reasons for his interest in the circumstances of Ophelia James's death. But, while she acted as though she served as some sort of custodian for Mrs. James's interests, it didn't seem to Steven that he could afford to accept her claim at face value. Nor were his doubts eased in the least by the presence at her side of Tal Chambers, whom Steven had found in the weight room on Friday. *I've been meaning to talk to you,* Chambers had said, but then never got in touch. Steven didn't understand where Chambers figured in any of this.

In fact, there were so many things Steven didn't understand that he found it almost impossible to talk freely.

"Have you told any of this to the police?" L.D. asked when he told her about searching through Timothy Warren's poetry for some clue to the circumstances that brought Timothy and Ophelia together in the weight room where they died.

"The police and I seem to be at cross-purposes," he answered evasively.

She drew back deeper into the cushions of the couch. "What do you want from Mrs. James?" she asked.

"I want her to tell me everything she can about Ophelia's relationship with Timothy," he said, but it felt cold and unnatural to talk about Ophelia's mother as though she no longer mattered in these deliberations. "I want you to help me," he added quickly, turning to face her, catching her just as she looked away.

Her shoulders trembled through the thin fabric of her faded dress.

"Yes, we can do that, Mr. Hillyer." L.D.'s soft, husky voice replied, seeming to float in the room, filling the spaces.

Victoria James rose to her feet, reaching a hand down to steady herself against the arm of the chair. Chambers was by her side instantly, bending to whisper something that Steven, only a few feet away, couldn't hear. She acted older than Steven or Miss Woods or Chambers, small and fragile and motherly. And yet for an instant, as her face came up to look into the eyes of the tall man standing over her, Steven realized that she probably hadn't been much more than a child when she bore Ophelia, and might have looked, if life had treated her differently, not much older than the three of them now.

"Please," she said softly. "I can't help him. Not against my girl I can't."

"Not against her," Chambers said.

"Timothy was a lost boy, Mr. Chambers. Don't you know what that means? Lost like that?"

"Then you did know him?" Steven asked.

Her eyes flashed as she pulled away from Chambers to turn on him.

"No, sir. I knew what he was."

"What was he, Mrs. James?"

"Do you know what the devil is, Mr. Hillyer? Do you know God and what it means to stand in God's light? He was a dark, ungodly child, that's what lost means."

"He believed in God, ma'am," Steven said as gently as he could.

"And accepted our Lord? You can't tell me that!"

Her voice was harsh with fear and distress. And in truth Steven couldn't tell her that, because Timothy believed without accepting.

"But you have to help him anyway," L.D. said, moving across the room to her, keeping her voice calm, insistent, inexorable, exactly the way she moved. "There was a connection between them and you have to tell Mr. Hillyer what it was."

"I put a stop to it," Victoria James shot back. "Why can't I put a stop to it now?"

"What did you put a stop to?" Steven asked.

The three of them gathered around her made her feel like a treed possum, and she knew better than to think she could escape.

"He called, he sent her letters. But I saw what he was. I stopped it."

"Were they love letters, Victoria?" L.D. asked, and at the same time Steven said, "What did you do with these letters, Mrs. James? Where are they?"

"I burned them, every last one in front of her eyes. Just to show her what it would come to, what she was dealing with. Burned them in front of her eyes, and she saw."

Her voice rose into the clear, shrill regions of hysteria.

"What did she see?"

"What he was, what he was doing. I didn't make her do things, Miss Woods, not ever before. I only had to tell her and she did. But this time I made her, made her fetch them to me right in that kitchen and I set them in the sink and put a match to them and they burned like sulphur, that's the truth. Like sulphur, because there was nothing decent or godly in them. Ophelia saw it and she was herself again after that. I didn't have to tell her again."

Her words called up before Steven's eyes an image of dark, dancing flames, the twisted sheets of Timothy's letters writhing under them like bodies in torment as the grim line of char swept up them.

"Are you sure?" he demanded hoarsely. "Are you sure you burned everything?"

Victoria turned on him angrily. "Everything," she said, her eyes flashing triumph.

"But she brought you the letters," he protested. "How do you know she brought you everything?"

Her face was set and stern, matching his stubbornness with her own. She looked into his eyes as long as she felt she needed to, and then turned to L. D. Woods. "I can't help him. Can't you make him go?"

"I can but I shouldn't, Victoria," L.D. said. "We both knew how hard this was going to be. But we both want the truth. So does Mr. Hillyer."

"No, I don't want it, I don't want it anymore," Victoria screamed. "I don't know why I listened to you."

"Where did she bring you the letters from, Mrs. James?" Steven asked, making himself ignore her anguish. "Where did she keep them?"

"We oughtn't be talking about this. Please."

"Tell him, Victoria," L.D. urged. "Let him look and we'll leave you alone."

"In her dresser? In her closet?" Steven persisted, reckless in his desperation.

"My God," Tal muttered, helpless before them.

"She brought them to me," Victoria cried. "I told her to bring them all and she brought all of them."

"Leave her alone," Tal pleaded, but L.D. said, "Then let him look," in a voice that cut through the woman's hysteria with its tone of cold command.

Victoria said nothing, wavering on the point of decision. Tal reached an arm around her shoulder and pulled her to him, let her rest in the lee of his strength. Her eyes fluttered closed as she tried to think it all through.

"I know how much this must hurt," Steven said, troubled now in the stillness by his own ruthlessness.

"But God doesn't care about pain," L.D. added softly. "He cares about truth. You know that, Victoria."

Victoria's eyes opened. "In the dresser," she said. "If she held anything back it would be in the dresser."

As Steven slipped into the girl's bedroom, the sound of the small, fragile woman's sobs followed him. He turned at the door and saw L. D. Woods holding Mrs. James to her bosom, hands stroking her hair as she cried. He forced himself to look away.

The room looked almost exactly as he would have imagined it, girlish and unadorned, so small it was barely possible to move around the narrow bed, the spindle-legged lamp table next to it and the chest-high dresser that made up the meager total of furnishings. A religious painting hung on the wall opposite the bed, a needlepoint sampler showing flowers in faded pinks above the bed. The coverlet, too, was flowered.

He took only a moment to look around and then moved quickly to the dresser, sensing somehow that he could lessen the sin of his intrusion by ignoring everything except what he had come to find. He heard Chambers's footsteps behind him as he set his hands on the faceted glass knobs of the dresser drawer.

"Christ, Hillyer," Chambers said. "Do you really think this is necessary?"

"Another boy was killed yesterday," Steven said simply.

Chambers swallowed back a breath, considering this. "There's a connection?" he asked.

"I think so."

Steven winced as the drawer opened with a squeak he couldn't muffle even by gentling it out slowly. He knew Ophelia's mother heard it in the living room.

One side of the drawer was piled with folded blouses, the rest of the space taken up with a meager assortment of cotton underwear, panties and plain scoop-neck chemises, all of it innocently childish and yet oddly stirring as his hands sorted through.

"She told me Ophelia wasn't wearing any underwear," Steven said. "Then she got very upset. That was when she called Miss Woods."

"No underpants," Chambers corrected. "She had on one of those undershirt things. It's a very touchy subject," he added, gesturing toward Mrs. James in the other room. "Check the next drawer."

Steven slid the drawer closed, letting the impact of what Chambers said sink in. He had been hoping it wasn't true, a nightmare fantasy of rape generated in the mother's mind by the girl's violent death. "She told you that, too?" he asked cautiously, tensing for the answer.

"I told her," Chambers said. "It was in the medical examiner's report."

"Was she raped?"

"She wasn't molested at all," Chambers said. "In fact, that's what I wanted to ask you about the other night."

Steven's mind was racing too fast for him to say anything.

"The only ones in the room were you and the cops. Someone had to take those underpants away."

Unless she wasn't wearing them when she got there, Steven thought. But that changed everything so much he felt the room spinning around him.

"I don't know," Steven answered, afraid to say more until he had a chance to think it through. "There were a lot of cops after it happened. I didn't see."

The drawer opened silently with a slight pull. Under a pile of folded slacks he found three opened envelopes, each of them bearing Ophelia's name in Timothy Warren's fine, small hand. They had been exactly where the mother said they would be, where Ophelia must have known her mother could find them if she chose to look.

They had trusted each other that much.

J I M M Y Franks wove across the yard in a pattern so random and intricate no defender, even an imaginary one, could hope to keep up with him. A dozen yards away his father darted back and forth, skipping and spinning to elude a phantom pass rush. He pirouetted neatly and cocked his arm back, the yellow sponge football bright in the growing twilight.

"What do you do? What do you do?" Jim called.

As the boy started toward him he let the ball fly in a soft, fluttering arc.

Jimmy caught it in both hands the way he had been taught and started toward his father, flinging childish fakes in all directions until he left the old man sprawled on the lawn while he rushed in for the touchdown.

"What do you do when your quarterback's in trouble?" Jim asked as he got to his feet.

"Come back to the ball," the boy quoted wearily.

"Well how come if you can tell me, I don't see it happening?"

"I forgot."

"Great. I've got Lawrence Taylor chasing me all over the backfield and you just run off on a pass pattern and leave me there," he teased. "I think dinner's ready."

He started toward the house but the boy pleaded for one more play. "One more," Jim conceded, putting a question in his voice that needed confirmation.

"Yeah, awright," Jimmy sulked.

"Even if you don't catch it?"

That was harder to agree to but the boy did. They huddled up under the kitchen window and Jim called for a slant-in over the middle. It was the one pattern they almost always completed.

Dinner, as predicted, was waiting on the table when they got inside, the girls bouncing impatiently at their places with their spoons poised over their soup.

"You didn't have to wait for us," Jim said.

"Mommy made us," Susan whined, dramatizing the injustice of it.

Lenny served the soup without sitting down herself, moving back and forth from stove to table to counter like a harried waitress. She brought in ham with broccoli, and went back to the kitchen. After a minute, Jim got up from the table.

"What can I help you with?" he asked.

"I'm managing fine."

He lifted a pot lid.

"I'll drain the yams."

"I'm managing fine, Jim. Sit down and eat."

How was she managing fine when they ended up eating like an assembly line, taking everything as it came down the chute? She always served that way when she was annoyed, and refusing to let him help was a part of it.

Let it play itself out, he thought. Now that he was going to be home all the time, he had to let these things slide. He went back to the table and served the ham, but waited to cut a slice for Lenny so it would be hot when she finally got around to sitting down. He asked Susan about the kindergarten play she had been rehearsing and promised to help her with her lines after dinner. The broccoli was served but Jimmy couldn't see the butter sauce on it and wouldn't eat any. There was no butter on the table, but as soon as Jim got up to get it, Lenny hurried across the kitchen to hand it to him.

"Thanks," he said.

"You don't have to thank me. There should have been butter on the table."

The rest of the meal went like that. When he reached over to cut Jimmy's ham for him because the boy was sawing at the meat like someone trying to cut lumber with a pocketknife, Jimmy protested that he could do it himself.

"I just thought I'd help."

"If he needed help he'd ask for it," Lenny said.

"I didn't say he *needed* it. People can help other people just to be nice, you know."

Actually, he hadn't done it to be nice but because sometimes the way the boy hacked at his food got on his nerves. At eight he should have been able to use a knife properly.

"He's not going to learn if you don't let him do it himself," Lenny added unnecessarily.

"I'm only delaying his development one meal, Lenny. Let's drop it," he said.

The yams arrived and Lenny sat down at the table at last. Laura asked for something to drink. By the time everyone had eaten and Jim and Lenny were alone in the kitchen, they both felt as if they had been locked in a small room together for longer than either of them could bear. Lenny got up to clear the table but Jim reached out and caught her wrist.

For a moment she stood there, a serving plate in either hand, the touch of her husband's hand surprisingly steady and tender and reassuring, pushing the irritation that had been building in her all day a small but perceptible way into the background. She met the generosity of his gesture with a wistful smile.

"Let's just have our coffee," he said.

"Let me straighten up the kitchen first," she countered, immediately annoyed with herself for not accepting his invitation. Whenever there was tension between them, it was always Jim who reached out to bridge over it. But his solutions weren't necessarily hers and she resented the way he imposed his settlements on her, acting like the only gatekeeper on the road back to serenity. "It will be nicer to sit down without this mess hanging over me," she added, to justify what she had said already.

He helped her with the dishes, neither of them speaking a single word more than was necessary in the process. *Should he save what was left of the broccoli? Where did she keep the foil?* When they were finished they sat at the freshly washed table over their coffee cups looking for a way out of the silence.

"Jim, is there some reason you're not telling me what you're doing?" she asked at last.

The quality of the silence changed from accidental to deliberate. He looked at her across what seemed like a hurtling distance, as though she were flying backward from him at indescribable speeds. Even to answer evasively took more effort than he thought he could muster.

"I'm not really doing anything," he said.

"Then where do you go?"

"I just have to see some people, that's all."

"You don't want to tell me?"

"Obviously I don't." She lowered her eyes, hurt. "I'd just like you to respect that, please," he added, which put it in another light. He was, no one knew better than Lenny, entitled to that much and more, a good father to the children, a good cop, a good husband to her. And the pain now was all his, the anguish and anger at his suspension, the uncertainty about what the Department would do with him, and not least the guilt she knew was eating at his insides over the boy he had shot. She wanted him to know she was available if needed, but he had the right to ask her not to push herself on him, encumbering him with help.

"You're right," she said. "I'm sorry," placing a hand on his, trying to put out of her mind not only the fact of the isolation he had chosen for himself, but also the fact that he took his gun when he went out in the morning. The empty shoe box told her that.

As he slid his hand out from under hers, remembering that he'd promised to help Susan with her play, the phone rang. Lenny, being closer, answered it. The voice of a man she didn't recognize asked for Jim. At least it wasn't Vince. She didn't want her husband involved in any of Donadio's madness.

"He's right here," she said. "Just a minute."

She held out the phone for him but Jim said he'd take it in the bedroom and hurried away.

Upstairs, he closed the bedroom door and picked up the phone. "Yeah," he said. "Hold on a second."

He waited for the click that told him Lenny had hung up the extension. Then he said "Yeah" again.

"Look, it's me," a voice said, giving no name in case Franks's phone was up. A cop, no one else thought that way. But what cop? He didn't place the voice. "I wouldn't have called except I thought you should know."

Then it clicked. Dwight Matthews. "Thanks, I appreciate it," Franks said. "What's up?"

"I don't know and I don't want to know," Matthews's voice came back low and fast, the words tumbling over each other. "That name you asked me to check out for you yesterday, he turned up dead this morning."

The news seemed to sizzle in Franks's head, setting off a spasm of unconnected thoughts. Yesterday he got nowhere looking for the boy. This morning he tried again, but met with only that strange passivity that warned him he was on a trail recently traveled by other cops. He knew he couldn't afford to run into them and went home. Now he understood what it was about.

He realized, too, how difficult this call was for Matthews, who had been worried about getting in trouble for looking up the name in the first place but still had the guts to call now that the trouble was real. A tear burned in Franks's eye until he blinked it away, refusing to concede he could be that touched by this small, brave token of an old friend's loyalty but touched in spite of denial, wondering the while if he was coming apart. *What's the matter with me?* he asked himself.

His silence made Matthews ask, "Are you there, Jim?"

"Yeah. I'm here."

"Look, I know it's none of my business. But are you going to be all right on this thing?"

It meant, *Are you mixed up in this in some way you shouldn't be?* It even meant, or may have meant, *Is there anything I can do to help?* There was something tender and touching in this too, the codes they talked in, man to man, burying their care under tough words.

"I'm fine. Really," Franks reassured him. "I'll fill you in when it gets straightened out. Thanks."

"Sure."

The phone went dead at Franks's ear. He laid the receiver down and sat heavily on the bed, trying to clear his mind.

The prophet in the poem, he thought, was the prophet Elijah, *daring the Lord to magic,* demanding that God heal the widow's child although his sickness was so sore that there was no breath left in him, according to the seventeenth chapter of the First Book of Kings.

But the boy Elijah was dead. Why? Because Jim Franks stuck his damn snout in, digging around, asking questions. He was dead because Franks was looking for him. Carve another notch in the gun.

O thou man of God, art thou come unto me to call my sin to remembrance and to slay my son?

Apparently, ma'am. (He hadn't thanked her for talking to him, but he left her a buck for the coffee. Big tipper.) He remembered the way the bullet looked when it leaped from the barrel of his gun, like a rope of fire, like a snake's tongue. They said it made an awful mess when it hit the boy's head but he couldn't be sure of that because he didn't watch it that far.

He picked up the telephone and dialed Steven Hillyer's number. He had called Hillyer earlier, just before he went out to play football with Jimmy, but there was no answer. And there was no answer now. (He had promised Susan he'd help her with her play. Or had he done that already? No, but he was on the way when the phone rang. One more call and that's what he'd do. He was a good daddy.)

He dialed the number and Donadio's voice answered on the second ring. It didn't sound as if he was drinking.

"Vince, it's me, Jim. I thought over what you said."

"Me too," Donadio said.

"Just follow this a minute, willya. I went to see the schoolteacher."

"That's the fuck that almost put us away."

"I know that. Just shut up a minute. All I wanted was some kind of handle on what the kid was up to. Hillyer gave me the name of a kid to talk to and now he's dead too."

"Hillyer?"

"No, the kid. All I'm telling you is there's something going on there, Vince."

"How does that do you any good?" Donadio asked.

Two weeks ago they had been partners, but nothing in Donadio's voice hinted at it now.

"I don't know," Franks said.

"Well it don't do me any good either. Is that the whole story or is there more?"

It was the whole story.

He hung up the phone and checked his watch, wondering how long it would be before the police came. Looking for the boy, he had left a trail even a blind man could follow.

In the play Susan was an apple tree, *bearing apples green and red.* A bird lived in her branches.

* * *

DONADIO thought of calling but decided to drive into Manhattan instead. He left a message on his answering machine telling Marla he'd be back in a few hours and to wait. She always played his messages anyway, so what the fuck.

It was late by the time he got to Headquarters but the fool in the lobby said the Chief of Detectives was still in and gave him a pass. Hell of a job for a cop, wasn't it, nothing more than a doorman really. Donadio took it as a reminder of why he had to play his cards right or he'd end up with assignments like that for the next eleven years.

Another fool outside the Chief's office kept him waiting almost half an hour. Just from the movement of detectives in and out of Terranova's private office he could tell things were popping. Finally the lieutenant said he could go in.

Terranova was eating as usual, and there was a black detective in his shirtsleeves watching him. Neither of them got up but the Chief waggled his fork around, signaling Donadio to come in. He swallowed a mouthful of food and said, "Vince Donadio. This is Detective Williams."

So that was the way it was going to be. *Vince* Donadio, *Detective* Williams. Williams only nodded. Donadio didn't nod back. "I just ran into something I thought you should know," he said.

Terranova ate the last bite of whatever he was eating and put the fork down. "Go ahead," he said.

"Do you have a new homicide of a kid connected to that school?" Donadio asked.

The look that passed between Terranova and his silent spade detective told Donadio they had already tied the new homicide in with the Warren case.

"You came to tell me something or ask questions?" Terranova said.

"Awright, it's about that homicide. I just wanted you to know my ex-partner was looking for that kid."

"Why?"

"Beats me. Franks got the kid's name from Hillyer. That's about all I know."

If there was a look between them a minute ago, there were sparks this time. Maybe they understood what it was about. Donadio didn't, and didn't care.

"Where'd you get this?" Terranova asked.

"What does that matter?"

"It doesn't."

Donadio didn't want to say he got it from Franks because something about the fact that Franks was still talking to him while he was talking to them didn't sit right. He could see from the way the Chief's small eyes seemed to pull back deeper into his face that he knew anyway. Fuck it, he thought, the idea here wasn't to be well liked.

"That's about all I can tell you," Donadio said. "I just thought you ought to know."

He had said his piece and expected Terranova to tell him to leave. Instead, the Chief crumpled up his napkin and jammed it into the plastic container he had taken his food out of. "Take a look in this box, Donadio," he said, pointing to the container. "Tell me what's in there."

Donadio looked at him as if he was crazy but stepped up to the desk and peered into the container. There was a whitish stain of some kind all over the inside of it. And the dirty napkin. If this was some kind of a riddle he didn't get it.

"How the hell do I know," he said. "It's just garbage."

"But it wasn't always garbage. Now get out of here before I lose my dinner."

For a second Donadio appeared to be about to say something but there wasn't, after all, anything he could say. He turned around and hurried to the door, pulling it open so hard it flew back against the wall.

"Donadio," Terranova called after him.

"Yeah?"

What the fuck was this? High school? Was he going to tell him to close the door?

"Do you happen to know a detective named West or Mullaney?"

Donadio actually shook his head in confusion, as though he had just been punched. Where was this coming from? He could have said no, but it was a matter of record anyway.

"Yeah, Fred Mullaney," he said. "He's my ex-wife's cousin. Is that all?"

He didn't get an answer from the Chief, but the black detective moved up to the door to close it.

"What was that about?" Williams asked as he made his way back to the Chief's desk.

"Mullaney and West," Terranova explained. "They're the ones who gave Hillyer a hard time when his apartment was burglarized."

"You think Donadio put them up to it?"

"Or they were doing him a favor. Comes to the same thing either way."

He scribbled a note to himself and slid it back on his blotter where he'd be sure to see it later. He didn't explain to Williams but he didn't have to. Just the way he pushed the note away said Donadio's career as a detective was over. Probably Mullaney's and West's as well.

"It's funny," he said. "I never minded a bent cop as much as I minded snakes like that."

"Yes, sir," Williams agreed, and then waited a moment before asking, "Do you want Franks picked up?"

Terranova nodded. "But don't call up to Dobbs Ferry. Send someone from here."

"What about Hillyer?"

"We've already got his apartment and his mother's place staked out."

Williams reached for the phone and dialed one of the squad detectives to ask him to drive up to Dobbs Ferry and get Franks. He hung up and said, "Hillyer and Franks working together. That kind of changes everything, doesn't it?"

Everything, Terranova thought. Franks blows a kid's head off without any witnesses except his partner and Hillyer. Hillyer's all alone with Lloyd Elijah when the kid nearly OD's, Hillyer's in a Bronx playground with a crack dealer named Charlie Wain, and Hillyer goes looking for Lloyd Elijah, only the kid must have known he was coming because he leaves school early. Like magic, Franks is looking for Elijah. Like magic, Elijah is dead.

Terranova picked up the container on his desk and aimed it at the waste basket.

"Do me a favor," he said with more weariness in his voice than Williams had ever heard there. "Get someone in here to empty this thing."

"G U Y like you in this neighborhood?" the gypsy cabdriver said, making it a question with his tone.

"Visiting a friend," Steven explained.

"Sucks."

Steven mumbled something noncommittal.

"Nobody works. I drive this piece of shit twelve hours a day. Wife don't work, don't even make dinner. Brother, the kids, nobody. Look at it."

He gestured around the Bronx streets as though the whole borough was populated with the indolent relatives he was supporting.

"Yeah," Steven agreed. "It doesn't look too good."

"Sucks."

He lapsed into silence.

Settling back in the seat, Steven felt in his pocket for Timothy's letters. He checked the light fixture over his head and saw that the plastic cover was missing and there was no bulb. He didn't mind waiting to begin reading the letters. He knew as certainly as if he had read them already that the answers to his questions about Timothy and Ophelia were in those envelopes.

Half a block from Steven's apartment they had to stop behind a yellow cab discharging a passenger. Steven's driver leaned on the horn and cursed in Spanish while a woman slid out of the cab dragging a collapsible stroller after her. She wrestled with the mechanism until it was fully deployed, reached back into the taxi for a squirming child, and tried to secure the tot in the stroller with a complicated tangle of straps.

"Never mind, I'll get out here," Steven said at that point, leaning over to dig into his pants pocket for his money. As he started to pay the driver, he noticed two men in a car parked in front of his building.

The moment he saw them he knew they were cops and realized with a clarity that surprised him that they were waiting for him. His pulse quickened. Why they were there or who had sent them didn't matter at all. He knew that he couldn't deal with them with Timothy's letters in his pocket. At least not until he'd had a chance to find out what was in them.

He leaned all the way over so that he could see his apartment windows. The lights were on, which meant that Rita was there.

"Look, I've got to stop somewhere else," he said without sitting up. "Just head over to Third."

The driver glanced around and must have noticed the cops too, because he turned to look back at Steven with an expression that conveyed a newfound interest.

When the yellow cab finally moved on, the gypsy driver followed, easing past the unmarked police car.

"Didn't even look. You're okay," the cabbie said when they reached the corner.

Still, Steven didn't sit up until he felt the car laboring up the hill on the other side of Second Avenue. He saw a phone booth on the corner at Third and asked the driver to wait while he made a call.

He dialed his own number. The tension in his chest and guts grew while he waited for Rita to answer, but it wasn't an unpleasant sensation. He felt alert and canny, and oddly pleased with himself for having made it this far. A few weeks ago he would have walked right into the cops without seeing them.

"It's me," he said when Rita picked up the phone. "Is anyone there?"

"Of course not. Where are you?"

"I'll tell you in a minute. There are two cops outside. Did they talk to you?"

"No," she said, carrying the phone to the window. "I can see them. I don't think they were there when I came in. Where are you, Steven?"

"Just up the hill," he said. "At the corner of Third."

"I'll be there in two minutes," she said. "You'd better have a damn good explanation for all this."

"Don't turn off the lights when you leave," he said.

He hung up the phone and went back to his cab. "There's someone meeting me. Can we wait a couple minutes?"

"Not for twelve bucks, man." That was what the driver had asked to take him from the Bronx.

"Fifteen."

"Twenty."

"Twenty and you'll take us where we're going," Steven said. "It's only a few blocks."

The driver indicated his acceptance of the terms by not answering.

Steven got back in the car to wait, turning in the seat to look out the rear window until he saw Rita hurrying toward him. Even at that distance, on the badly lit street, she was clearly a woman one wouldn't mind knowing, her long-legged strides almost provocative in their forcefulness, the sway of her hair, dark in the darkness around her, exciting him with promises. She slowed her pace when she neared the corner, hesitating as she looked around for him.

He swung the car door open and she hurried over, sliding in next to him, instantly washing the fetid air of the cab with the warm fragrance of her flesh.

"Did they see you?" he asked.

One of the cops had undressed her with his eyes as she walked past the car, but that wasn't what Steven meant. "No," she said. "Do you have somewhere to go?"

"No."

"We can go to my place."

He nodded and she gave the driver the address. As soon as the car was in motion, she said, "I almost didn't come over. When Hal Garson told me you'd left school, I was so mad I didn't want to see you again."

"Why did you?"

She was sitting sideways in the seat, facing him, and his hand stroked her arm, trying to reassure her with the pressure of his touch.

"Because I had to tell you how stupid you were. Only you weren't there and then I was too mad to leave."

"I had to talk to Ophelia's mother," he explained.

"You're only going to make everything worse. Haven't you figured that out yet?"

That was what he had said to Timothy. And Timothy said, *It's worse, man. It's already worse.*

Steven didn't answer her.

"Maybe that doesn't bother you," Rita said, nettled by his silence. "What in God's name would you want to bother that poor woman for?"

"She had some letters from Timothy."

She seemed as excited by the news as he hoped she'd be. "What do they say?" she asked.

He told her he hadn't read them yet and she fell thoughtfully silent. In a few minutes the cab stopped at the address she had given on 113th Street, a fortresslike project so numbingly devoid of design that it might have been carved out of a single gigantic brick. While Steven paid the driver, Rita hurried ahead to the front door. She was inside holding the lobby door when he caught up with her.

They rode up to the eighth floor without speaking, and then Rita led him down a grim institutional corridor. "I don't know why I'm doing this," she grumbled on the way. "I'm going to get nothing but shit from my mother and you're not worth it."

"I love you too," he said.

She glanced back over her shoulder to throw him a very grudging smile. At the door she planted a quick kiss on his lips. "You must be one terrific lay," she said. "Otherwise it doesn't make any sense."

The door opened into a living room cluttered with furniture slipcovered with intricately detailed floral prints. The pair of lamps on the end tables bore patterned shades that rainbowed the light like the stained-glass windows in a church. A small, stout woman drawn by the sound of the door materialized from a hall and stood with her hands clasped. Even though her features were softened by age and fat, Steven could see the resemblance.

"Mama, this is Steven Hillyer," Rita said. And to Steven, "My mother."

Steven offered that he was pleased to meet her, but Mrs. Torres responded with a few words in Spanish directed to Rita and then stormed out of the room.

"Take off your coat and sit down," Rita said. "I'll just be a minute."

She rolled her eyes in a comic and slightly sad intimation that the next few minutes weren't going to be easy and paced down the hall after her mother. Steven picked one of the morris chairs and sat down, keeping his coat on. He reassured himself that the letters were still in his pocket but didn't want to open them until he was alone with Rita. At one point he heard her shout, "Shut up, Mama," in English, and then she screamed it again even louder only a few seconds later. "Shut up, Mama!"

She came back into the living room, her face flushed, her brow wet with sweat. "Come on," she said in a crisp, unfriendly command.

She led him down a different hall past two bedrooms, stalking with an angry, mannish stride. "I'm sorry you had to hear all that, Steven," she growled angrily.

"I don't speak Spanish."

"I'm a whore, that's all I've ever been. That's the gist. You want the details?"

"No."

A bathroom stood at the end of the hall, the door open. She turned just before it and shoved open a bedroom door, stepping back to let him go in. There was a sports poster on the wall and a picture of a bare-breasted girl. Steven turned and looked at her questioningly.

"This is my brother's room. You'll sleep here," she said. "My room's here."

She went through the door opposite and he followed her inside. She closed the door.

"She knows you're going to come to my room in the night. I promised her I won't scream when I come."

"Take it easy, Rita," he said, helpless in the face of her raw and aching bitterness.

"Why should I?" she snapped. "I pay the goddamn rent on this place. That ought to entitle me to rant a little."

She tore off her shirt, wiped the sweat from her shoulders and breasts with it before flinging it into a hamper, and slipped on a printed T-shirt she took from a dresser drawer. A faded portrait of Mozart looked back at Steven from her chest.

She sat down on the bed, crossing her hands between her knees like a child. "I'm fine," she said, her lips taut with the effort of mastering herself. But the tension was still discernible just under the surface. "I'm calm and I'm fine. Now let's look at those letters."

He took them out of his coat pocket, the first time he had seen them since leaving Victoria James's apartment. He fanned them out in his hand and studied them a moment, three plain white envelopes that he hoped held the key to the deaths of three children.

Rita's hand came to rest on his. "I'm scared, Steven," she said.

He could see in her eyes that this was true.

"Of what?" he asked.

"For what. For you."

She pulled him next to her on the bed and kissed him, her hands sliding under his coat, her fingers working magic on the tightly knotted muscles of his shoulders, the skin of his chest. He felt the excitement of her mouth working on him, felt the stir of her moving down through his body to his loins and legs, felt her hand slipping down his belly to his waist, prowling its way in under his pants as her tongue flicked like fire over his lips.

Abruptly she pulled away, arching back from him, hands and mouth and body all withdrawn in an instant, and she looked at him through narrow, unforgiving eyes.

"Read your damn letters," she said. "From a dead boy to a dead girl. How the hell can I compete with that?"

A R T E M I S Reach drove around the city for hours, numb and defeated. He expected to feel rage, to feel the fire in his brain and belly and chest he counted on to light up the city and drive his enemies before him. But he couldn't make it come. Even his passions, it seemed, had abandoned him.

Who did they think they were fucking with, those downtown imbeciles who couldn't even control their own cops? The investigation had to be stopped or there'd be hell to pay. He'd made that clear to them. And what happened? The pussy Police Chief backed down from a confrontation with his Chief of Detectives and the smug little bastard from the mayor's office couldn't do a damn thing about it. Like no one was in charge. The cops had his school infiltrated, they were everywhere, inside and out, and they would stay until they destroyed everything.

When Boorstin threw up his hands and walked out of the P.C.'s office, Reach knew he was beaten and accepted it with a kind of resignation that was so out of character even he was surprised. He expected to hear himself making threats, denouncing the lot of them, to feel a surge of anger and indignation that would bring them all in line. For some reason the rage just wasn't there.

He left Headquarters in a fog, unable to understand why he was taking it like this. If ever there was a time to fight back, this was it. The rage was part of his power, the main part. He had always been able to have his way because he spoke for the wrath of his people, embodied it, containing it in himself, channeling it for use. They knew he was dangerous. That was the key.

Only now the key wouldn't turn in the lock and he found himself lost for the first time since he was a boy on these very streets.

Oh, not lost in the literal sense. He knew where he was, as if that mattered. Harlem. Lenox Avenue, as broad as a highway, One-Twenty-fifth, teeming like the markets of Marrakech, the dense huddle of St. Nicholas Avenue, the calm elegance of the mosque, streets named for Powell and King.

He didn't go to Harlem much anymore but he had grown up on these streets and they shaped him. Illusion and reality fought each other tooth and nail here, like Jacob wrestling with his angel, until no one could tell them apart. Behind some of the grimmest facades you could still find here and there a dining room with rich crystal chandeliers, a gaming room where the taps were gleaming brass and the bar a sixteen-foot slab of real marble, wealth and glory hidden behind a wall of blight as though they were things to be ashamed of. The stories his father used to tell of Harlem in its glory were filled with these paradoxes, and for Artemis Reach they were and would always be the last magic in New York.

He needed some of that magic now but couldn't connect to it.

> *Well I'm feeling like a stranger here*
> *I feel like a stranger everywhere*
> *Feel like I'd like to go back home*
> *But I'm even a stranger there.*

A girl on the avenue smiled as he drove past, thin-lipped, hair creamed to an intoxicating gloss. She had some shape to her and he eased the car to the curb, reaching over to open the door as she hustled up with the splay-legged clatter of a woman in high-heeled boots. Her thighs were bare from the top of the boots to her skirt. She could have been sixteen or twenty-five, it was impossible to tell.

Sliding into the seat next to him, she grinned and pulled the door closed. He eased the car around the corner and parked. Neither spoke. The street was deserted enough for their purposes.

He left the engine running and leaned his head back, her fingers already working the zipper of his fly. "This way a little, honey," she said softly, her voice sweetly southern.

He slid toward her, to be free of the steering wheel, and felt her shift in the seat, coiling her legs under her. She probed into his underwear with one hand, exploring, freeing him, and then he felt her shoulder against his belly and the warmth of her mouth on him, the teasing sharpness of teeth nicking and nibbling at his flesh.

Resting one hand on her head, in the oiled tangle of her hair, he slid the other down the back of her neck, under her blouse, his fingers brushing back and forth across her spine. He liked the feel of a woman's back, taut smooth skin stretched over bone, rising and falling like a wave with the rhythmic bobbing of her head. She knew her job.

Clawlike, his fingertips tightened into her back, digging for purchase as he felt the tension spread from his loins into his mind. His nails scratched into her bare skin, grasping for something to hold on to, squeezing tight and then tighter, biting into lean flesh. He heard a soft, muffled whimper of pain, felt her try to pull off him, but his hand on her head rammed her down on him hard, fingers knotted in her hair.

Desperate, she groped behind her, flailing blindly to free herself from the hand at her back that dug deeper and deeper until she would have screamed if she could have, tightening her mouth around him to finish faster, make him stop. He held her down, angered by her struggle, breathing low curses that came faster and faster until finally, still unsatisfied, he pulled her head back violently, jerking her upright, flinging her back against the door, gasping and terrified.

"Get out," he spat. "Get the fuck out of this car."

Her hand scrambled behind her for the handle but couldn't find it.

"Get out!" he screamed.

She found the handle at last, pulled hard and lurched backward to the curb.

"Your money, bitch!" he yelled, flinging a handful of crumpled bills out the open door after her.

The car streaked away, careening through a turn. Behind the wheel, Artemis Reach drove like a madman, his brain a blur of passion, as wild and erratic as the open door flapping with each turn as he wove recklessly around the traffic, speeding uptown. They didn't know who they were fucking with.

He bolted from the car in front of Community Board Sixty-one and raced to the front door, dragging the keys from his pocket. The ancient school building was dark, its cavernous lobby filled with sepulchral shadows from the stray wisps of streetlight filtering in, hollow with the echo of his own feet. He didn't know where to turn on the lights and didn't need to. Feral instincts carried him up the stairs, where he pushed through the door into his office and slammed it so hard that the glass shattered with the impact.

He groped to his desk in the darkness and fumbled with a small key until the lock turned. He yanked open the bottom drawer, where he kept a revolver and a bottle of whiskey, even though he rarely drank. When you got right down to it, those were the only protections a man had.

He picked up the revolver and held it in his hand for a moment, then set it down carefully on the desk. He had to walk across the room to the bookshelf where he kept glasses, but his eyes were used to the darkness now. Back at his desk, he poured out a few fingers of whiskey and took a long drink, then waited to feel the effect. Part of his brain was saying he had to stay calm, settle down, think. Another part said it was too late for that and he was better off not thinking at all. That pusillanimous asshole of a Police Commissioner caved in to his own Chief of Detectives and was going to let the investigation continue. It was too late to stop it now.

The only question left was whether Artemis Reach would go down quietly.

The telephone rang, startling him so badly he had to let it ring two more times before he could answer it.

He expected to hear the Commissioner's voice. Or Chief Terranova's. Instead, it was Barry Lucasian.

"I've been trying to get you all night," Lucasian said. "About Hillyer."

"I don't give a damn about Hillyer!"

"Well you ought to. He talked to the girl's mother. She gave him some of the Warren kid's letters."

"And?"

"I don't know. Depends on what's in them. They could be about what the two of them were doing."

There was silence for a moment and then Reach said, "That's your problem, it's not mine."

His voice sounded thick and slightly slurred, not much, not enough for anyone else to notice. But Reach noticed it and shoved the glass away. It toppled from the desk, shattering on the floor. Good. He was rid of it. He was aware of Lucasian's voice saying something in his ear.

"Give me that again," Reach said.

"I said if it's my problem, it'll be yours."

Reach laughed. "Mine?" he said. "I don't have problems. I make them, you ignorant asshole. It was your mistake from the beginning, and everything you've done about it only made it worse. Now you think you can turn on me like everyone else? It's not that easy."

"I'm just telling you . . ."

"No, you're not telling me shit," Reach shouted, springing to his feet.

Glass crunched under his shoes as he strode around the desk. "Don't you understand I don't give a damn how you get out of it? I don't give a damn *if* you get out of it. I don't give a damn if they send you to jail for the rest of your puny, meaningless life. It was stupid what you did with that girl and stupid what you did about it. You told me you took care of that other kid, and they find him in an alley two days later. Now you can take care of Hillyer or don't. But don't be stupid enough to think you can touch me."

He slammed down the phone and fell back into his chair, thinking for a moment about what he had to do. But there wasn't anything to do. It was over. Little by little it would unravel. Only a fool would pretend that wasn't so, and Artemis Reach wasn't a fool. There was nothing he could do to stop it, and he wasn't interested in trying.

Hillyer would be taken care of, and there was some little satisfaction in that.

But not enough. It wouldn't be enough unless they all paid.

He knew how to make that happen.

THE last houses at the end of Linden Lane backed onto thick birch woods where it was still possible to startle a raccoon in the night, where now and then an owl called. Paths were worn in it by kids who used the woods as nothing more than a shortcut from Linden Lane to Shannon. Sometimes on a summer night the leaves would hold the bitter smell of pot and Jim Franks heard panicked squeals and the scraping sounds of fleeing feet as he moved among the trees, ruining someone's good time.

But on a school night in spring he could count on having the moon-dappled space to himself. His shoes made soft, sucking sounds in the decaying leaves and the rub of budded branches against his shoulders filled him with a strange sense of well-being, as though he were surrounded by calm and silent friends. There was no place on earth he loved the way he loved these few stubborn acres of woodland that survived the domestication of everything wild around them. He loved them above all for the generosity of their solitude.

Tonight the wind scraped at the top of the trees and stirred down through the branches in swirling eddies of unrest. He hunched himself against the chill and plunged forward, eager to get in deep enough for the branches to blot out the street lamps he had left behind on Linden Lane. Then the magic could begin to work.

Only it didn't. He raised his hands in front of him to fend off stray branches as he pushed along one of the narrower paths that dwindled down to something less than a trail, more than an intent. In the moonlight the white skins of the birches gleamed like skeletons, and it struck him suddenly that he didn't know the woods at all.

Yet the woods had always been there, so it was he, James Anthony Franks, who was the stranger.

O

I saw her where she lets herself be seen, haunting-hovering. In thin close even though it was cold. She had a body once with breasts that might have nursed if there was time. Wrathe thin now I mean it hurt to look because theres no flesh at all just angles and bones.

On the shit again, thats the message. Eyes from another space and planet. On her way to being dead. Which in her case has reached the point of turning tricks on Lexington ave. Yes, I followed her even though I promised you I wouldnt and promised myself too. Dont be made at me, O. I break promises to every one, even promised her I wouldnt follow.

But she wasnt at the time dead yet, strung on shit with the light out of her eyes and yes purple bruises on her what used to be skin. One trick, thats my limit, all I saw and had to see but see I did, O.

I use your name like crying sometimes a neat circle that closes around and hugs itself. Just writing it feels better.

I'm telling you about her because shes the why of it, O. The shit in her veins thats drinking her blood from the inside out. Shes not your reason, you have your own. But mine. Its got to stop, doesnt it. I have to talk to you. God, I have to talk to you.

Are we really prophets? And who is listening?

The job as far as it went was over. Whatever they found about the shooting. Just for knocking on Lloyd Elijah's door, telling his mother and sister he was a cop. That by itself was enough to make him not a cop anymore. He couldn't remember not being a cop but maybe it was time for a change. In fact it was definitely time for a change. There were things in the job that disgusted him. It was time to try something else.

Jim had to laugh at himself for that because he said it so bravely, like hoisting a sail for the wind to catch and carry him off to Fiji or Samoa or somewhere he had been hearing about since he was Jimmy's age.

People didn't really do that, did they? It seemed to him he read a story once about a man who did. But that only showed how few people managed it. It only sounded simple. Pack up the wife and the kids and set sail.

He leaned against a tree trunk and thought it through. Elijah's mother would be distraught and might not tell them right away a cop had been to see her. (The daughter wouldn't remember, that was reasonably sure. But didn't matter.) *I knew something happened to him when that detective came around asking questions*, the mother would say sooner or later. And the two cops questioning her would look at each other and puzzle it out and say *No, ma'am, there haven't been any detectives asking questions* and she'd say *Sat right at the counter real as life and I poured him coffee.*

He'd given her his name to make it easy for them.

He'd left a trail on the street that even the least of them could follow.

Standing away from the tree, Jim pressed the button on his watch that lit the dial. It was only a few minutes past ten. Lenny was watching the news.

If he thought about it the right way, he could make it all come out for the best. Start something new. A blessing in disguise.

His strength, his virtue, really, was that he could think about it the right way when he had to. Now he had to. A man accepts what he has to accept.

Something ran before him, startling the undergrowth. But Jim Franks wasn't startled. He was calm, had reached calm, had made himself calm, which meant he had already accepted what would happen. The myrtle hugging the tree roots rippled and went still and Jim knew that a rabbit or a raccoon had come and gone.

He took a step after it, his sole crunching the shimmering myrtle. A second step, this time laid on the leaves so delicately it scarcely made a sound. The rabbit wouldn't have run far, would it? He didn't know, even though a good hunter would know the habits of all this little game. These were the things he would have to learn.

He stopped, poised between strides, acutely conscious of not making sense.

This is crazy, he told himself. He wasn't a hunter, had never hunted in his life.

And then he took another step on the myrtle, thinking that a man who shot and killed a boy should have no trouble at all with a rabbit, a possum or even a deer.

No trouble. No trouble at all.

I started a poem that says I am the moon before sunset and I could hear you in my head asking me what it means. The moons for the night, isn't it, silverwhite against the darkness, stars around. Some times comes out early, kind of useless and futile and trying to be a moon but what is it? I count on you to know what I mean.

Tell you the truth, O, I like telling my poems to you, trying to tell you after what they mean even though I have a rule against it. Mr H says you cant say what a poem means because it means the whole poem, but still there are things you can say although some times you have to find them when you talk because they werent there when you wrote the poem. I am the moon before sunset. I didn't no why until I told you.

I wish I could believe the way you do, in god I mean but sometimes I think if he really wanted me to believe in him he could be a little more convincing.

e is terrific and knows everything and I dont think he'll mess up again. He got someone to talk to me last night but I wont tell you who because I'm not sure if he'll join us. We'll never have 50 will we O? That was dumb but 25 would be enough. Ten would. e says its all changing and someone is giving it to them and everyones afraid to get it anywhere else. Guys he knows used to make crack out of coke but now they cant because no one is letting anyone do that. You have to get it from them or they break you if you try to sell it e says.

Maybe thats not bad. Because if a thing has a head and you cut the head off, it dies. If it doesnt have a head you just keep cutting.

Only you have to know where the head is.

Please be careful O. We cant stop them if they stop us. We have to be careful. They kill people every way there is.

The difference between you and me is I just hate them all and you dont hate anyone. Isnt it funny that it comes to the same thing?

Jim Franks drifted out to the edge of the woods around where Linden Lane bends to the right, even though he wouldn't be able to get home that way without cutting through Taylor's yard. Now, for some reason he couldn't understand, the woods made him think about the boy he shot and he decided he wouldn't be able to make himself stop thinking about it until he got out of there.

It was easier to get control of himself in Taylor's yard, where he could see the string of streetlights that led home. He skirted the swimming pool, keeping to the lawn so that his shoes wouldn't make any noise on the flagstones, slowing down when he reached the street. He'd start from the fact that it wasn't a good shooting. There was no point defending it because he'd never get anywhere with it as long as he did.

It was a mistake. He understood that. He was human and he made a mistake. Accept it, Jim. Accept it for what it is.

He did. A tragic, human accident like the kind that sometimes . . . *oh God it was ridiculous*, he told himself, making himself stop. A kid's head got blown off.

There was a car in front of the house. They had come already.

Get it straight now, he told himself. A mistake. You can't torture yourself about a mistake.

Except that you have to. Only a monster wouldn't. It was all right to feel this way, to see it in his sleep.

But how could he see it in his sleep when he hadn't seen it when it happened? Which he hadn't. He had closed his eyes and hadn't looked over at the body even once. He'd made it out of the room without looking.

Which wasn't far enough.

The car was a city car, he realized from the plates.

That was good. They could have radioed for the Dobbs Ferry police to pick him up, but instead they sent someone. A class touch.

Lenny, he imagined, was serving them tea.

We're not all children of God, O. Be more careful. No one would believe us so we have to know more. I'm sure your right they keep it there, because guess who I saw coming out? And you know he doesn't have a girlfriend. But dont take chances, we dont need to know that bad. Dont go in there again. If they catch you you know what will happen.

Don't say anything. Anything. Not even to e. I can talk to him, you talk to me. I used to think you were safe as a sparrow, shy Ophelia, gentle Ophelia, who would fear, who would hurt?

But theyr not children of god. Theyr killing all of us, why not you.

If it goes that high, how low? e can find out. But we cant do anything now. God I'm scared. Be scared too.

The two detectives stood up and turned to face the door as Jim came in. They were both black. One of them said, "Detective Franks?"

"Yes."

Lenny was standing between them. It all looked very natural, as though they had come for a visit.

"My name's Greg Young, this is Doug Phelan." His shield case was in his hand and he flipped it open and then closed. "We'd like you to come downtown with us?"

"Downtown?" Franks asked. "You're not with Internal Affairs?"

Internal Affairs had its offices in Brooklyn.

"No, sir. Chief of Detectives' squad."

Franks nodded. It didn't matter one way or the other. "Honey, I'll probably be a while," he said.

He had closed the door behind him when he came in and now he opened it again.

"You've already surrendered your service revolver, is that right?" Young said.

"That's right."

"But you have an off-duty weapon?"

"Yes."

"We'd appreciate it if you'd bring it."

Franks knew why and it hurt the way a knife hurts. They were going to do ballistics tests on it. They knew he had been looking for Lloyd Elijah and they were going to check into the possibility that he had found and killed him.

"It's upstairs," he said. "Maybe one of you ought to come with me."

Phelan started across the room but Young said, "That won't be necessary."

Phelan stopped in his tracks and looked at his shoes, embarrassed at having moved.

"What kind of weapon is it?" Young asked.

"Nine-millimeter automatic."

Young smiled. "Good," he said. "I wouldn't worry about it. We'll wait here."

Franks should have been relieved but he wasn't. As he started up the stairs he realized why. What bothered him wasn't that the Department considered him a possible killer. He didn't care one way or the other what the Department thought. What he cared about was that the Elijah boy hadn't been murdered until after he started looking for him. That made him responsible.

He heard Lenny say, "Is it all right if I go upstairs?"

He took down the gun from the closet shelf where he kept it and was stepping out of the closet when Lenny came in.

"Are you all right?" she asked.

Her voice had lost its steadiness and her face looked careworn and aged. He wanted to tell her he was sorry for that, but all he said was, "Yes, of course."

He turned away to look at himself in the mirror. He was still wearing the sweatshirt he played football with Jimmy in. He pulled it over his head and tossed it aside, not wanting to go to Headquarters dressed like that.

"What's happening, Jim?" she asked.

He took a fresh shirt from the drawer and turned to face her, tearing the paper from the shirt.

"I was looking for a boy who had some connection with the boy I shot," he said. "He was killed, and they want to ask me about it."

She didn't understand but couldn't bring herself to ask anything else. Her eyes clouded over, as though his telling her about two dead children one after the other was more than her mind and heart could deal with. Cops got used to those things, that's why he could say it so easily, but civilians never did.

"Do you want a tie?" she asked.

He tucked in his shirt and slid the gun in at his waist. She handed him a tie and picked out a jacket while he knotted the tie. She asked if the jacket was all right and he said it was.

"I'll just be a second," he said, and went into the bathroom. He could hear her crying softly until he closed the door.

He looked at himself in the mirror over the sink and noticed that the gun was in his hand.

He remembered that he had read the play with Susan and that his last pass to Jimmy was complete.

The barrel of the gun was bitter as a penny on his tongue.

The trigger was soft and yielding like a woman's breast.

FRIDAY

EVEN before seven o'clock Lieutenant Larocca had a feeling something wasn't right. Friday was his sixth day on duty outside La Guardia Junior High, and it had rained through much of the night, with high winds. The streets had that clean, washed and swept look that comes to New York only when the day dawns clear and bright after a storm.

The custodial staff showed up as they always did to open the school. They were used to the police by this time and usually exchanged words with them on their way in. This morning they said nothing, letting themselves in with keys from their heavy rings and locking the doors behind them.

Still, there wasn't anything Larocca could put his finger on. By a little past seven, he realized that the doors were still locked and the kitchen staff hadn't shown up at all. He called the Borough Command on his radio.

"I know this is gonna sound dumb," he said. "But is this some kind of a holiday?"

He was told it wasn't and went back to his post, where his men were drinking coffee and eating doughnuts. "Is it me or is there something funny going on?" he wondered out loud.

The men looked around indifferently. It must be him. There wasn't anything going on at all.

At seven-fifteen Larocca found out just how good his instincts were. Borough Command called him to say that one of the radio stations was announcing that all schools in District Sixty-one were closed for the day because of "police interference with educational processes."

Larocca had the presence of mind to ask for a confirmation before he did anything. By the time Borough Command called back, the school closing bulletin had been broadcast by virtually every station in the city, just as they did for snowstorms. A call to Community Board Sixty-one got a tape-recorded announcement to the same effect.

"Guess you might as well pack it in," the captain with whom he was speaking suggested, but Larocca wasn't so sure and asked to have the orders verified by Commander Norland himself.

He was still on the radio waiting when a group of between seventy-five and a hundred students came around the corner from the direction of the subway.

"Lieutenant," one of the men called, directing his attention to them.

Larocca got off the phone in a hurry and ordered his squad to form up. He took two men with him and approached the students. They were moving toward him in a tight phalanx that gave him a distinct sense of uneasiness. If they were going to close the damn schools, why the hell couldn't they announce it in time to keep the kids from showing up? And send someone to handle those who showed up anyway? It was a pain in the ass that he had to do their work. He noticed a few teachers, maybe half a dozen of them, in the crowd. They were the ones who usually came early, so that was okay. The odd thing was the kids. School didn't start until nine and there were never any kids before eight-thirty. Today, with no school, the kids were coming early.

When the students were still about twenty yards from the cops, a big kid, thick and tall, at the front of the column—he seemed to be leading them—held up one hand. The students stopped behind him, their ranks tightening.

The instant he saw that, Larocca knew he was in trouble. "Call the Borough Command, tell them we need more people," he whispered urgently to the patrolman next to him.

"There is no school today," he announced in a loud voice. "I don't have the details but the school board's announcing it on the radio. You might as well go home."

He could see a few of the teachers pushing their way toward the front of the crowd, but most were moving the other way, anticipating trouble and getting away from it.

"*You* go home," the boy who seemed to be the leader called back. "And take 'em all with you!"

Hal Garson shouldered his way out of the pack. Larocca was glad to see a teacher taking charge but doubted it would do any good.

"That's enough, Charlie," Garson said. "Give me a minute, let me talk with them."

"Talk all you want," Charlie Wain said. "But we ain't goin' if they don't."

Garson nodded his understanding of the terms and moved into the space between the police and the students. "Is it true?" he said. "The school's closed?"

"I'm only hearing it now," Larocca answered. "But yeah, that's what it looks like. Any chance you can get them dispersed?"

Garson turned to face the students and saw that a few of the other teachers had made it to the front of the pack. They were facing the students, their backs to the cops. The rest remained in the crowd, working their way back to the corner and out of sight.

"The police didn't shut down the school," Garson announced loudly. "They don't know any more about it than you do. But we're going to have a mess here if everybody hangs around. How about helping us out?"

"I told you what's gonna be, Mr. Garson," Charlie shouted back at him. "We don't go until they go!"

The kids ranked behind him shouted their approval. Looking into their faces, Garson realized he didn't recognize half of them. Many were older than La Guardia kids, dropouts probably, Charlie Wain's shock troops for a showdown with the cops. Christ, that meant Charlie had been ready for the closing before it happened.

Garson tried to think of something he could say to stall a confrontation, of some way to warn the cops that it was a setup. But before he could say anything one of the cops shouted, "Lieutenant!" in a voice filled with alarm.

At least sixty kids were coming up the block from the opposite corner, moving right toward the first group. Garson was swallowed up in the crowd as it surged around him. The two or three cops who had come onto the sidewalk with the lieutenant to parlay with Charlie Wain quickly fell back to the curb, letting the two groups meet, conceding the sidewalk to them. Garson fought his way free of the mob and rushed over to the cops, who were forming up quickly in the street.

"Listen," he said urgently, grabbing the lieutenant by the arm. "Most of these kids aren't from the school. Street kids, someone put them up to it, they're trying to get something started."

"Shit, are you sure?" Larocca asked but didn't even wait for a reply. He was on the radio at once. "We've got a hundred, hundred-fifty kids here and we can't hold our position," he shouted into his radio. "We need reinforcements immediately."

Around him, his men all had their riot sticks out, holding them in the ready position, two-handed, across their chests. But there were only twelve men, far too few to send into the mob.

And yet they couldn't just stand there. Passivity, Larocca knew, was like a red flag, a provocative confession of weakness. They had to move forward, at least to buy time.

"Take it slow, let's move," he ordered in a calm voice. Starting with a measured, deliberate pace, they moved toward the center of the pack of students directly in front of the school, hoping to hypnotize the kids with their movement just long enough for reinforcements to arrive. Already they could hear the wail of sirens approaching fast.

The kids weren't fooled. Or perhaps they sensed that it was the time to strike. They could hear the sirens, too, and must have known that once the cops were there in force they would all be locked into the positions they had claimed. "Get outta my face," Charlie Wain shouted at Larocca, taking a step toward him. The others followed, right on his shoulder, moving to meet the advancing cops.

A radio car flew around the corner and the siren cut out, dropping a strange quiet over the street. But there were only two men in the car and two men wouldn't do much good. The kids saw it and picked up the pace, moving faster, chanting derisively, only a few feet separating them from the cops.

Larocca could make out more sirens in the distance but knew he'd be facing a full-scale riot by the time they got there unless he got some space between his cops and the kids before anyone touched anyone.

"Back!" he yelled. "Fall back! Now!"

The dozen cops in his command broke ranks even before the words were out of his mouth, sprinting to safety across the boulevard, followed by a chorus of mocking cheers.

Like water rushing through an open sluice, the kids surged into the street, taking uncontested possession of everything in front of the school. A loud cheer made it impossible to talk for a moment but then subsided into a continuous stream of shouted taunts.

Marooned across the street, Larocca's troops huddled impotently. The pair of officers from the radio car raced up, eager to help.

"Whatdya want us to do, Lieutenant?" one of them asked, inanely enthusiastic, shouting to be heard above the noise.

"Do?" Larocca shouted back to him. "Don't do a goddamned thing!"

PARTS of the message in Timothy's letters seemed clear. Steven had come to know the boy's mind so well that the scattered fragments of information fell into place the way the jumbled pieces on a chessboard organize themselves in the mind of a player. The bright, intense boy, with no resources other than his own indignation, had opened a secret war on the drug dealers at La Guardia Junior High. How long it had been going on Steven couldn't tell, but it explained the bout of apparent paranoia Timothy went through a few months before he died, when he insisted that other students were trying to kill him. Perhaps they weren't, but they would have been if they had found out what he was doing.

At one stage he must have imagined he could get fifty kids to join his crusade, but he seemed to have settled in the end for only Ophelia James and Lloyd Elijah, *shy Ophelia, gentle Ophelia, safe as a sparrow,* and Lloyd, the prophet of his poems who had been a user and a dealer. Evidently, Elijah straightened himself out when Timothy went to live with him, but then slipped back. *I don't think he'll mess up again,* Timothy wrote, expressing what must have been a hope more than an opinion. It was typical of Timothy to stake so much on a boy as fragile and lost as himself.

The letter in which Timothy told about trailing his mother to a trick on Lexington Avenue echoed in Steven's mind with an aching pain for the boy's anguish. He ached above all with the feeling that if only he, Steven Hillyer, had done more, had fought harder to get Timothy the help he needed, his life might have been spared. But perhaps that was only an illusion generated by guilt and a desire to believe that roads not taken lead to other destinations. In reality it may well have been that the self-destructive recklessness so apparent in the boy was the only way Timothy could shape his life, the only choice he had. *I am the moon before sunset,* he wrote in a poem he never finished.

Apparently Timothy learned through Lloyd Elijah that the chaotic crack trade at school was being organized into a tight little monopoly. *You have to get it from them or they break you if you try to sell it e says.* He was naive enough to find a reason for hope in this new arrangement—*if a thing has a head and you cut the head off, it dies*—but he was also realistic enough to be afraid, especially for Ophelia's sake. *Theyr not children of god. Theyr killing all of us, why not you?* he wrote in his last letter of warning, pleading with her to be careful. *They kill people every way there is.*

But who were *they?* Ophelia must have come close to the answer, because suddenly the letters turned from brave to cautious. *I'm sure your right they keep it there,* he wrote, insistently warning her not to take chances, not to *go in there again, we dont need to know that bad.*

Go in where? And who did Timothy see coming out? The only clue Timothy left was that it was someone who didn't have a girlfriend. But that could be anyone.

Right now what mattered to Steven was the fact that Ophelia had probably disregarded Timothy's warning. Could that be why she was killed?

Just framing the question excited him. From the beginning he had wanted to believe that Timothy didn't kill Ophelia James. Now it seemed possible. *If they catch you you know what will happen*, Timothy warned. But how? And who?

Certainly Charlie Wain was one of them, but that wasn't the answer. He was in the middle of the La Guardia drug-trafficking network, the first on the scene in the weight room. He had undoubtedly lied to Steven when Steven and Rita caught him in the playground, and he had his henchman beat Steven to scare him out of questioning Lloyd Elijah. But Charlie Wain wasn't an organizer. He couldn't have been more than a soldier and enforcer on the low end of the chain of command. It went higher. That thought played over and over in Steven's mind as it had in Timothy's. *If it goes so high*, Timothy had wondered. How high?

High enough to frighten Timothy into caution. *No one would believe us*, he wrote.

Steven tried to explain it to Rita but she wouldn't listen. She met his excitement at first with cold indifference and then with mounting indignation.

"This isn't your world, Steven," she snapped. "Who gave you the right to police it?"

He had worked hard to make it his world. Maybe at too many points along the way he had almost given up. But he hadn't given up. That was what mattered. He came to District Sixty-one believing there didn't have to be the gulf between his world and hers that she insisted on, and he was beginning to believe it again. He wouldn't accept her verdict. "You were born here so that gives you a straight line into street truth?" he countered, matching his anger to hers. "That's bullshit."

"I'm not talking about truth," she said. "I'm talking about getting Lloyd Elijah killed. You're an English teacher from Connecticut, you don't know what you're doing. Who else will be killed if you don't stay out of this?"

"Is that how you fight this thing? Do you think the body count stays down if we all just leave the killers alone?"

"Who are you going to talk to next?" she answered, taunting him as though she hadn't heard what he said at all. "How about Jamal? They'll find him in an alley and you'll know you're getting even closer."

"I'm not involving anyone who isn't involved."

"Good. Then the only one killed will be you."

"I'm not looking to get killed."

"It won't be a meaningful death, Steven. It's not a martyrdom. Timothy Warren wasn't a prophet and you're not one either. Nobody rides up to heaven in a chariot of fire."

"So we just accept it?" he asked, not as a challenge but because he really wanted to hear her answer.

"I don't accept it," she said softly, reaching across her anger to lay a finger on his lips. "I fight it by giving them an alternative. I fight it by being a teacher and showing them there's another way to live. I fight it by doing my work and making love and living a life. There isn't any other way, Steven."

By that time it was morning and they talked awhile longer, in a quieter vein, and then they made love, forgoing the luxury of sleep. As he showered and dressed for school, Steven thought about Rita and wondered if she had made love to him in order to buy his acquiescence with the extravagant bribe of her body. Still, perhaps, just perhaps, she wasn't wrong.

They didn't talk about Timothy or the letters as they rode to school together, though the pressure of her thigh against his on the subway seat was enough to remind him of what she believed, and he couldn't respond.

As they got off the train and started up out of the station they began to realize that something was wrong. The wail of sirens from the street pulled them to the surface fast, along with the students on the train. Chaos greeted them.

Looking toward the school corner, they could see students clustered in a thick, milling knot, with more rushing to join them. Steven and Rita paused only long enough to exchange glances and then hurried forward to find out what was going on.

Ahead of him, Steven saw a girl fighting her way through a knot of students, trying to get away from the school as one kid and then another caught hold of her, refusing to let her leave. He broke into a run, and as he drew nearer recognized Maria Onofrio. Rita was right behind him.

"Let her go, leave her alone," he called, flinging kids aside in his haste to get to Maria.

By the time he reached her, Maria was crouched back against the side of the building, her large oval eyes wide with fear as Steven peeled the boys away from her. At half a dozen other places on the block other gangs of boys were detaining kids who wanted to leave.

"School's closed, Mr. Hillyer," Maria cried. "There's police all over and there's going to be awful trouble."

"Are you all right?" he demanded, afraid she might be hurt.

"I just want to go home," Maria wailed. "Please can I go home?"

"What are you runnin' out for?" one of the boys taunted.

"You gonna let 'em lock us out of our own school?" another boy called. "We gotta stick together."

Steven wheeled on him. "You stick together somewhere else," he commanded sharply.

He took a step toward the boy, who held his ground for a moment, weighing the consequences of fighting back. A dozen kids stood ready to help the boy if he decided to go that way but Steven didn't care. One way or the other he was getting Maria out of there.

"Did you hear me?" he demanded, stepping into the boy's chest, driving him back.

The boy, about Steven's size, shoved back with his forearms. Someone shouted that there were more cops arriving and that they were trying to clear the kids off the sidewalk in front of the school.

For a fraction of a second everyone hung fire, and then suddenly the knot disintegrated as the kids all turned and raced like hell toward the school, charging off for bigger and more exciting battles.

Down the length of the block the other clusters of boys dissolved just as quickly, leaving behind a few frightened children like stray strands of sea grass abandoned by the tide.

"Go with Miss Torres," Steven called to them. "She'll take you to the subway station."

While Rita led her charges back to the station, Steven dashed to the corner, seeing the signs of confusion multiply with every step. Across the street, away from the dense crowds of teenagers, he saw about a dozen teachers looking on helplessly. Others were probably hiding beyond the edges of the action, afraid to get involved yet duty-bound to stay.

The sound of police sirens was almost constant now as vehicles continued to pour onto the scene, most of them regular patrol cars with only a pair of officers, here and there the unmarked vehicle of a detective team. The block in front of the school was choked with traffic, the arrivals piling up chaotically behind the cars already on the scene, cops abandoning their cars to sprint forward on foot.

As Steven looked toward the school, the dimensions of the problem, with its potential for violence, were instantly and appallingly clear. The students controlled the block-long stretch of sidewalk in front of the school from corner to corner. The police had done nothing to secure the perimeters, so nothing prevented new kids from coming onto the scene. Every few minutes, as trains arrived at the subway station nearby, scores of children poured onto the sidewalk, adding their numbers to the critical mass already collected in front of the school.

The cops, as far as Steven could tell, weren't doing anything. They stood clustered together in the street, milling uncertainly. They had very little room to maneuver, hemmed in left and right by their own cars.

Heading toward the school, he heard an angry shout erupt from the students ahead of him, while behind him a siren shrieked so close it exploded inside his head. He whirled around to see the doors of a large police truck flinging open. Tactical troops in full riot gear, armored and helmeted, charged out, clearly with a plan, awesome and frightening in the grim certainty with which they moved. While the main body of new troops snaked its way toward the other cops in the middle of the block, a dozen or so broke away in an effort to seal off the street at the corners, where the crowd of students was thinnest.

Steven froze for an instant, overwhelmed by the shock wave of force that flowed from them, the anonymous threat hidden behind their faceless visors.

But only for an instant. He realized quickly that if he didn't get to the school before the police sealed off the sidewalk it would be too late. He felt he belonged there without even thinking what he would do.

As he raced for the school, the riot cops hustled forward, angling toward a point on the sidewalk between the school door and the corner where they would make their stand. Steven picked up his pace and so did the kids around him, propelled by the same urgency. Boys rushed by him, calling to each other to hurry, shouting warnings, a few cheering him on as they raced past. *C'mon, Mr. Hillyer. You with us, Mr. Hillyer.*

But Steven wasn't with them. He wanted to stop them, or stop the police, or at least get in the middle where maybe, just maybe, he could do something to forestall the bloody confrontation about to erupt around him. Hatred of the police, always intense among these kids, had been building to the ignition point for almost two weeks now. Once the violence exploded, nothing would contain it until it had run its course.

Three cops lunged in front of him, swinging around, sticks ready, blocking the way. *Keep back, keep back,* they called, their voices muffled, inhuman, in their gleaming masks.

Instantly half a dozen boys charged the line, a girl screamed at the cop holding her, a boy scrambled monkeylike over the roof of a car at the curb. A stick flashed out at the boy's feet, tripping him up, and he slammed flat against the metal roof, rolled away and was gone.

For an instant a space opened in front of Steven, a narrow gap, and he lunged for it, twisting sideways. "I'm a teacher!" he shouted into the visored face of the cop, who shoved him back into the pack of kids, knocking him from his feet.

He fell to the side, toppling to the pavement, but as the cop stepped past him to grab at a boy, Steven was able to roll clear and spring to his feet behind the newly formed police line. He ran toward the concentration of students in front of the school doors.

He was among the last to make it through as the police ranks stiffened behind him. From the street a bullhorn began to issue ultimatums in a booming, artificial voice. "Move to the corner in an orderly fashion," it commanded. "Proceed to the corner in an orderly fashion. You have five minutes to disperse."

"Time's up, pigs!" someone shouted back, his loud clear voice surrounded by a chorus of obscenities.

As if on signal, something thrown from the crowd caught Lieutenant Larocca on the side of the head and he staggered back, the bullhorn dropping to his side. It was a book, a large textbook scaled across the distance like a skimmed rock, and as it plummeted to the ground Steven caught the flash of color from the cover and his mind irrelevantly informed him that it was the eighth-grade American history text. After that there was no time for connected thought of any kind.

At the front of the crowd the students hooted with laughter, but from the back the book was followed by a barrage of thrown objects, more books but also bottles and soda cans, opened cartons of milk that came in streaming like comets, and then, more and more often, stones and fragments of brick that escalated the confrontation in a moment from mockery to battle.

The police in the street began to fall back under the bombardment, arms raised to ward off books and cans, ducking and twisting away with odd slapstick contortions. But one cop, blood running from his scalp where a stone caught him, changed all that in an instant. Screaming obscenities, swinging his stick wildly, he led a charge against the students.

The uniformed cops followed first simply because they were closest, but the helmeted riot cops were right on their heels, hard and invulnerable as a machine.

With the cops coming toward him and the pressure of the students at his back, Steven was trapped. He threw up a hand to protect himself and caught a blow on the shoulder that sent a shivering pain down the length of his arm. Someone shoved him and he staggered against a cop, who drove a forearm into his chest and flung him aside.

Kids were screaming, rushing in all directions, some fleeing from the police attack, others fighting back, but all of them running any way they could, dodging, darting, ensnared by the cold geometry of the street, cops at either end, fanning out from the middle, tangled in a hundred brawls at once. Mixed with the screams and shouts were the sickening soft thuds of clubs against flesh, clubs against skulls, the crack and shatter of stones and bricks against cars and shields.

A cop, tripped to the pavement, was kicked hard in the face. Another fell back against a girl, clutching his abdomen as though he could hold in the blood that gushed over his hands. A boy, clubbed in the neck, head lolling oddly, tottered back to the building wall and slid down it like a raindrop.

Steven ran to him. A voice not far away shouted, "There he is! Hillyer!" Before Steven could figure out what it meant or where it came from, something hit him in the side just below his ribs. He whirled, saw a boy with a knife, a boy he didn't know, and felt a warm trickle of blood where the blade must have caught him.

Christ, that was no accident, no act of random violence in the mael-strom.

"You're meat, man," the boy muttered, lunging forward as Steven stepped backward, the wall against his back. Behind the boy he saw Charlie Wain moving toward him.

Suddenly the boy with the knife lurched aside, stumbling, as a smaller boy flung himself at him. It was Jamal Horton.

"Run, Mr. Hillyer!" Jamal yelled, careening away from the boy with the knife. "You gotta get out of here!"

In an instant they were both running, Steven following Jamal's darting lead, letting the boy draw him away from the fiercest fighting. He glanced back to see Charlie Wain angrily shoving the boy with the knife out of his way as he waded through the mob, pushing people aside in his slow and relentless pursuit.

Steven looked away for only a fraction of a section but in that moment he almost lost Jamal. A few paces ahead the boy wove and darted, mag-ically finding aisles through the violence, glancing back to make sure Steven was still there. An explosive roar shook them all as one of the police cars burst into flames.

There was nothing to do now but run and keep running until they got to the corner. And around the corner to safety, if the fighting hadn't spread that far. Again Steven saw the looming form of Charlie Wain thrusting through the chaos, and again he disappeared as Steven ran after Jamal.

Lurching past the last thin cordon of riot cops and panicked children, they turned the corner at last. Ahead of them, among the huddled spec-tators driven back by the carnage, Rita stood, frightened, her eyes scan-ning the fleeing refugees and then finding Steven, calling to him.

Steven ran to her and she threw her arms around him. "My God," she sobbed. "I thought you were in the middle of it."

"C'mon, Mr. Hillyer," Jamal pleaded. "Charlie's got everybody looking for you. You gotta get outta here."

When Steven pulled away from Rita there was blood on her hands where she'd held him, so he knew he was bleeding, but he didn't feel any pain. He didn't see Charlie Wain when he looked down the street but couldn't afford to wait until he did.

"I have to go," Steven said to Rita, starting to move off, pulling away from the touch of her hands.

"Where?" she called after him.

"A lady on the Board. I'll explain later," he called back, turned and started to run.

He raced down the subway stairs without even realizing Jamal was no longer with him until he reached the turnstile and stopped to dig a token from his pocket.

"Forget it, man," someone called.

Kids by the scores were racing through exits, turnstiles and tokens forgotten in their rush to be out of there.

At the same time, new kids were pouring off the trains, charging up the stairs, drawn from other schools by news of trouble, ready to make more. The sight of them filled Steven with a numbed awareness that the riot upstairs had barely begun.

Above them and a block away, a candy store across from the school began to burn.

SURPRISED? Nothing that black son of a bitch ever did would surprise Boorstin. But closing the schools? Christ.

It was the most arrogant and reckless act Boorstin had ever heard of in public life. He had known there would be trouble when Commissioner Pound caved in to Terranova and let the investigation at La Guardia Junior High go on. The fact that Reach had said almost nothing when he left the Commissioner's office didn't fool Boorstin for a minute. There would be hell to pay.

But closing the schools? Not just La Guardia, but every junior high and grammar school in the district. Great Christ Almighty.

Between eighteen and nineteen thousand children attending those schools would now be on the streets. Summers were scary enough, kids on the loose with nothing to do. Every summer the whole city held its breath from the day school got out till the end of Labor Day weekend. Suddenly a Friday in spring had all the earmarks of the worst summers there had ever been all rolled into one. Even before the first alarms came in from the Bronx, Boorstin alerted the Commissioner to alert Tactical.

What could that maniac have been thinking? Did Reach imagine that everyone would be so upset about the boys and girls missing their classes that they'd promise to give him what he wanted next time? Hell no. He was thinking chaos, thinking there wouldn't be a next time, thinking Harlem, Watts, Detroit and Armageddon. Reach knew what the schools were for, and he knew what closing them would do. He was blowing himself up to blow up the city. Why?

What did it matter why? It was a declaration of fucking war.

Boorstin had slightly under three minutes to enjoy these reflections. For no sooner had he responded to the announcement of the school closings by alerting the police than the police began to call back relaying Lieutenant Larocca's urgent alarms from the scene. By nine o'clock City Hall knew the shit was hitting the fan.

At nine-fifteen Junius Ehrlich marched up the stairs from his own office to Boorstin's. It was the first time he had ever been angry enough to do that.

"Explain it to me," he demanded, storming through the door.

Boorstin was on two phones and his secretary Rachel was on a third.

Boorstin hung up both lines. "You can't explain a thing like this," he said. "I'll tell you one thing, though. That bastard Reach just fucked himself."

"Then how come I can feel his big black schlong all the way up to my kidneys?"

Rachel turned to face the window.

"She's giggling, for Christ's sake. Is she crazy or what? Get her out of here," the mayor said.

Rachel hung up the phone and scampered out. The mayor watched her go, shaking his head, then turned to Boorstin.

"Run that by me again," he said. "I'll try to listen."

Boorstin came around from behind his desk. "Long before me and long before you," he said, "Reach got himself where he is because he had one particular threat in his pocket—eighteen thousand animals he could turn loose any time. Those kids are his doomsday machine. He screwed in the warhead, he set the fuse and he ran it past the fail-safe point. Now he's got nothing left."

The mayor's head was cocked to the side as though he were considering all of this. "Why would he do that?" he asked.

Boorstin could only shrug. "Could be he's psychotic," he said. "Could be he's got problems we don't even know about yet."

"What kind of problems?"

"I don't know. But you should have seen him when Pound said he wouldn't call off the investigation. The air went out."

For a moment neither man spoke.

"I suppose you're going to explain to me now that we don't have a problem," Mayor Ehrlich said at last.

"Of course we've got a problem."

"And what are we going to do about it?"

Boorstin took a deep breath. "It might help if you went up there," he said.

"Do I look like John Fucking Lindsay to you? I wouldn't go up there yesterday. How the hell am I going to go up there today?"

"All right," Boorstin said, raising his hands for peace. "So you don't go. There are still things we can do."

Mayor Ehrlich lowered himself into the chair behind Boorstin's desk. "And I'll tell you what they are," he said. "We get every cop who's not up there at that school out looking for Reach, we bring him in in a straitjacket if we have to. And we make him stand up there and tell them all to go home."

Boorstin considered for a moment. That might quiet things down but it would give Reach the chance to play the role of peacemaker. "I'm not so sure, Your Honor," he started to say.

"I am. Make the call."

Ehrlich handed him the phone. Boorstin dialed the Commissioner's office and asked him to send as many men as he could spare to find Artemis Reach.

When he hung up the phone, the mayor had his elbows on the desk and his head in his hands. "A spade cop kills a spade kid and you tell me you can handle it," he mumbled softly. "Next thing I know the whole city's burning down."

It wasn't the whole city. It was only the Bronx. But Boorstin knew better than to argue.

The mayor looked up at his deputy. "We should have indicted that cop in the first place. I don't suppose it'd do any good to indict him now?" he asked.

Boorstin shook his head. "He killed himself last night. Blew his brains out."

Ehrlich leaned all the way back in the chair with a look of fathomless resignation. "Awright," he said. "You made the call, the cops are doing what they can. Get out of here, willya."

Boorstin smiled in spite of himself. It was typical of Mayor Ehrlich to take possession of a desk, forgetting he wasn't in his own office.

"Excuse me, Your Honor," Boorstin said. "But this is my office."

Junius Ehrlich sat up straight and looked Boorstin in the eye. "Not anymore," he said. And smiled.

EVERYONE in Congressman Kellem's office was gathered around the radio when Steven hurried in. The cut in his side had stopped bleeding but he hadn't taken time to clean himself. He looked as if he had just come through a war, the war they were listening to on the radio.

The staff of young interns rushed to him, anxious and eager for a firsthand report. But Steven didn't have time to satisfy their curiosity. "We've got to talk," he said as soon as he saw L. D. Woods pushing her way through the staffers clustered around him.

She was the one who had called for the investigation into the killings in the weight room. And Steven had found explosive ammunition for that investigation in Timothy's letters.

L.D. filled him in on what she knew about the situation at La Guardia as they hurried down the corridor to her office. Two or three buildings near the school were in flames but the firefighters were being driven off by rock-throwing adolescents. One cop was in critical condition from a knife wound, another had been shot in the shoulder, and an interview with an emergency room attendant unofficially confirmed that dozens of wounded students had been brought in, some of them critical.

There were reported outbreaks of violence at schools all over the city, in Harlem and Brooklyn as well as the Bronx, and most of the high schools near La Guardia had been abandoned by their students, who rushed off to get in on the action at La Guardia.

"What about you?" she asked. "What happened?"

She stopped just outside her office to get a cupful of water from a drinking fountain.

"I don't know where to start," Steven said as soon as they were alone in her office.

"With those letters," she suggested. "Open your shirt, let me see what that looks like."

"Before the letters," he said, peeling back the bloodstained shirt, then dropping into the seat opposite her desk. He realized for the first time how sore and fatigued he was.

Leaning over him, L.D. slid a box of Kleenex within reach, wet a tissue and gently dabbed at the dried blood on his side. The cold water stung badly but the cut had stopped bleeding and only needed cleaning.

"Timothy Warren was on some kind of antidrug crusade," he said. "His mother seems to have been a heroin addict. I guess that's where it came from. Ophelia and Lloyd, the other boy who was killed, were helping him."

"Ophelia and Timothy," she asked. "Were they lovers?"

"I don't think so," he said. "Not from the letters. They're all about getting other kids to help them. Someone was organizing the crack traffic at La Guardia. That scared Timothy, mostly for Ophelia's sake. She was trying to find out something but he warned her not to push it."

L.D. stared at him with a frightened look in her eyes, and then she quickly gathered up the bloody tissues from the floor. "There must be a first-aid kit," she said. "Let me get some antiseptic."

She moved quickly to the door, gliding with perfect and uncanny grace. But then she stopped and turned to face him, her eyes questioning.

"If they weren't lovers," she said, "if she was helping him, then why did he kill her?"

"I don't think he did," Steven said.

The raw skin of his side began to throb with a dull, insistent pain as it warmed back to normal temperature.

L.D. studied him, her dark eyes wide and thoughtful. "What do you know about Artemis Reach?" she asked softly.

"He was the reason I came to La Guardia," Steven said. But he knew she was on a different track.

"Yes," she said. "He wanted to change everything."

"We all did."

She shook her head sadly and there were tears in her eyes. "It's not the same thing," she said. "We were changing the system because we wanted something different. I don't know what Artemis wanted. I think he just hated it the way it was." She sighed. "I used to think he was a great man."

There was a knock at the door and she turned to open it.

Detective Hartley Williams stepped past L.D., ignoring her. A second cop stood in the doorway.

"You'd better come with us, Hillyer," Williams said.

And then he read him his rights.

* * *

WITH the fires still burning in the Bronx, anything having to do with La Guardia Junior High was headline news. Word that the Chief of Detectives was having a La Guardia teacher pulled in for questioning brought the reporters out in force, with microphones stabbing forward like lances and lights blazing through the lobby at One Police Plaza the moment Detective Williams led Steven through the door. But Williams, who had warned him of this possibility in the car, bulled past them without answering any questions and Steven did the same, ducking his head away from the cameras like an old-fashioned gangster.

He was escorted to the Chief of Detectives' office, where Terranova was waiting for him. "Sit down," the big man ordered gruffly.

Steven sat.

Terranova stalked around Steven's chair for a moment, studying him like someone checking out a used car. "You didn't go home last night," he said at last.

"No."

"Or to your mother's."

It wasn't a question so Steven let it pass.

"Where'd that come from?" Terranova asked Williams, pointing to the blood on Steven's side.

"It was there when we picked him up."

"Is that right?"

The question was directed at Steven and he nodded his head.

"When we're finished here get him over to Beekman and let them have a look at it," Terranova said.

"It doesn't have to be looked at," Steven said. "Do you mind telling me why I'm here?"

"Do you mind telling us why you were looking for Lloyd Elijah after school Tuesday?"

"He was one of my students."

Terranova was pacing in the space between Steven and the desk. Williams was somewhere behind Steven, where he couldn't see him.

"Missing homework? Something like that?" the Chief of Detectives asked.

"It was about school," Steven answered evasively, unwilling to say more until he knew what they knew and what they were looking for.

"And this is why you asked Detective Franks to look for him too? To get his homework in?"

"I didn't ask Franks to look for him," Steven said.

"But he did."

"I think so. You'd better ask him that."

Terranova looked up to where Williams must have been standing and then stalked around behind his desk. Williams took over the questioning.

"How long have you known Franks?" he said.

"The first time I saw him was when he shot Timothy."

"You didn't know him before that?"

"Of course not."

"And when was the next time you had contact with him?"

"He came to my apartment. That was . . . Monday night," Steven said, thinking carefully to keep the days straight.

"What Monday is that? Do you recall?"

"This past Monday. Four days ago."

The answer seemed to puzzle or displease Williams. He looked back at the Chief and then down to Steven again. "You saw him at the grand jury, didn't you?" he asked.

"I saw him," Steven said. "We didn't talk. There wasn't anything to talk about."

"Why was that, Mr. Hillyer?"

"Because I was testifying about him."

"And because you saw him shoot one of your students."

"That's right."

"But then he dropped by your apartment. Is that what you're telling us?"

Steven leaned around him to look at Terranova. "Can I ask him to sit down?" he said.

"I'm sorry," Williams said. "Am I making you nervous?"

Steven didn't say anything. Williams grabbed a chair and swung it around so he could sit facing Steven.

"Yes, he dropped by my apartment," Steven said, directing his response to Terranova. "He wanted to talk about Timothy."

"What about Timothy?" Terranova asked, carefully lowering himself into the chair behind his desk.

"Franks said he had a son. He said he was upset about . . ." Steven stopped and tried to think how he could say this. "About what happened," he continued. "He wanted to know what kind of person Timothy was."

"And what did you tell him?"

"We talked for a long time. A couple hours I think. I showed him some of Timothy's poetry."

"That's the poetry you took from the Bronx County district attorney's office?"

There didn't seem to be anything he did that they didn't know about. They didn't want information, they already had it all. They were only trying to trip him up. "Look, I think you better tell me what the hell this is about," Steven said sharply, getting to his feet.

"I'll tell you exactly what it's about, Mr. Hillyer," Terranova snapped. "Get your ass back in that chair."

Steven hesitated but then sat. Terranova's chair creaked as he leaned forward, resting his elbows on the desk.

"We've got two dead kids and we had a teacher running around meeting drug dealers in a playground," Terranova began. "He told us he was just asking around so we let that slide. Do you remember telling us that, Mr. Hillyer?"

"Go ahead," Steven said.

"Cut to this week," Terranova said. "The teacher tells the district attorney some bullshit story to get his hands on some evidence, he meets with the cop that killed the kid, and then the two of them look for another kid who soon turns up dead. That's what it's about, Hillyer. It's about the crack business at La Guardia Junior High. Somebody's putting it all together. Think it might be a teacher? He'd need some muscle. Think it might be a cop?"

"That's insane," Steven shouted, back on his feet again, fighting through the wave of accusations that made him feel he would be pinned there forever if he didn't move. "I don't have to listen to this."

Terranova was on his feet too, so fast his chair skittered backward on its wheels until it hit the wall.

"There's more, Hillyer," he growled, "a lot more. And I don't give a shit what you want to listen to. We try to find that teacher but he slips out of the school. We go to pick up the cop and he blows his fucking brains out in his own bathroom."

Franks dead. The news hit Steven like a blow, and Terranova's rage, the bitter, biting anger in his voice as he hurled his accusations at Steven, hit him again.

"I was told I don't have to answer questions, is that right?" Steven demanded sharply.

"You have that right, Mr. Hillyer."

"Am I under arrest?"

"Not at this time."

"Then you can't hold me here, can you?"

Terranova's eyes bore in on Steven and he didn't say anything for a long time. Then he said, "You're free to go, Mr. Hillyer. Count on being back."

Steven hurried to the door and pushed through as if coming up for air after a long time in a cave. Outside, he shoved past the reporters and didn't slow down until he found a newspaper kiosk and bought copies of the afternoon papers. He hailed a cab and began to study the papers while he rode home.

One newspaper had a whole page of pictures from the scene in front of the school, but the accompanying stories told him nothing except that the situation hadn't been brought under control by early afternoon, when the paper went to press. The paper said there were no "confirmed fatalities" among the students, but it wasn't clear whether this meant they had unconfirmed reports of students' deaths.

He threw the papers away when he got home and dashed inside. As he started up the stairs he heard movement behind him and his name, *Mr. Hillyer*, whispered urgently. He turned to see Jamal Horton dart out from behind the staircase.

The boy looked around nervously and spoke quickly, words tumbling over words.

"They said you was meeting Charlie up on the avenue," he said. "They said you met him at a basketball game. They was all saying that and I believed them. I thought you was one of them. It's not true, is it, Mr. Hillyer?"

"I met Charlie to ask him what he saw in the weight room."

"Is that the truth, Mr. Hillyer?"

"You know it is or you wouldn't be here, Jamal," Steven said gently. "Have you been here all afternoon?"

"I didn't know where else to go."

"Well, there's no sense standing here," Steven said. "Let's go upstairs."

"Miss Torres is there. I seen her come in."

"Saw," Steven said.

He led Jamal up to his apartment. They could hear the television even before Steven got the door open. Rita rushed to meet him.

"I was so worried. Are you all right?" she asked, starting to throw her arms around him and then stopping short as she noticed little Jamal looking up at her.

"I'm all right. What's happening?" Steven asked, gesturing toward the television.

"It's hard to tell. The kids are still at the school. They're inside now and out in front, two or three hundred at least. The police are negotiating with them."

"The fighting stopped?"

"Most of it. But there's still a couple of fires they can't control. What happened to you?"

They kept the television on to hear the news as he told her about going to see L. D. Woods and being picked up by the police. The television announced that the transit authority was closing the subway station closest to La Guardia Junior High to keep more kids from getting to the scene. The mayor had declared a nine o'clock curfew.

Rita made the sign of the cross when Steven told her about Franks's death, and then she said, "That poor man."

"The police think he killed Lloyd," Steven said.

"Do you?"

"They think I was involved, Franks and I," he answered.

Jamal's eyes grew wide with fear and concern. In his experience, the people the police wanted to put in jail went to jail. "What are you going to do, Mr. Hillyer?" he asked.

What could he do? Nothing, it seemed. For the moment at least Steven was satisfied just to be away from the police. But he knew that wasn't enough. The boy's question told him he had to do something, and almost as an answer a stray thought, connected to nothing that was happening at this moment, flew into his mind.

"Jamal," he asked, "does Charlie Wain have a girlfriend?"

Jamal shrugged. "Bunch of girls working for him," he said. "That count as a girlfriend?"

"Steven, what's this about?" Rita asked.

He pulled Timothy's letters from his pocket and leafed quickly through them, looking for something he was sure he remembered, hoped he remembered right. Yes. There it was. *I'm sure your right they keep it there, because guess who I saw coming out? And you know he doesnt have a girlfriend.*

Ophelia thought she knew where the drugs were stashed, where the deals were done. That much was clear from the letters. And Timothy confirmed her suspicion because he had seen someone coming out of there. Who? Probably Charlie Wain, because Charlie seemed to be in the middle of everything. But that didn't matter. What mattered was where. And now Steven thought he knew. It seemed so obvious he cursed himself for not having thought of it before.

The girls' locker room. Where a boy might sneak in and out for a clandestine meeting with his girl, but where a boy without a girlfriend had no business at all, unless Ophelia was right.

It was just a guess, but it made enough sense to make him want to see for himself. Because if it was true, then the locker room was where Ophelia James died.

He didn't explain. "I need your help, Jamal," he said instead. "Is there some way we can get into the school?"

WHILE Steven and Jamal waited for a train, Steven called L. D. Woods from the pay phone on the platform. He got an answering machine that said the office was closed but Congressman Kellem would return his call.

"This is a message for L. D. Woods," Steven said. "This is Steven Hillyer. I'd appreciate it if whoever gets this message would contact Miss Woods immediately. Tell her I was right about Timothy. I think I know what happened. And tell her I've gone to La Guardia to check it out."

He hung up the phone and rejoined Jamal. Even in the dirty yellow light of the subway station, the boy's eyes sparkled with excitement.

"I was just thinking," Jamal said. "About the watchman."

He hadn't mentioned a watchman when Steven asked him about getting into the school.

"What about him?" Steven asked warily.

"Could be he ain't there. On account of all that shit going on."

That made sense to Steven, too.

When a train finally arrived almost half an hour later it was as crowded as rush hour. Steven and Jamal had to force themselves through the door, where they were packed in so tightly they could feel the buttons and zippers on the clothes of total strangers. The loudspeaker blared an un-intelligible announcement about the deleted stops in the Bronx and offered free transfers for "surface transportation," which Steven was reasonably sure wouldn't be available either. He and Jamal got off the train about a mile from the school.

The sky to the north glowed a faint pink russet from fires that were now supposedly under control. Massive clouds of smoke and steam hung like cartoon balloons above the building tops. While the people coming out of the subway all around them paused to study the sky as though reading it for omens, Steven and Jamal hurried on without comment.

The closer they got to the school, the more the area looked like a territory under occupation. Police cars cruised the streets with slow and stately insolence, turning every block or so, weaving an intricate web over the whole area. For about half a mile around La Guardia the police were broadcasting reminders of the impending curfew over their loud-speakers. Pedestrians still on the street after nine o'clock would be subject to arrest.

Steven and Jamal quickened their pace. The best way into the school, Jamal explained, was through the shop annex. The two buildings were connected by underground tunnels. If the streets were anywhere near as crowded as in the morning, it might be possible to slip in unnoticed through a back window. Once the streets were cleared by the curfew, it would be impossible.

A fair portion of the stores they passed were already closed, sealed against violence behind heavy iron shutters or curtains of latticed steel. Steven stopped at a hardware store and pulled Jamal in after him. They bought two flashlights from a storekeeper who kept one hand under the counter the whole time they were in the store, probably on a gun.

"Good thinking, Mr. Hillyer," Jamal said when they were back on their way.

But Steven didn't see it that way. If it took the accident of passing a hardware store to make him think of flashlights, what else might they be overlooking? The fact that he couldn't come up with anything only meant that he didn't really know what they were walking into.

The mounting tension propelled them forward with a kind of mindless oblivion, which Steven at least was thankful for. Jamal busied himself loading the batteries into the flashlights and trying them out, clicking the beams off and on, playing them over the street.

"You'd better put them away," Steven advised as the light caught the attention of a cop across the street.

By time they got to the school, they had only forty-five minutes until curfew. From their vantage point on a low hill, a whole panorama of tense stalemate stretched in front of them. The curb across from La Guardia was lined with fire trucks, their hoses tangled on the sidewalk like a nest of snakes, pouring out torrents of water that turned into huge billows of steaming smoke rising from the smoldering buildings. The charred wreck of the police car that had exploded that morning still blocked the street, which was even more densely packed with emergency vehicles than before, including a pair of ambulances and two or three heavy blue and white police trucks.

The street was entirely occupied by police, the sidewalk controlled by students, perhaps as many as four or five hundred of them. There was nothing between them and the cops, nothing to prevent the police from wading in and clearing the area except someone's commendable reluctance to put a couple hundred kids in the hospital.

Both ends of the block were guarded by squads of riot troops packed shoulder to shoulder to prevent newcomers from joining the kids as they had done most of the morning. Beyond that human barricade, a crowd of spectators milled aimlessly on the side street. A few enterprising vendors had actually set up pushcarts from which they sold soft drinks, franks and souvlaki, turning chaos into a carnival.

Steven and Jamal plunged into the crowd of spectators, making their way toward the mouth of the alley that ran behind the school and the annex, bisecting the block.

They found a pair of cops stationed at the entrance to the alley, feet planted wide, sticks held two-handed at their thighs.

"What do we do now?" Jamal asked softly.

Steven's eyes scanned the crowd around them. He spotted a fair number of La Guardia students but didn't see any of his own students.

"I got an idea," Jamal said brightly. "Wait here."

He squeezed his way forward, disappearing into the crowd, then bobbed up again a dozen yards away, like a gopher popping to the surface from another hole. He was talking with a tall Hispanic kid Steven recognized from one of the other fourth-floor homerooms. The boy glanced in Steven's direction and nodded, and Jamal turned to make his way back through the crowd. In a moment he was at Steven's side again.

"Okay," he said, "when I say go, go. See them trash cans? Get in behind them quick as you can."

Jamal moved around until he was only a few feet from the cops at the mouth of the alley and looked up at Steven. "Any second," he said.

But seconds passed and nothing happened. Jamal looked up at Steven and smiled hopefully.

Suddenly there was a shout from somewhere in the crowd, which lurched sideways like closely packed riders on a bouncing train. Someone shouted an obscenity, someone shouted a warning, a woman screamed, and voices began to cry out, "Fight! Fight!"

The two cops at the mouth of the alley exchanged glances. "Take a look," one of them said, holding his place while he sent his partner probing tentatively into the crowd.

Steven understood now, and understood, too, that it hadn't worked.

"That cop's in for a surprise," he shouted to Jamal. "Did you see the size of that blade?"

The cop behind him grabbed his shoulder and spun him around.

"Which one's got the knife?" he demanded.

"Bunch of 'em," Steven said. "Right there, where your partner went."

The cop barked something into his radio and raced off after his partner, his stick in one hand, the other on his gun.

Jamal took off for the alleyway and dove for the space behind the trash cans as if he were cannonballing into a swimming pool. Steven slid in after him and the two of them lay tumbled together behind the cans, silently congratulating each other on making it this far.

No more than a foot or two away was a low half window only a few inches off the ground. A set of iron bars bolted into the brick of the building wall arched over it. "There," Jamal said, pointing to the grate. "Move your legs a little, I gotta get by."

He twisted around, crawled to the window and reached his hand up to the top bolt, trying to turn it with his fingers. It didn't move.

"You try," he whispered back over his shoulder while he directed his attention to the lower bolt.

The odds of unbolting a window guard with his bare hands didn't seem to be in Steven's favor but he twisted around in the narrow space behind the trash can and reached for the bolt, wrapping his fingers around it and twisting as hard as he could. Amazingly, it turned.

"It's loose," he whispered excitedly.

"Fucking A," Jamal whispered back.

They moved quickly around the window, Steven getting the bolts started, Jamal working them out. By the time all four bolts were loose, Steven's fingers were scraped raw. He held the grating in place so it wouldn't crash to the ground as Jamal slipped out the last of the bolts. Then the two of them lifted it from the window and propped it behind the trash cans where it couldn't be seen from the street.

Now there was just the window to deal with.

"Is it locked?" Steven asked.

"Are you kidding?"

Spacing his hands to distribute the pressure evenly, Steven pushed against the window frame. At first it wouldn't budge, but then it jumped back with a squeak. They worked the frame backward carefully, swinging the window up and in.

Jamal slid his legs in through the open window, held himself suspended there for a second and then suddenly disappeared, making a soft thudding sound as he landed on the basement floor.

Steven followed suit, backing in as Jamal had done, until only his head and shoulders were outside. He had no idea how big a drop it was to the basement floor. Taking a deep breath, he let go, felt the back of his head crack against the window frame, felt himself falling through space for what seemed a long time until he hit bottom. Jamal's flashlight was shining right in his eyes from only a few inches away.

"Not too good on style," the boy said. "You awright?"

"Hit my head I guess," Steven whispered back.

"You *guess*," Jamal muttered sarcastically. The light went out.

Steven followed as Jamal led the way from the window through a doorway and into a windowless corridor where it was safe for them to turn their lights back on. Steven could see numerous doors opening off the corridor to either side. The walls were a damp, unpainted plaster and the ceiling supported a set of thick pipes wrapped in heavy insulation. The corridor turned to the right about twenty yards ahead.

"D'ya know how I knew about that window?" Jamal said.

"No, tell me."

"Nothing much to tell. Some guys I know get in that way, boost tools from the shops."

"They must do it pretty often if they've got the bolts worked loose."

"Every damn weekend," Jamal said, then added, "Least that's what they told me."

They made their way quickly down the corridor, then followed it to the right about a dozen yards, where it branched off toward a set of double doors, on the other side of which was the basement of the junior high itself. The doors weren't locked.

They heard voices filtering down from the lobby over their heads the moment they let themselves in. They made their way to the back stairs, which would take them up to the fifth floor without going through the lobby. Jamal quietly inched back the fire door to the stairwell and slid through. Steven followed, easing the door closed behind him.

They clicked off their lights and started up in the darkness, lit only by the feeble light that made the frosted windows of the stairwell glow above their heads with a cold, pale phosphorescence. Finding no railing, Steven kept his hand on the wall and Jamal kept a hand on Steven as they climbed toward the first floor. Just below the landing Steven stopped dead in his tracks. The stairwell door was open. The kids occupying the lobby stood only a few feet away.

The voices were loud now, a heated argument about negotiations with the cops. One of the voices sounded like Charlie Wain, which made sense because he seemed to be the head troublemaker.

There was no choice but to run for it. Steven reached down and slipped off his shoes, holding them in one hand. Jamal did the same. Crouching low and keeping close to the wall, Steven ran up the stairs and kept going until he reached the landing between the first floor and the second. He dropped to a crouch and spun around, peering back down into the darkness where he could just make out Jamal's shape on the stairs below him. In the lobby the argument was still going on. None of the kids appeared to have heard or seen anything.

Steven held his breath and waited while Jamal gathered his courage for the dash up the stairs. In a moment he saw the boy darting through the darkness and he scrambled out of the way. Jamal flew past him and didn't stop until he gained the second floor, where Steven joined him.

The worst part was over. It took them only a few minutes to make it to the fifth floor. Steven put his hand on the flashlight button, then pulled the fire door toward him and leaned into the corridor. The coast was clear and he turned on the light, letting the beam play down the length of the familiar corridor. He slipped through the door with Jamal right behind.

The weight room door was locked, as he expected, but it was a simple slip lock, the kind people said could be opened with a credit card. Now was the time to find out.

He took a card out of his wallet and tried it, sliding it in until it jammed against the beveled bolt. He maneuvered the card up and down but couldn't get anywhere with the bolt.

"You got a driver's license," Jamal asked, "something with a little more bend?"

The license was a thin piece of plasticized paper, as flexible as a worn playing card. It caught the lock and easily slipped it back.

Once they were in the windowless storage room with the door closed behind them, Steven turned on the lights. The room looked exactly as it had the morning Rita brought him there, littered with towels and mats. Directly ahead of him was the door to the weight room.

Steven swung it open, the stark outlines of the machinery looming in front of him in a thick tangle of shadows. He turned on the light and the shadows fled, replaced by the weird hulking shapes of the equipment, cold metallic arms reaching in all directions.

He felt Jamal's presence at his side and forced himself to put everything else except why they had come here out of his mind.

"Okay," Jamal said. "We're here. How come?"

"Because there's got to be another way into this room," Steven said. "Another door."

"No there ain't."

Steven pulled the weight room door closed and strode across the storage area to the wrestling mat hanging on the wall. The ropes supporting the mat were tied to a shelf support. He freed the slipknot and released the rope, which slithered up through the pulley as the mat tumbled loudly to the floor, revealing a door.

"Holy shit," Jamal said. "Where does it go?"

"It's not supposed to go anywhere," Steven said. "They sealed it up when they put in the weight room."

The door was no secret. The kids who used the wrestling mats saw it every day. But until he read Timothy's letters, Steven never asked himself how Ophelia James had gotten into the weight room. Without thinking, he assumed she had come in from the corridor to meet Timothy.

"Come on," he said. "I'll show you what's on the other side."

Jamal followed him into the weight room, where Steven yanked a heavy iron rod used to secure the weights from one of the machines and handed it to Jamal.

But he didn't go back to the mysterious door. Instead, he hurried out to the corridor and headed for the gym, turning just before he got there down the short hall leading to the locker rooms. He pushed through the door into the girls' locker room and walked to the showers, a broad, tiled space with drains in the floor and a dozen shower heads spaced along two walls. The toilet area opened off it, with seven or eight toilets ranked side by side. Steven played his flashlight over the space until it came to rest on the sealed, padlocked door.

He reached back and Jamal handed him the iron rod. It wasn't necessary for either of them to speak.

Steven levered the rod in behind the hasp and leaned his weight into it, straining until his arms ached with the effort. The hasp bent and he worked the rod in farther, prying it up and down until finally the hasp cracked and split. He tossed aside the rod and opened the door, confirming what he had known all along.

"I don't get it," Jamal said.

"Ophelia wasn't killed in the weight room. It happened somewhere in here."

"Are you nuts or what?"

"Jamal, her panties were missing."

"So Timothy took her pants off."

"And did what with them? He didn't have them. They weren't in the weight room."

"Maybe she didn't have 'em on . . ." Jamal started but didn't finish the sentence. There were plenty of girls at La Guardia who might have slipped into the weight room without their underwear for a quick rendezvous. Ophelia James wasn't one of them.

"Follow me on this," Steven said, looking around to work out a scenario that made sense. He walked from the toilets back into the shower area. "Timothy and Lloyd and Ophelia were trying to get together some kind of campaign against the crack dealers at school," he said. "Did you know anything about that?"

"He said something once. I didn't want no part of it."

"Okay. Now Timothy's letters say Ophelia knew where they kept the stuff."

"And you're saying the locker room?"

"He saw a boy coming out who didn't have a girlfriend. Sounds like the girls' locker room, doesn't it?"

"I'm with you."

Steven paced through the shower area into the locker room itself. The drugs could have been kept anywhere. In a locker or an equipment cabinet, on the towel shelves. It didn't pay to look now, because after all that had happened, the operation had to have been moved elsewhere.

"All right," he said, working it out in his mind as he spoke. "The drugs are somewhere in here and the dealers come here to pick them up. When do they do that?"

"Before school. After school. Lunch."

"And Ophelia was found first period after lunch. It fits. Now you're Ophelia. You want to spy on them at lunchtime, see who's doing what. What do you do?"

"I sneak in."

"Maybe. Or maybe you're already in. You finish gym class. All the girls go to take their showers. You do too." He hurried back to the shower room. "You stay under the shower till the other girls leave. They get dressed and they're gone. You turn off the water and you wait."

"Here?" Jamal asked. He pictured Ophelia, naked and cold.

"Of course. If you go back to the lockers, whoever's coming in is going to see you. But maybe they won't check the showers. That's what you're counting on. You wait."

"Christ," Jamal said. "More guts than I've got."

More than anyone Steven knew. He shuddered at the picture in his mind, a tiny child, barely five feet tall, wet and alone and afraid. But she stayed. Strong men died in battle showing less courage.

"And then they come in," he went on. He moved close to one of the tiled walls of the shower, pressed back against it as if he were hiding. "She hears their voices. She knows who they are. I don't think they found her right away or she could have pretended she was just late getting out of the shower. They did their dealing, passed out the crack, collected the money. And Ophelia heard all of it."

He stopped talking.

In the silence Jamal said softly, "And then they found her. Jesus Christ!"

"Maybe she tried to pretend she was just there by accident. She probably swore she didn't hear anything. Or she wouldn't tell."

"But they killed her anyway."

"Now they're kind of in a panic. They've got to get the body out of there. So they stick some clothes on her and put her in the weight room. One of them goes to get Timothy, tells him Ophelia wants to see him in the weight room. Because no one's going to believe crazy Timothy Warren when he's found with a dead girl and swears he didn't kill her. No one's going to believe him when he says someone told him to come there. Only it never even comes to that because Timothy panics and he won't let go of her and then he's killed before he gets a chance to explain any of it."

Suddenly the room was flooded with light and a voice said, "Smart guy, aren't you, Hillyer?"

Steven and Jamal both whirled around. Charlie Wain stood at the end of the row of lockers.

"I got it right though, didn't I, Charlie? What did you do with her underpants?"

Charlie said, "Fuck you."

He moved aside and Barry Lucasian stepped past him.

"The police thought about the door, too, Hillyer. Only I told them there wasn't a key and they believed me. That's because they didn't have Timothy's letters. Let's have them."

Lucasian held out a hand as he strode toward them.

"Run, Jamal!" Steven yelled.

They turned around and split up, racing in opposite directions past the rows of lockers. Before Steven reached the end a tall, broad-chested boy stepped around the last row of lockers, blocking his path. Steven, remembering him from the beating in the machine shop, turned to run the other way and saw another boy coming toward him from the opposite direction, closing in on Jamal.

Steven darted sideways between two rows of lockers, praying Jamal was quick enough to do the same. He started to run but realized in an instant that Charlie could cut him off at the end of the aisle.

Turning, he threw his full weight against one of the lockers and the whole row rocked back and then settled again. He took a quick step back and hurled himself at it again, driving his shoulder into it. This time it toppled backward and crashed over, coming to rest against the lockers in the next row.

He lunged for the top and pulled himself up the steeply sloping plain.

A hand grabbed at his ankle and he felt a sharp pain as a knife sliced the back of his leg. He kicked out with his other foot and felt it hit home. He heard a sharp, gasping groan and hoped it was Charlie Wain's face his heel had just smashed.

He didn't look back to find out, but pulled himself up to the top of the tilted pile and scrambled to his feet. Good. That meant the blade hadn't sliced a tendon. He jumped to the next row of lockers and then the next, looking for Jamal. The boy was standing mid-aisle, Lucasian and the two others closing in from either end.

Steven leaped for one of the kids, feetfirst, crashing down on him, sprawling to the floor along with him. The knife clattered from the dazed boy's hand.

It was all the opening Jamal needed. He raced right over the fallen kid, past Steven, heading for the open space and the locker room door beyond it. At the end of the aisle he spun crazily as Lucasian yanked him from his feet like a roped calf.

Steven grabbed for the knife on the floor near him but missed it and didn't have time to reach back a second time. He lunged at Lucasian from the ground, a low tackle going for the legs, slamming the gym teacher to the floor. He heard footsteps running toward him from behind— footsteps he hoped were Jamal's—and he tried to roll away but didn't know where to go. Then a voice boomed, "Right there!" and everything stopped at once.

"Drop those knives. Now!" the voice commanded.

Tal Chambers stood in the locker room doorway, flanked by two detectives with guns drawn.

"Don't shoot," Lucasian yelled from the floor. "Don't shoot!"

Charlie Wain turned to run but there was nowhere to go. At the end of the row of lockers he stopped and raised his hands slowly above his head in surrender, then turned to face the cop, blood streaming from his nose and mouth where Steven had kicked him. The other two boys surrendered without a struggle.

Chambers reached down a hand to help Steven to his feet. "L.D. called me as soon as she got your message," he said. "You could have been in a lot of trouble."

"Yeah. I noticed," Steven said.

Jamal wouldn't come out of hiding until the cops assured him it was safe.

They walked down to the lobby in a slow procession, Steven, Jamal and Tal Chambers first, the cops and their prisoners behind. The students in the lobby moved back to give them a wide berth as they crossed to the front door.

Tal opened the door and stepped out first. "Let us through," he said simply.

No one understood what was going on but no one resisted. A path opened up before them and they made their way to the street, where L. D. Woods was waiting with Chief of Detectives Terranova at the front of the police line.

"Someone give him a hand to the ambulance," was all Terranova said. Two cops let Steven rest his weight on their shoulders.

"Wait a minute," Steven heard L.D. say as the prisoners were led past her on their way to a waiting wagon. He turned to watch.

She walked over to Charlie Wain and inspected him closely, then picked up his wrist to show Terranova the white-gold bracelet she had mentioned in her description of the boy who drove her to meet Artemis Reach in the park.

"This is the boy I told you about," she said.

The Chief stepped up to Charlie, whose nose was bleeding a steady river onto his chin. "You work for Artemis Reach? Is that right, son?"

Charlie stared at him through glazed eyes but said nothing.

The Chief shrugged indifferently. "No problem," he said. "Charlie here is a stand-up guy. He doesn't know any better. But the gym teacher's going to make himself a deal and tell us everything. Isn't that right, Mr. Lucasian?"

Lucasian didn't answer. Terranova tossed his head and the detectives led the prisoners to a waiting van.

When they were gone, L.D. said, "I guess that explains why Artemis was so incensed about the investigation."

"And why he pulled the plug on everything when he realized he couldn't stop it," Terranova added.

While Steven's leg was being stitched in the ambulance Terranova opened the door and leaned in. "We're going to need a statement," he said. "You've had yourself a hell of a day. Tomorrow morning will be good enough."

Steven nodded an acknowledgment.

"Need a lift home?" the Chief asked.

He went back outside to wait and when the medics finished with Steven they walked together to the Chief's car.

"East Eigthy-ninth, isn't it?" Terranova asked as the car began to make its way down the congested street.

"One Hundred Thirteenth," Steven said.

He gave the driver the address and when they got there he asked the Chief to wait.

W I L L I A M S and Phelan waited in their car in front of Community Board Sixty-one until the custodian arrived. He was a short, thick-bodied black man who didn't ask to see their warrant but they showed it to him anyway. It entitled them to seize and remove papers, appointment books and other effects from Artemis Reach's office that might constitute evidence in the wrongful deaths of Ophelia James, Timothy Warren and Lloyd Elijah, as well as any documents, appointment books or memoranda pertaining to narcotics trafficking or an unlawful order to close the schools under his jurisdiction.

"Radio say you be looking to arrest Mr. Reach," the custodian said as he unlocked the heavy front door.

"That's right," Williams said. "You wouldn't have any idea where he might be?"

The custodian grumbled a laugh. "Wouldn't be here," he said. "We close up real early, everybody gone home."

"Was he here when you closed?"

"Wouldn't know that. But I reckon he was."

The custodian led them across the darkened lobby and down a short corridor to the Chairman's office, jangling at least two dozen keys on a ring as he searched for the right one. Williams was a step in front of him and noticed the broken glass on the office door. He held out a hand to keep the man from going any closer. His other hand went to his gun but he didn't draw it.

"We'll let ourselves in," he said softly. "Go back to the front door and wait for us there."

He stepped away from the glass and waited with his partner while the staccato click of the man's shoes drifted back across the darkness. It faded almost to silence as he made his way into the lobby.

Without speaking a word to each other, the two detectives drew their revolvers and moved to positions on each side of the door. Phelan reached through the broken glass and felt for the knob. It turned in his hand and he let the door swing open away from him.

Quickly, the two detectives stepped through, moving to opposite sides of the door.

"Find the lights," Williams whispered.

A voice, a deep voice, came at them from the darkness. "Don't touch the lights. I've got a gun."

"We have guns, too, Mr. Reach," Williams said. "There are two of us and we're trained to use them."

The room smelled like liquor but Reach didn't sound as if he was drunk. Williams heard Phelan slipping off in the darkness, moving along the wall. That was good. Putting distance between them lowered the gunman's odds, and that in turn lowered the odds he would shoot. Reach, he thought, must also have heard Phelan moving, but he didn't say anything, didn't order them to stand still.

The thought flashed through Williams's mind that this man might shoot them anyway, might want them to shoot him. The fact that Reach was sitting in a darkened room with a gun in his hand didn't generate confidence in his judgment, intentions or stability.

"Put down the gun, Mr. Reach," Williams said slowly, as though speaking to someone who might have difficulty understanding. "We don't need no one else getting hurt."

"Did you come to arrest me?" Reach asked.

"Yes, sir."

Williams could just barely make out the shape of a man at the desk across the room. If he had to shoot into those shadows, he figured he stood at best a fair chance of hitting what he aimed at. On the other hand, he made a damn good target with the door just behind him.

"You're black, aren't you?" Reach asked.

"Yes, sir. I am," Williams said. "I'm going to walk over there. I'd like you to stand up and put your hands over your head."

"I can't do that. Stay where you are," Reach said.

Williams held his position.

"Good," Reach said. "Now tell your friend to stay where he is."

"Doug."

The faint sound of Phelan's shoes on the carpeted floor stopped.

"Is he black, too?" Reach asked.

"That's right."

"Black people listen to me," Reach said. There was no particular inflection in his voice. He was simply stating a fact.

Shit, Williams thought. This was going to take a long time. The man was going to tell his whole damn story.

"You know why?" Reach went on. "Because I make sense. I tell them what other people don't want them to know. You think this city wants a bunch of educated niggers? The hell it does. You have to fight for everything."

"Selling black kids crack? Is that how you fought for it?" Williams shot back as a challenge. He heard Phelan moving again, just a step or two, while Reach was talking and he wanted to keep him talking. He wished he knew where his partner was, but at least Reach didn't seem to know either.

"Is that what they say?" Reach demanded.

"It's what I say. You want to tell me why, Mr. Reach? Why's a man that's supposed to be helping our kids doing that?"

"It's lies," Reach shot back at him, his deep voice rolling across the darkness. "Did they wash that out of your brain when they made you a cop? Wash out all the lies? They lied about King and Powell. J. Edgar Hoover, right? You telling me you don't know that?"

"King didn't sell crack."

"And what? You got the damn gym teacher, right? White gym teacher. He's telling you that shit and you come up here like a white man, arrest the fool nigger."

"If you're telling me it didn't happen that way, then put down the gun, Mr. Reach. You'll get your chance."

"When?"

"Now. Starting now."

"You're a fool."

"I'm not pointing one gun at two cops, Mr. Reach."

The Chairman's laugh rolled across the darkness like a wave of energy. Williams had heard that laugh before, heard it in interviews on the radio and television. It was deep and self-mocking, a laugh filled with warmth and energy and the strength to mock and stand somehow above the mockery. All those qualities were still there, even in the desperation of the moment. Christ, it was incomprehensible, even to a detective who had seen all the paradoxes of love and depravity Williams had seen in a lifetime of solving mysteries.

"How the hell does it happen, Mr. Reach?" he asked, because that laugh made him want to know.

"I thought you were a smart nigger. Tell me."

"You're hooked yourself. You've got a habit to feed. Is that it?"

"Fuck you."

"Then tell me, damn it!" Williams thundered. "I got kids in this city. You were moving the right way, you were making a difference."

He heard Phelan move. Reach didn't.

"And what? And what?" Reach shouted back. "Those kids of yours gonna be cops, too, Mr. Cop? Listen to yourself, fool. You want truth? You don't want truth, wouldn't know truth. 'Cause truth is you're not listening, Mr. Yes-I-am-a-black-man. I'll tell you now and you won't hear a word because all you want to do is keep me talking till shadow man creeps up in back of me and makes his move. That's your answer, mister. That's this job, that's this title, that's Artemis Reach. Every last motherfucking bit of him. I was making a difference? What difference? Find it for me! Twelve, twenty, a hundred more educated niggers every year. You think that's a difference, then you're sorrier than I am, boy. I don't see any of it making a difference."

"It was a start."

"It was nothing!" Reach roared in the darkness, his voice wild and pained, careening on the edge of action.

In that instant Williams knew he had no choice. It had to end now. He took a step forward, daring him to shoot.

"Why, Mr. Reach?" he demanded as he moved. "Why?"

"No closer!"

But he kept moving. "Why? Tell me something, something that makes sense!"

"No closer!"

"Damn it, man, why?"

The noise was like a cannon, the flash like lightning. But the single shot whistled wide of Williams and the sound of shattering glass was followed almost immediately by the collision of two bodies and a brief but brutal struggle in the darkness.

Williams lunged for the desk, diving over it like a man leaping into a moving car, landed splayed across the surface, his gun ready, aimed at the space behind the desk where his partner and the suspect would be tangled on the floor, ready for whatever had to be done.

But there was nothing to be done. It was over. He heard a sharp grunt of pain as Phelan yanked Reach's arm back, could see Phelan kneeling on the suspect's back. His own gun was held in two hands in front of him, aimed straight to the floor where Reach's head was.

He heard the snap of handcuffs and then Phelan yanked the School Board Chairman to his feet.

Williams righted himself, holstered his gun and reached down to the floor to pick up the weapon that had been fired at him. Then he stepped around in front of Reach, their faces close enough to see each other clearly in the darkness.

"You still haven't told me why," he said.

"I am what I am," Artemis Reach said. "That's why. Do you think any of this matters?"

* * *

STEVEN knocked on the door and waited. He heard the muffled sound of movement from the other side and then Rita's voice asked, "Who's there?"

He heard the small metallic sound as the cover over the peephole was lifted back and then the hurried noise of the door being unbolted. "Oh, Steven," she cried as she stepped toward him.

Her mother was standing off to the side, glowering and groggy in a faded bathrobe.

"My God, what happened to you?" Rita asked as soon as she saw Steven's bruised face and bloody clothes.

She turned to her mother without waiting for his answer and said something in Spanish so sharp and peremptory that the woman turned and waddled back to her bedroom. Rita turned back to Steven, reaching past him to close the door.

"I figured you'd be here," he said. "It didn't make much sense for you to wait for me at my place if I wasn't coming back."

Rita took a step back, stunned, but said nothing.

"When I tried to talk to you last week in the cafeteria," he said, "you didn't want to talk about it at all. But after I talked to Lucasian at the basketball game, you came running to meet me. He called you, didn't he? Did he tell you to do that?"

"Steven, you don't understand," she said.

Her eyes were clear and soft, and even though he knew that everything she said would be a lie, he couldn't see anything in her face, couldn't hear anything in her voice that told him she wasn't the same woman he had known yesterday.

"What don't I understand?" he demanded. "That you sent Lucasian to kill me tonight?"

"I didn't, Steven," she pleaded. "I'd never do that. You know that."

"You called him tonight. You told him Jamal and I were going to the school. No one else knew."

"I didn't. I didn't."

"You sent him to catch us there. They were going to kill us."

"God, Steven. No, no, I didn't tell him. You have to believe me. I wouldn't do that."

"I don't have to believe anything, Rita. Why did you come to meet me in the first place? Why did you come to my apartment? Lucasian told you to do it, didn't he?"

"I asked you to stop, Steven. I begged you to," she said.

He saw the tears in her eyes as she stepped close to him, reached her hand out to touch his brow and brush his hair back. He let her.

"He told me to take you to see Charlie. We thought maybe that would be the end of it," she went on, her voice fast and breathless and out of control. "I wouldn't say this if I wasn't telling you the truth. When I came to your apartment it was because I wanted you to stop. He didn't tell me to do that. I came because I loved you, Steven. Because I was afraid you'd get hurt."

"Because you wanted to protect your drug business," he shot back angrily.

"I can't change what I am," she cried. "I can't change what I've done. You don't know what it's like to be poor, Steven. My mother, my brother, supporting them, never getting out from under it."

"So you sell crack to kids?"

"I won't defend it, Steven. Barry told me what was happening. He told me what Artemis was doing, taking control of it, bringing it all together. It was frightening. It was big and powerful and terrifying. And then he asked me to be part of it and I said yes. What did it matter anymore? Artemis. Barry. All over the district there were teachers doing it, and I was one of them. Do you think it would have stopped anything if I'd said no?"

He didn't answer the question for her because she knew the answer. He turned away but she moved in front of him and fell to her knees, clutching his hands, holding them to her face.

"I'm not like that, Steven," she pleaded. "It was a mistake. And when I saw you and we went up there to see Charlie together, and I saw how much you cared, I loved you for it. Because I wanted to care that much. I used to, Steven. I cared about those kids. And I knew that with you I could care again. I didn't want you to get hurt, I didn't want to lose you. I needed you, Steven. I'd never get out of this without you. Was that wrong?"

"You killed a girl, Rita. You killed that little girl."

"I didn't. Honest to God I didn't."

"Did she beg the way you're doing?"

The tears came freely now and she sobbed uncontrollably, gasping through the sobs. "Please, Steven, don't do this to me. I can't think about it, I can't go over it again. If I could bring her back to life, don't you think I would?"

"Did she beg, Rita?"

His voice was cold and hard. Hearing it, Rita knew she wouldn't bend him.

"No," she said, releasing his hands. "She didn't beg."

She slumped to the floor, her body sagging down over folded legs, small and shapeless and pitiable.

"And you killed her anyway."

"Not me, Steven. I tried to stop him." Her voice rose up to him, soft and distant. "There were some girls there, it doesn't matter who. They gave me the money they took in, I gave them crack. Charlie Wain turned in his money to Barry. We kept the drugs in the first-aid locker. We heard a noise when we were getting it out and one of the girls went to look. 'Hey, look what I found.' I remember that's what she said. And we ran over there. Ophelia was in the corner of the shower and she was naked and she tried to cover herself with her hands."

Rita rolled over on the floor in an odd, crumpled position, and looked up at Steven through tear-streaked eyes.

"Oh, God, Steven, it was awful. Barry told the girls to go and then Charlie grabbed Ophelia's hand and pulled her out of the shower. I tried to stop him. I put my arms around her and I could feel how cold she was. Then Ophelia said to let her go because Timothy knew she was there, and that's when Charlie grabbed her. He had her around the neck, yelling at me to let go of her. He kept choking her until she went limp in my arms. And she was dead."

"So you dressed her."

"They did."

"And you put her in the weight room."

"They did. Because of what she said. I think Charlie was going to kill Timothy, too, and say they fought when he found him with her. But Timothy had a knife. I think that's why he didn't. I don't know, I wasn't there then. It was crazy but I was scared and Barry was telling us what we had to do. She never cried, she never cried at all."

Steven said nothing, numb from all he had heard.

"Steven," Rita said after a long silence. Her eyes were closed and she said it almost as a question, as if she were asking if he was still there.

"Yes."

"They put her skirt and vest on, and her blouse. And Barry unlocked the door and they carried her into the weight room. And when they were putting her down on that bench, her skirt came up and she was naked under it."

There were tears in Steven's eyes too, now, and he looked away.

"Oh, Steven," she said. "I wished it was me there. She was such a little girl. I didn't want it to happen. Not any of it."

"Is that the truth?" he asked.

"Yes. Yes."

"And you didn't send Lucasian to get me tonight?"

"I swear it, Steven."

He looked down at her and tried to remember that only a few hours ago he had loved her. Then he turned away and opened the door. "Lucasian asked me for the letters," he said. "No one but you knew I had them."

Now it was her turn to be silent.

"There's a cop downstairs," he said. "He'll wait for you to come down. But if you don't, he'll come up."

And then he left.

EPILOGUE

In the morning Steven took the subway down to One Police Plaza and gave the statement he had promised. When he was finished, the detective who took the statement told him the Chief wanted to talk to him.

"I thought you'd want to know we caught up with Artemis Reach last night," Terranova said.

"You arrested him?"

Terranova nodded. "A couple years ago I would have sworn that son of a bitch was going to get the schools straightened out," he said. "How do you figure a guy like that?"

Steven didn't know. For some reason his thoughts carried him back to that moment in the nurse's office at La Guardia a week ago, when Artemis Reach refused to let Lloyd Elijah be taken out in an ambulance, directing the raw force of his will into the boy to make him stand. Why? What lies was Reach telling himself? Did he imagine he could give back through his strength and force what he had taken away when he or the people working for him supplied that boy with the drugs that almost stopped his heart?

And did that make it easier, a few days later, to order Lloyd's death?

None of these thoughts answered Terranova's question. Perhaps the answer was as simple as a lust for wealth or power. Steven doubted it. Bitterness, he was sure, had something to do with it. At some point the energy and ruthlessness that had always been the core of Artmeis Reach's strength turned the wrong way. L. D. Woods seemed to have understood it better than Steven ever could. The fires that fueled the man, she said, had never been anything other than the fires of rage and hatred.

And perhaps that was all the answer there would ever be.

"All we'll get now in any case," Terranova agreed. "Lucasian's already talking. We've got names of teachers working for Reach at a couple of the other schools. I'm betting it ran through the whole district. I'll keep you posted."

Steven didn't much want to know. "What about the riot?" he asked. "The radio said the kids gave up."

"Once we got Wain out of there, there wasn't much fight left. Chambers talked to them and that helped a lot."

Steven moved to the door. At least it was over.

"I guess I was wrong about you, Hillyer," Terranova called after him.

That was as close as he would come to an apology. In fact he had been wrong about almost all of it.

"No problem," Steven said.

Maybe for Hillyer that was true. It was sure as hell a problem for Jim Franks's widow. And his kids. Terranova didn't ask himself how it might have ended differently for Franks if the Chief of Detectives had figured it out earlier. His mind didn't work that way, refused to entertain alternatives to reality. What hurt instead was the realization that Franks had been, after all, Albert Terranova's kind of cop.

"Look," he said, "you're going to the funeral, right? Tell his wife for me . . ."

He stopped without finishing the sentence, and then he said, "No. You'd better not say anything."

Steven rented a car from one of the cut-rate agencies near the courthouse and drove up to Dobbs Ferry. There weren't many people at the funeral but enough to keep it from being more forlorn than it had to be. In addition to Franks's family there were a number of people who seemed to be friends and neighbors, and a handful that Steven guessed were cops.

He sat with the cops, and when the line of mourners formed to pay their condolences to the widow, he took his place and waited his turn. He told her his name as he shook her hand and said how sorry he was, but he could see that she didn't know who he was and she didn't ask. It was just as well.

He didn't go to the cemetery.

He drove back to the city but got off the highway in the Bronx and found his way to Victoria James's apartment. Tal Chambers opened the door for him when he knocked.

"I want to tell Mrs. James what happened," Steven said. "I think she ought to know."

Chambers motioned for him to come in and then went to knock on the bedroom door. L. D. opened it and then went back inside after Tal said something to her Steven couldn't hear.

"She's kind of sedated," Tal explained when he rejoined Steven in the living room. "L. D.'s been sitting with her. We've already told her a little. It's hard for her, but I think she ought to hear it from you."

A few minutes later L. D. came out of the bedroom with Victoria James.

"It's good of you to come," Mrs. James said. "Miss Woods was telling me how much you did."

"How much your daughter did," Steven corrected.

He told her as much as he thought she could listen to. He didn't tell her that Ophelia hid in the shower or that they caught her naked there. He didn't say how she was killed. He talked about Timothy and Ophelia and their brave and beautiful fight against the overwhelming power of the drug dealers.

Victoria listened gravely, nodding her understanding of everything he said.

"She had a good heart, Mr. Hillyer," she said at the end. "But she was just a child. A child without sense enough to know a child can't stop people like that."

He reached across the sofa and took the woman's hand in his. "She did stop them, Mrs. James," he said. "That's what happened last night. That's what Ophelia did."

They sat a few moments longer, but no one spoke. L. D. followed Steven to the door and stepped into the hall with him.

"Steven, I'm going to run for Artemis's job," L. D. said, and then laughed her warm, throaty laugh. "The chairmanship, I mean. I can't be calling it Artemis's job anymore."

"No," he said. "Don't call it that. I think you'll be very good."

"I'm sure it's too soon for you even to think about something like this," L. D. said. "But a lot of the community boards have teachers on them. I'd like you to consider it."

Steven started to say he wasn't interested, that he felt he belonged in the classroom, but L. D. put a finger to his lips and said, "Don't say no till you've thought about it. Don't sell the kids short. They deserve the most we can give."

He drove back to Manhattan and returned the car, then took a taxi home and fell straight into bed. He had hardly slept at all for two nights, but now he slept a deep, dreamless sleep that seemed to go on and on until finally he woke up and realized it was almost noon on Sunday.

He called L. D. at her apartment and said he wanted to talk to her about her ideas for District Sixty-one.

"Come on over," she said. "I'll fix breakfast and we can talk."

"I can't now," he said. "There's something I've got to do. I just wanted you to know I am thinking about it."

He showered, made himself a quick breakfast and then took the subway up to the Bronx, where he walked from the station to the address he had in his register for Jamal Horton.

Jamal's father couldn't get it out of his mind, despite repeated assurances, that his son must be in very serious trouble to bring a teacher around to their door on a Sunday afternoon. Mrs. Horton served coffee while Jamal's older sister was sent grumbling into the street to round up Jamal, who was somewhere in the neighborhood.

"There was something I wanted to do today," Steven explained when Jamal was fetched home. "I thought maybe you'd do it with me."

"I guess. What?"

"You'll see when we get there."

As soon as they were out of the house, Jamal turned on him. "What did you do that for?" he demanded. "My father's gonna kill me."

"I told him you were doing very well."

"No way he's gonna believe that," Jamal said.

Steven draped an arm over the boy's shoulder and they continued down the stairs. "I'm sorry," he said. "But you'll survive. Something tells me this wouldn't be the first time he was going to kill you."

"First time for something I never done."

"Did."

They took the subway down to Manhattan, all the way to the Fourteenth Street station, and then walked to Twelfth Street and across to Broadway. When Steven led him into the Strand Book Store, Jamal's eyes went wide with baffled wonder that was at least in part disappointment.

"This can't be where we're going," he said.

"Yeah. It is."

"What the hell is it? A library?"

"Bookstore," Steven said.

The store was as big as a supermarket, the walls covered from floor to ceiling with books. There were tables stacked chest-high with books, and books stacked on the floor. Placards above the tables bore signs that said things like "Review Copies" or "Everything on this table, $1.99."

"What's a buck ninety-nine?" Jamal asked in a furtive whisper.

"Anything on that table. Want to take a look?"

"Not especially," Jamal said. He looked around a little more and said, "What are you gonna do?"

"See if I can find something," Steven said.

He threaded his way through the narrow aisles jammed with customers to a doorway that opened onto a staircase leading down to the basement. Even the stairs were stacked with books, and the cellar seemed to have even more books than upstairs, if that was possible.

"Are you sure this ain't a library?" Jamal asked.

Steven laughed and led the way to a bank of shelves toward the back.

"What's here?" Jamal asked.

Steven pointed to the sign at the mouth of the aisle. "These are all books about education," he said.

"There's books *about* education?"

"Apparently."

It took Steven less than five minutes to find what he wanted. When he was finished he had three books in his arms and they started back for the stairs.

"What did you get?" Jamal asked.

"I teach literature," Steven said. "And a little grammar. I don't know the first thing about teaching someone to read. That's what these are about."

Jamal stopped in his tracks and even took a step backward, down the stairs. "No way," he said. "I thought we had that worked out."

Steven smiled but didn't say anything.

"Hey, what do you want to do this to me for?" Jamal protested. "I'm doing fine."

"Fine's good," Steven said. "Better's better."

They stopped on Fourteenth Street for a soda and some pie, and by the time they came out it was almost six o'clock.

The sun was still about an hour from setting and the streets were shadowed but not dark. In the east, at the end of Fourteenth Street, the moon had already risen.